W9-BRN-347

FIREDANCER

Tsia twirled in the center of the fire. Flames crawled up her calves and whipped around her thighs. The cats yowled in her head. She ducked and twisted, kicking up a dazzling flurry of sparks, then sweeping low and curling under an arc of orange-red gas that stretched out over her head. The fire hissed and crackled. Coals turned beneath her feet. Heat ate at her legs, her waist, her arms . . .

Still she danced. There was nothing but the fire, nothing but herself in the flames. Her voice sang to the coals, coaxing them up, up along her legs while she leaped even higher to avoid them. Her body glowed, clothed only in sweat and flames . . .

By Tara K. Harper
Published By Ballantine Books:

LIGHTWING
CAT SCRATCH FEVER

Tales of the Wolves
WOLFWALKER
SHADOW LEADER
STORM RUNNER

CAT
SCRATCH
FEVER

Tara K. Harper

A Del Rey® Book
BALLANTINE BOOKS • NEW YORK

This book is dedicated to my sister
Colleen Annice Harper
with the hope that she might someday call

Sale of this book without a front cover may be unauthorized. If this book is coverless, it may have been reported to the publisher as "unsold or destroyed" and neither the author nor the publisher may have received payment for it.

A Del Rey® Book
Published by Ballantine Books

Copyright © 1994 by Tara K. Harper

All rights reserved under International and Pan-American Copyright Conventions. Published in the United States of America by Ballantine Books, a division of Random House, Inc., New York, and simultaneously in Canada by Random House of Canada Limited, Toronto.

Library of Congress Catalog Card Number: 93-90872

ISBN 0-345-38051-7

Manufactured in the United States of America

First Edition: May 1994

10 9 8 7 6 5 4 3

1

Tsia was waist deep in the incoming tide. On a slow scan, she ignored the numbing water that pulled at her thighs. Currents eroded the muddy sand on which she stood, and she leaned hard against the swift sweep of water. When the thin strand of kelp caught on her trousers, she hardly noticed; her hands were busy with the underwater sensors which she kept on the edge of the demonfish run. The repulsor, tied to her waist by its safety thread, floated down and to her left in the murk. Its blue-coded lights blinked silently in time with the sonic pulses by which it repelled the fish.

Two more days, she thought, and she would have everything she needed to complete her study. She had been right: The demonfish were laying sparsely this year. Satscan from the orbiting node had indicated a close-to-normal run, but Tsia had seen signs along the inlets that the aggressive fish were acting oddly—the females were grouping in schools that were not from the same birth streams; the schools themselves were moving far too slowly toward the spawning grounds; the demonfish were going half-heartedly after food . . . It was as if they were unhappy, she realized. Or demoralized. She shook her head silently. A depressed school of fish? She should refer it to one of the older guides; there were two in the local guild who specialized in sensing the marine life of this planet.

The underwater scanner flashed its accumulating data, and Tsia scowled at herself for the silent suggestion. She was out here, up to her waist in frigid water and loose, green-slimed kelp because, after what had happened a week earlier, she was avoiding the guild. But however humiliated she felt about her status, she was still a guide. And as one of the newest guides in the guild, her obligation was clear: She must report the biologicals. This planet was still new enough to humans that half the major species were not even logged. If the demonfish had culture beyond normal schooling, the guide guild should be the first to know.

Another strand of kelp swept against her pants, catching on the first, and Tsia brushed irritably at it. The water rose another finger's width above her waist. Behind her, the shore receded suddenly as the tide breached a line of rocks and poured into the shallow, briny pools behind them. Barely aware of the change in sound and ignoring the constant churn of her stomach, Tsia concentrated on her manual scanner instead. She ground her teeth with frustration, coded the commands with awkward finger motions and cursed the lack of her temple link. With her temple link, she could have imaged the commands directly. But no, it would be at least two more months of manual work before she would get her temple link back.

She glanced at the repulsor that hung from her waist, noted the harmless biologicals registered on its code bars, then returned her attention to the demonfish. How fast, she wondered bitterly, would this scan be if she, like that old guide out of Ciordan, had biolinked to a demonfish? Abruptly, she quelled that train of thought. Work now, she reminded herself harshly. Dream later.

Her feet sank slowly up to her ankles in sandy mud, and she moved automatically to the next spot along the run. The slough bottom was harder here, but it would be only a minute before it, too, went soft beneath her weight. She scowled at the shifting scanner bars and tapped in more commands. The red blinking light went back to amber; the other amber lights went back to green. The school of demonfish curved away.

A mudcrab floated past, caught the tag end of the kelp on Tsia's trousers, and clipped its two side claws onto the slick strand. The soft, flat body of the crab hung for a moment, waving slowly in the currents. Then it crept up the strand. A code bar on her repulsor went yellow. Tsia did not notice. Instead, she peered toward the school through the murky water as a cloud of detritus began to pass. Behind her, the shore receded further.

One of the kelp strands slid away in the water; the crab reached Tsia's thigh. It pinched its foreclaw onto her trousers and clung for a moment in the surge. The repulsor, its emitters set for the frequency of the demonfish, flashed its automatic warning along the node, received no answer from Tsia's closed temple link, and burned the yellow light of its proximity bars into the water. The crab, following the faint scent of the organic circuits in the repulsor, edged upward.

The school thinned, and Tsia looked toward the sea to realize that the last of the demonfish were breaking around a massive deadhead that was being rolled back up the slough by the strong incoming current. She looked farther to the right. The tag end of the school was now behind her. That was a bit of luck. Had the fish shifted toward the deeper water of the inlet, she would have had to wade out to her neck to keep up with it.

"Not more than a hundred left to pass," she estimated in a murmur. She pulled her gear out of the water to read the scan lead. "Twelve hundred fish in this school," she muttered, "and only ninety-two jennies."

She turned and waded carefully toward the other line of fish that now swept between her and the shore. Underwater, the soft flapping of her trousers and the bumping of her gear against her chilled skin went unheeded in the struggle to remain upright. Her toes dug into the muddy sand. The repulsor, hanging only by its safety thread, floated back and waved behind her in the slough, while its passenger, joined by another crab, determinedly sawed away at the repulsor's protective case.

Tsia watched the narrow, rippling V that showed the approach of the new line of fish. Less than ten percent female, she repeated to herself with a frown. She imaged a query to the node before she thought. "Got to stop that," she muttered. "Goddamn thing can't hear me till I get my temple link back."

She held the scanner below the surface again, the water almost warm to her now-numbed hands. The oncoming demonfish avoided the two-meter circle created around her by the repulsor's protective fields. Instead, their spawning instincts pushed them steadily upstream, away from the sandy mud, toward the shallows where the Yellow River became rocky and filled with rapids and roiling pools. There, in the pools, the males would fight to the death for the privilege of mating with the females.

Tsia eyed the distinct, wickedly spiked shape of a jenny as the cold wind cut across her face and neck. With so few jennies, this year's fighting would reduce this single run to a hundred jacks instead of the usual thousand. She rubbed a wet hand against her nose and wrinkled her expression as the salt from the water dried quickly into a gritty crust. She thrust her hand back underwater and coded another command as she watched the heavier, grotesquely bulging bodies of the spiny males. Double rows of teeth protruded from the demonfish mouths; the heavy eyebrows were lined with stinging spikes. Each tail had stinging whiskers, each dorsal fin, a row of spines. Tsia found herself watching the fish with the same fascination she had felt when she had first seen them. Once these jacks and jennies mated, she knew, they would tear each other apart for food. The jennies that survived would eat their mates and lay their fertilized eggs in the male carcasses they buried on the river bottom. The jennies that died would be devoured themselves by their male counterparts.

Twelve hundred fish, she thought with disgust, and maybe only thirty or forty jennies would survive this run to lay their eggs. "When the mining guild blew up Floater-4 last week," she murmured to the school as she thought of the marine and freepick mining station off Black Flats, "that did a heck of a lot more damage to you than anyone thought."

She glanced at her scanner again. "Well," she told the silently passing school, "if I had been on the investigation board, the mining guild would not have gotten off with a simple matter of fines. The freepicks put in a lot of effort to comply with the biome laws. No guild miner ever does that. G-miners just take what they want and laugh while they pay the fines for cleanup." She stopped for an instant as a disgusted look crossed her face. "Daya!" She rolled her eyes. "Listen to me. I'm so desperate to be a full guide that I'm talking to fish."

She scowled and shifted her feet, and the current dragged at her legs. One of the crabs that dug into her repulsor clung with one claw for stability to the safety cord that held the gear to her belt. The current swirled; the crab clutched more tightly, and the cord, guaranteed against stretch, not slicing, was abruptly severed. The repulsor, its yellow bars flashing urgently, sank with both crabs into the murk at her feet.

The sand sucked, and the school of demonfish curved toward the shore. With a mutter, Tsia followed it. Behind her, mudcrabs buried the repulsor, and its signal faded.

A few seconds later she waded out of the two-meter field. The passing school hesitated. The scent of Tsia's skin was in the water, and the lead fish were no longer repelled by the sonics. Tsia, intent on her scanner, did not immediately notice. Then some change in the current made her look up.

The V of the demonfish was no longer straight. She scowled and reached for the repulsor. Her hand caught the safety thread, but when she pulled for the small floating box, the string came up fast and loose. Disconcerted, Tsia shifted her gaze toward the water—and searched the murky depths for a sign—any glimpse at all—of blinking amber lights.

There was nothing.

The fish uptide swept on past, but the V of the downtide school curved back against the current. Tsia felt her breath catch in her throat. Automatically, she imaged a command to the node for an emergency broadcast, but the silence of her temple link mocked her.

"Daya," she whispered. Her boots, standard guide issue, would protect her feet from almost anything, but her trousers were weatherproof, not protective, cloth. A demonfish could chew through that in a cold second. She should know. She had run into demonfish twice before. The memory of their ripping, stinging spines brought a rush of fear that chilled her twice as much as the icy water. In a second her feet pulled themselves free of the muck and struck out against the current, digging into the sand as fast as she could yank them loose and shove them down again.

The V of the lead fish had turned the school into a complete U now. And it was closer. Tsia spared it a frightened glance. She could not go through the rest of the school, even as sparse as it was. She leaned into the water. To lose her footing now would allow the current to sweep her right into those hungry, fang-full mouths.

The water swirled a greenish gray, and Tsia stared at its depth as she located the tag end of the school. Hurriedly, with the pounding of her heart choking the cold breath in her throat, she forced her way against the current. The hand that clutched the scanner swept through the water with her other palm, half swimming, half dragging herself along. She was now thigh-deep in the slough, and her toes dug into the mud with a vengeance. Something plucked at her knee—

Tsia's heart stopped. Her trousers tore in the teeth of the first fish, and the creature clung to the fabric with delight. It tugged and backed away from her legs, pulling back as she forced herself forward. Pieces of seaweed and detritus brushed slickly against her skin as the water was no longer filtered through her pants. Then a scaly fin slid along her calf.

Tsia panicked. She began to run in nightmarishly slow motion. She thrashed against the water, digging with her hands into the tide to pull herself away. The demonfish converged. Teeth shredded her trousers, tearing at the glistening fabric. She slipped against an algae-slick log half-buried in the mud and lost her footing. The current swept her into the school like a leaf. Stinging whiskers ripped across the back of her thigh. A set of dorsal spines cut across her calf. "Daya!" she cried out.

And then she burst out of the water and threw herself onto a rock. Her legs kicked at the bulging faces that followed. With a gasp that was almost a sob, she scrambled between the cracks in the stone and fell into the briny pools beyond.

Sand creatures shot away from her feet as she landed in the first pool. Wild-eyed, Tsia flung herself across the depth and up onto the next rock. She crouched for an instant like a cat, her chest heaving, the shreds of her trousers dripping and slapping against her skin in the icy wind and the churning of the slough that marked her escape.

Slowly, her heart sank out of her throat, but the stings in her thigh and calf now burned hotter with the cold wind that cut across her soaked and tattered clothes. Salt dried in her swelling wounds. The demonfish swirled out beyond the rock, their school disorganized as they hunted her scent. Small flurries marked the spots where males fought irritably among themselves; the jennies, more determined to spawn than to eat, turned and began to swim back upstream. Tsia stared at the V that reshaped itself in the slough. Two minutes, and the tag end of the school was hidden by the rippling of the current. Only the stinging of her calf and thigh reminded her of her risk.

Without ointment, the burn from the demonfish stings would last for hours. She tightened her jaw against the rising agony. The first time she had been stung, she had swum face-first into an aggressive jenny that had jabbed her whiskers into Tsia's cheek—Tsia still had a tiny line of puncture scars to prove it. The second time she had been stung had been four years ago, when she had been roughhoused off a Floater deck by her brother. She did not fault her brother; it could as easily have been he who fell in. Besides, he had used his own hands to distract the fish and push them away from her body as she climbed out.

Something cut into her hand, and, taking a breath to steady herself, she glanced down with a puzzled frown. The scanner, she realized, was still in her fist. Around it, her knuckles were scraped and bleeding from grabbing at the rocks while she held on to the gear. She stared at it for a long moment. Then her lips twisted. All that, she thought wryly, and she had not lost her data. Her friend Cullen would be proud.

She started to rise, and the movement set off another burning pain that faded as she finally regained her feet. Her legs shook. Carefully, wishing she could image some med commands to her body from the node, she slid off the rock and waded the rest of the way to the shore.

The tide had compressed the beach into a thin strip of sand, and

Tsia eyed it warily. Sandflies bred this time of year, and a careless step could mean immersion ankle-deep in a nest of stinking insects. Unlike the carnivorous shapers that swarmed in the fall, sandflies did not sting or bite; they exuded a rancid fluid that stained human skin and came off only in a molecular scrub. Tsia, looking down at her bare legs, made her way back to her cache of gear with care.

A few moments later she dragged her pack from under its sheltering sinktree and turned off its repulsor field. She had been gone from it only half an hour, but even in that time the estuary windmites, like whatever had gotten her own repulsor, could have dug into the sensitive organic modules stored in her pack. The First Droppers had learned quickly: On this planet unprotected gear was gear that would never be used again.

Intent on finding her medkit, she shoved her one spare jumpsuit aside, hesitated, then tossed it out onto the protruding sinktree roots. "Daya-damned demonfish," she muttered as she found the medkit under a layer of carefully packed samples. She fumbled with the manual catch of the kit as the pain in her thigh and calf increased. With an oath, she ripped the box open. The laser knife, the watergen and molecular scrub, the generic skin grafts—everything fell out into the sand. Tsia grabbed the antisting in midair and had the seal off even before the last bits of the medkit had stopped tumbling. Then she gritted her teeth from the added burn where the salve and demonfish venom interacted.

"At least guides heal fast," she muttered, slapping the seal back on the antisting. Even without the med commands imaged to her body from the node, the swelling would go down and the sting holes would shut within two days. Since she was not due back until after the gale hit, none of the other guides in the guild would notice, thank Daya. And it would be a cold day in hell before she trusted a safety thread again, she told herself as she repacked the medkit.

Shivering from the growing wind, she stripped the rags of her trousers from her legs and changed into her spare jumpsuit. She made a face at her boots. The boots were thermal, but the insides were always gritty after being immersed in the slough.

She glanced at the sky. She did not have to be a guide to know that a storm was blowing up; no biolink was necessary to feel the gusting chill that swept in from the sea. She would have to get her samples back to the skimmer and move the craft before the weather really hit. Her landing site was convenient to this finger of the slough, but it was also exposed, and no personal skimmer could stand up to one of the gales that so regularly smashed into this coast.

Feeling the wind again where it lifted her short hair, she grimaced. A second later she stuffed the scanner into her pack against the other hand-held units. Then she closed the bag, shouldered it, and made her way back to the trail. She did not envy the rep for the mining guild when she made her report to the marine guides. She grinned wryly to herself. She suspected that the mining guild wished she would delay her return as much as she wanted to herself.

A kilometer later, as if to remind her more forcefully that she did not want to go back, Tsia's pack began to whine. Hearing a second tone of complaint in the rising sound, she paused and scowled at the pack controls on her arm straps. Then she cursed softly. Her stabilizers were going out.

She imaged a command with her mind, then cut it off in midsend in growing frustration. With an angry gesture she dropped the pack on the ground. Manually, she reminded herself savagely. Everything had to be manual now because she did not have a goddamn temple link. Like the rest of the colonists, she was used to relying on her link to warn her of these things. She did not think to keep her eye on the manual readouts. If she had still had her temple link, she would have noticed the instant the pack started to destabilize.

Frustrated, she wrenched in vain at the controls. "Daya dang it," she cursed slowly. Of course the stabilizers were not working. She had forgotten to put the pack repulsor on again, and the node had not reminded her because it could not image the caution through her disabled temple link.

As she stared at the readouts, the stabilizer dial dropped even farther into the dead zone. There were, she thought hopelessly, probably dozens of windmites chewing at the pack circuits even as she watched. Chewing, eating their way toward the antigrav unit. And her samples and scanners.

"My samples!" Snapping out of her reverie, she tore into the pack. "Daya help you," she warned the windmites, "if you've gotten into my gear . . ." Torn trousers, medkit, everything went flying once again. Tsia did not care. She grabbed each scanner and pack of samples and brought them into the light, breathing in relief only when she saw that each one's shielding was still intact.

By the time she turned her attention to the stabilizers again, the unit was completely dead. The antigrav was in the green, but just barely—she could almost feel the module straining—and there was no way she could haul the pack all the way to her skimmer with both the stabilizers and the antigrav out. With the weight of her gear, at least one module had to be working or she could not even have lifted the pack, let alone hike with it.

"Useless, low-end piece of litter." She shoved the pack away. "Cursed windmites and Daya-damned demonfish," she added in frustration.

She rubbed the back of her thigh as if the thought of the fish made the sting wounds burn again. Then she cranked the pack repulsors on full.

"The way my luck is running," she muttered, "this will probably stimulate the windmites to eat more quickly."

She regarded her pack with disgust. If Cullen was around, maybe he could jury-rig the stabilizers through the node or give her a lift. If not—she kicked the offending module again—it was still six kilometers to her skimmer, and whether or not her stabilizers were working, she would have to make that distance fast.

2

She had hiked for an hour before Cullen met her where the Quill Trail branched north and east. Warned by yet another burn-out light, Tsia was struggling again with the pack, hauling it by brute force down the trail. Without any of the stabilizers and with half the antigrav unit down, the heavy weight of the bag jabbed painfully against her ribs. When she saw Cullen coming, she simply gave up and dropped the unwieldy thing on the path.

Cullen's black eyes crinkled, and he met her frustrated expression with a laugh. "I have never seen a more sour look on any guide's face."

"I need help," she returned sourly.

He glanced at the row of flashing red bars on the control straps of the pack. "You don't need help; you need an overhaul."

"Cullen, please," she said desperately. "I forgot to watch the controls manually, and the windmites got into the stabilizers—and the antigrav," she added, "but I think they are stopped now."

"You think?" His voice was teasing, but his eyes were sharp as he imaged his queries to the node and read the status of her pack through his own temple link.

Tsia shrugged helplessly and tried to punch in another manual command.

"Give me a minute," he returned absently, "and for Daya's sake, put that manual link down. I can image the node a thousand times faster than your clumsy fingers, and the maintenance jocks will do almost anything before they spend time trying to talk to you through a manual link."

With relief, Tsia tossed the manual linkbox aside. "I thought you would never get here." She grinned.

He raised his eyebrow. "I *hoped* I never would have to."

She scowled at him. "Yaza."

10

"Call me names and I won't fix your pack," he warned.

"I would rather you gave me and this gear a lift to my skimmer," she suggested.

"Can't. Got my craft locked into a two-day scan cycle that has to complete before the gale hits. I would lose both days of data if I broke out of the scan now."

"Then how did you get here so fast?"

He imaged a series of commands to the node and watched the status bars on Tsia's pack respond. "I was over on Rider Island," he answered absently. "Caught a waterjet across to Fern Creek off Black Pony Slough and came down Backlash Branch to the main trail. Couldn't go around to Yellow River. The tealers are running before the gale, and you know how sensitive they are to sonics—the jet would have panicked them back into the bay."

"Oh."

"Don't sigh so heavily," he said with a grin. "This—" He imaged a final command through the node. "—should hold you till you reach your own ship."

"Thank Daya," she breathed, rolling her shoulders when the weight of the pack suddenly lifted as Cullen reset the antigrav.

"Not me?"

She made a face and got to her feet. "Last one to the Backlash Branch is a mudfooted nake."

They strode off quickly. Even with the jury-rig, Tsia found walking awkward. Her body fought with odd muscles to turn her on the trail when the pack tried to continue in the same direction in which she had started. On top of that, her stomach roiled with nearly every step. She stopped for a moment to rest her calves, sighed, and rubbed her hand through her short, dark hair. Beside her, Cullen shot her a sympathetic glance.

"Goddamn useless stabilizers," she muttered.

Cullen chuckled. "Could have cached the pack."

"And risked more windmites?"

He shrugged. "Repulsors might have held out."

"Might have," she agreed noncommittally.

He grinned. "You going to cart that pack all the way to your skimmer?"

She nodded stubbornly.

"You'll catch hell if any of the guides find out."

Tsia's other hand rubbed the back of her punctured thigh guiltily. "Who's going to tell them?" she demanded. "My temple link is down and will be for another two months. The only way they can trace me is through my ID dot, and that only tells them where I am, not what I'm doing."

The dark-haired man frowned as he examined her antigrav unit again. The module was on its last legs. Even now it was holding up only half the weight of the pack. Cullen eyed Tsia, surreptitiously taking in her flushed cheeks, her frustrated ice-blue eyes, her short-cropped hair, and the stubborn set of her chin. "You took the guide virus only a week ago," he cautioned. "You know you should not be carrying that kind of weight."

She shifted her lean body against the awkward weight of the pack. "You could carry it for me," she suggested slyly.

He barked a laugh. "No chance. If I don't get back to my own scans, I'll have to reset the entire test." He started hiking again. "You coming or not?"

She dabbed ineffectually at her forehead with the back of her hand. "I am as soon as I take a breather."

Cullen halted, and his gaze narrowed as he looked back. "Your breath is quick," he said flatly, "and your skin is sweating. That is not a good sign."

"Actually," she retorted, "the one thing that is good is the sweat. If I didn't sweat, I would think the virus had not taken well in my body."

Cullen raised his eyebrow. "Heavy exercise means a faster-working virus," he reminded her sternly. "Your mutation rate is probably high as a skyhook right now. And after seventeen years in the guild," he admonished, "you, who have finally become a guide, should know better."

Tsia's lips set. "After seventeen years of training, three worthless stabilizers and half an antigrav unit are not about to stop me from making schedule. Don't worry about me. I know my limits." She rolled her shoulders and started after him again.

Cullen turned on his heel. "Last time you said that, it took four of us and a gale net to get you off Red Needle Rock."

Tsia smiled reminiscently. "That was hotter than riding the turbo hook to the station when the cable gave way. Remember that jump? Before we caught that updraft, I thought we were going to—"

"Tsia," he broke in, looking back over his shoulder, "you are changing the subject."

"Is it working?"

"No," he retorted. "If your mutation gets out of control, the guild will deactivate your virus. You know that. You said yourself that it would be the worst thing that could happen to a guide. And you," he accused, "with all the problems you have had taking the previruses, have spent three times longer than normal in the training classes. Seventeen years in the preps, and you could lose it all because you do not want to give up a little bit of data."

She rubbed her stomach absently, wishing its churning would stop. "I have been through three sessions of warning holos, Cullen. I have a pretty good idea of how much exercise the virus will take before it gets out of control."

The dark-haired man snorted.

Tsia glanced forward shrewdly. "If I were you and you were me, I bet you would not give up your gear."

He had the grace to acknowledge that truth.

"Hauling this pack might increase the rate of change in my body, but it will not strain the virus's effects past a viable mutation."

Cullen gave her a dark look. "I haven't known you to be this stubborn since you got rights-conditioned, in spite of the guild."

Tsia gave him a sour look. "If I wanted to learn to use a flexor, I had to get conditioned. It's the only legal way to get a weapon license. You can't carry more than a raser without one."

"Yeah, but why did you need to learn weapons, anyway?"

She grinned. "Jak wanted someone to practice on. It was fun," she insisted. "And I got good enough to be required to take rights-conditioning whether or not I went into the guide guild."

Cullen glanced back. He looked unconvinced.

"It has been useful," she reminded him. "Or have you forgotten the time you walked into that brawl? If Jak and I had not been there—"

He cut her off with a sour look. "Jak, Jak, Jak. The only man you ever talk about is Jak, and he is not even here—he's off in the tradelanes." Cullen's expression suggested that he hoped the other man would stay offplanet, too. "Why don't you, for once, forget him?"

"Like I can forget the effects of this guide virus?"

Cullen smacked his forehead with his palm. "I ought to be used to this by now," he muttered.

"Ought to be," she acknowledged, "but it sure doesn't stop you from nagging."

He glared at her, then chuckled. "I still think you should have kept your hair."

Tsia rolled her eyes and stared sourly at the slough as she passed a break in the heavy brush. Orpheus and Eurydice, Risthmus's two moons, had been aligned for days, and the tide was coming in like a flood. The short slapping sound of water against sand and mud was a constant, irregular rhythm, in contrast to her footsteps. "I took the virus for this—" She gestured toward the slough, the dikeland to the right, and the choppy gray bay beyond. "For the link I would get to the world. For the chance to taste the dust in my nose and feel the air changes like fingers on a second skin. I have dreamed of this since I was eight—to balance a biome as naturally as I balanced myself on my legs. When I finally hit twenty-one and got my temple link, the first thing I did was image every hologen on the work of the guides." She shook her head slightly. "To be a guide is to live, not just create the crops and creatures shipped out to planets I will never see."

Cullen's voice was thoughtful when he answered. "And wanting that so much," he said quietly, "you risk it all here?"

Tsia flushed slowly but refused to answer.

Cullen paused on the trail. When he turned to face her, his expression was sober. "In the time it takes you to get to your skimmer, you could push your mutation rate far past the viable rate of change. You could end up as a mutant—a guide without a virus, without a biogate. For all the years you have put into this, you could end up being no better than a naught."

For all the years ... Tsia's lips twisted bitterly as she came to a stop, and she hid her retort. She might as well be a naught for all the good her new biolink would do her.

Unconsciously, her fingers rose to tap the tiny temple insets. Without the active link, only the background noise of the node cushioned the thoughts in her mind. Irritating as it was, at least her link had not been shut off completely while the virus changed her brain patterns. Only rare trainees—and the odd religious zealots and criminals, she acknowledged—had the complete silence of the node in their minds. No access. No images to call up, create, and communicate to other minds through the linking of the orbiting nodes. She eyed Cullen enviously.

Beside her, Cullen's gaze followed her hands to her inactive temple sockets. "Wish you still had your link?"

She nodded sourly. Her fingers brushed the newly short strands of her hair from the surface of the tiny sockets with a wince.

He grinned. "Wish you still had your hair?"

Tsia made a face at him. Her gaze flicked to his thick, black hair. Black like the peaks of the Vulcans. She glanced up beyond the trees to the mountain range that blocked the south end of the sky. Sixty kilometers away the slough disappeared abruptly into those rising ridges. Up there, where the demonfish fought and bred and devoured each other in a frenzy, the brine of the Yellow River Drainage became clear, icy runoff; the lowland ferns and pipeplants became the hardy brush and sparse trunks of the alpine fir. If her body took the virus well, the Federation would award her this entire watershed, from coast to cliff, as long as she wanted it. Her own land to design, to plant, to mutate, to test and change. Here, like a tiny god, she could create life, destroy it, and build it up again. Here, where the twisted fingers of the slough branched back from the swollen, whitecapped ocean, where the grasses swayed in the gusting wind, she could be the one who imaged life into being.

She motioned for him to continue, and he eyed the faraway look on her face as he turned back to the trail. "So how many in your class took the final virus?"

"Four."

"You, Geri, Starr, and Idonlia?"

She shook her head. "Idonlia's virus did not take. The fourth was Sian."

Cullen made a rude sound. "Sian the artist?"

She nodded her own disgust. "How he can take the virus just for the firedance, when there is so much more to being a guide . . ."

Cullen gave her a sidewise look. "You have to admit, of all the side effects the guide virus has, the firedance is one of the most beautiful."

"Oh, it makes my blood sing to dance in the flames," she admitted. "And my skin glows to feel the the sweat pouring out between me and the heat. But when it is over and the firepit is empty, I realize every time that the firedance is still just movement. It is just a dance. It does not change *dreams*."

"Only a shallow-brained artist would try to take the guide virus just to get a firedance."

"The smart ones," Tsia agreed, "try to buy a guide to use the firedance in their art." She brushed at a cloud of gnats that hung over the trail and ducked beneath a fallen branch. Ahead of her, Cullen paused at the fallen frame of a moss-covered horitree.

"Did you ever look at the offers you got from the art guild?" he asked as he half turned to step over the log.

"Didn't bother. The firedance is the least of what I wanted from the virus. I wanted the biogate—the sense of another life-form as my own. Besides," she added in a smug voice as she accepted Cullen's help over the log, "I had four offers from the top biodevelopment companies. Two more came direct from Gea."

"Two from genetic engineering and analysis?" Cullen sighed wistfully. "They must want you badly."

She nodded. "So, even if I was interested in working for an artist—which I am not—it would be hard for them to top the other offers." She grinned to herself as Cullen strode ahead. Seventeen years, and the final virus had finally taken. And once it was finished changing her and she became a full guide—

Tsia's thoughts stopped abruptly. She would never be a full guide. That she must not forget. The most important part of being a guide was the biogate, and her own gate was useless. Seventeen years to take the preps. Almost half her life growing more and more stubborn about the goal of becoming a guide, and then this—a week ago, to have the phage mutate in the one way she had not expected . . .

Above her, dull sunlight caught her gaze as it shifted among the leaves and made her sensitive eyes flinch. The twisting shadows seemed to mock her with their dancing light. The sky, she thought angrily, should reflect the roiling gray of the oncoming gale, the cold set of her heart, or at least some bitter disappointment— anything but the bright blue of summer and Cullen's smiling face and that picturesque line of peaks that hid what Tsia could never, ethically, touch.

She turned her head and stared back at the distant Vulcans. Somewhere in that mountain range ran the descendants of the first scoutcats—the cougars and panthers that had come down before even the First Droppers had hit ground. Somewhere beyond those ridges more cats prowled the Sinking Plains. Tsia's own grandmother, like the other First Droppers, had come in with the scoutcats. For eighty years, before Risthmus was opened for colonists, her grandmother had lived on this world and run the hills with the three-toed deer. Even helped engineer some of the servals and cougars. Servals and cheetahs and cougars—scouts, Tsia knew, for every terrain. The cheetahs, with their long, lanky bodies and short, coarse hair, had taken to the plains in a flash. The cougars had gone for the rocky ridges and forests. And the tams, with those furry, sensitive knobs between their ears, had taken to the heights of the Cheba Rift. All across the planet the scoutcats had taken to Risthmus as if it were old Earth itself.

Tsia stared at the Vulcans and the way they mocked her biogate. Every guide's virus settled into a resonance that let the new guide feel one aspect of her world. With time, the new guide could become sensitive to dozens—sometimes even hundreds—of life-forms, leading the life-forms into new mutations, new paths that could be used on this and other worlds. Seals, mudcrabs, demonfish, trees . . . Some of the First Droppers could sense more than a thousand life-forms. Daya, what she would have given to have been one of them: the first to see the Dry Mountains, to find the evie ores, to feel the shifts in the biomes that came from the presence of the scoutcats . . . Her envy rose again, and she tasted it with a bitter tang. Seventeen years . . .

She said in a low voice, "Did you never dream of being a guide? Of being the one whose work influenced the grass and trees on other worlds? To know that your work would live on in biomes so new to humans that the bones of the first colonists had not yet rotted?" She fingered her short hair. "I wanted the virus more than anything. After almost two decades of preps, giving up my hair seemed a small price to pay."

Cullen glanced back, then away. "I would have paid that price," he said quietly.

Tsia glanced at the set of his shoulders in surprise. "You are jealous?"

He gave her a steady look, then grinned. "With the guide virus in your body,"—he motioned with his chin at her lean figure— "you will be able to pull twice the contract offers a flat ecologist like me will get. A couple of years, and your credit chit will be fatter than a summer reaver on a full root dike."

"Pretty clean deal, huh?"

"Hell. If I had even had a chance . . ."

Cullen's words held real envy, and Tsia glanced at him sharply, then hurried forward to touch his arm in apology. "Cullen, I did not mean to tease." His mouth set in a thin line, and she nudged him until the corners of his lips twitched. "Besides, of all the people on Risthmus, you are the last one to need the guide virus. You have more instinct for the slough than I have ever seen in anyone except the guides themselves, and we both know the guides are no competition for you. There aren't even that many guides here."

He sighed. "Too much ecological balancing, not enough newness or challenge."

"Don't be bitter. Challenge is what you make it."

"Now, that sounds like something a guide would say."

She laughed. "Sorry."

He gave her a lopsided grin. "You will have to leave the slough now, won't you?"

"Probably," she said bluntly.

"Do you have a choice?"

"I don't know. The other new guides already shipped out on assignment. Geri to Tipler Ridge, Sian to the Rushing Forest—even an artist has to pay off his training." She grinned maliciously. "And Starr to Paddleback Creek."

"She waited so long to choose, I wondered if she would take that contract."

She shrugged. "Gea contracts are always good."

Cullen motioned at the roiling currents in the water. "Good as the one you have here?"

"Pretty much."

He caught the hesitation in her tone. "But?"

She glanced wistfully toward the peaks of the Vulcans. "I love it here," she admitted, "but sometimes I feel . . ." She hesitated. "Locked in place." She nodded, more to herself than to Cullen. "Yes, locked in place by the smell of the sea."

Cullen glanced over his shoulder at her. Her sun-darkened skin was weathered with tiny lines around her eyes and mouth—good lines, he thought: lines of humor and determination. With the stiff wind, her short hair ruffled softly. "I can't imagine you away from the coast," he commented. "What would you do for fun if there were no storm sets to swim out in? No gales to bend the trees around your ears?"

Tsia gave a low laugh. "The sound of the sea—it is too much in my blood," she agreed. Her lips twisted. "Of course, with all the time it has taken for me to get through the preps, the guild is waiting to see whether the guide virus takes fully before they assign me anywhere else."

"Virus or not," Cullen said slowly, "I would not want another terrain."

Tsia's gaze rose again to the Vulcans. "My grandmother was firstgen. She scouted this coast with a cougar and a three-toed deer. My father was born in her second cycle, when she was 154, and he followed the white stalkers, took the sea assayers' guild all the way from the headwaters of the Yellow River to the mouth of the Grodnik Bar. Both my brothers are up on Black Flats, creating microcosms of mud that are shipped out every month to Oasis— that new planet on the rim. And I—" She touched the soft soil at her feet. "—am here. My older sister is the only one who did not want to be a guide, and even she left the coast for the trade stations. Last I heard, she was up on an orbiting hammer, docking ships and checking cargo and slapping the smugglers' hands when they got too obvious for even her to ignore." Cullen grinned, and Tsia nodded at the currents that boiled even closer now, where the tide and the flowing river met.

"I think of my sister, looking down on this planet. Every day I wonder if, while she checks my work through some trader's hold and seals it for some colonist on the rim, she ever longs for something more. And then I smell the storms rising from the sea, and I want to dive in, let the current take me out past the land, far away—anywhere—just to see what there is beyond this stretch of sand."

Cullen plucked a shred of tall grass from a clump beside the trail. "Curiosity?"

She shrugged. "Risthmus is so new. There are places not even the miners have staked."

Passing another clump, Cullen tossed his crushed grass aside and picked another. "Might be places they never will," he commented, crunching down on the new green spike.

She snorted, remembering the decimated demonfish run. "If the freepicks have as much coring gear down now as they claim, the mining guild will have to fight for every ore deposit left on the planet."

Cullen chuckled and leaned into the trail as it climbed a small hill. "They are at each other's throats," he agreed. "Did you hear about what happened in Pulan? As soon as the ores in the subterranean vaults were cleared for staking, some freepicks beamed in on a narrowwarp gate. They had half the deposits staked before the mining guild even knew they were there." He plucked another grass from the clump and chucked his currently crushed blade. "Between the freepicks and being kicked down off Cheba Rift, the guild is smoldering."

Tsia grimaced as she fought her pack up the hill. Its weight wanted to go forward, not up, and she struggled to keep her shoulders upright. "Don't see why they are all churned up over Cheba Rift," she complained. "The Landing Pact is clear enough. The scoutcats got all the land in Cheba Rift and half the land in the Vulcans. The miners should have tried to stake something else."

"They are trying to stake everything they can before the Pulanese prophecy comes true."

"Prophecy? Oh, you mean the one from the First Droppers? The one about some great leader who would come and unite the colonist factions of this entire planet?"

Cullen reached the top of the hill and nodded. He glanced back to see if Tsia needed a hand, but she gave him a back-off look, and he grinned. "Esper guild reconfirmed it last week," he explained. "Something about it centering in Pulan—around the ores.

That the next leader in the council would weld all the mining factions together. Of course, the mining guild does not want to share anything with the freepicks. They want to make sure that if anyone unites the mining factions, the guild holds most, if not all, of the ore deposits. Everyone remembers what happened on Vendetta."

Tsia nodded slowly. When the planet Vendetta had been staked, the mining guild had pulled only a quarter of the ores. It tried to buy out the freepicks and ended up being kicked off the planet. When they retaliated, they used microbes and viruses. Now the entire planet was blacklisted. The only people dirtside on Vendetta were scientists, criminals, and revenge challengers who never went offplanet once they landed to fight out their differences. Vendetta was a planet that took all comers. It was a place where people without hope went to die. The mercs called it heaven.

Tsia glanced out toward the ocean. "Mining guild," she murmured. "Probably blasted Floater-4 on spite. As long as they stopped another freepick holding, they would not care whether or not they killed the marine biologists there, too."

Cullen nodded again and hiked along the top of the rise. "Bet it's an all-out conflict before the year is out."

"At least the merc guild would be hiring then. They fight a hell of a lot cleaner than the miners ever did."

"Ah, yes, the errant knights of the Federation." Cullen grinned and paused to look out at the estuarine race. "I wonder if, while we dream of fish, they dream of war and flexors."

She came up to stand beside him and gave a short laugh. "I used to wonder," she said, "when I was a child—when both moons rose and the tides came in—what dreams they brought for me."

" 'They bring the dreams of life,' " Cullen quoted softly. " 'The lines, the tidelines that barely hold the water from the sea—they wait to greet the land flowing down and to give back to it the brine of the sea.' "

" 'Oh, let my heart with fire be filled,' " she finished softly, " 'So then to be quenched in this sea.' " She squatted and, as the pack settled down, jabbed her fingers through the slough bank, the sand and mud clinging to her hand before she washed it off in the lapping water.

Cullen squatted beside her and reached out to take her other hand.

The tide was still rising, and another school of demonfish made its way upstream. Restlessly, Tsia shifted her irritated calf. Across the water the mud flats were dark and flooded, and the white stalkers and blue-spotted creepers picked their way along the shallows. Tsia watched them silently move along the tideline until a watercat crept to the water. Her gaze sharpened abruptly.

Tail twitching, the watercat crouched in wait for the stalkers. Tsia ran her tongue around her lips. She could almost sense the cat. Involuntarily, she leaned forward, and the eagerness in her eyes was palpable. Her longing, her disappointment fell away. The biolink she had just gotten from the virus—this was it, she realized: this sense of life. This feeling that her heart beat not here, in her chest, but there, across the water, in the body of that cat. She could almost touch it, guide the creature with her mind . . .

Her train of thought shut off abruptly. She had no right to guide a cat. Touch it, yes, but not lead it. All that training, she spit at herself, and she would, the first time she felt a feline, give in to the one thing she must not do. The cat's ears twitched, and her cheek muscles flinched with her sense of it. She forced herself to lean back, to rub her calf casually, as if the disappointment that swelled within her were nothing.

It should not matter that her biolink was stuck on the cats, that her resonance had settled in the gate of the felines. The virus was a gamble, she reminded herself harshly, a challenge to oneself to change one's own future. The work, she told herself, the ecology, the biology—that, at least, would never be a loss.

Cullen regarded the water absently, then helped Tsia back up. "Remember when I dared you to cross that fireline over on Black Pony Slough two years back?"

On the opposite bank the watercat slipped back into the brush, and Tsia's eyes glinted. "Sure." It was difficult to keep the emotion from her voice, but Cullen did not notice. "You dared me," she agreed, "and, as usual, I did it."

"Yeah." He laughed. "And singed your toes while you were at it. I've never seen anyone hit Roan Creek so hard in my life." He pushed her lightly onto the trail.

Tsia forced a grin. "I hit your credit chit, too. You owed me for two weeks after that."

"You never could resist a dare."

"I should have refused that one. I thought they would throw me out of the firedance classes after that. And you should have seen the look on Jak's face when he found out. I thought he was going to take the next trade ship off the docking hammers without ever speaking to me again."

Cullen stretched his neck, twisting it from one side to the other until it cracked. When he looked back at her, his eyes were somber. "You know, that day was the first time I really believed you would pass all the tests."

She glanced at him in surprise, and he nodded.

"You had just come from the guild, and you were sick of the pity behind every word of instruction you got. They were trying one more time to convince you of some other career path—I think it was with the builders guild that time—they had an opening out in Korshan where the desert ran up against the Dry Mountains, and they needed someone who really knew soil to help them plan the retaining walls for another cargo skimmer pad on the southern side of the Cheba Rift."

She nodded slowly.

He chuckled and began heading down the other side of the rise. "You were so angry by the time you reached the slough that even I could not make you laugh. The way you faced the fire . . ." He shook his head. "You were so determined, so stubborn. That was two years ago, and you had spent fifteen years training to be a guide, but you were still working your way through the prep viruses. You had more feet in the coals—spent more time there, I mean—than any other guide since your father took the preps, and for once, here, nothing was going to stand in your way, not the fire, not the lack of the virus. Nothing."

She raised her eyebrow.

"I had the feeling," he admitted, "that my dare was secondary."

Her eyes shuttered. Cautiously, she started down the slope after him. Her pack whined softly, and its antigrav-supported weight almost lifted her feet from the earth.

"You wanted to go through that fire," he stated flatly, watching her descent. "If I had not been there, you would have done it anyway, just to show yourself that you could."

Tsia said nothing. She could walk the fire better than half the guides on Risthmus, but she could never use her link . . . She forced her mind to the mud-slick path.

"You did the moves like a veteran," Cullen added. "Even without the final virus to help you sweat, you danced your way across just like a real guide. It was as if . . ." He regarded her probingly. "As if you thought that the fire was just one more obstacle in your way, one more discouragement you had to face to become a guide, not something that could burn or scare you away."

She gave him a wry look. "With fifteen years in the coals, fire was the last thing that could scare me." She hit the bottom of the slope and caught her breath with relief. The weight of the pack was beginning to cramp her shoulders. "I think the longer my prep took," she admitted, "the more I wanted the final phage."

"Wanted it?" Cullen snorted. "You needed it."

She wrinkled her nose at him.

He nodded. "I've thought about this quite a bit—it is the prerogative of friends," he teased as he continued, "to think often of each other." He grew more serious. "But you do need this virus," he repeated. "You need to best it, to show that you, too, are strong enough, stubborn enough to be a guide."

"And stupid enough to walk the fire when my body does not know how to sweat."

Cullen grinned. "Why let stupidity stand in your way? Nothing else has."

"I had fifteen years in the coals," she protested virtuously. "My feet were so used to the firepit that I hardly even felt the heat anymore. What harm could a little fireline like the one in Black Pony do? It wasn't even a hot flame. Anyone could have done it."

"Most of the guide wannabes do not even make it out of the coal classes," returned Cullen. "Half the rest do not make it through the preps, and only one in four can tolerate the final virus. That does not even count the ones who drop out because it requires more work than glamour." He turned on a tiny switchback and shot her a considering look. "After watching you go through the preps, I am beginning to think that it is not genetics that makes a guide but mule-headed determination."

Tsia's eyes crinkled. "That is the most tactful you have ever been in calling me a stubborn fool."

"Stubborn? I'll go with the second half of that: fool." He had the satisfaction of seeing her eyes narrow in mock anger. "You had neither the final virus nor the sweat it now brings to your skin, and yet you were dancing your way through the flames. You took my dare as if it were a splash of water, not a firedance you had no approval to do."

"Well, I firedanced my way to the bottom of the class list once again."

"And got your status. They had to acknowledge what you did. And you have not seen their pity since."

Tsia's face lost her humor. No, she had not seen pity for the last two years. Not until a week ago, when she finally took the guide virus and became linked to her biogate. The bitterness that rose in her mouth tasted like rotting mud, and she had to swallow to rid herself of the sensation. She should have let the demonfish have her for supper for all the good she would do the guide guild. A guide without a gate. Now, *that* was a joke.

Unaware, Cullen walked on. "I always wondered what it would feel like to have a biogate like you do now. To be able to feel, not just study a biome." He motioned at his deep black eyes. "I got my vision from my parents. Naturally," he teased with a grin. "Not as a forced mutation like you. I can see what others don't, but sight does not add to my other feelings. To be a guide, now, that is a goal. To feel the life-forms in a biome as much as you would feel your own skin . . ."

Tsia shifted her pack, cursed as its assisted weight made her stumble against a tree, and used the time to get a grip on the bitterness that wanted to sharpen her words. "I can't feel much yet," she returned steadily. "I took the virus only a week ago, and—damn these stabilizers." She stopped abruptly against the bole of a sinktree. "I will probably have to go the entire year before I stop feeling nauseous and start feeling biomes."

Cullen got up and hauled her to her feet, balancing the pack for her. "So," he said curiously, "you going to tell me?"

Tsia turned away, hiding the slow flush that spread across her cheeks and down her neck. She knew what he was going to ask. "Tell you what?" she stalled, rubbing her calf again.

"Don't play dumb. I saw you staring across the slough back there. What biogate did you get with your virus—at what resonance did it stop? Did you link to the sea lions? The sinktrees? The—" He leered evilly. "—watersnakes?"

Tsia smiled in spite of herself. "No," she said truthfully, "I did not get the watersnakes."

The hand steadying her pack suddenly removed its grip so that she tottered on the bank of the slough. "Cullen," she protested, laughing. She grabbed his arms so that she would not fall.

He pursed his lips as if thinking. "The black-tailed gris?" he suggested. He followed her gaze. "The hungry demonfish? The reavers? No, I've got it—the smelly pipeplants!"

"No," she said, pulling free. "Never, and absolutely not."

"Well, what, then?"

Tsia's eyes flickered across the slough. Cullen stooped to stare into her face. "You are blushing," he said, puzzled. "You are . . . embarrassed? Tsia, look at me. What kind of biolink could make you look like this? You're a biologist, an ecologist even. In your position, a windmite would have value."

Tsia looked down at her feet, noting absently the clay that still clung stubbornly to her thin jumpsuit. She brushed the pants so that the wet dirt slid off, dropping with tiny plops beside her now-dry boots. "Why," she complained rhetorically, "can't they invent skin that would shed dirt like our clothes do?"

"Tsia," he went on, ignoring her subterfuge, "what is wrong with you? You are the newest guide in Ciordan. New guides are dying to tell the world which resonance their virus set their gates at. Every other guide does."

"Maybe I'm not like every other guide."

"Maybe," he acknowledged slowly, his eyes steady. "But ever since I met you you have been telling me about buying one of those live-in skimmers. You have been assaulting my ears for almost two decades now, boasting that once you got your virus, you would have the ship in half a decade. You are the one," he reminded her, "who told me the guide spiel so often, it has haunted me in my dreams." His voice took on a node broadcast tone. " 'The newest guide—guaranteed to land a job with any of the eighteen guilds, catch any Gea contract the Federation offers, hire out custom to the colonists, earn five times the credit a yaza like me will make. Any job you want is yours: biologist, ecologist, agfa, even dirtside scout. Just like the First Droppers—tap into your biogate and let the senses flow. Better than a scanner on full sweep.' "

Tsia's lips set in a bitter line. "Better than a scanner. Right."

Cullen eyed her warily. "What the heck is wrong with you? Didn't the virus . . ." His eyes widened, and his voice trailed off. He remembered the guide who had lost her virus. "Didn't it . . . take?"

"It took." Tsia's voice was flat.

"You touched your gate? Had your first sweat? Did the firedance? Come on, Tsia, talk to me."

"I had the sweat. I did the firedance."

"And?"

Tsia looked up. "I will tell you about my biolink, Cullen, but only once." She stared off at the mountains, one hand rubbing along her stomach as if the motion alone would calm her guts. "After that," she said flatly, "I do not want to talk about it again."

"Tsia, I don't understand."

"My virus," she said curtly, "resonated to the felines."

"Tsia—" Cullen's voice broke off abruptly. He stared at her. "The cats? The cat family?"

She nodded.

The tall man ran his hand through his dark hair. Staring at her, he demanded, "You are sure?" He motioned sharply. "Reaver dung," he cursed, muttering. "Of course you are sure. It is your goddamn biogate."

Tsia stared at the towering peaks of the Vulcans that rose above the trees to the south. Like cats' ears, she thought bitterly, sharp and conical. Cats. Hell, even the resonance of a demonfish would have been a better biolink. At least with a demonfish, she would have been able to guide the runs so that they recovered quickly from that blast out on Floater-4. She tightened her lips. Or a reaver—linking to them would have been an estuarine guide's dream. To be able to lead their work where it was needed along the coastline, to build dikes where the tides would otherwise destroy a fragile breeding ground, or dig out the earthen walls to open a meadow to the brine . . .

But no, she had the felines. The one link that, on the entire planet of Risthmus, could not be fully used or even completely explored. Once the work of the scoutcats was done, the felines had slunk away to the wilderness they had been awarded. The Landing Pact gave them the choice of their future, and they chose isolation. To have a link with them . . .

Tsia forced herself to stop rubbing the back of her thigh. Daya damn her, she thought with tight emotion, but seventeen years of prep and she was no better than a cripple. A . . . naught herself—a guide without a gate. One who felt but not one who created action or balance. She would not be able to live with the cats the way the other guides lived with their gates, so she would never grow beyond her link to the other life-forms. For a genetic ecologist there could be no more useless link.

Soon, she knew, she would feel the felines more strongly than she had sensed that watercat on the bank. Her biogate would taunt her with the sleek power of the cougars and tams, their blood lust, their hedonistic senses, their range from plains to mountains to sands . . . And all she would have was the fire and short hair that marked her as a guide. She would have what only an idiot like Sian wanted: the coals and flames that seared the oils from her skin and, with them, burned the bitterness into her brain.

Cullen's voice, when he spoke, was low and gravelly. "God, Tsia, I'm sorry."

She met his eyes. "I would appreciate it—" Her voice almost broke, but she steadied it. "—if you did not spread the news around just yet." She motioned sharply at the trail.

"Tsia, no one would make fu—"

She cut him off and pushed ahead of him. "Cullen—" She threw the words back with bitterness. "I am the oldest new guide to take the virus in eight planets and three centuries. I have caught flak for that for the last eleven years. Now, with a biolink to the felines, I will be the butt of every other stupid joke and rude remark for the rest of my life. I am no better than a blind guide, and if that isn't a joke, what is? I can dance in the fire, but I cannot use my biogate. The only thing the virus gives me is sweat and short hair and a too-damn-sensitive nose. The part I dreamed of, the part I need, the part I have given half my life to get, is the one thing I cannot have: a link that I could use to feel the land—the biome—like a sense, a link that would be the voice of this earth always in my mind." She clenched her fists so tightly that her knuckles whitened. "I might as well be like that artist, Sian. With my link, I am nothing more than a . . . than a naught, myself," she forced out the words.

Cullen caught up with her and grabbed her hand. "Tsia, I—"

Tsia pulled her hand free. "Please, Cullen." She took a deep breath. Some of the tension eased from her frame. "Let me be."

He looked at her for a moment, taking in her close-cropped head and tanned skin, the stubborn set of her jaw, and the bitter glint in her ice-blue eyes. "I guess," he said softly, "it will take a little while longer to build up that credit chit, huh?"

Tsia gave him a sour look. He mimicked it back so exactly that she found she was laughing in spite of herself. "Cullen," she said helplessly, "you are my best friend, but—"

He raised his eyebrow suggestively. "I was hoping I was more than that."

Laughing, Tsia turned back to the path. "You know why you are not."

He snagged her hand and, turning her, swept her hand to his lips, catching her weight and steadying her as her pack kept swiveling around. "But Jak is away," he said persuasively, "and you could grant me just a little hope. Even a microrad of promise would sustain me for yet another year of dreaming: marriage, family, kids . . . little black-eyed guides hanging off my legs and yours . . ."

Tsia lost some of her smile. Even if the virus did not leave her barren—which happened about half the time and was the reason the guide guild kept samples from each guide in stasis—she was too old now to have children within her first set of cycles. Her first menopause had occurred a year ago. She would not go into second cycle till she was well over a hundred. Daya alone knew if, with all Tsia's other troubles assimilating the virus, she would be able to have children then, either.

Cullen caught her expression and misunderstood. "It's Jak Volen and my foul karma that has come between us again," he lamented. "I can have any woman in the sixty-four worlds except the one I want."

"Uh huh."

"Tease."

Glancing back, she raised her eyebrows and missed the turn on the trail. Her pack pushed her forward, and the slope of the ground made her misstep. Two feet, and she was into the slough, knee-deep in the water and ankle-deep in mud. "Daya damn it!" she cursed, trying to stop herself before she got in much deeper. The pack whined; her momentum forced her another foot forward. Behind her, Cullen started to laugh. She twisted to glare at him, and the current pressed against her legs while she sank into the mud.

"Dammit," she swore. "Cullen, give me a hand, will you."

Cullen, his black eyes dancing, choked his laughter into a cough. "Of course," he said slyly. He dropped his own gear and started clapping.

"Cullen," she wailed. "If I turn around, I will fall. I cannot afford to get my gear wet, and—dang it all," she cursed with exasperation, "I'm sinking."

He took pity and waded out to get her. It took both of them to get her up the undercut embankment off which she had stepped. It took another five minutes for him to jury-rig her pack again. In the meantime Tsia fidgeted from foot to foot, the water in her boots squishing with an unpleasant sound. She would have to hike with it now; getting the pack on and off once Cullen had adjusted it was even worse than walking in water-slogged footgear.

Cullen adjusted the weight of her pack as best he could. "Okay, I think this will do it." He trailed off. "This time, follow me. And watch where I step."

"You mud-footed yaza," she snapped. "I have been hiking this slough since I was born."

"It shows, too," he teased.

Tsia let out her breath in disgust.

"Your gate," he began. "Is that the reason you came back to the demonfish run so soon after taking the virus?"

"It was not obvious?" she retorted.

He followed the trail around a stand of immature rednut trees. "Is it wise to be away from the guild right now? Don't you want to find out all the mysteries of being a guide? Now that you have the virus, even your father can finally talk to you about it. You can get the answers to all the questions you have saved up over, let's see now, how many years has it been?" He started counting on his hands. "Eleven, twelve . . ."

"Seventeen, you reaver-toothed mutant."

Cullen glanced back. "You say you need time to adjust, but it is pretty isolated out here. You ought to be with the other guides. This is your first week with that stuff in your body. No telling what it will end up doing." He began to twitch his arm as he hiked. "You could begin to feel claws stretching out of your hands . . ." He batted at the air. "You are," he added slyly over his shoulder, "and even you admit it, very old to become a guide."

"You flat-faced yaza—"

"They say," he went on, voice dropping to a whisper, "the virus is harder to adjust to the older you get. You are thirty-eight. It might not even make a clean mutation with you. Your eyes, why, they could begin to slant like a suncat in a week."

"Cullen—"

"You could grow a tail," he suggested with interest.

"You—" She jabbed a finger at his back. "—have been through this already with your cousin. Did he sprout wings? Grow feathers on his back? You know the changes are subtle. Besides," she added, shrugging into the pack and trying to adjust its position against her sore hips, "I have plenty of time to ask my questions later, just like the other guides. Right now I want some peace."

"Before the battle?"

"Before the war."

He chuckled.

"So," she said, changing the subject, "what was the word from the orbiting node? About my stabilizers, I mean. Can they do anything from their God-on-high position? Or must they admit to a more dirtside pursuit of their mechanical errors?"

"They can't do anything remotely," he answered.

Tsia grimaced. "So if I want this pack fixed, I will have to drop the whole thing off tonight for service?"

"Uh huh." The trail forked, and Cullen paused, waiting for her to catch up. When she did, he checked her pack again. "At least it isn't far to your skimmer from here. You could have followed that run of fish all the way in to the breeding grounds before the stabilizers cut out."

"My luck runneth over."

He grinned and let his eyes run over her dark, cropped hair. The brown hair framed her face, making her look, with her ragged eyebrows, vaguely catlike in the cream-colored jumpsuit. The splash of forest green that marked the sides of the clothing somehow caught the blue in her eyes, making her gaze brighter than it had been before. He watched the play of muscles in her arms as she shifted the pack again. She had, what, four genetic engineering and analysis degrees now? And every one of those Gea degrees was in biology and ecology. Even though her link had settled at the felines, this entire planet was geared for genetic research, and she would still be a guide in demand.

Unaware of his thoughts, Tsia tried to shift her pack again, and Cullen gave her a hand. "I've set the antigrav on as high as it will go," he remarked, "so remember your momentum."

She gave him a sour look. "I can hardly forget it," she retorted. "When I went into the mud flats back there, I was thigh-deep before I could stop without falling on my face. And you," she accused, "were less than helpful."

"Humor *is* helpful," Cullen insisted piously. "Listen, I have to get back to my own scans. If you get stuck again, give a yell. I will be over on Rider Island for at least three more hours, then I'm heading up to the meadow above Frail Falls to dig in before the wind hits."

She nodded. "All right. If you don't hear from me, don't worry. I should have gone on in by the time you finish up on the island." Her shoulders bent forward under the weight of her pack. "By the time I get to my skimmer, I will have barely enough time to set the backup unit for tomorrow's work and still get this piece of trash back for service."

Cullen frowned. "You will lose four hours of work today. You want me to call in on my link and get you a new schedule?"

"No, I'll use the manual link. I have to wait anyway till I know how long it will take to get my pack back. There are no extras at base, and the center is still backed up with the agfa equipment that was damaged in the last gale."

"So even a guide has to take what she can get?"

"I will take you and dump you in the slough if you don't let me get on with my work."

The black-haired man grinned and disappeared around a bend in the trail, and Tsia's expression faded to worry.

3

Time, she thought as she watched Cullen stride away. Everything was a matter of time. Time to take the viral preps, time to get used to her biolink, time to follow the demonfish runs, time to fix her pack. She was short of nothing but time, and her scans had to be completed by the end of next week. Unfortunately, the slower speed of her backup unit would drop her scan rate to three kilometers a day. Her entire schedule could be shifted.

Stubbornly resolute, she caught her stride quickly and made her awkward way between the rocks and roots that littered the path. The trail wound along the slough, crossing four, then five small creeks that added their tiny flow to the estuary. To her right a long, low monument stone curved down into the flooded inlet beyond the dikes. Cullen's mention of family had brought to the fore her memory of the children who had drowned and suffocated in the mud flat: three of those children had been the sons and daughters of guides, guides who had hit their second menopause and for whom there would be no more chances to try to have children again. Tsia quelled her own uncertainty. Most of the guides in her family had been lucky, but there were no guarantees. Her fertility, not just her hair, could have been sacrificed to get the biogate of the cats.

Tsia shivered. The monument stone was like a white beacon in the flooded bay, and the images of the dead children were sharp in her mind. Those small, slender bodies sinking, chilled into hypothermia, screaming in gargled terror as the tide swept in and choked off their lives. Hands, her brother's hands, her own hands numbed by the icy cold, gripping, hauling futilely at those tiny, tide-slick wrists. Voices, Jak's voice, her own voice urging, shouting, screaming at them to keep their lips on the hollow reeds, to keep their eyes shut from the claws of the mud crabs that she

31

caught, heedless of the stinging hairs, and threw out of the water. Screaming at them to breathe, breathe through the broken reeds— She closed off her thoughts abruptly. The sea did not give gentle death.

As if the thought of the churning sea had brought it on, her nausea rose and swept her guts with savage suddenness. With the full weight of the pack tipping her forward, she groaned and stumbled against a sinktree, missed her grab, and ended up scraping her arm on the tree's roughened bark. Her other hand grabbed her stomach. Her lips twisted, and her teeth clenched against the sensation. The silent struggle ended a moment later as the wave of queasiness passed, only to be followed by a second rise of bile. Her mentor guides had said it would be bad the first couple of days—but this bad? As with the demonfish stings, she could not even use her temple link to image the med commands to her brain. All she could do was listen to the background noise of the node while her guts scrambled themselves below.

With the third wave of nausea, Tsia dropped her pack and went to her knees in the dirt. She stared at the earth for endless moments while her stomach roiled and the nausea flared, then subsided, then surged up again. The sweet scent of the dirt was strong in her nose, but it mixed disgustingly with the acrid bile in her throat.

The convulsions faded. For a long moment she remained on her hands and knees, thanking Daya it had not happened in front of Cullen. That mortification would be more than she could stand. She looked down at the scuffled dirt, pulled a pocket of her pack open, and drew out a thin watergen, sucking deeply at the straw while it hummed and shifted its molecules to create the fluid she needed.

Sitting back while the cool water soothed her throat, Tsia scooped dirt in her fingers, letting the dry nodules crumble through her fingers. A scent somehow familiar, somehow new assailed her nose, and she drew her breath in deeply. The odor tickled her biogate. This musky smell—was it the scent of the cats? It was an odor that clung to the soil like a shroud, and Tsia found herself analyzing it, rolling it over and dissecting it through the sense of her gate.

She was not yet used to the change in her own personal odor, and the now-sweeter oil of her skin was still novel to her nose. The wind gusted and stole the scent of both herself and the soil from her nostrils, and its chill made her shiver. She rubbed the back of her neck absently. Odd to feel the wind there. She had not realized how much her hair had protected the nape. But there was a good side to that: Even with this wind, there were few tangles to comb out. The virus would not allow her hair to grow long, and she would no longer have to braid and clip her hair back to work outdoors, fly top-down in the skimmer, or even swim across the bay.

Tsia noted the bay currents absently as she crossed to one of the taller reaver dikes. Older dikes like this one were no less than six meters tall and wide enough that the sides were as thick as a cargo skimmer was long. The winter storms rarely stole more earth from the dikes than the reavers added in the spring.

Tsia's gaze followed the dike down onto the reaver meadow behind it. The flat was already thick with clumps of tallgrass that hid the reaver dens; the reavers themselves were not sleeping. They would be under her feet, tearing out the roots they had planted months earlier in the dike. As with the dirt, she did not need to scan the thick dam to know the reavers were there; even with the brine of the slough in her nose, the scent of the rodents came to her more quickly than the readout on her scanner. Tsia's grin soured. The changes she had felt this last week alone: roiling stomach; short, oily hair; tanned, softer skin; and sharper, sensitive nose ... Before she had taken the virus, the older guides had warned her only about her hair and the nausea. Besides her skin and scent, what else had they neglected to tell her about?

Maybe she should have stayed at the guild base, let the changes happen, asked her questions of the other guides. But she just could not face them all yet, not while all the others were still excited about their gates. Not when she herself was ashamed.

Soon the other new guides would be preparing for their next dance. The virus would be strong enough in all of them to make the sweat flow freely for dancing the high flames they had dreamed of. And Tsia would have to meet them there, in the heat of the fire, across the light of the pit. Her feet, her body would dance the flames as they did. Her eyes would watch; her ears would hear them revel in their links, feeling their bond grow stronger with this world. And she herself would be crying silently, bitterly, feeling her biogate and reaching for the cats that she could never touch.

That first night, before she had known what her link would be, with the virus raging through her blood and the fever flushing her cheeks ...

Her pores had exuded their sweetness across her skin, making the sweeps a sweaty flight of limbs instead of the searing touch of flames. It had been incredible—the sweat had beaded and hissed on her skin like tiny, darting snakes. The fire itself—with her eyes closed, she had sensed its heat waves like winds. Hot currents had whirled and coiled behind other dancers so that she had felt, more than heard, their movements. The fires had not been high—they never were for a first dance—but they had been hot enough to burn to a yellow-white bed of coals.

Remembering in the wind of the slough, Tsia flung out her arms, stepped high, leapt, then twirled, as if she were dancing the flames there, on top of the dike. The pack threw her balance off, and she laughed out loud. Then she stopped so abruptly that she almost fell.

A group of traders were watching her from the other side of the dike. Her left leg was still in midair, and she dropped it down slowly. Her face flushed; the weight of the pack dug into her ribs and hips.

On the other side of the dike the traders waited without speaking. Tsia hesitated. She could feel the heat of her flush, and futilely she wished that the wind would chill the embarrassment from her cheeks. Although her nose was overly keen, she could not smell the traders; the wind that cut across her face swept their scents downstream to the drowning monument stone rather than across the dike to her. Finally she raised her hand in half greeting, then crossed the dike.

There were five of them: three men, two women. One of the women was brown-haired, skinny, and of medium height. The other was blond, unusually tall, and as heavy as the first female trader was thin. The tall blond woman and two of the men were similar enough in build to be siblings. At a glance the only discernible difference between the two tall, heavy men was the color of their hair. Where the tall woman's hair was a true yellow-blond, the first man's hair was a pale yellow-white, the other's a reddish-yellow.

The fifth figure had light-brown hair, slender hips, broad shoulders, a bony face, and fat, full lips. With his nondescript clothing, he looked as out of place with the three siblings as the skinny woman did.

That fifth man made Tsia pause and feel a slight unease. He could be an agfa man, a tax man, or one of the academy teachers for all she could tell. Where the others wore trader insignia on their sleeves, this man wore nothing with badge or color. She longed to flick his image to the node, but without her temple link, she could only do it manually. Manual requests were both obvious and rude. Besides, the traders were probably just going to offer her contact as the other guilds had done.

Resolutely, she reached the end of the dike, then skidded down the slick path to land clumsily in front of the group. Nothing like good balance to mark the walk of a new guide, she thought with self-derision.

The scrawny woman looked at Tsia, then glanced at one of the tall men next to her. "Let's hope," the woman said abruptly, "this guide is a hell of a lot more graceful than that."

Tsia stared. What kind of greeting was that? "Who are you?" she demanded slowly.

The fifth man, the nontrader, gestured. "Take her." The others stepped forward.

Tsia stepped back. Her unease turned sharply into fear. "What do you think you're doing? Get away from me! I have a class-four Gea 'shed permit—" She broke off, scrambling back up the dike, her feet slipping in the wet clay. One of the men grabbed at her legs and closed his hands around her calf where the demonfish had stung her. Tsia kicked out. Her foot flung chunks of mud in his face. The man flinched, but the awkward weight of the pack threw Tsia's balance off again. The larger woman, lunging at Tsia's side, caught one of the loose pack straps and yanked.

"Watch her feet!"

"Let go of me, damn you!" The pack crippled Tsia's movements, throwing off her momentum with its mass. She twisted, slamming it into one of the men, knocking him down in the mud beside her. She slid to her knees. One of her flailing arms clouted the thick woman on her cheek; the woman staggered back, holding her hand to her bruised face as she glared at Tsia. "Hesse," she said softly, "we need the rod in here." The fifth man, Hesse, nodded. Watching Tsia's struggles with a speculative eye, he pulled a black-tipped rod from his belt and stepped forward.

Tsia kicked at the two men who gripped her legs. One of them, unaware of the demonfish punctures, dug his fingers into her thigh so that she cringed. Her butt was cold and growing wet, pressed down into the mud. Her pack jammed her against the soft clay so that she had no leverage for her blows. She felt like a turtle on its back. In a second the scrawny woman had scrambled above her. Talonlike hands caught the top of the pack and forced Tsia to stretch out on the muddy slope, her head just over the top of the dike and her legs spread down its bank. Tsia twisted, then tried to jackknife. "What the hell do you want from me?" she snarled. "Space-spawned liver flukes, let go of me!"

Hesse pointed the black-tipped rod at her. His face, tanned and smiling reassuringly, was somehow evil in the very semblance of its pleasantness. "Just a minute," he soothed. "Trust me. Everything will be fine."

Tsia hesitated, and in an instant the iron grips of the four traders had locked her more firmly in place. Pressing down on her joints, they held her so that she could not move without pain. Her back was arched farther over her pack, and the edges of her scanners jabbed into her ribs and guts. Upside down in her sight, the white, curving line of the monument stone wavered in the rising surge of the tide.

Her eyes were wide in her pale face. "What are you doing to me?" she whispered.

"Do not worry." Hesse stepped between the two traders holding her legs. "You will not feel a thing."

The rod tilted down, moving in slow motion. It seemed to hover over her right arm. Then it touched. Tsia did not think she screamed, but someone's voice was rising higher and higher in pitch so that it would break her ears in another second. She was blind with an agony of fire, as if acid were chewing through her arm. The flames touched her other arm, and this time she knew it was she who screamed.

Something moved in her field of vision, and she saw Hesse's shadow looming over her face. She struggled weakly, unable to stand the motion in her arms until she realized with a sob that he was not going to touch her again. Instead, he was laughing. This Hesse, with his tanned, bony face and full, fat lips—he and the others were laughing while she writhed in the dirt. A spark of anger felt its way through the nausea in her guts. With a curse that caught the tall man by surprise, she wrenched her right leg free in a catlike motion that surprised even her. With the same motion, she jammed it up into Hesse's crotch with all her strength. The force of the blow lifted him to his toes.

"Ahhhh . . ." Stunned, he folded, toppling backward and falling to his side in the mud.

She snapped the kick back but missed the tall trader as he jerked away from the blow and punched her inner thigh instead. The others jumped back on her body, digging their knees and elbows into nerve gates, wrenching her joints into pressure holds even tighter than before. Tsia cried out, then shrieked. The tall man recovered his grip and twisted her knee, forcing her leg to the verge of breaking it. They held her there, watching expressionlessly as Hesse recovered. Minutes passed. Sweat ran down Tsia's forehead and stung her eyes. The burning in her arms seemed to fade before Hesse crawled to his knees, his head down and one hand gripping his crotch.

When he raised his head, Tsia's heart seemed to stop at his expression. Time did not exist except as the means to measure that painful crawl toward her body. The black-tipped rod was again in his hands. The bony face came closer. Tsia's lungs did not seem to be working right. She tried to draw a breath, but even that was constricted in a strange, anticipated scream. The nerve rod reached toward her chest.

Her voice finally broke from its horror. "I am a Gea ecologist," she begged, her voice rising to a scream as the rod came close. "I just work in the slough. I am not worth this."

The black rod dropped. Hesse regarded her like a demon. "You are a guide," he said softly, "so you are a firedancer." He nodded at the nerve rod. "And as a firedancer, you are worth every credit." Then he tapped her outstretched hands until her wrists, then her arms burst into mental fire, burned from the n-rod pulse that pierced her veins and tore through her muscles. Red flames hotter than any firedance. A blaze that ate at her sanity and did not end until he released her and let her shrink into a fetal huddle as she dragged her wrists and arms around herself.

"Check her," Hesse ordered curtly.

The scrawny woman, knees in the mud, yanked the pack from Tsia's back. One of the men lifted it away while the woman put a scanner to Tsia's chest. Crying, Tsia struggled weakly. The woman brushed her hands aside. "She's a guide, all right," the woman said with satisfaction. "FOF, too—fresh off the fire. Node trail was right: She took the virus only a week ago."

The other tall, stocky man looked at Tsia curiously, his flat eyes following her movement as she turned her head away in shame. "Seems old to be taking the virus now."

The woman shrugged. "You know what they say: Some come late to the flames." She glanced at the scanner again. "She is thirty-eight. Scan says she is a second-level mutation—her gene line is pretty mixed." She gave Tsia a sharp look. "From the look of some of these scans, she probably took twice as long to assimilate the previruses as the other candidates." She closed the scanner and answered Hesse's unspoken question. "It will not make a difference with the way the guide virus sets," she reassured, "except to drag the mutation effects out a bit in the beginning and make them more intense in the end." She got to her feet. "You want the resonance scan now or later?"

"Later." Hesse nodded. "Plug her."

One of the traders grabbed Tsia's head, and she cried out. She tried to shake off the man and scramble to her feet, but her legs and arms were covered in mud. She slid farther into their hands. Wrestling her off the dike, the heavy-fleshed woman stepped on Tsia's knee to hold her down, smiling at the involuntary cry she elicited. Then rigid fingers dug into Tsia's jaw and forced her head forward. At first she did not understand.

Her head was jammed in a vise. Something silver approached in her peripheral vision, and Tsia began to struggle in earnest. The silver clips latched around her head. A tender tentacle lifted the tiny skin flaps from her temple sockets. Wide-eyed, Tsia cringed from its reach. Another gentle, always gentle tentacle brought forth a silver metaplas plug.

"No—" Her voice was incoherent.

"Hold her, dammit!"

"It's okay. Right side is locked."

"Going in."

The silver plugs touched her temples. The steely touch invaded her mind. With it came no pain, no further torture, only silence, a blankness that swamped her. Abruptly, the subtle sense of the imaging node was shut off. The voices and pictures that had formed the mental noise she had known since she was twenty-one were gone.

The blackness of the isolation struck her like a flood wall. She froze in the traders' arms. Then her mind burst free of its icy fear to beat commands at the nothingness like a claustrophobic child. There was no response. She screamed at Hesse as if she were mad, struggling against the hands that gripped her jaw. They tightened their grip and removed the pincers. Then they slapped her to her knees and touched her with the n-rod again.

When her body stopped shuddering, Hesse helped her gently to her feet, wiping the mud from her clothes himself. The softness of his voice belied the strange glint in his eyes. "Come along," he said gently. "We don't want to be late."

She balked, fear showing deep in her eyes.

"Do we want to be late?" He raised the rod a fraction.

Tsia cringed, her breath hiccuping with the humiliating tears that streamed down her face. "No—"

He smiled. "Everything will be fine. Trust me."

She shuddered, her body crying, the shame of it burning in her cheeks like a fire that would not go out.

"Get her pack."

The shorter man in the group grabbed it and swung it up, then grunted. "Goddamn stabilizer's off. No wonder she was so awkward."

Without further words they left the path and took off north, moving along the reaver meadow. Tsia stumbled in Hesse's wake. She was cold from shock. She barely noticed the drying mud that flaked and fell cleanly from her clothes. The traders were not so lucky. Tsia's garments were made of weathercloth; they repelled most substances automatically and sloughed off almost everything else when they dried. The traders wore new dirtside clothing, and although the heatsuits must have been comfortable in the cold estuarine wind, the smell of the reaver mud made their noses wrinkle.

A half kilometer. A kilometer. They hiked into the trees, then onto a small path. Ahead, light seemed to blur, then sharpen. Tsia blinked. She seemed to see a heat wave, which made no sense in the coolness of the wind. But as they neared the blurring, she realized it was no heat wave but a distort under which the traders' skimmer was hidden. When they entered, the air waved, then solidified above her, so that it looked like a fish-eye bubble beneath the trees. The faint scent of grease came to her, and some part of her mind identified it as the oil in the hinges of the skimmer's dark hatch. The body scents of the three traders who waited for Hesse by the skimmer came to her before the men strode out to meet Hesse. Tsia tried not to flare her nostrils at the odors. All she could think was that one had an acrid scent, one had a scent that was sweet, and the third had mint-stinking breath.

Hesse motioned for Tsia to stop, and she obeyed. To her shame, she could not help cringing from his touch as he slid his hand around her arm like a ring of steel. "Ghost line picked up her skimmer yet?" he asked one of the three new men.

The man nodded. "Ran the full line as soon as you plugged her." He indicated Tsia.

Hesse motioned at the skinny woman. "All right, Chun. You have fifteen minutes. If you can't get the rest of the scans in that time, we will wait until we reach Gamma Base and Oren can set a better line of ghosts."

Tsia, her shoulders hunched, her body shivering with the aftermath of the burning of her nerves, followed their conversation without comprehension. Why scan her body? Why not simply call the guild for her mutation report? And what did he mean, set a line of ghosts on her skimmer? One used a ghost line only when one was hiding one's real movements. They could not be thinking to steal her skimmer, too?

The scrawny woman was quick but thorough. As the trader read the data that imaged through her link, her eyes widened.

Tsia's lips tightened. She knew what the woman had found. Her cheeks flamed further.

"Well," the skinny trader drawled. "What do you know, Hesse. We have ourselves a dud."

He glanced at her in surprise.

"Don't worry. She *is* a bioguide." Chun closed the scanner and tossed it to one of the men. "It is just that she is about as useless a guide as any thirdgen or naught could be."

Hesse stared at Tsia's burning face and started to laugh. "You mean . . ."

The woman nodded. "Her biogate is keyed to the felines."

Tsia swallowed her shame. She told herself that it would have been much worse if her body had rejected the virus outright than that it had settled at the resonance of the felines. Better a crippled guide than a true naught, she reminded herself harshly.

Hesse wiped his eyes. "So," he said, taunting Tsia with a slight smile, "how does it feel to be useless in your new trade? You should have been born two hundred years earlier—you would have been worth at least a few credits to the guide guild then. As it is . . ." He touched her cheek. "They will not even think of this as a loss."

"You cannot do this," she said hoarsely. "The nodes will—"

"Will what?" Hesse cut her off, leaning forward. "Register your absence? Your link was deactivated a week ago. All the node needs is a confirmation dot to think you are still alive, and you do not think we have forgotten that, do you?" He gestured at the scrawny woman. "The scanner sends your dot just like the node thinks it should. And when Oren here gets through with your skimmer, there will be a line of ghosts behind you that even the node will believe."

"What do you mean?" she whispered. "The node—my family, my friends will never believe anything you set there. Cullen knows where I was today. He will trace you. They will all find you."

Hesse smiled sympathetically, his full-fleshed lips somehow horribly composed. "You hold on to that thought. It will help in the days to come." He turned to the man who had caught the scanner. "Oren, you have what you need there. Make it good and tight. No loose ends to trace back here. No shaky ghosts."

The tall man nodded. He pulled a hologenerator from his belt, linked it to the scanner, and grinned. "Not to worry. Except for the nodies among the mercs, I'm the best line runner in the business."

"You had better be. Guild is paying enough for this one job to put both of your kids through the academy." He gestured Tsia forward.

One of the other traders scowled. "Don't forget to wipe her skimmer down," the heavy woman said to the tall man. "You don't want one of the guides to get a whiff of your scent on the internal scans. Better take a couple molecular scrubs from the stock."

"Right." The man changed course in midstep, falling back into place behind Hesse and Tsia.

The skimmer was thirty meters away, and Hesse forced Tsia to trot after him like a dog. Every pound of her feet brought the burn back in her arms. Her eyes watered as her heels hit, while in her head the voice of Jak Volen slammed into her brain: "You are letting them take you like a doll? Can't you fight? Have you forgotten how to use your strengths?" And another voice, that of her guide mentor, snapped beside his: "Are you some kind of coward that you follow meekly in this trade dog's steps? Were you too old, too weak to take the virus, after all?"

Something settled in Tsia's gut, and for the first time in a week it was not nausea. She stared at Hesse's back and felt the presence of the traders at her sides. Then the anger took hold, and even as the tears blinded her, she forced her body to move.

She whipped around, slamming her palm into the tall one's stomach. In one smooth move she snatched the raser from his belt and followed up with her elbow to his gut as she switched the weapon on. The heavy man grunted and dropped slowly to his knees, his mouth working without taking in air. Tsia whirled. Sobs cut through her breathing, but she ignored them, slicing through the scrawny woman's wrist, where a second raser suddenly appeared.

There was no pause or horror in her as the trader's laser knife, still clenched in stiffened fingers, dropped to the dirt, splashed with dusty blood. Her ears were closed to the woman's scream. Tsia followed her victim forward. In an instant she carved a third man's guts from his bones till he gargled like a dying hen. Then she followed the sound of shrieking to the heavy-fleshed woman and turned the raser on her. A flick, a slice, and the heavy woman fell silently to the ground, her legs kicking with the throes of her death. Like a cat in a flock of pigeons, Tsia snapped past the other big man and punched the raser through his ribs, stopping only when her fist hit bone. Hesse screamed commands; the other two threw themselves on Tsia.

"Space scum," she screamed. She did not bother to draw the raser out of the heavy body she had thrust it into. She jerked the beam sideways instead. As the burly man clutched her arms in shock, she cut through his torso, spun him away, and followed the beam into the thighs of the next man in. The black-tipped n-rod slashed down, and she twisted with feral grace to avoid it. The raser flicked; the other man screamed and fell back stupidly.

And then Hesse grabbed a small black box from one of the bodies.

The r-con. The control for the plugs in her brain.

Hesse took one look at the sprawled and twitching bodies where the raser had cauterized his wife's expression and cranked the r-con on full. And left it on. And listened to Tsia scream.

4

Hours passed. The agony of the n-rod burned away from her limbs, and Tsia's tears dried hard and crinkly on her cheeks. She did not know how long it was before she realized that it was not her sight that was at fault for the fog in her eyes. There was no fog. The cloudy view came from the smoky walls of the box that surrounded her. So close to her were those walls that she could have touched them by leaning a hand span to either side.

She blinked—Daya, but even that seemed painful—and tried to focus on the figures she saw outside the tiny coffin. Something hurt her lip. She moved her mouth and realized she was biting it. Her mind came back to her abruptly. Those voices . . .

Beyond the walls the inside of the skimmer was too bright for her sensitive sight. There was a glimpse of figures moving, of bodies stacked and rolled against the crowded wall. Then her eyes watered and bleared the images into nothingness. She closed her eyes, squeezed the tearing from their tortured sockets, then opened them again to see Hesse standing before her. His bony face swam into focus, staring grimly into the transport box. Behind him the scrawny woman held a medpad over the stump of her wrist.

"You owe me for this," the woman promised Tsia viciously. "It will be years before they can grow me a new hand. I will have to have a prosthetic." She glared at the guide. "But I promise you, every time I close its fingers, I will think with pleasure of how I closed these fingers—" She flexed her good hand. "—on your—"

"Chun," Hesse snarled, "you are not to touch her."

The woman's gray eyes bored into Tsia's blue ones with a hatred that made Tsia reel. "I won't mark her, Hesse," Chun said softly. "I won't even touch her skin."

Tsia felt faint and steadied herself against the wall, then cried

43

out. "Ahhh—" The movement triggered a radiant pain that shot up along her forearm to her shoulder.

Chun's lips stretched into a vengeful smile. She shouldered Hesse aside. "Feel that?" she demanded. "You will feel a hell of a lot more before you reach the Black Well."

Hesse eyed the restraint-control box with tight anger. "I told you to keep the r-con on level six."

The skinny woman shook her swathed wrist in his face. "And get nothing for this?"

"You get hazard pay, same as Arhbon."

Chun barely cast a look over her shoulder toward the only other trader left alive. The man was hunched over the console of the skimmer, his holotank generating a continuous series of three-dimensional images that blurred and flicked from one contour to the next so quickly that the eye did not register the tank's content. The generic skin graft that covered the slash over his ribs would heal in days, but Chun's hand would never be reattached. The cauterization from the raser would not allow it. The woman eyed Hesse in disgust. "Dismemberment should warrant me extra cred—"

Hesse cut her off with a cold anger. "You get what you signed on for. Nothing else." He smiled at her fury. "You want to dispute it, take it up with the trade board."

Chun bit back her comment. She turned back to Tsia. "Move," she suggested nastily. "Shift just a little. Give me that much satisfaction."

Tsia shook her head in mute rebellion, stopped instantly as the lance of pain struck through her neck and head, and ground her teeth to keep from crying out.

The woman trader watched Tsia's face whiten. "What you feel now is nothing," she promised softly. "The r-con will hold you in that position until hell freezes over if we don't release you first. Move again," she begged vengefully. "Move against it now and often. It is stimulated by the nerve action in your muscles."

Tsia licked her lips. She stared back at Chun, and her stomach roiled. "Next time I am free," she said through gritted teeth, "I will cut more than the hand from your body."

Chun laughed nastily. "Next time you are free, I will be the one to—"

"God, Chun," Hesse snapped, "shut up. This whole thing has shifted our schedule by over an hour. See if we can make it out of here before that wind front hits."

With a muttered curse the one-handed woman stalked to the

holotank at the front of the skimmer. The other man had his eyes
riveted on the holotank, which was still flashing a series of images
almost too fast for the eye to see. He frowned faintly, relaxed,
then frowned again while his hands absently tapped his temple
links as he lay the ghost lines in the node. Threads of false images
spread out into the histories and scans of the node and hid Hesse's
skimmer. Ghosts covered Tsia's pain. She knew what they were
doing. Guides did not usually learn to lay a ghost line, but Jak
Volen had never really believed that Tsia would be a guide, and
he had taught her well. With every inhale, she watched the trader
lay more ghosts to cover her existence. With every exhale, she
watched her own presence disappear.

Chun glanced back, saw the recognition in Tsia's eyes, and
smiled grimly. She split the holotank without disturbing the other
man, then imaged the wind currents into the tank. She studied
them for only a moment. "Wind front already hit, Hesse." She
motioned for him to examine the tank himself. "It is not bad right
now, but at eighty-six kilometers per hour, we cannot lift without
drawing power from the node."

"Damn." Hesse studied the split image, keeping his eyes from
the other side of the holotank. The flickering shapes could make
a man dizzy if he watched them without being linked to their
forms. He glanced back at the bodies stacked against the side of
the skimmer. "Arhbon," he said, interrupting the other man's
work, "can you include cover for a force-three power suck with
a ghost line?"

The flow of images in the holotank barely hesitated as the man
answered with a silent shake of his head.

Hesse glanced toward the con. "We are grounded, then. We will
have to wait it out."

Chun motioned at the line of bodies. "What about them?"

"Leave them hissing in the sand. By the time the gale is over,
all traces will be gone. We are as safe dusting them here as we
would be dusting them in Noirelle."

"It will take hours," Chun warned.

"Didn't you get merc composites?"

She shook her head. "Uh-uh. Too risky, the way they track their
surplus microbes." She dug a pair of slender blued metaplas pipes
out of stowage. "Had to settle for guide-scout surplus. The compounds in these tubes are old mixtures, actually date back to First
Drop. They work better in heat than cold, and they will take
hours, not minutes, to disintegrate a body completely. But," she
added, "they are guaranteed traceless. One hundred percent de-

composition." She gave Tsia a cold look. "The guides are, at least in their gear, as biome-minded as they claim."

Hesse released the hatch, turning his face from the force of the wind that whipped inside. A cold rain was beginning to whirl in the growing storm, and thick moisture dappled his clothes as he stooped and caught the body of his wife by the arms. He hesitated. Then, without ceremony, he dragged the dead woman to the opening and shoved her out onto the growing mud. If there was a thud when the body hit the ground, the wind hid that sound as well as it hid everything else but the rushing of air through the sinktree canopy. Without a word Hesse turned back to the next body.

Limp heads banged against the floor and the sides of the doorway. Feet caught awkwardly on the frame of the hatch. Rain pressed inside and made the floor slick, but Hesse ignored it. When there were none but the living left in the skimmer, Chun turned to Tsia and smiled. There was one thing more. She stooped and caught up her own hand—her cold, severed hand—and fingered it as she watched Tsia's expression.

" 'Thou, who has parted me from me,' " she quoted, " 'give me to my destiny.' " She smiled then. "Come out," she said, "and watch your funeral." She shoved the hand into her pocket.

Tsia held herself still.

Chun ordered Arhbon to stay on the ghost lines, then tucked the hisser tube under one arm. With her good hand, she took the r-con box from the side of Tsia's coffin. A moment later she was connected to the r-con through her own temple link. Hesse was already outside, standing in the whipping rain, oblivious to the drops that slammed into his side and plastered his short hair against his scalp. Chun opened the transport box and began to walk to the hatch.

Locked to the trader's movements by the r-con, Tsia could only follow. Her muscles imitated Chun's steps through her plugged temple link. When Chun reached the hatch, Tsia was still at the wall, and, with a tiny smile around her lips, the trader jumped down without hesitation and ran quickly forward two steps. Tsia's legs, following the trader's motions, bent, then threw her body into the wall. She could only turn her face and jerk back, blinded by the pain that shot up her neck as she resisted Chun's face-forward movement, to take the blow on her chin and chest instead of her face.

Chun released the link and poked her head back in. "Oh," she said, shaking her head. "That was clumsy of me. I guess there is a reason why one uses an r-con only in an open space."

Tsia said nothing. Released from the r-con for an instant, she dragged herself up. She was not prepared for Chun to grab her with a strong hand; when the woman jerked her from the skimmer, she fell to the mud on her knees.

The ground was soft and she was not hurt, but her teeth grated together unpleasantly. The biting rain fell against the thin material of her jumpsuit and soaked her skin, but it slid off the weatherfabric like glass. Cold water ran down Tsia's forehead and then her nose, dripped off her chin. She stared at the hands that were sinking in the mud. Daya, she prayed, her ice-blue eyes hard and grim. She would never again ask for much if she could just get her hands on that woman.

Chun reached down and jerked her again just before she got to her feet, and Tsia sprawled forward onto one of the bodies. With a cry of disgust, she yanked back, slipped in the mud, then turned the motion into a spin with which to throw herself on the trader. And shrieked with agony. She could not help it. Chun had activated the r-con just as she had launched herself. Her body writhed, unable to find the position of least resistance until she once again stood upright, sobbing with the pain.

"Enough," Hesse said softly.

Chun nodded without argument. She took her severed hand from her pocket and, fingering it one more time, tossed it on the top of the heap. Like a hand of Daya, it lay on the face of Hesse's wife and pointed its cold, dead fingers at the trader. Chun glanced from the hand to his face, then took the tube from under her arm and passed it to him.

"Ashes to ashes," he said. "Dust to dust." Rain had turned his brown hair black, and he did not seem to notice the water running down the sides of his face. "Back to the earth, what has come from its soil." He raised the tube. "I leave you hissing in the sand."

A flash of light sprayed from the tube and briefly covered the bodies. In the rain it was difficult to see, but a dark stain spread across the pile and began to eat at the flesh. Within seconds all the shapes were black. The hand on top of the pile wrinkled and sagged as they watched. Hesse stared at the shapes for a long moment, then, handing the hisser back to Chun, turned and climbed back into the skimmer.

Tsia stared at the bodies. Using the r-con, Chun forced her back to the ship, made her body climb inside and drove her back to her coffin before, at last, reluctantly unlinking and hanging up r-con. Hesse glanced back. Unsmilingly, he followed her anticipatory look toward Tsia. "Do not worry, Chun," he said softly. "I will take care of this guide."

Chun closed the hatch against the wind without answering. Leaning against it slowly, she looked at Tsia and then, gazing at her with cold eyes, smiled.

An hour passed. Then two. The nodie—the man who was laying the ghost line—worked at his console tensely, without comment. Chun, the expression wiped from her face, sat at the nodie's side and manipulated the holotanks as he directed. Beside them, then behind them, then interrupting them as he needed, Hesse worked to pull in the distort till it clung to the sides of the skimmer itself and no longer encompassed the clearing.

Tsia watched and waited and strained against the r-con till she found its pain-delineated limits. She could move her fingers and toes, yes, and the small muscles without agony, but her arms and legs, her head, her shoulders—their movement caused a blinding agony along the muscles and tendons. Her chest rose and fell with a growing panic, and she stared at Hesse and Arhbon and Chun with all the hate she could muster. Five, at least, were dead; Jak had taught her the artery points well. When he heard . . .

Tsia's breath caught, and she pushed the images of the dead traders out of her mind. Involuntarily she raised a hand to wipe the tears from her eyes, then cried out. Chun, working at the holotank console with the pilot, glanced over her shoulder. She looked involuntarily back at the stump of her wrist.

"Do not disappoint me," she said softly, her words as clear as if she were in the transport box with Tsia. "Move harder."

Tsia stared at the woman and bit her lip till it bled. These traders could not stay here for days. Cullen would come, she told herself resolutely. He would have sensed something in the node. He—someone—would hike along this trail and see the waves of the distort. She set her jaw and deliberately shifted her stance. The white-hot lance that shot up through her calves and thighs to her buttocks made her whiten once again.

Hesse followed Chun's gaze, then came to stand before Tsia.

Silently, her fury growing with every second, she stared back at his bony face.

"Wishing me dead," he said gently, "will not even make me nervous."

"How can you do this?" she demanded harshly. "When I am free . . ."

Hesse regarded her curiously. "You think this is some kind of hazing from which you will wake? An initiation to the guild that abandons you now? You are no better than a naught." He gestured at the consoles that reflected the growing force of the wind in three-dimensional tanks. "The winds are up to 140 kph. No skimmer can land in that. So no guide will risk this gale to save you. They do not even know where you are."

Tsia's heart beat rapidly. "Remove these plugs," she said finally. "I have rights to the node."

"Rights? You committed murder. You are a common criminal now."

Murder? Tsia felt a wash of sickness. "No," she returned tersely, the whiteness around her eyes refuting the strength with which she spoke. "I am no criminal. I am rights-conditioned and licensed for full-force defense. I killed within my license."

"Rights-conditioned, were you?" Hesse smiled pleasantly. "But can you fight for your rights now?"

Tsia stared at him. She had no need to fight for her rights. "The mercs—"

"Mercs? Who will petition them to search you out? Who will pay them to find you or apply for a kidnap grant? You? You are locked in a coffin where your own breath must be making you sick." He eyed her face. "Can't you smell it? You are new to the guide virus. Your nose must be terribly sensitive. Does it not," he inquired, "gag at the stench of that space?"

Tsia's stomach churned at his words, and her face paled further. Bile rose, and she tried to hold in her guts. But her stomach heaved, and Hesse laughed, and as the vomit clogged Tsia's throat, her body jackknifed with the convulsion. The r-con seared her back and front; Tsia screamed. She choked. The vomit poured over her chin.

She sobbed in humiliation and pain as the vile matter dribbled down her front. When she looked back up, Chun was standing there with Hesse. The woman laughed while Tsia gagged again at the stench.

"Leave her like that," Chun suggested.

Hesse nodded slowly. His expression, as he met Tsia's tortured gaze, was quiet and filled with nothing but the thought of the next task he had to do.

Acrid fumes clogged Tsia's nose. The sweet scent of her body odor mixed with her vomit and sweat until she gagged convulsively again and again. Each time her body shook, the r-con burned her nerves. She could not raise a hand to wipe her mouth or chin; she could only lick her lips and swallow the acid-burned chunks on her tongue.

Another hour. The waves of nausea passed more closely now, and Tsia began to feel faint. The traders ignored her, securing the skimmer as the winds rose to two hundred kph. Ground hooks dug into the earth below the craft; Tsia could see their representation dimly in the holotanks at the consoles. A repulsor field was added to the distort to keep the trees from breaking over the ship. Another hour, and the wind rocked the craft in a rough rhythm.

Tsia's thoughts seemed frozen. How? she asked herself again and again. How could this happen? Why did they need a guide? No, a firedancer, Hesse had said. If they needed one so badly, why did they not get one on contract? Her fury abated suddenly, and dread grew in its place. What was it they wanted to do that a contract would not allow? Her stomach began to heave again, and this time she controlled it. Daya, she thought desperately, the plea ending on a humiliating sob, would not these traders open this coffin even once to let her clean herself? To let her breathe?

Night fell, and still Tsia stood. To her left, Chun slept restlessly in a bunk; Hesse brooded silently at the con. The third trader ignored her completely. Tsia's calves ached; her feet were swollen from standing, and even the massage pads of her boots could not keep her heels from complaining. Her arms and hands were coated in mud and salty grime. Her eyes were dry and hard with thirst. And on her chin and neck and the front of her chest the vomit clung like worms. Every breath brought with it fear. And after the fear came terror, terror that swept her chest like an incoming tide, until she shivered almost constantly in the coffin.

At midnight the wind slacked off, and the skimmer settled into a dull vibration. Tsia fouled herself with her urine. The hot and sudden fumes were more than she could bear. She began to gag. Unbidden, her body bent against the r-con, and as the fire seared through her muscles, she began to scream.

Hesse looked up to see her choking. He looked at her for a moment as if he were trying to recall what distressed her, then rose slowly to stand in front of the coffin.

Tsia saw his shape only dimly. She could not stop convulsing. Every sob tore at her throat; every gag pulled at her stomach. The r-con read each impulse and burned it through her chest. Her legs, locked in place from standing so long, rocked forward until she fell suddenly against the front of the coffin. Her face turned instinctively sideways so that her cheek, instead of her nose and lips, struck the wall; her back stiffened to take up the shock, and her answering shriek of torture deafened her. Hesse did not even wince.

Calmly, he reached for the r-con. To his right, Chun pulled a pillow over her head to shut out the noise.

Tsia, leaning against the front of the transport coffin, begged Hesse silently to release her. When he did, she crumpled with a gasp to the floor of the box. Her legs screamed anew; they had been locked too long in one position. Her knees and ankles burned as they collapsed in the confines of the coffin. She retched dryly. Even as her stomach convulsed, the door of the transport box opened. Hesse stepped back. Unable to hold herself up, Tsia fell, sprawling, across the skimmer floor.

The hot urine in her jumpsuit rasped against her skin, and she pushed herself onto her elbows and dragged her shoulder cloth across her chin to break off the dried vomit. Staring up from Hesse's feet, Tsia could see only the smile that grew faintly on his bony face—that slow, gentle expression that did not touch his eyes.

"Let me help you, Tsia-guide," he soothed. He reached down, but the n-rod was in his hand, and Tsia cringed back.

"No," she whimpered. "No, please . . ." Blindly, she tried to crawl back in the transport box.

"Trust me, Tsia," he said softly. "It will not hurt at all."

A day of this: no food, no water, nothing but the virus raging in her blood and the flame of the n-rod on her skin. Nothing but the burn of the r-con searing through her nerves. She could not help herself. Her voice began to rise as she pleaded. "No. Please, Daya, no . . ." Her mind beat in silent thrusts at the temple plugs that blocked her frantic calls to the node. Her arms cowered over her face. As the rod dropped, her voice rose to a shriek. Crouching, huddling, she cringed against the walls of the box. When the rod touched her arms, her muscles spasmed, bashing out to the walls so that Hesse reached in between them and touched the rod to her chest. Her screams rose abruptly in a piercing note.

"I'll kill you," she shrieked out. "I swear it on my grave."

"I laugh," he said softly. "I spit on your hope."

He followed her movements, touching her on her shoulder, her knee, the back of her calf. She burned from the rod until she choked on her own screams and could move no more than the rise and fall of her chest as she sobbed.

When he paused to let the pain burn in her limbs, he was still not done with her. "Is this the best a guide can do?" he asked quietly. "Are you, this cringing specimen, the new generation of the flames?" He regarded her with a pity that did not touch his eyes. "Who will want," he said gently, "a naught like you?" And with his fat, full lips, expressing the concern in his thin-boned face, he touched her almost tenderly with the n-rod, on her cheek.

And Tsia, her humiliation burning as hot as the fire that seared her face, could not stop her screams. Her eyes seemed blinded— she could not see her future.

She had not realized it was no longer hers.

5

Even after her muscles stopped their spasms, Tsia's dread and fury grew together like tangled cats. When she did not report in, she told herself, when her scanners disappeared and Cullen or one of the guides—someone—checked up on her contract work, Hesse would not get away with this. There was no way he could hide his traces so well that no one would suspect something wrong. The guild could not let her go so easily. People disappeared all the time on this world; it was still untamed enough to take lives as a child took candy. But not guides, she thought. Guides were tracked. Every death was verified. And Hesse—he could hide her, but he could not keep her without the guild finding out.

She hurt too much to sleep. Even her eyes seemed to burn, and every time they closed, the throbbing of her pulse awakened her.

In the morning, when Hesse came to her again in her coffin, she clenched her fists and dug her nails into her palms and gripped her sanity the way a dying man clung to the light. It was not she, she told herself, who clenched her jaw to keep from crying out. It was not she whose bones were made of fear. Some other body writhed in that cage. Some other woman was seared from the inside out.

She ignored the spittle on her chin, the mud and grime on her skin, the dried vomit on her clothes. She had fouled herself that night. Hesse looked and sniffed and shook his head. He let her out to fall on the floor again, then hit her with the n-rod. And outside the walls of the skimmer the gale whipped the trees back down as Hesse whipped her nerves and fired her hatred hotter.

By the evening of the second day her throat was so raw that she could barely croak against the agony from the n-rod. It was then that Hesse showed her the holos of herself. Holos taken by the skimmer's automatic recording system. And she was forced to

53

stand and watch herself cringe, cry from the pain, beg for them to
stop, vomit and foul herself while her muscles were locked by the
r-con and her bowels moved beyond the r-con's control. She stood
and watched the fear, the abject terror crawl across her holo face
while she shamed herself in front of Hesse.

She stared at the holo, imprisoned as much by her humiliation
as she was by the r-con in Hesse's hand. Her eyes did not focus,
but her mind saw, as clearly as if she relived it, every supplication
she made. When Hesse turned off the holotank, Tsia tried to
speak. She choked on the dryness of her throat.

Outside, the gale had blown itself out to a strong wind. "I need
water," she croaked at last.

"Of course." He turned from the holotank and opened the door
of the transport coffin. Then he gestured at the watergen straw
that lay on the skimmer's metaplas worktable. "Please," he said
politely. "Feel free."

Her body convulsed involuntarily. The r-con burned. She whitened, then touched her tongue to her dry, chapped lips.

Hesse regarded her quietly. "You have been active the last two
days," he remarked. "The virus must be raging by now in your
blood."

"Daya damn you," she whispered. She bit her parched, dry lips.
With the thirst that rubbed her throat raw, a desperate need had
grown in her guts for justice against these trade dogs. That need
gnawed now at the insides of her stomach like a thousand tiny
paws clawing and tearing at the flesh. She stared at Hesse and
saw him smile. Despair swept across her face. No glint of triumph
reached Hesse's eyes, but she bit her lip again savagely to draw
herself together.

If she had been a full guide, she could have called through her
biogate. If she had been linked to a deer or even a tree, she could
have called through the gate to another guide. But, Daya damn
her, she was linked to the felines. And the cats would never listen.

She had seen a firedance once, by a First Dropper, a guide 261
years old who had lived through the slaughter of her family during the Third-Year War on Chaos and had then shipped out to
Risthmus to become a guide. Tsia remembered . . . The hairs had
risen on her neck and arms with every step of those wrinkled,
wizened feet. There had been death in that dance, though her
mentors had disclaimed it. Now Tsia thought she understood those
steps. Life, her mentors had said, gave the greatest depth to the
dance, but Tsia, remembering the twist and flick of the woman's

naked, glistening body, looked at Hesse's fat-lipped smile as he flicked the n-rod on and felt a different melody move her heart.

Hesse watched her expression change, and he smiled. "What kind of courage do you have, Tsia-guide?" he asked quietly.

Tsia's hands clenched as if they wore claws instead of nails. She stared at the watergen. She stared at Hesse. Something clouded her sight, and she reached instinctively through her biogate as if she could draw the strength of the felines to her. But the r-con held her still, and as she shifted her legs for that first step, she bit back her cry and lost her hold on her gate.

Pain lanced all the way up her back. Her face and neck went rigid, and she ground her breath into a silent shriek. She stepped, then, against the r-con. She forced one step and then another, blind with the burning pain. She knew where the table was; she could smell Hesse standing next to it like a cloud of odor. She groped forward with a hand eaten away by nerve-seared flame and found the metaplas table. For an instant she just stood in her rigid-locked stance while the r-con burned away. Then she reached for the watergen straw.

A slender hand removed it as she forced her burning fingers open. She cried out in despair.

Hesse smiled. "Trust me," he said softly. "You would not want this now."

Her eyes locked on the watergen; she swayed in despair. *Are you a coward?* Her mentor's voice seemed to ring in her head. "What kind of courage do you have?" Hesse's echo disparaged. Against the burning, against the fire in her hands, against Hesse's words, she forced her fingers to reach for the straw.

The trader, watergen in one hand, raised the n-rod with the other. And Tsia, caught in the muscle lock of the r-con, could do nothing more than scream.

6

∽◦◉◦∽

Two more days of torture. Two more nights of dreams. In the dark, while the skimmer sat and hummed in the wind and Hesse sat brooding at the edge-lit skimmer's console and holotank, the sky closed in on her sight and the ground reached up like a claw. In her nightmares her short hair grew down to her ankles, covering her in the tawny coat of a cougar. Her muscles stretched and screamed with the stretching until her arms lengthened and her jaw spread out and her limbs became those of the cat. Her claws dug into the earth and were trapped by the soil itself. They dug, then rooted in the ground and became trees, thickening with every breath. The trees became the walls, a solid wall that surged closer with every pulse of her heart until she crouched in the slave box and clawed against its closing surfaces. And when she stared in her dream at the smoky-clear walls of her coffin, her cat-slitted eyes picked out the colors in the dull, dirty gray shades and saw only a latticework of rods, of n-rods, their black tips touching and arcing into her nerve gates until she woke, screaming silently, covered in sweat. Licking the salt that stung her lips. Shivering with the chill of clammy skin, while inside her stomach turned with fear.

No one bothered to speak to her now. Water and food—she ate with Hesse and Arhbon, locked in place by the r-con, raising and lowering her hands as Hesse did to eat his own meal.

On the fifth day the gale calmed to strong winds that only bent the treetops instead of breaking their trunks. In grim silence Tsia watched Hesse and Chun and the pilot until the holotank filled with the air patterns and the transport foam surged up and filled her coffin. It was porous; it did not stop her from breathing. Even with its fibers blinding her to the con, she felt the skimmer vibrate and lift.

56

"Daya," she whispered. "How could you give me up like this?" There was no answer. No one heard.

For one week, then two, they traveled along a ghost line laid out by the nodie pilot at the holotank. Following the line of false images he created in the node, they skimmed along the coast and landed in the north, then in the east, where Chun left them silently. Three weeks passed; then four. They flew south, and Arhbon got off. But his ghost lines ran on, listing the false images, spinning a web of lines that told no truths to the node.

Somewhere along the journey Tsia changed. She no longer worried about her watershed. She did not wonder who was caring for her biome. By now her gene maps would have been assigned to someone else. The haywort would be planted, the arrowroot thick on the dikes. It was close to the end of summer, and the ponytrees would be dropping their filament hair, and some other guide would be playing God in the slough.

In four weeks, she thought bitterly, why had no one come? She had spent too many years in the preps to be given up like chaff. Everyone in the guild—even those who had discouraged her from becoming a guide—admitted that she would be one of the best if the final virus took. And it had. She could feel her senses growing with the strange expanse of the biogate. She could even smell Hesse better than she could see him now. She *was* a guide. Even if her gate was nearly useless, she still had that.

So she chafed in the coffin and breathed while the heat grew, and the air dried further, and the box that let her stand but not sit was skimmed and carted and packed and driven south, ever south. A day in a warehouse, two on a transport, three more at the loading pad for a partial ride on the hook . . . A month while her brain beat at the plugs in her link sockets: metaplas plugs, r-con plugs that kept her mind from the nodes and held her thoughts captive in her own skull. A month of standing, sometimes frozen by the r-con in her coffin, while the r-con itself hung just outside the box and taunted her with its winking locks.

On the eighteenth day she took Hesse's lash and remained on her feet. And when, finally frustrated, he struck her with his fist, she smiled.

That was the day Hesse first felt fear.

7

Tsia stood silent before the Black Well. Another moment, and the restraints would jerk her forward; the nausea made her sway. She raised her wind-chapped hands to her burning, sun-dried eyes. Her teeth grated in a tight feral grin. The smile was stiff; the familiar agony of the r-con lanced through her nerve-restrained wrists like a dozen slender knives.

Catlike, her sun-seared eyes tracked Hesse's movements while he held the r-con tightly. He stared at her teeth-grinding smile and nervously licked his lips. Still they were fat, moist lips, thick with the water denied to her own dry mouth.

She eyed the trader tightly. This journey had changed him, she acknowledged. He was no longer calm. He turned suddenly sometimes. Glanced to see that she was still. Some time, some second, he would relax just a hair, loosen his grip, or look away, and she would take that n-rod away from him. She looked at him with a fierce steadiness. Her cheeks ached with her smile.

Imaging his commands to the node through his own temple link, Hesse rigged the skysail for full collapse.

Traders. Laser-burned lung worms, she thought vehemently. Except for Jak Volen, she would never have given the trade guild much thought, so remotely had traders been connected to her life. They brought the marine tools she used to plant the black oyster beds. They took the gene maps and samples she made from her watershed. But beyond that? Never in a dozen worlds would she have thought they would become the focus of her existence. Her life had been the guide guild, even in her dreams. Biomes and gene scans. Fire and water. Now it was the r-con that burned each synapse, guided her every thought. As it had done ever since Hesse and his trade dogs had caught her alone on the dikes.

Four weeks had passed since that morning in Ciordan. Four

long weeks of Hesse's festering, moist-lipped smile. Thirty-two days of shattered nerves that left no mark on her skin. Don't want to damage the merchandise, he told her gently. Don't want to mark down the wares. Can't firedance, he said, if your body's full of scars . . .

Tsia, locked in the transport coffin with her lungs aching for the cold, open air of the sea, ground her teeth and bit her lips to keep from crying at the bitter irony that made her a guide whose only worth was the sweat that let her dance.

She stared up, willing the heat of the Risthmus star to burn Hesse's guts from his bones as he had seared her nerves, but the sky itself mocked her. This was not the sky she knew at all. There was little blue up there; where she was used to the deep hue of Ciordan skies, here there was only a white-blue, bleached-blue matte. On these sands it was the cruel n-rod, not a cool, coastal wind, that cut across her shoulders. And this heat . . . Dry and smothering with the hot breath of an open oven. How could one live in this place? There were no rivers here, no sloughs or ponds or streams. Just yellow grass and gritty sand and burning, furnace heat.

Heat waves walled her in. Clumps of sage and redroot barely pierced the waves with spikes of dusty green, while far away the dry and crumbling mountains faded in the growing haze. Hungrily Tsia's eyes fastened on the peaks. Beyond their dead-brown, hollow-brown crusts was the Cheba Rift, then the Sinking Plains, and after that the red-green steppes of Reydina. And beyond the thin trees of Piuten Woods, past Drum Valley where the Wailing River flashed deep and fast in the Rocky Bottom Drainage, that was where the Vulcans rose. Tall, jagged peaks where the lava had flowed like mud a mere five hundred years before. Where the narrow, blackened cones thrust toward the sky like a smoking army poised on a rim of red-tipped stone. Where the lightning caught their tips in nights of fire and ice . . .

Hesse's shadow fell like a vulture across her face. Tsia focused slowly on his visage. How, she wondered, could he look so normal, so like any other man in this world, with his mind so terribly twisted? She stared at him and felt her fingers clench. Forceably, she relaxed them.

Above, the faint rippling of the collapsing skysail was like a wind that had no breath. Hesse's hair glinted, and he grimaced at the heat as he moved around her warily, ignoring the smile on her face. He used his temple link to release the cargo lock; his right hand clenched the n-rod until his knuckles whitened. Tsia's eyes, those icy blue-gray eyes, followed him like a coiled snake, forcing a shiver from deep inside his spine up his neck and onto his scalp. He ran a hand over his thinning hair. When he brought it away, it was wet with sweat, and he glared at the moisture. This woman was half his size, trapped in the restraints, and helpless as a desert digger out on the rocks, and yet ... She could get used to the r-con—yes, it was possible—but fight it completely? Not in his lifetime. He wiped his hands on his hood as he yanked the heatcloth back on, then set the r-con high. An hour, no more, and he would be rid of this woman's cool, taunting body, her stubborn predator smile, her catlike, close-cropped head—everything but the credits he would take in her place. He tapped his temple jack irritably, linked himself to the controls, then tuned his thoughts to the r-con. Without looking back, he stalked down the path.

Loose sand scrunched beneath his feet before it was shunted from the metaplas path by the underlying power net. With savage satisfaction, he thought of the tight edge to Tsia's taunting grin. She was hurting still from her last lesson, and he was glad.

Behind him, Tsia's legs and arms were not her own. While Hesse walked, the r-con sent its pulses into her brain, forcing her body to walk in his wake and mimic his long stride with her shorter legs until the backs of her limbs ached and then cried out against the strain. She could not pause or slack her stride. Subtly, Hesse lengthened his walk so that Tsia ground her teeth, her feet slapping hard against the path as her body fought to keep up. Already the heat reached up through her bare heels. Blown sand gritted between her toes, wearing at the dance calluses that covered her soles. Above her forced and rigid smile, her eyes bored into Hesse's back.

He could feel it. Tsia's gaze was a raser carving inch by inch through his spine. Her silence was a laser scalpel, slicing each layer of cartilage from his bones. In her head she sensed the nearness of a desert cat and tensed. An instant later it was gone. Tsia swallowed her bitterness with her bile. A link with the cats, and she was already a slave. Not just to Hesse but to despair, which washed her every time she sensed the quick hot breath, the twitch of a whisker on her skin. The cats—the only link that could not save her.

Ahead of them, in the smooth, marbled, columnlike walls of the Black Well, sudden movement reflected. Hesse tensed, then cursed himself in a dozen silent tongues. Tsia's reflection chased him like a dog. "Slave dog," he muttered under his breath. Tsia smiled. She could almost hear his thoughts. She was no dog, she promised silently. She was a cougar, waiting to take his heart.

She forced her head to turn against the r-con so she could keep the mountains in her sight. The pain, dull at first, sharpened with each degree of turn. She kept her smile. It was the only defiance she had left.

Ahead, the walls of the Black Well stretched up, shimmered, and dissolved into the bleached-out sky. Yellow-white sand pushed up against the smooth, black sides of the column, drifting close but never quite touching. The energy net that hugged the outer walls took its power from the sun, the sand particles that struck it constantly in the wind, and the wind that stripped Tsia's skin further even as it gave energy to the well. Up close, the black marbled walls were a faceted surface, alive with deceptive depth. Tsia stared at its darkness. There was motion there . . . Currents . . . The energy net sucked her sight as it sucked the light from the sun. She forced her gaze away.

Hesse wiped at the sweat on his forehead, and Tsia's hand rose without volition to mimic his move. She had to stiffen her fingers so they did not poke her own eyes. But she smiled until her cheeks ached. And walked in his wake like a human 'bot. How did that saying go? You can't beat a 'bot, but you can bribe a 'borg . . . Not many robots or cyborgs on Risthmus. Just colonists and guides and miners and traders . . .

The touch of the n-rod frayed and snapped her nerves, stifled and fragmented her thoughts. Concentrate, she told herself. All the trade wells were guild. And there were only twenty-two wells, one at every skyhook port on the planet. Someone would be here to help. She forced her shoulders to relax. And if no one came, then she would break this r-con herself and cut Hesse apart like a bird.

Time, she thought, was on her side, not Hesse's. The longer he used the r-con, the more she learned its inner ways. Like a 'bot, she might walk in his wake, but give her a chance—just one instant in all the weeks he had kept her—and she would bet her left eye that she could break his control and find her own way home. Over his dead body.

Step, swing . . . Her own body forced itself toward the well. Behind her two other lines of humans jerked along in their shadows. Was every one of those men and women a criminal doing labor for penance? Did those lines of hard, hopeless faces hide another ghost like her? She forced herself to watch the ragged steps of the other prisoners. There were three mutants in the first line—the blue-gray skin of the convicts standing out where the others had tanned to browns. The second line was almost standard stock, except for one woman, whose thin frame towered over the others like a flagpole. Behind the wavering lines of slaves, the other trader sails were still collapsing. Their sails were larger than the one flown by Hesse. How many coffins did they hold?

Tsia breathed deeply, hugging down the nausea it wrought in her stomach. She had never been afraid of small spaces, but that shipping box and its transport foam had tested her will more than all the n-rods combined. Smoky walls, cold metaplas, suffocating pads . . .

Hesse paused, and Tsia, caught in the r-con, did also. He waited, and the wall dissolved before them, leaving a portal clear. In unison, in sync, they stepped inside. What had Jak Volen said a year ago, when he had bought nav rights for his trade ship? "Through the demon door itself, where the souls of the damned are silenced."

The sensor scan swept her body like a chill. Hesse's stride forced her forward. The temperature dropped with each meter until, in spite of the remaining heat, she began to shiver. Inside, blank walls made a cold, colorless facade for the corridor. The bare surfaces smothered her thoughts until she had to fight the urge to run. She clenched her jaw and forced herself to study the walls. In Ciordan, the trade well was painted and light-shifted in the corridors. Here, where the walls closed her off from the land and sky she needed, there were no color patterns, no doors to hide even the hope of a trade. To keep a slave off balance? A muscle jumped in Tsia's jaw.

No other scans tingled through her bones; no links on the walls let a body think to the node. This place was as lifeless as her coffin. She smiled grimly. Her coffin. The words echoed in her mind with a finality that chilled her more than the box had. Bound by the r-con, then by the walls—was it any wonder that she ached to stretch her legs? Did no one understand what it was like here, locked in this coffin while she knew the wind blew along the coast, and the breakers surged on the rocks, and the topoff cedars whipped below the dark heights of the Vulcans? Daya, but for one breath of cold, salty air . . .

She gazed at the corridor. Close by, perhaps on the other side of these walls, would be the guild offices: agfa, profs, techs and spacers, shipping, coms, psychs and med . . . All trades bought or sold work rights at some time or another. Some, like the art guild and the mercs, bought lives. And almost any guild could use a guide.

She caught herself. She was, in Hesse's r-con, no guide. She was a firedancer. Nothing more. So here there would be no techs to hire her skills. No Gea people with whom to lock a contract.

Spacers? They would not waste their credits on an entertainer who could not go offworld—the guide who left her planet could not support the virus that also let her dance. Those who left Risthmus left their biolink behind.

She was entertainment. Tsia invoked the word deliberately and used the anger it brought to keep her mind controlled. No one here cared if her degrees were Gea, whether she had two or ten years experience with the gene maps. Her skills were nothing here. Only her sweat—she clenched her fingers—had given her body value. And that only to an artist.

In spite of the heat, a cold snake squirmed up between Tsia's shoulders. Of all the buyers in the Black Well, the thought of an artist could freeze her into terror faster than the frost baths of the northern pole. The art guild ... The contracts they offered new guides did not allow the artist to maim a guide in a firedance. But there had always been rumors. Criminals, cut forever from the node, were ghosts. And ghosts, it was said, could not sign a contract or protest their treatment in the courts.

Artists ... They used humans—and aliens—as they used paint or light or stone. Disposable minds. Experimental bodies. No torture clause for them. What had Jak Volen said? Guild art can touch your soul, but don't ask its price. Tsia swallowed. There was no mortality clause for a ghost.

Once, six years ago, she had met Ebatan, the sculptor who had done *Twisted Body Rising from the Rocks*. The torso of the sculpture looked as if it had been dragged inch by inch up out of the lava itself. The horror and despair on its face had haunted her ever since. She had taken Jak's dare and asked Ebatan how he had achieved it. The artist had laughed. Then he had pointed at the inscription. Eighteen years, he had said. That long to find a subject strong enough to survive the completion of his work.

Tsia looked at the restraint controls in Hesse's hand and hid her shiver. The art guild had no gene-manipulation clause, either.

Hesse reached the end of the corridor and locked the r-con in place. Obediently, Tsia's body stopped, her nausea rising, and she swallowed carefully, letting her mind picture Hesse's heart carved from his body like a piece of dinner meat.

Hesse's narrow face made his eyes stand out like a hawk's. He examined her carefully. When he met her eyes, he raised his brow at her stubborn smile. "Do you still hope the guild that gave you your virus will save you, Tsia-guide?" He leaned forward. "That even now your mentors search the nodes for your presence? Do you pray that the sensor scan back at the door alerted a team of mercs to rescue you?"

Tsia focused her gaze beyond him, and Hesse's face tightened. He stepped close, staring down into those distant blue-gray eyes. "Your presence"—he smiled gently—"in the sensor nodes was deleted four weeks ago. You don't exist anymore. You are not even a sentient being anymore—not to the nodes, anyway. You are a ghost. Just a shadow on a very large ball of orbiting dirt."

Tsia stared silently. A fist, caught at the apex of a punch, seemed to have slammed into her gut. But no, Hesse had not moved—it was her own body, frozen somehow in shock.

Hesse's complacent gaze cut across her like an icy wind. "Did you wonder how we could bring you to a guild well for trade?" He ran his hand along the length of the n-rod, caressing it like a lover. "Your scansign," he said softly, "was traded with that of a body that was buried." He raised the n-rod and tapped her forehead with its black, unactivated tip. "Buried four weeks ago."

Tsia wrenched her gaze beyond him. It was no fist in her gut. It was an adder, cold and deadly, which had settled into her stomach. If her scansign was no longer in the nodes—she felt Hesse smile with her comprehension—her temple link was useless. She was no more than a resonant shadow in the node. A shadow, not a person. Not Tsia.

"With all the hunts and ventures on this planet," Hesse said, tracing her cheeks with the n-rod, "with all the challenges made and lost, no one bothers to question the accidents."

No one . . . No guides, no parents, no mentors. Something blinded Tsia's eyes. She saw no corridor, no Hesse, no n-rod with its promise of pain. Only a void stretching out through her chest. Her scansign was no longer hers. The node no longer knew her. Her family . . . Cullen . . . Jak . . .

"You want to know the irony of it?" Hesse breathed in her face, knowing she could not flinch. "You were burned to death. You—a guide. Fresh from the flames of Daya herself. Seared to a stain of blackened ash. And," he said, beginning to laugh, "best of all . . ." The sound chilled Tsia's lungs so that they could no longer take air. "Best of all," he repeated, "they accepted it. You had the arrogance of a new guide. You took a dare that killed you. And they believed it. They never looked for you." He turned away, laughing. "They never even checked."

〜◦◦◦〜

8

Tsia stared blankly at the ghosts. Node ghosts. The line of their bodies stretched before her like a human ladder to hell. Her thoughts were frozen. The Ciordani thought her dead. The node no longer knew her. Even if she got rid of the plugs in her temples and linked in, the node itself would not recognize her pattern as real. It would read her, then discard her as junk. She would simply be a simulation, another image floating through the data. Never breathing. Never hungry for the freedom of the sea. Never real.

She stumbled as the line moved forward. Her temples ached where the node plugs fit into her link. The r-con was not on; with the manacles, it was no longer needed. Besides, slaves moved better with their own grace, not the jerky movements the r-con forced. And she, Tsia, was a slave. A ghost in the nodes. Worse than a naught, she was a nonbeing. In an hour the art guild would own her. And how long would they keep her? her mind demanded. They had no need of an ecologist, a gene mapper, a biologist from the coast. They needed only her sweat, her feet in the flames. How long would it be before they burned her to death? Or molded her into some kind of atrocity? Like Ebatan's *Twisted Body*, she could be an experience trapped in stone forever. Or a flaming memory sold to the minds of the blind . . .

Tsia stared down at the chains that ringed her wrists and ankles. She chafed at their metaplas coils. She could force her body to move against the r-con, but this steel . . . Daya, this metal on her skin . . .

She hated the white that surrounded her. They had taken her jumpsuit and boots, given her the scrub, and left her the white of the slaves. No footgear now, she snarled to herself. No, it was bare feet for the ghosts of the well.

A short woman walked down the line with a fat watergen tube. "Drink," the woman said to each slave. With the thirst born of the desert, each ghost slave took the straw. Reluctantly, each relinquished it to the next. Tsia could smell the water long before it reached her. When the watergen arrived, she was already grabbing at it, sucking desperately to relieve the parched thinness of her throat. Her thirst was a secondary torture in her lungs, her mouth, her eyes. When the woman tugged, Tsia could not let go of the straw, and the woman yanked it finally from her grasp, leaving Tsia to glare after her, shivering with need.

When the woman was out of sight, a thickset man walked down the line with a vial, stopping at each slave. "Breathe," he said softly, tipping the vial. Golden dust curled out. "Breathe," to the next. Another tiny cloud of dust. Another slave. Another breath. "Breathe." Two ghosts away from Tsia, one man refused to inhale. The trader did not even pause. He blew gently, and the golden cloud curled up and sought the reluctant one's face. Tiny flecks clung to the ghost slave's lips and nose and eyes. The man blinked furiously, wrinkling his nostrils against the sensation. He rubbed his face against his shoulder, trying to wipe off the powder. The dust seemed to crawl inside his lips. Tsia stared blankly. Hydrophilic—the dust was hydrophilic. First the water, then that golden dust . . . The powder sought the moisture of their mouths.

The trader was beside her now. Tsia tried to dry the lips that had been so parched a moment before. "Breathe," said the man before her. She could not. He blew the powder; it touched her lips. "Breathe," he said to the woman on her right.

Tsia could not raise her arms more than halfway to wipe her lips; the chains linked her feet to her waist, and her waist to her hands. Metal, always metal. She clenched her lips closed. The dust crawled between them. Her nostrils tickled. Her eyesight blurred. Her lungs began to ache. Daya, did it matter? She was a ghost now. A slave. Something dissolved on the inside of her lips. A metallic tang touched her tongue. Her breath stifled. She seemed to sink into the floor, her body pressed in from all sides. Was this how it had felt to those children? she asked herself. Sinking in the mud of the slough, knowing only that the tide would steal their breath and life as it surged toward them in the hands of time? She shivered and forced the memories, the claustrophobia, the guilt of death away, and her body did not respond. Her breath was a gale between her teeth. Time compressed.

People moved beside her. Bodies walked away. Time—did it still move forward? Two dozen slaves, then two, then five more disappeared. Tsia stared blankly at Hesse when he came back to claim her. He gestured. The motion was too quick for her sight. Stupidly, she followed him, leaving the other slaves behind. Corridor walls swept past her gaze. The floor rose to meet her feet so that she paid careful attention to its lack of design. She walked. She stopped. Hesse went away, and she waited. Patience, was that what dulled her mind? No, it was the dust, the powder of the sun . . .

How long had she been standing there? Noises rose and fell, but there was no source for the din. She tried to focus her gaze. It was minutes before she realized that the opening before her was shielded. Of course she could not see through it—it had not been cleared.

She shifted from foot to foot. She wiggled her hands. The effect of the powder was wearing off. Should this be happening? The slaves back in the corridor had not seemed alert when she was taken away. Her body, which had been lethargic, tried to stretch. Like a heron craning its neck after a fish, she reached up with her chin. Stretched, twisted . . . Did they know? Did they guess she could move? She could think? Her mind cleared for an instant. The virus did not accept drugs easily—it would even fight med commands from a node, commands that would stimulate her immune system to respond—and if these trader drugs were almost gone from her system, she could then fight her way free of this metal and get herself to the guild. She focused on the idea until it grew fuzzy and she lost her train of thought. The ache of her body tugged. She strained up, her muscles trapped and tight, cramped, as if she were caged in a box half her length.

When the portal cleared, Tsia's toes and fingers burned with returning sensation. Her mind cleared again with the door, and she relaxed her involuntary fist as Hesse grinned at her in the doorway. The dull din that struck her ears was suddenly full and loud, and she half raised her hands to her head. Hesse caught her arms, forcing them gently down. "Come," he said, his voice satisfied and full. "Trust me. Everything is going well."

She balked. His voice was a shiver that stripped her back of heat, and she stared at him as an idea suddenly grew in her mind. It was not, she realized, the drugs or the metal on her wrists that held her in thrall but the voice of this man, this "trust me" that echoed in her head and caught at her reason and made her try once more to believe. She could break the r-con, the manacles, because she could see them. But how could she break free of Hesse?

She could see beyond him now, on through the opening where

float chairs wafted through the air. She clung to the images and tried to fight the waves of fuzziness that washed her. In the hollow column before her, voices merged and swelled like a snake so that the haggling, laughing, talking bodies that filled the center of the well created a seething, coiling mass. The layers of traders darted and drifted from one spot to another. Chairs maneuvered closer to or farther from the lower levels. Half of them locked into semistructured hoverspots and left only the spanning walkways and supported disklike platforms clear.

Slowly Tsia followed Hesse out. Inside, the vast column, like the one in Ciordan, was white. Ivory-white. Bone-white. White walls that stretched up to a bleached-white sky. The sun, hanging at the edge of the well, splintered its filtered light off white mosaics that traced their pale worm patterns delicately up the walls. Patterns merged and changed. Tsia had seen similar mosaics before; they were the design biographies of every colonist who had landed at this site. The lives of her own grandparents were traced in the guild well at the base of the Vulcan Mountains.

Before her, odors rose from the sea of bodies and wavered in the air before being sucked into the fan channels that coiled between the floating tiers. Clumps of colors swam before her eyes: a miner in the gray and silver of his guild, Korshani in the sand-toned desert dress, a trader with her new, brilliant dirtside clothes showing her offworld origin, as if she had worn her e-suit down instead of woven planetary robes.

But the color that blended most with the well, the one color Tsia herself wore, was white. The white of trade. The clean palette—the blank of opportunity, as the trade guild said. Here the white made pools of the ghosts among the colored buyers. Indentured workers had some variation to their robes—they wore white with woven patterns. Only free workers—those fourth-class workers or better—wore clothing of their choice, and even they sported the white bands that said they were looking for work.

Hesse led Tsia to a platform in the center of the din. Other, higher platforms were empty at the moment; the guilds seemed done for the day. Tsia stared at the round stage. Her legs would not move toward it, and Hesse pulled her forward until she stumbled up. She did not kneel. Inexorably, his fingers like spikes in her shoulders, he forced her to her knees. "Relax," he said softly. "Trust me. Everything is fine."

She shuddered. He had trained her well with those words. Even now she expected the touch of the n-rod on her shoulder.

"Im heyta kahneketa," he called to the crowd. *"Hie a bo kai-van."*

Heyta? Tsia struggled under the weight of Hesse's hand. In the southern tongue, the language of Korshan, *heyta* meant "slave." With a twist, she forced her way up onto one knee. The metaplas chains slid gratingly across the stony floor. In front of her a languid woman leaned closer from her float chair. The woman's offworld cigar sent up a pale curl that twisted over her shoulder like a viper, then dissipated into one of the fan channels. Beside her a spacer's swarthy, half-shaven face provided an odd contrast to the polished green bars that stretched along his shoulders. Two figures drifted into Tsia's sight in a duet of float chairs: a lanky woman with an iron-gray streak in her red-auburn hair and a black-haired man in a startling blue jumpsuit. As they passed, the woman looked down. Tsia smiled grimly, unaware of the animal ferocity of the expression.

Above Tsia, Hesse called again. *"Im heyta kahneketa. Hie a bo kai-van."* More floats gathered around the platform, darting into the hover slots like rats diving home.

Tsia crouched under Hesse's heavy hand, ignoring the pressure of those hard, slender fingers. The crowd shifted out of focus, then snapped sharply back, and she blinked. She struggled against Hesse's hand, and the movement brought a shattering pain to her shoulders as his n-rod touched her briefly, reminding her to behave. Lips clenched, she shuddered silently, enduring the aftermath.

Damn Hesse. Damn him to the depths of space. Her blurry gaze focused on the floats that stabilized in the hover slots. Somewhere in her drug-dulled brain she recognized a pattern. Stairs. Float tiers were like manual stairs. And like stairs, they led to the top of the well. Her eyes sharpened. Far above her, the trade gates were open—she could see them. She could see the colors and symbols of the professions like tiny squares against the blinding white of the well. All she needed was a simple raser . . .

Or a flexor, she thought as her gaze darted to the traders' sides. They sported spacer blades—variable blades and fingernail knives. There must be one among them who carried a flex sword. Years ago, when Jak Volen had rights-conditioned her to fight, he had taught her to use a flexor first. She had loved the feel of the weapon, the way it changed with her movements to become the shape she needed. The closest thing to thinking one's way through a fight, he had told her a dozen times.

She glanced across the tiers. The two closest floats held traders

armed with nail knives. Beyond, another trader carried her variable blade in a back sling, but it was not the sword Tsia wanted.
She looked again at the chains that chilled her skin and glared at
the light that glinted back. Daya, she cursed, but could not that
sullen sun pierce the well at some other angle? The shadows
streamed away from the platform as if she were standing in a
spotlight. In Ciordan the sun would have been low, spitted on a
tree line as it tried to cross the sky, not high and swollen like an
angry eye above her. A flame-fed eye in the sky . . . The chem-
icals in her blood made her vision blur again, and she clung to the
memory of fire. Firedancing. Biogates. Gods, if she could only
think how to use her biogate, if she could touch a feline in this
place, catch some sense of its clarity to hunt and strike . . .

Hesse spoke again, and Tsia's lips thinned to a predator grin.
Her mentors had said her strength would grow as the virus took
hold of her body. What had been a tiny thread of feeling in
Ciordan should be at least a line by now . . .

She opened her senses and felt a fierce joy in the vastness that
rolled toward her in her mind. It did not matter, she snarled to
herself, that the cat gate was useless to a guide. It was all she had.
And if the guides themselves would not lift a hand to help her, let
the cats decide what was within their will.

And what would she get from them, anyway? her inner voice
asked.

Shut up, she told herself savagely. Even the sense of their speed
and claws would be a weapon here.

How long did it take her to find the suncat? Seconds? Minutes?
Hesse was still pitching his sale to the traders, his voice rising and
falling with dramatic intent. Tsia ignored him. The link she found
was weak, and she cursed Hesse for taking her from Ciordan before she had learned even the simple task of focusing through her
gate.

Calming herself, she swallowed her frustration. The suncat was
indigenous and did not have the engineered intelligence of the
colonists' beasts. She did not care. Even if she could not call it to
her, she could at least feel it and use its hunter purpose as her
own.

She tried to tighten the link. An itching tickled her thoughts.
The hunger of the cat hunter was like a sharp scent cutting
through a fog. Exhilaration at its senses caught in her throat. To
feel, to touch . . . Just as the exultation filled her, a savage disappointment curdled her thoughts. To touch and never to call . . . Furious, Tsia turned on herself, cursing herself silently until she

turned despair to bitter rage. Her guts seemed to tighten and
surge. The link expanded. With a roar of triumph, she threw off
Hesse's hand and staggered to her feet. The massed sound around
her hiccupped with the slap of her fetters.

"I fight you," she shouted angrily, swaying upright. And then
her cheeks flamed because her voice had as little strength as she
did. The buyers laughed, their teeth white and flashing in their
space-darkened faces. An olive-skinned trader in the back lifted a
finger from the hilt of his flex sword; the languid woman rubbed
her nose thoughtfully; and to the side, a lone yellow-robed figure
raised his eyebrow into a quizzical expression that was out of
place on his cold, emotionless face.

"Emekka al vana," Hesse said behind her. He imaged her history out of the node to a dream channel, where the buyers could
tap in and feel it as their own. Like an unwanted lover, his long-
fingered hand caressed her naked arm. *"Jit kai-al,"* he said. *"Jit
nyeka."*

Kai-al: "guide-firedancer." She knew that much. And *nyeka*?
Female fighter—something like "one-who-fought-with-grace."
Her face tightened. *Nyeka* was not what Hesse had called her that
first day when she had killed his wife and four of his friends.

"Al brey im bo heyta," he encouraged as the swarthy man hesitated. *"Jit kai-al, jit nyeka."*

The yellow-robed man nodded slowly, his flat amber eyes disinterested. The languid woman tapped the arm of her float. The
swarthy man cocked his head.

Tsia gathered the sense of her gate into her hands. Hesse's eyes
went greedily from the swarthy man to the yellow-robed figure.
And then Tsia struck him, whirling and snapping his wrist as if it
were old wood.

Hesse grunted, his tanned face paling suddenly. She kicked out
his knee with her heel but buckled along with him as her feckless
muscles refused to stand up to her weight. Not a trader in the
crowd moved to help him. A red-robed woman tugged at her ear,
countered by another bid from the man in yellow silk, and Tsia's
head rocked back with the brute force of Hesse's returning blow.
Her lip tore, but she made no sound as she hit him again. Hesse
grabbed for her chains. She swung them back, but he yanked
hard, jerking her feet out from under her. She hit the platform on
her shoulder, smashing into the stone. She gasped as the air leapt
out of her lungs. She rolled desperately across the stones. A raser
. . . anything . . .

The swarthy man nodded; the yellow figure coughed. Tsia

snapped out in a lunge and caught the edge of a float. She hauled herself over the arm, ignoring the fat man's saucer-eyed look of horror. Her teeth snarled as she ripped the smooth handle of his flexor from his belt. Unable to stretch completely, she dropped to the arm of the float beneath him and leapt back to the platform, facing Hesse as she tried to balance the blade for her hand. It was awkward, set for the fat man's hand. It curled into a claw, then straightened as she whipped it toward the trader. Hesse jumped back. Still, no bidder—not even the man from whom she had stolen the blade—moved to stop the silent, straining fight. Tsia did not wait to find out why. She severed her chains at the waist to free her arms, then lunged.

Hesse leapt back again. Scrambling to the edge of the platform, he jerked an n-rod from the hands of a woman nearby. Tsia froze for an instant. Her hesitation cost her dearly. When she came in, she came in short, slicing Hesse's hamstrings instead of his back, and the loose-hanging chains slammed brutally against her arms as they followed her blow. Hesse cried out. Tsia lunged again. The n-rod slashed the hand she threw up to disarm him.

She spared one glance at her limb as it hung nerve-deadened and limp at her side. Then she spun, snapping the flex blade into a narrow, twisted point. She shifted its mass down. She knew its balance now, but Hesse lunged inside the long blade's reach. Tsia cut awkwardly at his wrists, but her limp, left arm dragged her balance back. She whipped the blade into a hook and clawed at his gut. Her foot slipped in a splash of warm blood. With the motion, her leg chains slung around her stable ankle, and she fell to one knee.

Hesse clutched wildly. Missing, he grabbed inside his baggy tunic and, fumbling, tearing at the sack, hurled a handful of the golden powder at her face. It blinded her, but her wild stab impaled him, the now-straight blade thrusting deep into his gut. She felt it hit home and wrenched it up into a hook as she caught his ribs. She dragged it through his stomach with a sob. His carcass kicked at her feet while his gray-pink guts spilled out across the stone.

She stared down. The spray of pink-gray guts mesmerized her eyes, and her breath rasped in her lungs. His limbs seemed to thrash forever. Daya, how long was it before the yellow stain at his crotch mixed with the red splash of blood? It was not until then that Tsia broke from her frozen stance and sank, trembling, to the stone. She buried her head in her hands.

She tried to think and found that her breath came more easily when she opened her mouth to take it in. She was free. She shuddered. Then she stood, kicking Hesse's limp leg aside so it no longer sprawled. The movement sent a fresh surge of guts hanging over his abdomen, and Tsia pressed her hands against her stomach. Like the blurring lights that dulled her eyes, the nausea rose in waves.

Her lips tight, she bared her teeth at the faces in the floats. She could see all the figures before her, the bottoms of the upper floats, and the undersides of the narrow spans. She grinned in exultation, her sight still clear, then she stooped and gripped the flexor. With two blows she severed the links on her right leg as close to the manacle as she could.

A second later a movement close beside her caught her eye. She glanced up. Was someone coming to clean up the mess? No, there was no one moving yet from the lower door. She looked around and saw the floats still gathered. There the languid woman touched her ear again, and the yellow-clad trader frowned, coughing twice.

Tsia blinked. This could not be real. They could no longer bid—she was no ghost now. She was free.

The officer pulled at his beard, and the lone figure tapped his chin.

"Daya," she whispered, "have you no eyes?" She straightened. "Hesse is dead," she said more loudly. The faces swam suddenly in her sight. "I am not his to sell."

The figures did not respond, and Tsia gripped the flex sword tighter. The Black Well became suddenly stifling. In her grip the sword shaped itself into a narrow, tapering spike. Tsia stared at the blade, wiping her foggy eyes without success. The light was bright—too bright. She must be seeing things. But her breath came quickly, and her hand did not loosen on the sword.

The trader in yellow coughed again. The languid woman looked thoughtful. Tsia shook her fists at them, heedless of the slap of hard, loose chains against her arms. "I am a guide," she shouted. "I am not some ghost you can ignore."

The languid woman eyed her and tapped the arm of her chair. Tsia tried to scream her rage, but she choked on her breath. Her eyes blurred again.

"Damn you," she whispered. She looked around wildly. The lower door was shimmering open. "Damn you all," she snarled.

Her heart pounded. Another trader was coming through the door, and in his hands was another black-tipped rod. She glared over the edge of the platform, then up along the floats. If she could reach the guild levels, someone would have to listen.

There were no walkways between levels here, but there were the floats themselves. Like steps, the tiers were stacked between the arching spans, stairs that she could climb on. Her vision blurred again, and she wiped desperately at her eyes. A spot of red caught her attention. She stared at the spot until she realized it was a head of hair. The woman with the red-gray hair. The chair drifted disinterestedly past, on its way to a hover spot above, and Tsia focused on the advancing trader, then leapt.

She landed half on the red-haired woman's arm and half on the blue-gray chair. The flexor dropped from her grip as she grasped the arm of the float. Their eyes met. The woman shifted, her lips moved, and the sword, falling gently through the curving fan channels, landed somewhere below.

Tsia leapt again. Another float chair—its occupant jerked away to avoid her feet—and she gained the outer edge of the circle. Above, the sky beckoned. If she kept her hands on the wall, the outer energy net would slow her fall, taking her potential energy and adding that power to its own. She knew that, but the thought was sluggish in coming. Her left arm still hung limply, and her teeth grit tightly as the remaining chains jingled with her jump.

Odd, the way the traders moved. Their shapes vacillated in the white heat like mirages. They avoided her, floating silently aside, and she had to leap long to grasp one of the balcony railings. Her breath was ragged, and her breasts heaved with the exertion she forced from her body. She dragged herself over the balustrade with her good arm and fell heavily to her knees on the other side. She knelt blindly, her right hand on the railing, her left limp on the floor.

White floors. White robes. Ghosts. She lifted her head with effort. The portal before her was a huge, shimmering surface, green, with the colored bands of the economists. She hauled herself up and took a step toward it, then went again to her knees. No one was in sight. The door remained closed. Or could she trust her sight? Above, the sky glowed red, then yellow, then pale blue as she blinked. The walls rose roughly, swarming with white mosaic. White, she thought. White for the ghost in the traders' Black Well.

The feeling crawled back into her left hand, dimming the pain but barely. There was a murmur, and she whirled awkwardly, her back to the portal. Below in the hovering tiers, one of the black-garbed traders accepted the nods from the other bidders. The float of the other black-dressed man began to rise, while below, a cleaning 'bot appeared and moved toward Hesse's body.

"Oh, Daya, help me," Tsia whispered.

The top of the well beckoned. The tiles were like steps . . . Another level, another banister to climb. No door would open to her without a link to the nodes. But there would be skysails outside, and those could be put on manual. She lunged up, her hand catching the bottom rail, and one bare foot scratched for a hold on the white, always white tiles that burned beneath her lightly callused soles. The chains snagged, then jerked free. If she could make it to the top of the well, the energy net outside would slow her descent.

But the sun was so far away . . .

She was halfway up the next rail when she fainted.

9

In the midst of dreams tall trees stretched their limbs to tease each other's trunks. The sun was warm and light in the air. Dancers circled the fire, caressing the flames. Among them, Tsia stepped with the beat: in, out, back, side jump . . . The fire crackled to the drums. Embers grew, glowing in the fire line. In, out, spin, side jump . . . Sweat ran down her body. Sweet, oily runnels welled constantly from her skin. Out, back, sweep, side jump . . . She touched the fire, kissed it with her feet. Sweat balled and rolled across her soles. Drop, lunge, roll, side jump . . . Skin glowed. Cheeks flushed. Stein, slender, graceful Stein, danced across the fire line. Dunn, with the laughing lips, skittered, mocking the light that hung above the coals. In, out, leap, side jump . . . The fire beckoned. Tsia's feet found the flames. Coals crushed gently beneath her soles. She danced, twisting away from the wave that breathed of singeing heat. Glory! She flung her arms up, turning and twisting like a coil above the coals. Back kick, leap, sweep, side jump . . . Sing with sweat. She leapt and turned, and then, in the midst of a step, a bobcat flashed across the flames. The drums faltered.

She stumbled. Her hands and knees hit the fire. Coals scattered beneath her. Down, she fell endlessly into the flames. Endlessly into the glowing furnace until her back slammed against the white-gold wall and she lay, stunned, in the heat. She was frozen, without breath. Her sweat began to burn away. The fire ate at her like acid, burning away the last sticky moisture, vaporizing hair, then charring skin and tearing into flesh. She screamed, and the nightmare sounds were swallowed by the hissing of the fire. Heat? No—this was a fire of ice. Cold, it froze the flesh on her back. Cold, smooth, the coals like a sheet of ice. A white sheet beneath a sky of blackened stars. No light. No trees. Only the darkness burning into her eyes. Only the ice on her back. Steel hands crept out of the ice and seared her wrists, hugging her close to that frigid skin. Steel hands crept from the white and locked her feet to its glaze. The black pressed down. The white ice burned. Her chest compressed. The black invaded her lungs, choking her breath from her chest.

Tsia blinked. Cold still burned through her skin with the dregs of her dream. She lay, frozen, against the floor. She tried to breathe, and her lungs obeyed reluctantly, as if they had forgotten how to expand. Her breath stank in her nose. She licked her lips, her tongue catching roughly on her dry, chapped skin. The cold floor—it was real. The darkness . . . real. She rolled to her feet and caught her breath as the hands of steel came with her. Chains. They scraped across the floor with her step and swung around her ankles as she stopped, slamming into her bare feet and bruising their still-tender skin. And then the absolute blackness filtered through to her brain.

She was blind.

In spite of her clenched lips, a low animal wail escaped her. She jerked back, then lost all control, tearing at her wrists. She wrenched at the chains around her hands until she flung herself back. Her shoulders slammed against a wall. Terrified, she yanked at her ankles, trying to tear them from the metaplas bonds. "No . . ." she cried again, flinging herself away. The chains followed her back. She beat them on the floor, sobbing, and the short, stout chains from her arms slashed across her face. The jagged blast of pain shocked her, and she slid down the wall, her breath coming in gulps as she huddled in the dark.

Her stomach was a pit. Fear was a cold knot that choked her breath. She touched her eyes but could not see her hands. She pressed hard against the sockets until waves of fuzzy color rose in bursts on the insides of her eyelids. Had they blinded her?

Her temples ached. The thin flaps of skin that covered her temple links had been bruised when Hesse had clouted her back in the well. Beneath the skin, the r-con no longer clogged her temple socket. Now a flat plug filled the slot for her link. The fit was smooth to her searching fingers; the plug itself was a blank to her mind. As with the r-con, she could not think against it. No response—not even an echo came back from the plug. Her fingers scratched at the metaplas in despair.

Tsia groped her way along the wall, cringing at the sound of the chains that followed her. "Please, Daya," she whispered. She leaned against the wall, her shoulders cold where they touched the stone. Her hands pressed flat in front of her. Were they watching her even now? Listening to her pray to a god that did not answer? She clenched her jaw to keep from crying out.

Her cheek throbbed angrily, and she touched it, wincing at the radiant pain. A sharp needle of sensation cut through the center of the bruise, where a sticky trickle of blood dribbled down. She flushed with the humiliation of the mark. The tiny punctures from the demonfish had shown only as an imperceptible line. This slash would scar. The mark would be with her forever. And it would not sweat—it would burn instead.

She had once asked her father why he no longer leapt the flames with the other guides. He had pointed to the four claw marks that ran from chin to chest. "A firedancer scarred," he had said, "is barred from the flames." Guides healed quickly, he had told her, but sometimes even their skin was too marked to sweat. And there were other guides who, after their first year with the virus, did not dance in the firepit simply because the fire was never as strong a call as their gate.

Tsia pressed her hand against her cheek. This was a warning, she told herself harshly. The kind Jak would have given her with his flex sword to teach her control.

She shifted, and the chains grated over the skin of her wrists. She forced herself to store the sound in memory. How long would they leave her here in the dark? They would have to come for her sometime—they did not care about her as a guide. They would only want her for the firedance—Daya damn the flames. And the blindness . . . She clenched her fists. Guides did not need their eyes to feel the heat. Most guides walked the flames with their eyes closed, anyway; they used the expanded senses they acquired with their gates.

She stood abruptly, and the chains banged noisily into the wall. In the blackened space the sound rang on and on until she grabbed the metaplas to muffle the sound. Artists, she thought with a curse that was more a half sob. They could take what they wanted from her without her even knowing what they stole. They could strip her memories with the help of the sensors that had to be stored in these temple plugs. Force her to live sightless. Force her to dance blind, then sell her mind images to the first alien with enough credit to buy. No sight. No light. Never to see the sea again, to watch the tide line sweep across the slough, to gaze at the trees twisting and snapping in the bristling winter gales. Her thought ended on a stifled breath, and she leaned against the wall, hugging herself tightly, rocking unevenly on her heels.

Were they watching now? Were they laughing at her pain? Recording the moment for their experience? In her stomach the knot of shame tightened. Were they listening to her ragged breath? Storing her brain patterns in the plug that filled her link? She breathed out slowly, letting the fear go with it until it was only a thin thread of air between her teeth. She had learned one thing, at least, from Hesse.

She breathed quietly for a long time. Perhaps she dozed; in the dark, she did not know for sure. At length she stood, ignoring the rage of thirst that swept her body. Someone had told her once that thirst was something felt in the throat and mouth. That only one's lips would dry. She snorted. Thirst with Hesse had been a raw thing, aggravated by the burn of bile in her throat. The thirst within her now was a tightening of every muscle, a shrinking of her tissues so that it seemed as if even her bones cried out for water. She raised her hands to rub her temples, and her cracked lips pursed painfully at the clanking sounds that followed. She refused to cringe from the noise. Instead, she flattened her hands against the wall and began to search for the door.

There was, she realized, no slick feel of metaplas to these walls— the surface was natural stone. Nor were there any textured seams for doors. In her lungs the air retained the dryness of the desert. A cargo hold? There were no lingering scents to indicate trade, no vibration to indicate a transport or skimmer or sail. Beneath her feet there was no dirt or dried packing gel, no wisps of foam, no sand, no grit, no wood. Nothing but that smooth and solid stone.

She paced the room end to end, but nowhere did she feel the subtle tingling that accompanied the molecular scans of a door's filter fields. Nor was there a freegrav plate—unless it was hidden—in the floor to indicate a transport channel. No links in the walls for node access. No windows. No gouge or dent to break the smooth density of the dark.

How much time had passed while she breathed in that black desert air? Was this a test? Or was she simply to be ignored until needed? Her stomach gnawed at her ribs. There was no place to relieve herself of the concentrated piss she had to pass. There were no comforts at all, not even a therm on which to sleep. There were no cracks of light in the panels that seamed the room. There was no roof to her seeking hands. There was nothing but the pacing of her feet. The scrape of the chains. The silence of her breathing. The endless, timeless dark.

It was a tiny rush of hot air that warned her. Tsia woke instantly. A brilliant shaft of light cracked the darkness like lightning. Even as

her eyes cringed from the opening door, she gasped at the sight.
Light! her mind shouted. Not blindness! Unthinkingly she lunged.

With a strength born of fear, she threw herself at the portal—
and slammed into the silhouetted body that was thrust through.
The two women tangled. Tsia hit the floor hard. Even as she
scrambled back to her feet, the door thudded shut again. With a
cry, she flung herself at the panel, ignoring the bruising slash of
the chains across her calves. But the door was closed as tightly as
if it were welded shut.

"Damn you," she breathed in the dark, staring where the door
had been. Her eyes still watered from the sliver of light she had
been allowed. Light—she was not blind. The words repeated in
her head like a chant.

Finally she judged the distance of the other person by the rustling cloth in the dark. In the flash of light from the door she had
seen only a blur of loose robes and a glimpse of the seamed,
weathered face of the woman who had been thrust in. Of the
room, all she had glimpsed was the stark white of the floor.

Silent seconds passed. The other woman grunted softly.

"Stay still," Tsia commanded abruptly, her voice coarse and dry
from her thirst.

The voice that responded was calm. "I will not hurt you."

Tsia's eyes narrowed. "What are you?"

"A slave," returned the low voice, "like yourself."

Tsia bit back her curse. "Is this Korshan?"

"Yes."

"What city?"

"The trade base Noirelle, in the northern quarter of the Korshan
desert."

"What date?"

"The second day of the third month of the desert horse."

Tsia snapped a translation command to her link before she
thought, then cursed under her breath at the blank wall that
stopped the command. Five weeks should have taught her the fu-
tility of that. "In standard," she said, forcing herself to be patient.
"What is the date in standard?"

"It is no longer important to you."

"I think I can still figure out what is important to me."

The other woman made a soft sound. "It is midsummer," she
said. "The moons are both full, and it has been three months since
the last rain. The date is standard nine-two."

Nine-two? She had lost a day somewhere. Perhaps they had put
her under the scanners. Without access to the automatic node

clocks, she would have no way of knowing how much time had passed. "Do you have a link?" she asked with less hostility.

"Inactive."

"May I have some water?"

"Yes."

But the woman did not move, and Tsia eyed the darkness with a growing sense of dread. "What do I have to do," she said slowly, hating herself even as she asked, "to get some water?"

There was approval in the voice of the other woman when she answered. "One thing," she said softly. "And one thing only."

Tsia felt the knot of shame harden into a fist.

"Submit."

Tsia clenched her fists and turned away. Noirelle, she breathed to herself. The black city on the southern edge of the silver mines. The city in the center of the Korshan desert. There was no better place, she thought with bitterness, to trap an estuarine ecologist. Cold stone for a firedancer, and a desert for a marsh biologist. She gritted her teeth until they caught on her dry lips, splitting her lower lip with a sharp, tiny pain. Tsia licked the spot, her parched lips giving up no blood and her tongue giving no softness to the split.

Tsia paced back to the slab that had opened. She traced its outline again with her hands, searching for a control panel she might have missed. But there were no depressions, no small squares . . . "Damn you to Daya's endless fires," she cursed, hitting the wall with her chains. She turned her back to the wall, letting her shoulders slam angrily against it. She knew the other woman was still standing where she had left her. She could smell her like a cloud of presence: her body odor, her breath, the stench of her apprehension.

"Why do you speak Ciordani and not Standard?" Tsia asked abruptly.

"Because I know it."

"You did not learn it in Ciordan."

The woman's clothes rustled. "Other *Jingas* have been brought here," she replied slowly. "Ciordani among them. I learned from one of them."

"I am not a *Jinga*," Tsia spit. "I am a Gea ecologist. Bound by contract for another two years."

"You are a firedancer. That is all that matters here."

"I am a guide," Tsia returned stubbornly.

"You're a slave."

"Not for long. I will get my link back, and then I will find justice."

The woman sighed with a rustle of cloth. In a patient voice she said, "Your link is inactive; your node thinks you dead. Even if you got rid of the plugs, you would not be freed of those chains. Neither of us will leave this room alive until you learn what I have to teach you."

"Learn?" Tsia snorted. "What? How? Where are your hypnotapes? Your holotank? Did you bring your memory pattern transfers with you?" She stared into the darkness. "You are a ghost like me. You cannot even turn on the lights. What can you possibly teach me without an active link, when the node does not even know your name?" She flared her nostrils, trying to pick up the sense of the woman's emotions in her scent. "It doesn't, does it? Know your name?"

"Names are not important here."

"You have no name?"

Tsia could almost sense a bitter smile on the other woman's face as she answered, "Ghosts have no need of designations."

"No name at all?"

The woman was silent for a moment. "Vashanna." She said the name hesitantly, as if it had been a long time unused.

Tsia scowled.

"My name is Vashanna," the woman repeated patiently.

"Vashanna. And what," Tsia returned with equal patience, her words increasingly tinged with derision, "is it that you think to teach me, Vashanna, slave of Korshan?"

The older serf laughed then, and a low, bitter sound it was. "Why, slave of Korshan, to swallow your pride and obey your master."

In her anger, Tsia could do nothing more than choke on her retort. "Obey?" she snarled. Hesse had not even tried teaching her that. Just the n-rod and the r-con for every meal. If it was obedience they wanted, they would get it only in her death.

"Give in, comply, take it lying down, but whatever you want to call it, obey."

"Are you space-crazy? I will *never*," Tsia swore, "take orders from some credit-grubby trader or kelp-slimed artist who thinks he can steal people from their jobs and their families and turn them into ghosts."

Silence hung between them until the other woman spoke again. "You are young. You are stubborn. That can be a fatal combination. If you think to resist, think again. The only thing pigheadedness brings is a great deal of pain. To both of us."

"You can no longer threaten me with the n-rod, Vashanna—"

The other woman cut her off harshly. "Your experience with

the n-rod has been minimal. Your mind functions. Your body is not scarred."

"And yours is?"

Vashanna did not answer for a moment. "You will learn," she said softly, "just like all the others before you. It has been much easier to teach *Jingas*—" She said the term deliberately. "—like yourself once the artists discovered your weakness for children. Being mostly barren makes the guides feel more for what they might never have. Do you not know," she asked softly, "what it is to long for something?" She waited, as if she knew Tsia's past. When Tsia did not answer, she continued. "You will learn," she said flatly. "Or your first punishment will be pain, of course. The second will bring with it the pain of a child. And later, the deaths of those youths. Slow deaths. How many children will you be responsible for, dance-fighter of Ciordan?"

Children. Tiny faces, Tsia thought with sudden guilt. Her hands on tiny wrists as they sunk deep in the mud. Her lips shouting at tiny, fear-twisted faces to breathe, breathe through the straws . . . And then Tsia's own face staring at her eggs at the guild cryo room, her eggs stored in stasis with her DNA sample. Her thoughts wondering if she would ever carry a child. Cullen's words: ". . . family, children, little black-eyed guides . . ."

She swallowed soundlessly, but her voice, when she answered, showed no expression. "Why not, just use the r-con?"

Vashanna shrugged. "An r-con must be monitored. That and, over time, one can become used to the r-con, even learn to withstand its pain. But to know that you are responsible for the torture of children . . . To see them, hear them as they are burned and flayed by the nerve rods . . . To know that their pain, their death is your guilt . . . That is a punishment not easily diminished."

Tsia held herself still, swallowing images until she felt she could control the rage that built in her at her helplessness. In the dark, the older servant took her silence as a sign that she would comply.

"Water, food, clothes, those you will receive after you prove that you're willing to learn." Vashanna's robes rustled. "In Korshan you have to earn the bread you eat and the clothes on your back. Language is your credit here. Learn your words, your sentences well. If they're pleased with you, they might open a window and let us see the sun again."

Silently Tsia cursed the woman who stood in the dark before her. "What purpose is served by forcing me to learn this language without memory patterns or hypnotapes? Why," she demanded bitterly, "should I learn without a link?"

"Because it will condition you to obey."

Tsia stared in her direction, peering uselessly to see an expression in the quiet words. "You told me that deliberately. Why? Now that I know, I will resist your conditioning as I would your torture."

The rustle of cloth made her think that the other woman had shrugged. "It does not matter if you know you are being conditioned. You will still learn to flinch at the pain and cringe on your knees at commands. Knowledge does not stop the process. Only death."

"And if I choose to die instead, and to hell with your threats and chains?"

The other voice was silent for a long moment. The woman released her breath, and Tsia knew she was afraid. The voice, when it spoke again, was harsh. "Then know that I also will die, and others you condemn with your selfishness. Do you think they can't hear us here? Do you think they have turned their sensors off? That they do not judge us as we stand here in their cursed night? You know nothing of pain that you stand and scoff—" Her voice sucked in, and Tsia knew the woman's nostrils were pinched with the same fear that laced her voice. "By your words alone you already bring torture to us both, and if they think you will not learn at all, you will die. They will take your memories anyway, but you will die."

Tsia smiled grimly. "Let me see this master of yours, Vashanna. Let me hear his voice tell me how he thinks to make me a slave."

The other woman was silent for a long moment. When she spoke again, her voice was quiet and persuasive. "You are new. You are uncertain. It can't hurt you to give a little at first."

"*Jit kai-al, jit nyeka,*" Tsia said softly in the dark. "I am what I am, Vashanna. And right now the fires of Daya burn hotter in me than they do in the sun itself."

"So you accept the pain instead?"

"I accept nothing."

"By what right," Vashanna said slowly, "do you condemn me to your punishment as well as yourself?"

Tsia turned to the wall, stiffening her shoulders against an accusation that already brought a pang of guilt. She cast her words over her shoulder. "You're just a ghost, Vashanna. Like me. We are not even real." She continued, determined. "You and I—we have no need of rights."

Her words still echoed in the silence when the marble shifted suddenly under her fingers. "Daya," she whispered eagerly. She lunged at the opening and caught a blinding glimpse of figures moving outside before her eyes blurred with painful tears. Then she cleared the opening and barreled into the mob, kicking and twisting to avoid their grabbing hands. Her eyes were pierced with the light; she fought by feel, not sight. She kicked and thrust, wrenching an n-rod from one man's belt as he fell beneath her. She had the wrong end and could not turn it on even manually, so she struck out instead, jabbing the hard bar into a woman's gut before slamming it up into another man's neck. She scrambled over his flailing arms.

And then she was assaulted by a child's scream and an indescribable fire at the same instant. Frozen in the grip of agony, she tumbled to the floor. Her legs were paralyzed by the searing touch of the rod. She hardly felt the shock of her knees smashing brutally into the marble; the shrieking sensations in her spine blotted all else from her mind. In her eyes only a red haze floated. Daya, was this an n-rod or was her death burning in her even now?

Dimly, the child's high-pitched wail rose up again. Vashanna cried out, "No, not mine—please—she is young—she will learn, I swear—*Passa ji heye!*" The woman's voice rose into a scream. *"Hukche passa ji bayen . . ."*

Massive hands closed on Tsia's arms like the twin jaws of a tooth-edged trap. Lifted and tossed without effort, her body slammed, then rolled across the marble, flaccid and fainting; her head cracked sickeningly on the stones. Her teeth snapped at the impact. She could not even writhe against the pain.

To her left, the angled square of light that cleaved the shadow-black floor was filled abruptly with the struggling and cringing shape of a child, and Vashanna screamed, throwing herself at the soldiers' feet. It did no good. They hauled Vashanna away from the child and cuffed her with the rod. The woman fell face-down, contorting and racking with spasms. Tsia glared dimly, her ice-blue gaze glistening with hate and pain as the rod reached over to touch the face of the child. She could not stop them—she could not even move to ward off the rod that slashed across her own chest, could do nothing but lie there and clench her teeth and shudder as her bones tried to explode within her body. She shrieked in her mind. She writhed in the blast of pain that wracked her from shoulder to waist. But she was young and strong and proud and so could not even escape to the dark void of oblivion.

When finally Tsia struggled out of the red haze, Vashanna was still sobbing. Tsia breathed in and stifled her own cry; her body cramped from the shooting pains. The dark was punctuated by the grate of the chains that thrust in constant rhythm across the stone from the twitching of her legs. In the blackness Tsia dragged her legs beneath her. She tried to reach her feet but fell heavily to the stone. For long moments she lay like a dying bird. That had not been the touch of a simple n-rod. From Hesse she had taken such pain and stood and smiled. What they had just done . . . "Vashanna," she croaked, gathering up the shreds of her voice. Her right leg kicked involuntarily as her muscles convulsed.

The ragged mother beat her bare hands on the floor. "*Ji bayen,*" she wailed. "That they used my own child."

Tsia shuddered again, and the clanging of the shackles across the stone made a demonic harmony to the mother's cry.

The older woman struck herself in the chest. "Ah, gods, to burn them in a thousand hells of oil."

"I am sorry, Vashanna," Tsia whispered.

The older woman moaned unheeding. "There were others who could have been brought. And for this? For this slut of the north-lands? For this arrogant dance-fighter, this dung of the flames, I lose my child? My last child . . ."

Tsia closed her eyes, her face twisted with pain. "*Jit kai-al, jit nyeka,*" she said hoarsely, painfully in the dark. She crawled toward Vashanna's voice. Her hand jammed against Vashanna's thigh, and she found the woman clutching the body of her child. She lay her hand on the other woman's arm. "Vashanna—"

"Yaza *nyeka*," Vashanna spit, violently shaking her off.

"Daya," Tsia whispered. "Forgive me, Vashanna."

"Forgive this? How could you? I told you what would happen. Did you think I was joking?"

Tsia clenched her fists. "Damn you," she cursed. "Did you really think I would submit by your words alone?"

The old slave hiccupped, and Tsia thought she could feel the heat of the woman's dark passion even through the cold, caliginous black. Vashanna spit. When Tsia heard the sluggish splat on the cool marble, she knew that it was blood. "Vashanna . . ."

"Truth here comes with pain, not peace. When I speak, you listen. When I command, you obey."

Tsia clenched her jaw. "I can't."

The body of the child was suddenly thrust into her arms, and the acrid scent of piss rose in her nose. She struggled to contain the limp form. "Feel him," the other woman spit viciously. "You are a guide; your nose is sharp. Breathe him in and smell him. Take him in your arms and taste the death of his body." Her voice broke.

Tiny wrists. Thin, fragile arms. "Oh, God . . ." Tsia tried to give the body back. Vashanna shoved her away, and Tsia struggled to push the child into his mother's arms. "I did not know he would be killed," she pleaded, her voice tight. "Take him back."

"He is yours," the woman said harshly. "Your arrogance bought his death."

"I won't." Tsia thrust the body into Vashanna's lap, and the little boy's head cracked against the stone. Both women froze. "I," Tsia said in a choked voice, "am rights-conditioned. Even if I wanted to, I could not kill him if he did not harm me. I did not kill him, any more than you did."

Vashanna gasped. Her hand slapped Tsia brutally in the dark. "His blood," she cursed, "is yours. Had you listened, he would not be dead. Had you believed, he would be breathing now."

Tsia's breath was ragged. "I am sorry," she cried out.

"And what is that worth?" Vashanna choked on her own rage. "What value has your apology? Is it worth his heartbeat? His thoughts? One gram of his body?"

Tsia could not control her shivers. The chains grated on the floor with the cold.

"Or does it mean as little as the sound of your fetters on stone?" Vashanna's fingers clutched the little boy and rocked his body. "Your sorrow, your guilt," she said to Tsia, "are nothing. You are nothing."

"I am a guide." Tsia whispered.

"You are a slave."

"Never."

"Now and always. You condemned yourself with his death. By that one act you put your own chains around your soul."

"Then I can take them off."

"You don't even know how to try."

"I will never submit, Vashanna, not till the last breath leaves my body as limp as the boy in your arms."

Vashanna did not speak for a moment. "And how many of these boys will you leave dead in my arms?"

The question halted Tsia like a fist in her gut, and the silence stretched in a long, forbidding moment.

"The word—" The older woman's voice was a deadly calm. "—the word for 'slave' is *heyta*." Her breath halted for a moment, and Tsia knew that she was rocking herself until she could speak again. "The word for 'hate' is *kobe* . . ."

10

How much time could one spend in a prison? Was each hour an infinite measure? A week of words earned for Tsia the water her body craved and the submission her heart despised. Another week earned a dim light so bright to her eyes that they watered for days. A month of false subservience earned a shower coil that burned her skin with shame more than it cleaned her with its molecular scrub. Each bite she took caught in her throat with the Korshani words in which she begged. Each month of heat made the gnashing of her teeth harder to still.

Twice she rebelled. The first time she deliberately broke her arm by landing on it in a slamming roll against the wall. Instead of forcing the guards to take her to a medlab, it earned her another punishment. This time they locked her body in the r-con and set the bones while she stood, tortured, unable even to scream because while she was locked in her stance, they laid the n-rods across her shoulders and legs as they set her arm. One did not damage an artist's goods, Vashanna told her flatly. Not without incurring the wrath of the artist.

The second time she rebelled, they brought in another child to punish with her. This child did not die. But as they carried the young body out, the only sound from the small, shocked mouth was a constant, tiny piteous mewling that haunted Tsia as she lay on the cold stone floor. And in the harsh, blinding pain that kept time to the jerking of her body across the stone, there came, beneath the mewling, the scream of a cougar in her mind. The claws of the mental cat tore into her muscles with the n-rod that slashed her nerves. She gasped in the hot, putrid breath of the cat. She screamed silently at it to taunt her no more with its life, its power, its freedom. And when its claws skittered along the inside of her skull as the searing pain subsided, the sounds of the mewling and snarling faded till only the scrape of her chains rang on the floor.

The sense of the cats grew: The vastness of the air they breathed choked her with the closeness of her own walls. As the link grew in strength, the room seemed to shrink till it was nothing more than a tomb in the midst of the desert. And Tsia crawled into herself and hugged herself together and cried silently, without moving. Cried in her mind so that she did not cry before Vashanna. She, Tsia, had given half her life to be a guide, half her life to have the biogate that would free her from Ciordan. And now she had nothing but the mocking snarl of the cats that ate the memory of freedom from her mind.

Fire was what trapped her here and made her hate the heat. But the virus shifted the cells of her body, bringing her sweats in the middle of dreams, tossing her to wakefulness in the hours of dark and night. The sweat that would let her dance in the firepit she had seen only once—it pulled her like a lover to the image of the flames. She dreamed of fire in Ciordan. She dreamed of fire in the sky. Lightning-struck grass fires that blazed in the Sinking Plains, too hot and suffocating for the dance . . . Firebug fires that crept cold along the ground of the sandy dunes off Black Pony Slough . . . Man-made fires in the hammers that flared out into space with the unshaded light of a burst of gas . . . She dreamed them all and danced each one in her head—wild animal motions that neither chains nor gravity could stop.

She firedanced day and night. Even without the flames, even before her arm healed, she danced her cell as if it were a pit and danced it in bitter irony. She swept across the floor, kicked at the height of the ceiling, and leapt like a bobcat after a black-spotted gull. She scorned the tiny sensor dots embedded in the walls, sensors that could no longer hide their subtle tingling from her skin. She swung and punched, blocked and ducked, and through it all she found nothing but the white walls, white floors, and white— bone-white—stone ceilings. Nothing in her sight but the pale surface that held its coolness even in the desert heat. No patterns marred the floor on which she stood. Nothing relieved the constancy of the white except Vashanna's twisted skin.

Tsia had stared at Vashanna the first time the room had held light. Like crumpled fabric, the nut-brown of the woman's skin was ridged and seamed and wrinkled. Her chin was corded and slick with burn scars that reached to her cloth-covered neck. Not even her eyes were even. Her eyebrows were tufted, as though the hair no longer knew which way to grow. And beneath the heatcloth of her cowl, her hairline was patched and ragged. But in all that marked and twisted flesh Vashanna's nose was straight. Unbroken, unmarred by any line, the nose was an artist's joke in the midst of melted skin. Tsia could draw Vashanna's face now from memory. The seams, the scars, the strangely perfect nose, the patchy shading where her skin did not grow evenly ... Vashanna had not hidden her face, and there had been nothing else to see.

Four months, five months. Six months. Seven. Hating herself as she did it, Tsia earned a window that barred her from the desert only with its filter field. Through that, with her hands pressed flat on the field, she stared at the smooth black walls of Noirelle.

She stared at Noirelle as if she could divine the inner halls from the shapes of the outer wall. For the thousandth time she stored in her head the smooth ledges that arced around the buildings and implied curves where none existed. Carved spouts faded in and out of the stone, reaching from ground to roof, where they directed the unexpected water flows from the rage of desert storms. Corners held black figurines captive. Set into a physical painting of rolling gardens and flat stone plazas, every building was lined with decorative fences of black metaplas spikes. In some places, the desert shrubs climbed the spikes; in others, plants left the fences bare.

Windows looked out on the plaza patterns like diamond-shaped eyes. The shadows of the walkway spans curved across the gardens and crept along the lines of spikes so that illusions of tracks and darkened roads appeared beneath the desert sun. And patterned—it was always patterned in precise aesthetic angles, so that the eye was caught by designs of black metal and yellow sand. Nowhere did a true green relieve the striking contrast. Nowhere did any color penetrate beyond the purple-gray of the sage. And always, as she stared across the shining solar installation, the cat feet skidded in her skull and made her clench her teeth to keep from crying out at the irony of the tawny-colored gate that taunted her black and white enslavement.

By the end of the year she could tell the change in weather by the smell of the air. She could identify a woman's perfume from an archway span and sense the subtle mind smell of an esper. She could tell from the taste of the dust when the Noirelle horses pulled away from the base and followed the long, curving tracks in the desert. Risthmus horses, she knew, engineered for the desert and mountains. And she could smell those mountains as if they were beside her. Cruelly, the wind brought her that scent, too, to remind her of the life she had known before.

Life—she could feel Vashanna's very essence, like a second pulse that echoed against the walls of her cell. When she stretched in that indefinable way, she could almost see the other woman as well as she now saw the cats in the desert—like shadows that flickered across her eyes. She closed her eyes to the shapes and focused instead on Noirelle.

Seventeen years of stubborn belief . . . She watched the skimmers rise from the pads and dart out over the desert with their Gea loads—genetic engineering and analysis. For seventeen years she had trained to take those Gea contracts, and then this—these chains. She pressed against the filter field until it hummed the strain on its pattern. Now it was eighteen years, and she had nothing within these walls but her will. No wind, no sea, no gales to whip the ground beneath her. Only the biogate that bound her to everything she no longer had.

Did she even remember the feel of a storm in her hair?

"Daya," she whispered, her face tightening. "Through this gate, if you must, but do not let me forget my freedom."

She raised her eyes to the window and stared at the distant running horses as if willing them to turn, to see her through her crippled link with the cats. And this time, instead of cutting off the sense of life that came to her through the gate, she welcomed it.

Tentatively she tasted, then immersed herself within it. And the sense of the cats swept in. The dust through a dozen mouths, the air through a dozen lungs. It was as if she were alive in a dozen places at once. She stared at the rolling land and watched the horses canter farther from Noirelle. She could taste their dung. She could smell the sweat of their hides.

"One day," she whispered to herself. "A single day on a horse . . ." She could be halfway to the dry winter mountains that blocked the north horizon. Another day and she could be within those peaks, hidden by the ridges that climbed toward the sky. She stretched farther and almost did not recognize the feathery touch at the edges of her gate. A cougar? Her heart leapt. Two days on a horse and she would be there beside it. Running with the very cats that taunted her dreams each night . . .

She stretched and breathed, and as the gate widened, the tide of sensation became a flood. Suddenly she was drowning in the desperation to claw and dig her way through the floor of the room, to find the reality in the shadow shapes that nudged the thoughts in her mind. Her hands clutched her arms; her chin was rigid to stem the animal sounds that threatened to burst forth.

No! It was too much. Too much sky and sand and space to be trapped in a mind that saw only stone walls. She began to shake and held herself more tightly to stop the shudders that crept down her arms from her shoulders. Slowly, deliberately, she shut the gate that gaped between the cats and her mind. Haltingly, despairingly, she sealed herself off until her eyes no longer swam with the images they had seen, her ears no longer hummed with their growls.

That night, as they did on every other, the thin stars pierced the darkened skies. The tiny shapes of Orpheus and Eurydice shifted across the window like a pair of white-blue eyes. Eyes of the nightcats winked on the sands; Tsia could feel their presence through her gate. Their feet itched in her mind like tiny claws scratching at her skull. On the sill, her hands clenched, and she sensed Vashanna moving up to the window. She closed out the cats abruptly, hiding the desperate, feral gleam it brought to her shuttered ice blue-eyes.

"What is it," Vashanna asked quietly, "that you see when you stare out so?"

Tsia forced herself to relax her pressure on the window field. Her voice was soft with bitterness when she answered. "A slave's road," she said finally. "A road where my soul dies a bit each day and my feet keep moving so that another's heart might beat."

Vashanna was silent for a moment. "You no longer think the sacrifice is worth the life of a child?"

Tsia stared at her. The ridged scars that seamed the other's face no longer made her wince, and she searched the wrinkled lines for some expression. The puckering beside the left eye and the tightening of the white patch near the perfect nose spoke of tension and anxiety that she could almost smell in the dark. "What do you fear, Vashanna? That I will be punished again? That you will be punished with me? I have learned your words too well. I speak the language you require."

"You speak with one tongue and think with another."

Tsia snorted. "You presume to teach me philosophy as well as language?"

"Dance-fighter—"

"Don't call me that," she snapped. "I am a guide, not just a firedancer or fighter."

"Tsia," Vashanna said softly. "Do not tempt the one who owns you."

Turning from the window, Tsia paced the room restlessly. "Why not?" she demanded wrathfully. "What have I left to lose? Your artist—my . . . master—" She spit the word. "—can take my freedom, my name, my body, my will, and my mind, all without my say-so. I signed no contract to be here. I consented to no such subservience. Yet you use me as if I were nothing more than a tool or toy for your amusement. What can I say? If I do not do as you wish—as you say your artist wishes—her guards torture a child." She glared at the other woman. "What responsibility do I have for these children?" she demanded harshly. "Was it I who brought them into serfdom? Was it I who put them in chains?"

Vashanna's brown eyes glinted.

Tsia's chest heaved with the fury that seemed to burst out of her mouth with every breath. "How," she glared, "could you, who have felt the n-rod yourself, birth a child to be such a slave?"

The other woman became very still. "You think I had a choice?"

"Did you not?"

"Whether I did or did not is not yours to judge."

Tsia let her breath out in a silent snarl. She turned abruptly to the window and pressed her hands back against the field. It tingled in her skin like the cat feet that clawed again in her skull. Let me be, she screamed silently at the teasing, taunting paws. Stop torturing me! Her back was tense, and her knuckles white.

Vashanna stared at Tsia's stance. Her voice was low when she said, "You have no ground from which to challenge me, *kai-al nyeka*. There is no wisdom in your words, no compassion in your heart." Her voice grew derisive as emotion began to burn in her own twisted, brown eyes. "What are you," she accused, "but a crippled guide who chafes because your freedom—which you never considered before—is now at someone else's mercy?"

Tsia whirled. "It is *my* freedom."

"It is not."

Tsia took a step toward Vashanna, her fingers clenched like claws in the palms of her hands.

Vashanna looked her up and down scornfully. "So what, if you wear the metal of a manacle on your wrist? Is that any different from the binding of your biogate on your soul? No, it is not." She answered her own question, cutting Tsia off abruptly. "And what if you think you are trapped in this room? Is that any different from being trapped on this planet by your virus? You earn your food and your keep here. Is that so different from your contract at the slough, the terms you signed with Gea? You learn a language with me, a private tutor. Is that any different from private lessons elsewhere?"

Tsia stared in disbelief. "How can you make analogies between the guide guild and the artists? The guides do not hide the terms of their virus—"

"Do they not?"

"No!"

"Do you know why you shake when you stare out that window?" Vashanna gestured with her chin, and the force of her words made Tsia take a step back and wrap her arms about herself to stop the shudder that automatically began. "Do you understand the pull of your gate?" the woman pressed. "Your longing for the fire? The changes in the way you think and feel? The restlessness—and the relentlessness," Vashanna added deliberately, "of the felines in your mind?"

Tsia whispered, "How do you know how it feels?"

Vashanna merely watched her, waiting for her answer.

Tsia clenched her fingers tighter. "I wanted the virus," she said in a low voice. "I gave myself to it, and I am glad—yes, I am glad of my gate. Even if it is to the cats. Even if it binds me to this world as tightly as death itself."

"And still, that is not slavery?"

"I wanted to be a guide," Tsia cried out. She hurled her chains against the window field, and the hum went supersonic at the force of it. The window instantly opaqued. "I never wanted this!"

"But the one has undeniably given you the other."

"Damn your words," Tsia burst out. "Damn you, Vashanna. And damn your artist to the depths of whatever hell her art comes out of." The window began to clear again, and she jerked up the chains on her wrists. "I will never accept these fetters. Not while there is breath left in my body to breathe."

"Like the breath you left in the body of my son."

"You are space-crazy to dwell so on this thing."

"I am his mother."

"You were his mother," Tsia corrected, "and you gave him to the art guild with his birth." Her face tightened as she went on, as if the strength of her words would deny her culpability. "And if you still think I will take the guilt for the death of your son— simply because you say it is mine to feel—you have lost more brain cells to the n-rod than you think." She glared at Vashanna. "I told you. I am rights-conditioned. I could not harm him unless he attacked me."

"Rights-conditioning." Vashanna's voice was soft and thoughtful as she ignored Tsia's other statements. "Is that not yet another form of slavery? Obedience to an ideal, an ethic given you by someone else?"

"I agreed with it," Tsia shouted. "I wanted it. I asked for it."

"And trained for it."

"Yes," she agreed, her voice suddenly quiet. "I trained hard to get it. I worked as hard as my teacher."

"As you do with me."

Tsia did not answer.

"And yet you think, with all the changes to your body, the sweeping sense of life and death in this world, the sweat that forces you toward a fire you can't even feel, the sharpness of your nose, and the nausea of your guts . . . The way you think now, not so much about the work you used to do but the life you now can feel . . . You think your virus has not changed that rights-conditioning in you, as well? Has it not made you the least bit susceptible to the influence of your gate?" She glanced at Tsia's fists. "You could not, for example, feel the urge to strike me now?"

Tsia could not answer.

"And the death of my child did not even touch you."

"Children are sacred to the guides," Tsia whispered. "The barrenness that comes with the virus makes us value our families all the more."

"And yet you still believe," Vashanna pressed, "that even though you refused to act, you have no responsibility for the death of my little boy?"

The air seemed to pause and hold its breath.

"If I refuse to learn," Tsia said in the sudden quiet, "am I responsible for the death dealt to one by another? What god," she snarled, suddenly vicious, "gives you the right to make me guilty of another's crime?"

Vashanna raised her hand partway. The billowing white of her robe let Tsia glimpse the twisted skin of her body, and Tsia steeled her eyes for the sight.

Vashanna followed her gaze. "There are no gods for ghosts," she said, and pushed back the fabric that hid her arms. The melted ridges rippled as she shook her forearms and fists. "There are no salvations," she said vehemently, clenching her hands tightly, "to save you from the chains you wear on your wrists or to free me—" She hit her fists on her chest. "—from those I carry in my soul."

Tsia's breath came harshly in the quiet that echoed after

Vashanna's words. Outside, the hum of a skimmer filled the window, then faded. The Dry Mountains, lost on the horizon with the purple-black sky, were as silent as the walls that listened in.

Vashanna met her gaze deliberately. "You have no god but yourself, dance-fighter." She shook her robe back down so that the sleeves covered her forearms. "Your honor, your integrity, your self—these are the things that stand between you and the chains on your skin. And between you and the pull of your gate."

Tsia's jaw tightened.

"You say you want to give up your guilt." Vashanna stepped forward, but Tsia did not flinch. "Do you not realize, child—" She touched Tsia's cheek gently. "—that the guilt is the only piece of your soul they cannot take away?"

Tsia stared at her. Vashanna's words seemed to hang in the air.

"It is the only tie, the only memory that keeps you human."

But, Tsia cried out silently, it is guilt itself that enslaves me. Not the chains but the guilt at the death of your child. The guilt for the deaths of Hesse, his traders. Even though they were wrong to kidnap me, I carry the memory of their presence in my mind. She tried to speak, choked, and realized that her throat was tight against the nausea that had risen in her stomach.

"I will not be slave to guilt or guile," she said, her voice low but vehement.

"You are already a slave, Tsia-*Jinga*."

"No." She set her jaw stubbornly. "I am enchained, but I am no slave."

Vashanna raised a twisted eyebrow. "I see no difference between your words."

Cat feet skittered inside Tsia's head, and the skin around her eyes whitened. The longing for the plains, for the surging sands, for any space but this room made her skin crawl. She wanted to scream at Vashanna, to beat her fists against the walls, tear the filter field of the window with her fingernails. To feel the freedom of the cats while she was thus imprisoned . . . If she were a full guide, she could call them, beg them for help, pass an image to someone in the guild . . .

It was a long moment before she spoke, and when she did, her voice was impassioned with denial and anger, longing and despair. "When I accept this—this slavery," she said vehemently, "then I become a slave. I could no longer be enchained, because I would have given myself up to blindly serve another. To serve your artist. And when I give up my humanity and become no more than a tool to be used, then I *am* a slave. No rights, no responsibility.

I would be a slave only if I agreed to that." She stared down at her slender hands, the weight of the metaplas chains hanging like a hundred weights from her wrists. "If I am enslaved," she added with clenched hands, "but do not accept myself as a slave, then I am not—I cannot be—a slave. I—" She struck her chest with her fist. "—still have a sense of responsibility, of rights, of individualism. I have not become so lost and confused as to give up my will to someone else. I will be no such victim."

"Tsia, *heyta*—"

"I am *en*slaved." Tsia spit out the words. "I am *not* a slave. I give up nothing," she snarled. "Not to you, not to your artist, not to any cursed body in Noirelle do I give an inch of myself. Only when I accept these chains could I be the slave you want. And—" She stared at Vashanna with tight, hard eyes. "—I would rather die."

Vashanna was silent for a moment. "To be a slave takes less than blind acceptance. You have not lived long enough, Tsia-guide, to understand the words you speak."

Pray Daya, Tsia thought, she never did.

11

⚬⚬⚬⚬⚬

Dawn was hot and muggy, and the overcast light of the sky gave no relief of rain to the dryness of the desert. Tsia stood at the window and stared at Noirelle as she had the first day she had seen it. She remembered that at first she had thought Noirelle a cage. It was no cage, she told herself now with a grim, humorless smile. It was just a hard wart in the dry, rock-dotted desert that stretched to the mountains beyond. A wart that she would some-day burn down to its dry, gritty skin and then mess in its ashes like a sandcat pissing in the dirt.

Behind her Vashanna stirred.

Tsia did not turn. "What do you see," she asked quietly, "when you look at me, Vashanna?"

Slowly, the other woman looked up.

"We have been here over a year," Tsia said. "A summer, a monsoon, a winter, and a spring. And now another summer. You—you are always the same. And I . . ." Her voice trailed off.

"And you?" Vashanna prompted quietly.

"Have . . . changed."

"In what way?"

"I do not know. I am . . . restless. I dream about cats. I dream about fire."

Vashanna watched her closely. "You feel sick?"

Tsia hesitated. Her anger and fear had brought tremors to her body for weeks when they argued. But was that not natural? After being held in the same room for over a year? Her nausea, at least, was the same. "No more than usual," she answered finally.

"How long has it been since you took the virus?"

"Daya," Tsia took a ragged breath. "It has been a year, three months, twelve days, and two hours."

Vashanna pursed her lips. "Three months more than a year? You are sure?"

"Not a day has escaped my notice," Tsia assured her bitterly.

"And you feel . . . changed?"

"I can feel in my bones that I am different."

The other woman's eyes flickered. "Perhaps," she said casually, "you have become the slave that you refuse to be."

"I am no slave."

Vashanna's voice was irritated when she retorted, "What are you, then?"

"An ecologist. A biologist. A guide. Slavery"—the skin around her eyes tightened—"is still in *your* mind, Vashanna, not mine."

Vashanna's anger was sudden and all-consuming. "A year and three months, twelve days, and two hours, and still you do not learn? Perhaps you just do not like to hear the word for 'slave': *heyta?* Is that it? You prefer some other term? Then, of course, you are right. You are not a slave. You are a tool," she agreed scornfully. "A toy for an artist. A novelty to be explored and soiled and discarded. Is that what you are, Tsia-who-is-not-a-slave?"

Tsia trembled and clenched her fists at her sides. "To be a slave is shameful."

"You think you eat shame?" Vashanna's voice was quiet, its softness bitter as thinroot. "You have never even tasted it."

Tsia's eyes grew hard. "And you have? You sit there in your heatcloth robe and meditate till my head spins. You cram words in my mind as a miner crams tailings down a recovery shute. You tell me nothing of the world outside this window—did the demonfish runs recover? Did the freepicks win out in the Dry Mountain mines? Did that prophecy come true about the leader of Pulan?" Has Jak returned to find me missing? she asked silently, bitterly. And will I ever touch the cats with my hands, or have them in my real nose the way they clog my mind? She stared at Vashanna with a cold despair that began to burn in her guts like gas. Her hands shook harder, and she ignored them, her anger growing to match Vashanna's. "You make me beg for every sip of water," she said heatedly. "You make me beg for every bit of food. For every human decency. And that, you say, is not shameful?"

Vashanna did not answer. Tsia, who was a guide. Tsia, who now is a slave. The words might as well have been said, they echoed so loudly in her ears.

Tsia thrust herself away from the window and paced the room.

"How can you accept this?" she demanded. "What rationale goes through your head to justify your constant serfdom at the expense of others? Do you say to yourself, 'I am fed and clothed; therefore, I must pay for these services with my body and blood? I am told I am needed; therefore, I must pay with my soul'? Is it not just your flesh but your heart that is enslaved?" She stopped at the window and turned to face Vashanna. "Do you know nothing else besides this?" She shook her wrists, and the jangling sound echoed off the smooth interior walls. "What do you see here, slave of Korshan, when you look at me? What do you see?"

Vashanna met her violent gaze quietly, her brown eyes glinting with a fierceness that belied the tone of her voice. Then the fire died, and her eyes were dull and brown again.

"I see a *Jinga*," Vashanna said softly. "Nothing more."

Tsia passed her hand over her forehead and turned abruptly to the window. A skimmer zipped into her field of sight, dropped below a black building, and was followed by another. Something about the look of the ships caught her attention, and she stared after them sharply, her hostility forgotten. "Vashanna, quickly— come to the window. Those skimmers—look there—they are merc-style ships."

Vashanna moved up.

Another skimmer dropped. "That one—there. Look. And that one landing now."

Thoughtfully, Vashanna watched the skimmer slow, then disappear behind a building.

Tsia's heart beat in a slow, heavy sound. "Are there mercs here?" she asked slowly.

Vashanna glanced at Tsia. "Not ones that would free you."

Skimmers—and mercs. The thin flame of hope that burned in her chest seemed to ignite. Tsia did not know that it lit her eyes with an icy fire. "You think I still hope for freedom?"

Vashanna smiled slightly, the expression twisting her lips into a ridged, macabre gash. "With every fiber of your body."

Tsia watched another skimmer land. The pilot was in a dangerous hurry—the ship's wings folded back even as it dropped from the skies.

"Desert wars are small," Vashanna said flatly, following her gaze. "Even if there were actions here, it would be over before you knew it had begun."

"Six skimmers in half that many minutes does not seem such a small force. How many mercs per skimmer? Seven? Eight?"

Vashanna shrugged.

Tsia did not turn from the window. She stared at the sky while another sleek white shape dropped to disappear behind the black facade of the walls. Eight, then nine skimmers in all. And any one of them able to take her away.

Mercs. Here, in Noirelle, she thought. She wiped irritably at her face; the coolness of the floor was the only comfort her body accepted. She held her sweat with difficulty. Uneasily, she wiped again at her brow with a shaking hand. She had to get out of here. She could last in this cell no longer. Trapped where the dull heat of the overcast sun was her only trigger, the virus swarmed in her flesh, chilling her blood, thickening and slowing her movements so that she ached to stretch and, once extended, strained to stretch again.

Vashanna broke into her thoughts softly. "Cekulu will want to see you soon."

"Cekulu the artist?"

"Yes."

Tsia's heart stilled. Mercs, here, and she would leave this cell without their help, after all. But at what price? Absently, she twisted the manacles on her wrists. "The skimmers were slow when they landed," she said, as if she had not heard Vashanna. "Heavy cargo or a lot of mercs?"

"Mercs: *merishkan*," the other woman corrected her automatically.

"*Merishkan*," Tsia repeated. She studied the descent line of the skimmers. "Why now?"

Vashanna shrugged. "They are guards for a prisoner who arrived this morning. The mercs hire out as guards for a fee, not just fighters for the causes they accept."

Tsia's eyes flickered. "So all these fighters are here simply to condemn another luckless ghost to death in the chains of the artists?" A small voice inside her spoke up: It had been Tsia who had condemned Vashanna's child to death with her disobedience. It had been Tsia who had tortured the other child with her rebellion. When would she pay those debts?

Shut up, she told herself harshly.

Vashanna gazed out the window, her facecloths slipping in the hot breeze so that several inches of her wretchedly scarred face were exposed. "The woman is no ghost," she answered as she secured the cloth again. "She is the pregnant council leader of Pulan."

Tsia felt a quickening of her blood. She almost turned. A councilwoman? No wonder Noirelle was hiring mercs. Even if the conflict was small, there could be days of fighting between Noirelle and the county of Pulan.

But a woman who was expecting? Unconsciously, Tsia touched a hand to her own abdomen. Her expression hardened an instant later. The barrenness of the guides would not matter to her if she did not first escape Noirelle. "Why this woman," she demanded, "if she is pregnant? Why not some other councilperson?"

Vashanna gave her a sober look. "It is the unborn child, not the councilwoman, who is important. Although," she added almost as an afterthought, "were it not that a councilwoman bore this child, the child would not be needed."

"Pulan will retaliate," Tsia said harshly.

"If they trace the hostage here."

"You think they won't?"

"Not in time to do any good. The woman is needed only for a day."

"One day?" Puzzled, Tsia turned and again tried to read the expression in Vashanna's face. "How could negotiations for her return be finished by then?"

Vashanna shook her head. "There will be no negotiation. The woman is not just a hostage. She is a . . . gift."

Tsia regarded her warily. "To whom?"

"To the artist Cekulu."

Tsia could not hide the tightening of her jaw. "To be used for the sake of her sculpture? As I am to be used?"

Vashanna nodded slowly. "If the councilwoman survives, she will be returned to Pulan, and the art guild will pay the retribution negotiated by the courts. If the woman dies . . ." She shrugged.

"You speak of the woman," Tsia said harshly. "What of her child?"

Vashanna did not answer.

"You said it was the child who was important."

Reluctantly, the woman nodded.

"If children are half as important to Pulan as they are to the guides, Pulan will not send a mere nine skimmers of mercs over the Dry Mountains. The Pulanese mercs will come in force, and they will come in vengeance."

Vashanna shrugged. "By the time they realize it is the artists, not the miners, who hold the woman, it will be too late. Cekulu will have done what she needs to do. And no one, not even an entire county such as Pulan, can reach inside her guild to punish her. Besides—" Vashanna glanced in the direction of the skimmer pads. "—war in the desert is not the same as war on other parts of the planet. Here one does not have to be stronger, just smarter."

"Because of the heat?"

"Because of the environment."

Tsia glanced out toward the desert. She had forgotten about the laws of war, and what Vashanna had said was true. The soil here was thin, lying on top of sand and rock. Only the tiny, threadlike roots of the desert grass held it in place like a sparse, silky tapestry that did not allow the wind and rain to steal the skin of nutrients. No large-scale movement or wide-range weapons would be allowed in such a place. The soil could not withstand it. And any merc who damaged such fragile soil beyond repair . . . She shook her head. Environmental laws were strict. She should know: The guide guild helped enforce them; her own work with the demonfish runs had been in that context.

But still, there would be some kind of fight. There would be some kind of weapons. The mercs, she thought, would use breakers to shatter human bones, and spec lasers, which affected only human tissues; few animals or plants suffered as mistaken targets. Gases were human-specific but difficult to control; viruses were prohibited completely, except for use by assassins. And there were no long-range weapons on any colony planet. The only thing that stood in her way was the strength of the walls of her cell and the size of the fight. Vashanna was right: A desert battle, by its very nature, had to be small. And a small force would scarcely create the confusion necessary for her escape.

A thought struck her, and she became suddenly still. "How do you know all this?" she asked Vashanna slowly. "You have been locked in here with me since I arrived." Locked by Hesse and then Cekulu, she snarled silently as the cat feet clawed her mind. Trapped for a year and three months while outside the grasses bunched and ran in the wind and the sand grew bleached and dry. She stared at the other woman. "How do you know these things about the hostage? You have not spoken to the guards. You have no link to the node—" She paused, and her realization grew. "Or have you?"

Vashanna's brown gaze was shuttered.

"Do you—" Tsia's hands tensed into fists, and she took a step forward. "Do you have a partial link?" she demanded. "Can you read the net?" Damn her voice—the sensors in the room would pick that up and store it with her sweat. Her eagerness could be used against her.

Vashanna's gaze drifted over Tsia's body, and finally the other woman nodded.

"How long have you been able to—" Tsia halted. She did not want to know. "You have full access?" she asked tersely.

Vashanna nodded again.

"So you *know*."

"Yes."

Tsia forced her mind to hold itself back from beating at the blind, blank temple plugs. Vashanna could image the net.

Vashanna watched the flow of emotions across Tsia's face. "You can bargain for a partial link, *Jinga*."

Tsia's jaw tightened, tiny muscles jumping. She was a guide, not a *heyta*, not a *Jinga*, she screamed in her mind. Carefully, thoroughly, she wiped her face of expression. "What would I have to do?" She forced the words out.

The other woman shook her head. "You have accepted your learning with a pretense of giving in. You have never lost hope of escape. Never acknowledged your owner completely."

I have no owner, Tsia raged silently. I have a life. I am a guide, not a slave! She gritted her teeth to keep her voice steady as she said, "I am a ghost, Vashanna. I have no reality outside of that."

"You are a *Jinga*," Vashanna said harshly. "When you learn that, you will earn your link."

Tsia smiled slowly, her lips stretching without humor into a predator grin. Vashanna stared back calmly, refusing to acknowledge the shiver that felt its way along her bones. She turned back to the window. "We will discuss Pulan."

12

In the cloud-dulled light of the afternoon Vashanna's words echoed in Tsia's head. Her forehead rested against the arm she pressed on the filter field. Her other hand rubbed the thin skin flaps over her temple plugs. Her feet itched. Her muscles felt strained with disuse. She hated the heat, and she needed it to burn away the oils that gathered on her skin—no simple shower could ease its feel. She needed to dance, needed to walk the flames, needed to feel the wind in her hair and the wet mud of the slough beneath her feet.

Round and round, her fingers traced the outlines of the plugs. Her brain reached out to them, spitting images at the plugs, and was blocked, leaving her cursing at herself when she realized what she was doing. Unbidden, her senses stretched out through the biogate until she felt the heat of a suncat that lay sprawled in the rocky dust. The suncat growled low in its throat, then sprawled on its other side. Tsia trembled with the strength of her gate.

But then the shakes crawled up her shoulders and down through her legs, and she realized with sudden clarity that the shakes were not tied to fear or anger. These shakes were in her body like starry-night plague, the disease that had caught the First Droppers. She stared at her hands until the tremors stopped. Was she herself sick? Was this the virus? Instinctively she knew it was, and she shivered, but it was not the virus that caused that quiver but the memory of the time she had damaged her arm and the punishment it had won from the artist. If they thought she was sick, would they do the same again? Had the room scans not picked up her symptoms? Unobstrusively, she slid her fingertips away from the tingling fields that told her where the scanners were embedded in the walls.

If the artist wanted Tsia soon, would she care if Tsia was sick? Vashanna had said she cared for nothing besides her art. She would not care if the mercs swarmed the very walls of Noirelle as long as she got what she wanted from Tsia and that leader from Pulan.

Tsia rubbed her nose, then her cheek against her hand and felt the depressed smoothness of the lightninglike scar that had torn her cheek that first day in the dark in this cell. She felt the tremor of the virus touch her muscles again with a pang of fear. Would she end up as scarred as Vashanna? As twisted and marred by fire?

Would it be the fire of the coals or a fire hot as lightning? The gray heaviness that covered the sky brought a stagnant wind to her nose. Distant desert hills, yellow-brown against the gray, roiling sky, taunted her ice-blue eyes.

"Pulan lies behind those peaks," Vashanna said. Tsia had not realized the other woman was watching her. Vashanna joined her at the window. "The Pulanese—they will be sitting beneath the dry clouds, cursing the war and playing the nodes while Noirelle holds their leader here."

Tsia did not look up. The filter field between her face and the sky lay coldly across her expression. "It has been hours since the mercs arrived. Has it begun?"

"I cannot tell. There is nothing in the node about it."

"They would not broadcast their performance."

"No," Vashanna said, motioning out the window. "But those here, in Noirelle, would react if it had started."

"They would set up ghosts, wouldn't they?"

Vashanna nodded.

"What about those?" Tsia asked. "Why don't you see if the node readings of the Pulanese and Korshan mercs are real?"

Vashanna shook her head absently. "I would not know the first thing about tracing ghosts."

Tsia thought about that for a moment. When she spoke again, she had a thoughtful expression. "What were you, Vashanna, before you were a slave?"

The woman flicked her a glance.

"I have asked you a dozen times," Tsia persisted, still staring at the mountains, "yet never have you answered."

"It is not important."

"Perhaps it is to me."

"And perhaps," Vashanna said softly, "the answer would destroy the little bit of belief you have left within you."

Tsia turned her head on her arms to regard the other woman with a look half-mocking and puzzled. "Is that not your job—to destroy my belief in myself, to make me the perfect *Jinga*? The perfect slave? Besides," she said, shrugging, "what could you ever have been to take away my trust now?"

The woman shrugged and stared out at the mountains.

Tsia's eyes were suddenly wary. "You say you don't know how to trace a ghost. There are not that many fields that don't use tracing techniques of some kind in the nodes. If you knew even the rudiments of tracing techniques, you could figure out how to trace a ghost."

Vashanna did not answer.

"Artists don't use traces," Tsia said more to herself than to Vashanna. "Neither do developers, crystallines . . ." She went on through the listing of fields. Her voice faltered. "And guides," she finished abruptly. The stagnant air seemed to choke the filter field.

Tsia stood suddenly straight. "Were you . . ." Her voice trailed off, and she tightened her jaw. "Vashanna, were you a guide?"

The other woman regarded her silently. Tsia reached halfway to the woman's scarred face, then stopped, her hand halted in midair. "Vashanna . . ."

Vashanna faced her steadily. "What do you see when you look at me, Tsia-firedancer?" The heatcloth covered her head and neck, leaving only her face bare to the twisted flesh and broken cheeks. "What do you see? A slave?"

Tsia let her fingers touch the brown, ridged flesh. "I see flesh, tortured flesh."

"Do you see a homeland? Do you see a past? Can you see my birthplace or my rights?"

Tsia stared at her, then shook her head slowly, painfully.

The woman reached up and dragged the heatcloth back from her head. The patched skin was rough, the hair stubble short and thick. She split her robe in the middle, ripping it from her body. "Look at me," she demanded. Tsia gasped.

Across Vashanna's body, in rows and ridges, were folds of skin and scars. White tissue alternated with the brown until it seemed as if she were a spotted animal, not a human being. Lumps of bone and calcium pushed out across her ribs; one hip had been displaced. Her legs were dark and blue-white shiny, as if the skin had been seared so deeply that even regeneration could not rid the body of its memory of fire. Like Tsia's, her pubic hair was short and coarse, her genital flaps completely protective and horribly twisted in those shiny warps of flesh. Tsia stared at her, then down at herself. She did not have to remove her clothes to recognize what she saw. Stunned, she raised her eyes to Vashanna's. Guides healed quickly. For a guide to be so heinously seared . . . "You—"

The other woman cut her off. "If I am what stands here now, dance-fighter, what then do you see?"

"I see—" Tsia drew a ragged breath. She looked again at the woman's twisted body, the short stubble of a firedancer's hair, then up to the links in her temples. She paused, then met her eyes with compassion. "I see a slave," she said quietly.

"Then," Vashanna's voice was suddenly harsh, "there never was a guide within this body."

The older woman's hands fumbled with her robes, and Tsia lifted them back to Vashanna's shoulders. She studied Vashanna's face then, as if she could see some sign of the guide virus in her tortured skin. The short hair was hidden again under the heatcloth; the darkened skin was disguised by the tan. There was nothing but the sweet scent of the woman herself. It was that odor, Tsia realized suddenly, that perhaps was the most damning evidence of all. Why she had never thought about Vashanna's scent . . . She shook her head to herself. She had left the guild before she had asked if the virus caused the same changes in all new guides. And it had not occurred to her to question the slave Vashanna.

Then another thought coalesced, and her eyes grew hard. "You are my teacher because you were a guide, because of what you used to be."

Vashanna nodded.

"And," Tsia guessed with a slow anger, "to show me my future if I do not learn to submit."

Vashanna shrugged. "You are a ghost," she reminded Tsia. "Like my son, you have no future here."

With a stubborn set of her jaw, Tsia met Vashanna's eyes. Their gazes locked. "I have the future I always had," she said flatly. "And no one—not you, not Daya herself—will take that away from me."

Vashanna settled the heatcloth back on her head. "It is not the gods you have to fear."

Tsia glanced around the rounded cell. "This room, the coldness of this stone . . . Was this the way Cekulu treated you?"

Vashanna stared out the window for a long moment. "Tsia, I tell you this as a warning. I tell you this because once you leave this room, you will not get a second chance. I know you. I see in your eyes even now that should the artist—should Cekulu—ask for the firedance, you will walk the flames for Daya but not for Cekulu. And of all the artists in the guild, that one will surely know it.

"I danced the flames for Daya, and Cekulu knew. So she bargained for my own eggs from my guild—only Daya knows how. She made me pregnant, then forced me to give birth in the flames. She caught it all—Cekulu did—the holos, the memories. The music of the screams. The heat of the flames. The smell of the skin that seared and flaked from my baby's bones." She shuddered deeply. "The guide virus can make you sweat," she whispered to herself, "but not even that virus can keep the flames from your body when you lie in the coals. And you can't dance—" Her voice choked. "—when you're shoving your child—" Her voice broke. "Your firstborn child in the fire. You can't just roll off the white-hot brands when he's born. All you can do—" Her neck muscles became taut, the cords making the twisted flesh stand out even more. "—is pray that they let you die with him."

Tsia shuddered. Sweat blurred her eyes, and she blinked, only to realize that the moisture was not sweat but a tear. She clenched her jaw and swallowed her compassion. "You did not die," she pointed out callously, hating her voice, hating her own words.

Vashanna's brown eyes grew hard. "I tried three times to die. But death here is a privilege, not a right. I did not have a chance." She looked down at the blistered skin of her hands. "They took me," she said bluntly, "then they broke me."

The image of Vashanna's child rose in her mind, and Tsia hid her guilt with a cold look, despising herself even more as she did so. "And you—" she forced the words to be steady—"have been a slave ever since."

Vashanna's eyes narrowed. She regarded Tsia as she would a snake on which she wanted to step. "You were brought here for a purpose," she snapped. "Cekulu cares about her work and only that. Obey her and you can live, even if it is here, in Noirelle, in chains. Deny her and you *will* die for her art."

Tsia's fingers bit into her palms. "I would rather die."

"You do not even know what you're saying."

Tsia's jaw tightened. "I say what I mean. I would rather die than become a slave like you—lose my will, lose my identity, lose myself in the trappings of life just to sustain my breath in a body."

"And how long does it take a guide to die, Tsia-who-is-not-a-slave?"

"What do you mean?"

"How long would it take you to die?"

Tsia shrugged scornfully. "A second, a minute. An hour."

"An hour? A mere sixty minutes? You think Cekulu would allow that?"

The vision of Vashanna's naked body rose before Tsia's eyes, the twisted, melted flesh blinding her to the woman who stood in the light of the window. She found herself unable to answer.

"Think of years," Vashanna said in a low voice. "Think of a decade of pain. Think of endless months while your body is eaten away and your eyes feel burned by the light and your skin never stops screaming for the agony to stop. Think of your bones stretching and shrinking and making you shriek in the night. Think of your children growing in pain, birthed in pain, burning to death in their only experience of life." Gently Vashanna touched Tsia's face, sliding her hand into the firedancer's stubble of hair. "Think, Tsia, of this." Abruptly, viciously, Vashanna gripped the younger woman's head so hard that Tsia cried out. "Tell me you would rather not live as a slave."

Eyes wide, Tsia stared at Vashanna as if she had never seen her before. When Vashanna released her, Tsia stumbled back.

"The scars . . ." Her voice trailed away. "You got the scars in the fire?"

The woman turned her back on Tsia. "Those small marks?" Her voice was gentle, emotionless again. "They were nothing. The scars you see here were achieved in the fires that followed the births of my second child, and my third."

"Vashanna—"

"You have been punished, Tsia, but you still do not know the meaning of the word *heyta*. You have never really been pushed. You have never been broken. All you have been is trained."

Trained, Tsia agreed bitterly, like a dog that did tricks. Rights-conditioned, virus-conditioned, slave-trained to speak on command.

More to herself, Vashanna continued, "They will not repeat to you what they did to me—it would not be good art."

"No," Tsia agreed facetiously.

"For you—"

Tsia nodded slowly. "There will be something else. Some other experience to survive."

"Or not to survive." Vashanna glanced at Tsia. "You could be thankful."

"For the chance to die?"

Vashanna merely looked at her, her brown eyes deep-set and shuttered in her twisted brown face.

Tsia rolled the chains on her wrist, letting the clanking sound grate in her room. "You are right, Vashanna," she said softly. "I have much to be grateful for. A great debt to the art guild which I will take an endless time repaying."

Vashanna frowned at her words. "If you obey Cekulu, you have a chance to lead a normal life. If not . . ."

Tsia glanced at the distant mountains. If not, she would have to kill Cekulu to get free. Somehow the thought did not bother her.

In spite of the heat, the older woman shivered and drew her thin robes close.

13

A moment later Vashanna stiffened. Tsia, glancing at her posture, turned from the window. Warily she asked, "What is it?"

The other woman pulled the head cloth self-consciously over her brow, hiding the blistered fissures of her skin. Her hand was not quite steady. "It is time. Cekulu will see you now."

Tsia started to move toward the door, her shoulders tense, but Vashanna's low voice stopped her. "*Kai-al nyeka*," the woman warned softly, "If you value your life at all, dance for her, dance for her art—dance for whomever she orders, but not—" She bared her twisted, fissured arm. "—in rebellion. Not for Daya." The cloth dropped back over her forearm, and Tsia nodded once, curtly.

The door slid open, and Tsia almost crouched to spring through. Belatedly she forced her body to relax. Outside, four guards stood and waited. All were taller than she was; the two women were as broad in the shoulder as the men. On all four chests and thighs were the dull, metallic grays of their blunter suits, guaranteed to deflect a sensor or take the punch of a handball breaker without shattering the bones inside. They wore harnesses to hold their weapons, and from each set of straps hung a black-tipped n-rod, the blue-gray box of an r-con, and the deactivated grip of a variable blade. One of the guards carried a flex sword in the hook position; another had the thin, shaped pad of a breaker at his side.

Tsia had seen a breaker once before. Jak Volen had brought one back after his first trip out on a ship. He had run into blackjacks— pirates coming out of Indrisi Five. He had not known they were armed with breakers when he had lost his flexor and had to go hand to hand. One of the blackjacks palmed the breaker and got a grip on Jak's arm, and Jak's humerus cracked in two. Jak finally forced the pirate's hand to the man's own neck, but not before he lost three ribs and a chip off his cheekbone to the breaker. Dirtside, breakers were illegal, but in space, the pirates preferred them; the breaker did not damage e-suits to get to the traders inside, and blackjacks could always use the extra gear.

Tsia glanced again at the guards. She would have been lying if she said she felt no fear. And yet her fingers itched to take that breaker pad in hand, her arm tensed to yank that flexor from that nearby harness. Just one n-rod, and she would—

The lead guard cut off Tsia's thoughts with a gesture. "Walk smoothly," he said. He took one of her arms in his hand, and his iron fingers ringed her bicep as inexorably as the chains around her wrist. Pulling on her arm, he forced her to walk on her toes. Instinctively, she struggled. With a warning glance, he dug his fingers into her bones, making her lips tighten in a feral grin before she acquiesced.

The blue-gray glove of the guard contrasted oddly with Tsia's white tunic. The blunter fabric of his jumpsuit rubbed gently as he walked, but his booted feet were as silent as hers. The only sounds she heard were the metal-gray shackles singing against the stone and the pounding of her heart beating down the hall. To be out of that room, her thoughts clamored. To be free of the walls of that cell . . .

Standard doors alternated with the opalescent filter fields of the link-controlled portals. Each time they approached a filter field, Tsia tensed until the fingers of the guard dug farther into her arm.

The walls appeared drab and dirty next to the shimmering fields; the standard doors were separated from the field doors by rough, blackened beams. Above, the ceiling was arched and filled with skylights of silvered metaplas. The diamond windows created blocks of shadow and light on the pale, silver-veined floor. The effect was deliberately unnerving, half-dingy, half-jewellike. As she stepped from one shadow to the next, Tsia realized that the angle of the sun in the skylights would never let the beams touch the dull metaplas walls or roughened metaplas posts. Light from the sun would shine only upon the opalescent doors. The effect of the juxtaposition made her feel somehow as trapped as if she still paced her cell. As they did outside, the light and dark of Noirelle sat side by side, each neither moving from nor ever free of the other.

Far down the hall a shimmering field ended their walk until the door wavered, then cleared, and the lead guard stepped through. Tsia hesitated, one foot poised before the other, and the guard let the side of his n-rod drop against her arm so that she jerked back and almost stumbled in spite of her feline grace. He hauled unceremoniously on her arm, yanking her through.

Another hall, a turn, another door . . . The route became etched into Tsia's brain. South—they were heading south, where Vashanna had told her the warehouses sat. She matched their way to her mental map. The warehouses were beside the stables; the stables were next to the skimmer pads. She waited impatiently for the next door to open. Her muscles bunched under the guard's iron hand, and he closed his fist more tightly till she forced herself to relax.

Seven people dressed in somber jumpsuits passed without even glancing at Tsia's small group. Single men and women strode confidently in the halls. Tsia itched as each one passed, the scent of their bodies like acrid waves that broke over her head. She had been so long in that room. Her nose was no longer used to any scent but the sweet molecular-scrubbed and sanitized odor of Vashanna and herself. Tentatively her mind sent a command to the plugs that fit in her temples, and she ignored the silence she felt. If they were going to use her soon, they might give her back a link.

They passed through each series of filter doors one after the other without hesitation. The room beyond the first light-edged frame was unfurnished, bare of color, and without windows. The second room was dim and contained pallets and jacks, trade boxes and globs of packing gel. The musty smell of old gas lingered, as if the goods unpacked had not been from Risthmus. Curious, she would have hesitated, but the guard dragged her through the room without regard for her feet; she stepped in a puddle of gel and flinched from the cold blob that oozed briefly between her toes before snapping back to the floor where it had first bonded.

The third door through which they passed had a full scan in its glowing frame. Edgy and distracted, Tsia jumped at its touch and almost bolted. The man beside her clamped his hand more tightly on her arm and hauled her through. Behind her the others closed in so she could not step back. She would not have wanted to: The direction they had come must put her somewhere near the eastern wall of the compound.

The scan shivered through her body; the door shimmered shut. Before her, the warehouse room that opened out was large. Quickly her eyes darted from side to side, taking in everything, then scanning the space again while she methodically cataloged the details. She was quick but thorough. She had waited more than a year for this.

The area was rectangular; the walls were tall, without windows; and the ceiling was high and unfinished, crisscrossed with structural beams. Wide skylights let in the indirect light of the sun, shading the room from the blistering heat of day. Below her feet the floor was shockingly cool, its silver-veined stone cut in tiles, as the halls had been before. She could feel the energy net beneath its surface like a tickling along her skin.

In the center of the room was a ring of metaplas flooring, edged half a meter high by solid bricks. Men and women crossed the room on errands, disappearing through the glowing frames of the doors on the other end of the hall. Near the center a white-haired woman gestured expansively to the small man beside her, listened briefly, then motioned sharply again. Finally the short man nodded.

Tsia's guard led her toward the metaplas ring and the woman who regarded it now with concentration. Faced with the gray-lit expanse, Tsia ignored the woman. Her feet itched to run. Her legs strained against her stride to prance and kick and leap away from the guards. She must have quickened her pace, because the guard twisted her fettered wrist so that the metal ground against her nerves and cut her skin. Her stride shortened abruptly. It was a small thing, she told herself, her jaw tightening at the unexpected pain.

They circled the ring until they arrived beside the white-haired woman. She glanced at Tsia but continued to talk with the short man, and Tsia had to force herself to stand and listen impassively.

She stared at the tall woman surreptitiously. Was this Cekulu? Her eyes were a startling violet-gray, standing out almost violently against her golden skin. Her skin itself, tanned and smooth, revealed her age only in the tiny stretching along the sides of her eyes and neck. A hundred fifty? Hundred seventy? Tsia could not exactly guess; the shock-white hair was not any indication. And even with her age, she was as voluptuous as a woman could ever want to be: tall, shapely, striking in her looks. She would not, Tsia guessed, show her years until she was well over two hundred. With her towering, glistening hair and exotic eyes, she made Tsia feel short, unfinished, and ridiculously prepubescent.

". . . ready tomorrow, I think," she was saying critically.

"And you want her to do at least one dance in the ring tonight?"

The artist nodded. "It will give her a taste of the fire—whet the appetite that runs through her veins."

The short man raised his eyebrows. "Five years of preparation, Cekulu, and we will take just one day to do the form?"

The woman gave him a dry smile. "Kern, I have worked with firedancers for eighty-seven years. I know their abilities as I know my own skills. One day only is what I need. Preparation is important, but the art is in the dance itself, and that cannot be repeated. This subject—" She indicated Tsia with a possessive nod. "—is as perfect as possible."

Tsia bristled, but the fingers that dug into her upper arm held her stiffly in place.

"The sculpture mask *is* perfect," the artist continued. "I see no problems with any aspect of the dance."

The short, brown-haired man looked wary. "There is still the mole," he warned.

Cekulu's violet eyes narrowed. "You were supposed to get the new molecular manipulator—the MT30—on shipment three days ago."

"I did, but—"

"But what?"

"Your new composite for the ice room—the mole re-forms the material just as you wanted, but it re-forms the metaplas slowly. If speed was not so important—"

"Damn it, Kern, speed is everything." The white-haired woman began to pace back and forth. "I have the Pulanese woman only for a day—her nodies have been on every link since we snatched her, and the merc tracers hired by the Pulan council are some of the best. Even if they have not yet figured out that we have her, they will within a day. And—" She tapped her temple link irritably, imaging a set of commands to the node almost in the background. "—the reparations I would have to pay for the use of her fetus could make the difference between making a profit and making a bust on this sculpture. Literally," she snapped as Kern choked off his chuckle. "The woman must have no choice," she snarled. "The fetus is mine. The mother is nothing. Remember that." She glared down at the man. "If this does not work, I will have to start all over again, and it took three years of waiting just to come up with *her*." She pointed at Tsia. "If the Pulanese woman is traced or the mole doesn't work—"

"This is the best model on trade for the compounds you specified," Kern soothed. "And it should be. It cost more than any three others I could find. Don't worry. It will work. It just might not work as fast as you wanted."

Cekulu stopped pacing and, with her hands on her hips,

faced the brown-haired man with a vicious expression. "Speed is *everything*," she snapped. "The transition from memory to sensory perception and then to the mole must be real-time. If the mole manipulation is slow, the dancer's timing will never fit the sensations."

Tsia stared from one to the other. "You can't," she interrupted, "change the timing of a firedance. You can't possibly combine memory with the spontaneity of the flames."

The two broke off and looked at Tsia slowly. Cekulu eyed her for a moment, then nodded slightly at one of the guards.

An n-rod struck Tsia in the back. She stiffened and stifled her scream, but her mouth opened and her throat went taut with the effort. Her body convulsed once; she fell heavily to her knees and then her side. In the haze that followed she heard Cekulu's voice rising and falling like a wail that beat in her skull with the scream of the cougar through her gate.

Seconds, minutes later one of the guards hauled Tsia back to her feet, ignoring the spasms that shook her legs out from under her. With her back burning from the nerve whip, she saw only blurred figures before her while her legs were rubbery and faint.

"Well," Kern said finally, "do you want to see if your dancer is at least worth the credit?"

Cekulu nodded and ran a hand through her white hair so that it cascaded around her face with the motion. "Set up the fire," she directed over her shoulder at another man who walked by. "Run the reflection fields down along the sides of the ring . . ."

Tsia forced herself to stand. With effort, she focused on the ring, taking in its dimensions as two men and a woman brought in a double flat of wood coals and spread them around the space. Cekulu noticed her attention.

"The area, *heyta*," the artist said, "is the same as the room in which you stayed for the last year."

"This is the same size as the ring you will have me in tonight?"

Cekulu regarded her curiously. "You are defiant, aren't you?"

"You did not answer my question."

The woman stared at her, then laughed softly. "It is too bad we will only have a day together. I think I could actually like you."

"And I think I could hate your guts." Tsia heard the words come out of her mouth. Her face paled as she realized what she had said. Then she clenched her jaw and braced herself for the touch of the n-rod.

Cekulu cocked her head. "You are more than defiant," she said consideringly. "You are damned insolent. But," she said more to herself, "that sort of emotion could actually be rather useful."

Useful, like a tool. Like Vashanna. Like the pregnant woman and her child. Tsia's blue-gray eyes were cold.

"Do not look so offended," Cekulu said soothingly. "Trust me; your dance will be a feat that even your mentors will envy."

A shiver shook Tsia's frame as she heard Hesse's "Trust me" echoed from Cekulu's tongue.

"Ah, I see that I have frightened you," the artist mocked. "Do not worry; I promise that you do not have to be the one who gets burned."

Tsia ground her teeth together. "I have no fear of you," she forced out.

"No? You should." Cekulu's voice was suddenly hard. "I do not even need an hour to twist your mind like you could wring a cloth. I can burn images into your brain that you could not have conceived in the deepest hell of the hottest star of all the systems in the Federation."

"You can burn me," Tsia acknowledged bitterly, "and you can scar me and twist me and leave me shaped like Vashanna, but I swear you cannot make me yours."

"Perhaps not before you die." Cekulu regarded her for a long moment. "But then," she said softly, "your death is not the one I need. How far will you go, *heyta*," she asked curiously, "to save another?"

Tsia refused to answer.

Cekulu continued speculatively. "You are rights-conditioned. Don't think I do not know; it is what gives you such guilt over the punishment of a child. And," she added thoughtfully, "it is what will force you to act in order to help another. If it were not for the firedance, I could have any merc here to do this for you. But I do not need a simple rights-conditioned fighter. I do not need the simple ideals they hang on a flexor. I need—" She fingered the scar on Tsia's cheek, and Tsia stood it without flinching, her ice-blue eyes as cold as space. "—a firedance with a conflict of interest." She dropped her hand. "You have already proved that you can be manipulated by the pain—by the deaths of others—but all you were asked to do for that was obey against the voice of your pride. What if you had to act?" She regarded Tsia curiously. "What if you had to move to help someone? How far would you go to keep them from death if it were the voice of pain—not pride—telling you to resist your duty?"

Tsia hid the shudder that trembled in her bones. Was this the purpose of the artist's firedance—to make her keep someone else from the flames? Vashanna's words about the births of her children rose in her mind. That pregnant woman . . . Tsia glanced at the fire ring. Four more flats of wood had been brought in, floating above the ring in their antigrav beams, and the flames were already building.

Cekulu smiled. "I see, *Jinga*, that you understand."

"You cannot expect me to keep another body from the flames."

"I don't expect anything from you, *heyta*," the artist said deliberately.

"I am not your slave—" Tsia snapped. Her voice broke off. "How," she demanded slowly, bewildered, "could I do the firedance to keep the Pulanese leader alive? If you put her in the fire, she will burn like any other woman whether or not my body sweats to protect mine."

"It does not matter how you perform," Cekulu explained patiently. "The images will be set whether or not you keep the woman alive. Either way, it will be emotive."

Tsia stared at her. "You are going to burn the woman to death—and force me to be there, helpless to prevent it—just to record the emotion?"

Cekulu nodded, her violet eyes lost in her vision. "It will be one of my most powerful pieces."

Tsia was speechless.

"It might," the artist added almost to herself, "even rival the performances of Vashanna."

Tsia felt faint.

Cekulu's eyes focused on Tsia with amusement. "You should be thankful, *heyta*, that I never repeat my art."

"Yes," Tsia whispered.

Cekulu brushed her hair back. "If you perform well, I should be able to sell the original set of senses for more credit than you can imagine. Then I can sell the copies to the dreamer channels and museums for royalties that will keep me in sculpture for the next decade. Vashanna's images did," she confided, maliciously watching Tsia's reaction.

The flames that leapt in the metaplas ring made an orange corona around Cekulu's white hair.

"Daya, but I love to work with firedancers." The woman smiled dreamily.

Tsia swallowed, her throat so dry that she choked. "I won't do it."

The other woman glanced at her. "You have no choice."

"I will fight you."

"With what? Your words? Your sticky sweat?" The woman laughed. "You have nothing but what I give you."

"I have hatred."

"It's not strong enough. If it was, you would attack me as I stand."

Tsia clenched her fists. "I am a guide, not just a firedancer. I will not dance the flames for you or your art."

Cekulu shrugged. "I have you, so I have your will."

"You cannot force me to dance for you, and I swear by all the sixty-four planets that you will not keep me here long enough to find out."

The other woman laughed again. "The sixty-four planets is an odd oath to use for a guide who cannot leave her own world. And on this planet you are caught not only by Noirelle's walls but by the desert itself. Even if I set you free at the gates of this base, there would be no place to which you could run."

Tsia stared at her. The cat feet skittered in her skull. Her expression was too revealing; one of the guards dug his fingers into her shoulders, yanking her back and making her writhe.

Cekulu's full lips thinned in a smile. "Too bad you are not more comely," she said softly. "It would have made the dance much more aesthetic."

Tsia's face paled. Two red coals burned in her cheeks, relieved only on the one side by the the scar that stretched, long and thin and ragged, across her bone. She had forgotten about that mark. It was small enough, she knew, to let her dance in the flames; she had not realized what it had done to her looks.

Cekulu gestured at the guards. One of the women touched her temple link, and Tsia's shackles sprung open, dropping the arm chains onto Tsia's feet before she had time to move them away. She did not cry out, but her jaw tightened as they hit. Daya, she whispered to the cats in her mind, she wanted the heart from this woman's body.

And then the weightlessness of the absence of the chains registered in her mind. For an instant she stood frozen. She was not aware of moving, but the fingers of another guard were already grinding back into her shoulders, holding her in place. Her muscles stretched. Her stomach unknotted. Her arms felt weightless, lifting themselves into the air. The hands on her shoulders tore into her nerves. She flinched beneath the grip, unable to prevent herself from writhing.

"You want to dance, don't you." It was a statement, not a question.

Tsia stared at Cekulu, her ice-blue eyes meeting the brilliant violet of her gaze. "I—need the flames," she choked out.

Kern regarded her curiously. "It is as you said," he said in wonderment to the artist. "For a new dancer, the urge to walk the flames is irresistible. As long as the virus holds her like this— look at her sweat—she must have fire to burn off the oils. It has been over a year for her. She must be nearly desperate."

Cekulu nodded. "A year and three months. It is a good thing we got the Pulanese woman now. This guide would not last much longer without the fire."

The flames were hot now, the wood turning quickly into coals. Orange lights flickered inside the heat fields. Tsia could almost feel the convection waves of heat that beat against the shields. Her body swayed, reacting instinctively. Her skin glowed and glistened with sweetness. Trembling, she stared at the pit.

"See," Cekulu said to her assistant. "She is so caught up in her senses, she does not even understand what the longing, the tremors mean. She is perfect."

Tsia shivered beneath the hands of the guards. "Whether I walk the flames or not," she snarled, forcing the words out, "I will do so for Daya, not you."

"Do you know," Kern demanded, "how much trouble Cekulu went to to bring you here? The timing it took to have you ready when the Pulanese woman could be taken? Even at that, we are a month late with you and a month early for the Pulanese leader. This is the third time Cekulu has tried this, and this is the first time we have gotten the timing close enough to use. Cekulu has had to wait almost five years for this."

"She should have had to wait forever," Tsia snarled.

Unoffended, Cekulu smiled. "You do not know how tough it is to turn a guide into a ghost," she said gently. "Only one in three have to be isolated from the link nodes when they take the virus, and we had to have one like you, isolated from the link. And then we had to catch you far from the eyes of the guild . . . I was quite impatient to have you by the time you ran away to the slough."

"I did not run away," she snapped. "I had work to do."

Cekulu raised her perfect eyebrow. "Five years waiting for you," she continued. "Another year letting you sit and stew and yearn for the dance you could not have. You are sweating, dance-fighter," she observed. "Do you think, after a year of cold stone, you can resist the heat of the flames here and now?"

The glowing circle beside her was flaring up now. With the last flats of fuel, the coals had spilled out to the very edges of the pit, coloring the metaplas that lined it with white ash. Tsia stood silently, her muscles quivering, her stomach twisting, her heart hating the flames, but the desperate hunger for its heat in her face and the sweat running down her taut body so that the white silk clung as if it had been drenched.

Cekulu motioned abruptly, and the guards lifted her unresisting. And threw her, through the heat shield, into the fire.

14

✧✦✧

Tsia rolled, stripping the silk from her body even as the fabric was consumed by the heat. She twisted. Only barely did she breathe in the blistering air. Her feet landed in the coals, and she lunged up like a spark. Here, her lungs and her skin were free; here her limbs could scream their defiance. Daya! She flung up her arms, and the sweat ran across her skin like snakes. The flames now licked only to her knees, hissing on her oils as they beaded and rolled across her skin, holding the heat away from her body.

Shimmering waves wafted across her flat, toned belly, and she danced to the side, moving into the cooler convection currents with catlike grace. Her eyes were closed. A burst of flame was followed by the snapping of the coals, and Tsia leapt across the cloud of sparks. She no longer thought. The bitterness that the virus had left her only this—only the flames—was forgotten in the beauty of the heat in her lungs and the singing of the sweat on her legs.

Under her feet, sticks shifted. Heat-weakened wood snapped and crushed with her weight. But her skin glowed and the breath of the fire was like wind to her face. Instinctively, she ducked and sucked the air from a pocket that formed and disappeared as quickly as a light went out. "Daya, mother, Tsia, me," she chanted under her breath. With a twist of her supple body she jumped and kicked away from a blast of heat, dancing beyond its reach. "Power links, and fire binds. The grace of the cougar; the strength of the cougar is mine."

She did not see Cekulu. She no longer saw the fire except in her mind. The color of the flames was the touch of heat on her skin; the heat was merely the warm hand of Daya. Her short hair was soaked in the oil of the virus and was glistening in the light.

123

She ducked, then leapt high over a flare of orange light. She stretched her arms up. In the roiling air her skin streamed and steamed with evaporating sweat. Only where the ragged scar cut across her cheek did the searing heat pierce her skin and tell her of its fierceness, but the scar was small and the fire large, and Tsia, free of the chains at last, did not care.

From where Cekulu stood, it seemed that Tsia made love to the flames, her body touching and teasing the blaze so that it burned brighter where she stepped in it and lay down before her when she stooped to take its kiss. Though she had seen this a hundred times before, the artist found herself leaning forward, holding her breath with the grace of Tsia's movements. The crackling of the fire hid any sound Tsia's slender figure made, but Cekulu thought she heard the slave-guide chanting. And when finally Tsia leapt through the heat shield and stamped the ashes from her feet, her body was glowing as if drenched. With her feet still prancing on the cold stone floor, she threw her head back and yowled. No one spoke.

Tsia's face was a feral grin. Her eyes were alight, their blue-gray depths reflecting the yellow-red fire like a star demon. She stalked toward Cekulu and Kern. One of the guards moved to block her, but Cekulu motioned him to stay.

When Tsia reached them, she opened her hand, revealing a glowing brand she had stolen from the ring. "Hiiyuh," she snarled inarticulately. "Shall I teach your assistant the dance of the flames?" She raised the smoking red-white coal to the short man's face. He jerked back. She grinned, then thrust it at Cekulu, who stood her ground.

"Kern does not trust the flames as you do," Tsia taunted. Her hand sizzled with the sweat in which she rolled the coal, and with a laugh she tossed it back through the heat shield. It had lost much of its heat going through the shield or she would not have been able to hold it that long. Going back, the coal lost the rest. It landed in the still-burning pit with a splash of ash and spark.

Cekulu regarded her contemplatively. "Clean yourself," she said calmly. "I will need you tonight."

She turned away, leaving Tsia, her chest still heaving from her exertions, to stand and stare after the artist, the feral expression still on her face. Kern followed Cekulu but looked back at Tsia once. His hazel eyes caught the hunger in Tsia's gaze before he looked away.

One of Tsia's guards picked up her chains from where they had been discarded and moved forward. Another tossed a clean white tunic and pair of pants at her feet. The clothes dropped to the floor unheeded, and she glared at them, her eyes instead on the chains. Her arms, her feet were free. They could not put metal again on her skin. Behind her the fire in the metaplas ring was quenched by a quiet spray of gas, and Tsia felt her sweat leak away with the heat as her guards warily advanced. The icy cold of the floor crept through her soles. She shivered.

"Clothe yourself," the lead guard ordered, gesturing at the pants and shirt.

Tsia did not move. Her muscles were tense, and she could not help the way her body rocked onto the balls of her feet, ready to leap. Deliberately, she stretched through her gate and felt her lips stretch in an answering snarl. Joy surged fiercely through her limbs.

The n-rod in the lead guard's hand went active. "The tunic," the man repeated. "Put it on."

Tsia shifted, kicking the clothes to one side. The lead guard grinned. When Tsia leapt, he was ready. He caught her lightning-fast blow on his forearm and used her momentum to swing her past, into the arms of the other two guards. The one thing he had not counted on was the rigid foot that landed wickedly in his throat. Toes dug in, then were torn away. The man stood stunned for a moment, then dropped slowly to his knees, his hands at his neck.

Behind him the other two guards caught Tsia in midair. She smashed an elbow into one woman's gut, felt an n-rod hit her side, gritted her teeth against the pain, and slammed her elbow lower, driving it viciously into the other man's inner thigh. Another n-rod hit her, and this time her left leg crumpled. She yowled again, and a rod scraped her arm. Then she was down on the floor, the icy touch of the stone stunning her between the burning touches of the rods. Expressionlessly, they hit her with the n-rods until her body convulsed repeatedly. She began to retch.

It was close to an hour before she could walk. The guard she had kicked in the throat was left on the floor until the medtech restructured his trachea so that he could be moved. When he was taken away, another guard took his place. The four stood loosely and impassively a meter away while her limbs thrust and scratched the floor and she cursed violently under her breath. Even before she could stand, she was worrying at the chains, twisting her ankles and wrists. After the freedom of the fire, the weight of the metal on her limbs was worse than it had been all year. And along with the unnatural feel of metaplas, the cat feet skidded across her mind and taunted her with their movement. She wanted to scream at their presence.

Finally she was hauled to her feet, and her clothes were thrust into her hands; she would not be allowed to dress until she reached Cekulu's suite. Instead, jerkily, her grace undone by the pain and muscle cramps that made every step a radiant agony, she followed the guards. She no longer struggled. Her defiance was hidden again in her eyes.

Just as she had come to the warehouse, she was led with her upper arms clenched in the fists of the guards. They marched silently, their n-rods swinging in their hands, their disinterested eyes belying the instinctive sharpness with which they noted Tsia's movements. This time Tsia stepped in two puddles of packing gel. The only indication she gave of the slime was the narrowing of her eyes as she shook out her foot. When the door scans hit her body, she did not even shiver. Her thoughts were already like ice.

Have to kill Cekulu, she told herself grimly. Maybe the Pulanese leader, too. The art guild would not be able to hide that, not with the Pulanese mercs looking for her so sharply. The councilwoman's death would force the mercs into Noirelle faster. She herself would need a flexor—maybe a breaker pad—if she could get one. And if she could not remove the plugs from her temples, she would have to have an r-con, too—something to keep the other control signals at bay. She had clothes, she noted absently, her hands clenched around the scuffed white fabric. Her nakedness did not disturb her; the chill she felt in the hall was there only because of the sweat of the dance. Had she not had the fire on her skin, the air would have seemed as warm as it had before. But her feet, her mind continued—she would need boots, some kind of footgear. Maybe a variable suit. This was the desert— there would be emergency gear like that somewhere. The flexibility of the suits would be controlled by the node links, but she could find a way around that. She stared ahead as she marched in the hall. Her stomach was twisted again, and her hands itched to scratch at her temples. Inside her skull the tiny, silent cat feet tickled at her brain.

Two doors short of her previous cell the lead guard paused at a portal, and Tsia's gaze sharpened. The filter door shimmered open, revealing another hall, and the guards and Tsia went through. There was little difference between this hall and the previous one, but Tsia ground this one's dimensions into her memory. North—they were going north now. They were already past the boundaries of the warehouse.

She counted her steps, burning the number into her mind. One hundred paces . . . one hundred ten. Three women passed, a man, and then a couple. They went through another door, this time to the left. As they crossed the glowing frame, a group of children squeezed past, ignoring her and her guards in their play. Did they even know what a ghost was? Tsia had never thought of such things when she was a child. And, she recognized, unlinked to the node as all children were, she would not have understood, either. She listened to their shrieks of laughter. When they were gone, the new hall became minaciously silent except for the pounding of her burning pulse, the scrape of her chains on the floor, and the thud of the guards' booted feet.

The last filter door led into one of the gleaming black walkspans between the buildings. The walls were dark but not completely opaque, and the scent of monkeybrush and horses struck her nose. She dragged her feet, her gaze piercing the walls as she tried to map her location to the images in her mind. There were sharp edges of buildings, angled shadows of the paths. She stared at the plaza she could barely see. The spiked fences made bars to hold the dry gardens in; the shadows of the buildings made angles in the sand. She quickened her pace. The tap of a cold n-rod, unactivated, brought her steps back to normal, but her mind could not help its churning: She was on the north side of Noirelle. There was just one wall between her and the sands. One wall to the desert beyond.

Tsia did not want to leave the walkway when they reached the other end. It took a shove from the guard behind to push her through. Then another hallway and another door, and they were at the artist's suite.

The lead guard used his link to activate the filter door; it opened almost immediately. In the doorway, Kern waited. Tsia glared at him, her eyes still feral and wild. The short man stepped back carefully, and the guards hauled Tsia in. They left her there, nude in her chains, her clothes in her arms like old laundry.

"This way."

Tsia hesitated, glancing back at the door.

Kern motioned patiently. "The rooms are already sealed."

Tsia let her breath out raggedly. She stalked after him, the scrape of the chains muffled on the blue and cream carpet. The man led her to a comfortable room decorated in cream and cool green and purple. Pointing to the shower block, he touched his temples. Tsia's chains dropped with a rattle. This time she moved her feet before they hit. She stared down at them, then looked at Kern. Her wariness must have shown in her eyes.

The man shrugged. "Cekulu doesn't want you scraping the carpet with those things." He turned to the door. "Clean up. Get comfortable. We will get started with your part of the firedance in a few hours."

Tsia stared after him. She still felt wild and uncontained. With a shiver she stooped, grabbed the chains, and slung them over her head in a wild circle.

She stopped as abruptly as she had started. The links swung to a halt in her hands. What had she intended? To smash the chains into the wall?

Daya, she whispered to herself, what was wrong with her? This Kern had freed her of the metal again just so she could provoke him to put her back in chains? Idiot, she cursed herself. She threw the shackles away, letting them slide into the corner of the room. Then she wrapped her arms around herself and dropped to her haunches, rocking back and forth, trying to contain her feelings.

The dance. It must have been the fire that had made her lose control like this. It had been so long since the flames had touched her skin ... "As long as the virus holds her like this ..." Cekulu's words echoed in her head. It had been sixteen months since she had taken the virus. And she had been old to become a guide. The effects—what had they said about them? Drawn out in the beginning, shortened and more intense in the end ...

In the end. A pang of fear touched her sharply. Was she supposed to have this virus in her body for more than a year?

And why this desperate need for the fire? Because that was what it was, she acknowledged with a sense of dread. A need, a raging hunger for the flames to burn the oils from her skin, to breathe the heated air, to somehow scald the crawling cat feet from the inside of her skull. And those cat feet ... Were the felines somehow reaching her? Here, within this base? The virus— making her shiver like an ague? She wrapped her arms around herself, holding in her shudders. Her left hand dug into her right ribs; her right hand gripped her left shoulder. She could feel the tremors in her bones. In all the years she had trained to be a guide, she had seen no other dancer shake. Was this from the semblance of freedom she had tasted in the firepit? Was it the helplessness that came with the chains? The rage that still grew in her guts?

She stared at the fetters in the corner. She felt like the riptide, tearing herself apart. Her hands went to her temples and became fists, pressing against the plugs in her head. The crawling sensation in her head was unbearable. She could see sandcats stretching and stalking from their cool, dank dens. She could smell the sterility of the air around her and choke with the sense of the mountains beyond her reach. The biogate had become an abyss of biofields, pulling her senses with its energies. With every breath she seemed to inhale it. With every step she came closer to the void.

A strangled sound escaped her lips, and she leapt up, pacing the room, ignoring the doorway that remained open to the area beyond. Her tension was like an acid taste in her mouth. Her restlessness had grown in the fire until she felt hemmed in by the very air in this base. She turned suddenly and saw Kern standing in the doorway. Silently, the man regarded her. Tsia halted, panting. Then, with a curse, she turned her back, made for the shower block, and buried herself under the molecular scrub.

In the shower the oils of her skin tasted weak with salt. She bent her head against the strength of the scrub and licked her lips. With a shock, she realized she was crying. The keening she could hear, so soft and steady in her ears, was herself. Tsia gripped herself hard, not caring that Kern might still be watching from the door. Head bent, she stood in the tingling cloud long after the scrub had lifted the ash and firegrime from her pores. She stood until her arms, her back, her legs were flushed from the scrub, until new oils rose to soften her skin.

She felt chilled when she stepped from the scrub. Even the heat of the shower had not removed the shivers from her skin. The sweet scent of herself was back in her nostrils, and she wrinkled her nose at the dusty smell of the carpet beneath her feet. It was not dirty; her nose was just too keen. The awareness of the life around her clogged her lungs so that she almost choked, and she stepped gingerly across the rug, as if by walking carefully she would not stir up the scent. When she shook out her clothes, she wrinkled her nose again. A dirty footprint marred the cleanliness of the white silk trousers. The tunic was scuffed on the side. Absently, she noted that she should not have kicked them earlier, and she smiled grimly at herself for her concern. These clothes would burn in the dance tomorrow, just as her others had today.

Kern was waiting for her just when she entered the larger room. "The scrub must have felt good," he remarked in a friendly fashion. "You are calmer. Less tense." He smiled faintly. "You don't smell so much like oil and old ash."

Tsia glanced at him once, then ignored him and examined the

room instead. There was one door opposite the hall exit, another to the side. No windows broke the walls; they were lined with holopanels instead. "What," she asked coolly, "is your part in all this?"

Thoughtfully, Kern watched Tsia pace the room. "I prepare the rooms, the sculptures."

"The subjects," Tsia stated.

He nodded. "You will be the seventh firedancer Cekulu's had."

"Vashanna was the sixth?"

"The third," he corrected. "The first two died before Cekulu figured out how to get the images she wanted. The others were too far beyond their first year when the other subjects were ready for birth."

Kern's voice was casual, unconcerned. Tsia stared at him. "Do you know what you did to them—to Vashanna?"

Kern crossed his legs and tilted his head at her. "Of course. Vashanna, she gave birth in the fire. It was one of the most powerful pieces I have ever witnessed—even out of Cekulu." He shook his head, trying to explain his memories, and found himself leaning forward on the couch. "The realism," he said. "The images—they were so strong that it has been almost twenty-two years since we completed those pieces, and all three of the Vashanna dances are still sharp in my mind."

"You . . . prepared—" Tsia had trouble with the term. "—Vashanna for the fires each time?"

He nodded, leaning back again. "She was a challenge. After the first birth she tried to refuse to dance."

Tsia licked her lips. "What did you do to make her comply?"

"We gave her a choice."

Tsia watched the man. She noted the perfect leanness of Kern's shoulders and the ideal bones of his smooth-skinned face, and she saw imposed upon it the twisted flesh of Vashanna. Something icy settled into her guts, and she placed the feeling beside the hatred growing for Cekulu. "A choice?" she asked carefully.

Kern nodded again, stretching his legs out in front of the couch. "She wanted to die. We said we would allow it."

"So she danced the second time."

"It was incredible. The desperation, the hope, the determination—all of it came through as if it had been shouted over the flames into the memory images themselves."

Tsia licked her lips, which were dry again after the molecular scrub. Kern must be crazy. There was no other explanation for a man who could sit and discuss the performance of torture as casually as if he were critiquing a dreamer channel. Tsia ran her hand over her shortened hair. Or was she crazy for talking with him? Should she not be outraged, tearing into him for his part in a mother's torture?

"After that dance," Kern went on, "Cekulu wanted to try another set of emotions. Vashanna was scarred, but Cekulu figured she could make it through one more fire."

"How—how could you do it?"

"Get her to agree to dance?"

Tsia's mind screamed, No, put Vashanna—scarred—back in the fire. Put her where she would burn.

Kern shrugged. "Cekulu told Vashanna that the firedancer could have the death of any other slave she wanted."

"Any? Such as you?"

Kern nodded. "She chose the woman who first put her in the flames. Vashanna took the woman with her when she danced, and she burned her to death while she birthed her third child. Cekulu caught the whole thing on full-dimension holo—senses, memories, skin—everything. Gods, you should have seen them—the twin images, one thin, one heavy with child. The screams of the unmother, the determined silence of Vashanna, and then—"

Tsia cut in harshly. "You want me to do the same thing, except with the leader from Pulan?"

"No." Kern surprised her. "Vashanna took the slave woman in the flames to die. It was an execution of sorts, a trade of life: the babe for the slave. Your dance," he said, pointing at Tsia, "will be completely different."

Tsia had been mistaken. Crazy could not begin to describe the man who sat before her. "How so?" she asked, her voice tight and hard.

"Because," Cekulu's voice said behind her, "you bear no antipathy toward the leader of Pulan."

Tsia whirled.

From the doorway Cekulu smiled. "You are clean. Good." She stepped inside, leaving in the hall the four guards who had stepped forward as Tsia had moved involuntarily toward the door. "As soon as the mole—"

"Molecular manipulator," Kern explained in an aside.

"—is finished setting the patterns, we can begin. Do you want something to eat?"

Tsia ignored her question. "Why will my lack of hostility make a difference?" she demanded. "The situation is almost identical to the one you had before: A woman is pregnant, like Vashanna; you will have a firedance, as you did before; and a woman will probably die, as Vashanna's victim did before."

"Because, *kai-al nyeka*," Cekulu said, her voice caressing the syllables, "in this dance you will be trying to save the woman— not kill her—for the sake of the child she bears."

Tsia found her hands shaking at her side. "Perhaps," she said vehemently, "I will help her find her gods more quickly instead."

Kern laughed, and Cekulu raised her bone-white eyebrows. "I doubt it," she answered. "You are not that ruthless yet."

"You don't know me."

"Your rights-conditioning betrays you," Cekulu returned, unconcerned. "You have already proved that you cannot stand the pain of others. Do you think I cannot help you feel a little more for the others that you pity?"

"You cannot."

"Then I will have to prove it to you. Would you like to meet the Pulanese woman before the dance?"

"No," Tsia snapped.

Cekulu smiled, a slow, languorous smile that made Tsia's stomach turn with queasiness. "Are you afraid you might think of her as a person? Afraid that she might make you dance as Vashanna did?"

Tsia set her jaw.

"Kern," Cekulu commanded, "bring her in." He rose and left through one of the side doors, leaving the two women alone in the main suite.

Tsia watched Cekulu silently.

The artist tossed back her white hair. "You will be the first guide to dance in my ice room," she said conversationally.

Tsia frowned. "Ice?"

Cekulu nodded. "In some ways it was a good thing that the timing of the other guides we had and the timing of the pregnancies did not match until we found you. It has taken me fourteen years just to perfect the dynamic ice effect I needed. Another year went into controlling the vapor before I could sculpt the freeze room—"

Tsia interrupted. "I dance in fire, not ice."

"Of course you do."

"Then what—"

"—am I talking about ice for?" Cekulu finished for her. "Think of the imagery . . ." Her voice grew dreamy. "The juxtaposition of the white-blue ice and the frozen vapor in the air, set against the yellow-red fire in your mind . . . The balance of opposing realities on two different planes—internal and external . . . The intensity of the dichotomy will stun anyone on the dreamer channels, and if I open the ice room to dancers themselves . . ."

The side door opened, and Kern returned, bringing with him a woman in the last month of pregnancy. The woman was pale, her hands curved protectively over her belly, but her eyes were hard and her mouth tight. Tsia refused to look at her. "To do this," she asked, "you will feed the memories of a firedance into my mind?"

Cekulu came out of her imagery. "No," she returned calmly.

"Then how—"

"I have analyzed the sweat of your body. The chemical composition of the ice vapor will react with your sweat. At colder temperatures it will burn your nerves like an intense heat. At warmer temperatures the combination will break down, becoming less active. Nearest the ice, I imagine it will be like rubbing undiluted acid along your flesh, something like the effect of the n-rod on your nerves." Cekulu gestured for the Pulanese woman to sit. Kern took up a stance behind the hostage. Cekulu continued. "I will record your memories throughout the dance," she said, "and interpret them as fire. Then I will combine them with the visual and physical record of the ice to create the sensual juxtaposition I want."

"The ice . . ."

"Will melt and set up convection currents in the room, just like a fire in its ring. The vapor will act as the heat waves. Hot air rises; cold air falls. You will dance to avoid the coldest vapor, just as you used to dance to avoid the heat."

"But I will know it is ice—my memories will reflect that."

Cekulu shook her head. "Like all guides, you dance with your eyes closed. Part of your memories will reflect the knowledge that you move through a dynamic structure of ice, but the reality of your senses will record the heat of fire on your skin. That, too, will create the conflict of the senses versus the mind."

Tsia felt pain in her hands and looked down. Her fingernails were digging into her palms. "And the woman?" She nodded her chin at the pregnant Pulanese.

"She will be coated with a substance—"

"That also reacts like acid to the vapor," Tsia finished harshly.

"Not exactly." Cekulu glanced at the Pulanese woman. "Yemene will feel real fire."

"How?"

"The coating on her body will react with the vapor as the mist warms in the air. When the mix on her skin reaches a certain temperature, it will spontaneously combust."

Tsia swallowed against her nausea and choked instead on the dryness of her throat. Vashanna in the flames. Vashanna's child in the flames. Vashanna's child, warm and dead in her arms, on her flesh, on her skin. A guide, watching her own children die.

Cekulu watched her impassively.

Tsia forced herself to speak. "So I can dance the vapors like a fire and stay where the air is warmest. If I do that, I keep the acid from building up on my body. But—" She licked her lips. "If the woman—"

"Yemene."

"If Yemene stays where the vapor is warm, her skin bursts into flame."

"Yes."

"And she will not know where the vapor is coldest unless I guide her."

"Yes," the artist agreed.

"And if I guide her to the coldest areas, I burn."

Cekulu smiled gently. "Yes."

Tsia stood shaking, her breathing ragged and uncontrolled with the fury that seemed to blind her. "What temperature," she said harshly, "will keep the fire from growing on her skin?"

The artist watched the shivering take Tsia's body like a cold wind. "The temperature where the acid burns you the most."

"And the baby?"

"It will be coated with the fire fluid as it is born. It should burst into flame as it exits the birth canal."

Yemene made a strange strangled sound.

Cekulu ignored her. She motioned at Kern and followed him to the side door. "You two may get acquainted," she said over her shoulder. "Yemene speaks nine of the desert tongues, including Korshani, so even without a node link, communication—" She smiled at Tsia. "—will not be the problem between you. You have an hour."

Tsia stared after them. Her head pounded, and her fists were still clenched. Before her the pregnant woman sat on the couch and watched. Light fell across the woman's face and made it seem more pale, the thin hardness of her cheeks unnatural against the rounded protrusion of her belly. Her fingers curled.

"How many years have you been a guide?"

The question made Tsia's eyes turn slowly toward the woman. Cold, hard, unrelenting, she identified the tones in the woman's voice. But stubborn, too. She regarded the woman silently. If it were a child in her own belly, how would she feel toward herself?

"How much experience do you have walking the flames?" the woman repeated.

Tsia shuddered, ridding herself with difficulty of the trembling that seemed to have taken over her bones. The shakes were worse than they had been the day before, and her unease at her weakness made her stand taller in the face of the councilwoman's question. How much experience? She smiled, and the feral grin forced the other woman's jaw to tighten. "Almost none," Tsia answered softly.

"None?" The woman blinked, then stared at her, incredulous. "You are, what, thirty-five? Thirty-eight? You must have at least ten years in the flames." She paused as if she were trying to access her link to the node.

Tsia's teeth parted. "It's tough to ask for someone's ID dot when you don't have a link, isn't it?"

Yemene dropped her hand from the temple plugs.

"I am thirty-nine," Tsia said, watching her discomfiture. "I took the virus over a year ago. I have walked the flames twice since I became a guide."

The woman's nostrils flared with her breath. "You are lying."

Tsia's eyes narrowed. She took a step closer, defying the woman's words without saying a thing.

"New guides walk the flames every month. You are either lying about the number of times you have danced in the firepit or you are lying about when you became a guide."

Tsia's voice was soft. "If I am your one hope to stay alive, you should at least pretend some respect for my words."

"Why?" Yemene demanded instead, struggling to push her heavy body to the edge of the couch. "Respect to a woman older than I, who by now ought to have fifteen years experience in the flames? What are you, some kind of throwback? An aberrant mutant?" Her voice was sharp and vicious as she levered herself awkwardly to her feet. "A guide who should never have taken the virus at all to come to it so late?"

"I am a twelfth-generation guide," Tsia said slowly. Her voice was as cold and hard as the other woman's face. "I am a third-generation guide on this planet alone. And I am the only guide you have. If I am an aberration, you had better hope I am a damn good one in order to keep the fire from your sullen face."

"Pah!" Yemene glared at Tsia. "With barely two steps in the flames? You will not even know how to protect yourself."

"I spent seventeen years in the coal classes."

"Coal classes," the woman snorted in disgust. "You know nothing."

"I know enough," Tsia snapped. "I *know* I need fire to burn away the oils on my skin. In Cekulu's art I will have that fire, but only if you burn, too. If I help you and stay out of the flames, my skin will be chemically-seared from my bones. If I don't help you, I can stay in the heat. I will stay unscarred and alive."

The woman glared at her. "If you don't help me, this baby will die."

"So will you."

Yemene's face was suddenly hard. "In the hands of the artists, I probably have no choice. But this baby—" She curled her hands around her belly. "—must not die. This child has to survive—he has to live."

"Why?"

"Have you ever had a child?"

Tsia shook her head.

"Then you should not ask that question."

Tsia absently rubbed and crushed the smooth white fabric of her trousers against her taut thighs. "You said *this* baby. Not *my* baby. Why?" She took another step forward until she gazed down at the woman's cold face. "Why?" she repeated softly, her voice so low that it was almost a growl.

Yemene met her gaze steadily. "There is a reading attached to this birth. A vision, if you will."

The esper reading? The one Tsia had heard about so long ago in Ciordan? She paused. Were her first instincts right? Did Cekulu have something to do with the prophecy?

"The esper guild," Yemene continued, unaware of her thoughts. "They matched my fetus to the prophecy that was made two hundred years ago at First Drop. They confirmed it again a month ago. This child is important to Pulan."

Tsia, thinking, did not respond, and Yemene made an irritated sound.

"Do you not believe me?" the councilwoman demanded. "From Catmount Ridge of the Cheba Rift to the wasteland of the Sinking Plains, all Pulan's industry is based on our mines. Our council sits in the midst of the guild and freework buildings, surrounded by the influence of the ores. Right now there is so much conflict between the freepicks and the mining guild that to move from the council building—from any building—is to court death from a hidden sharper." She made an angry snort. "It takes only one sharper sighting in off the node to kill a councilman. We cannot work with that strain, knowing that any step outside could mean a tight beam to the skull. Most of the contract bids are on hold. Eighty percent of our ore cannot be worked. Future stakes are in jeopardy. We *need* a leader," she repeated. "An esper leader who can bring the factions together, force peace if necessary. This child—" She touched her belly. "—will be that man."

"You cannot force peace," Tsia said softly. She rubbed at the manacle marks that still ringed her slender wrists. "Nor can you force this child to fill the role you have in mind for him."

"His destiny is already in place," Yemene returned wearily. "He will understand that as he grows up. Pulan cannot afford to go the way of Vendetta. To be destroyed by war so that none may ever live there again. The mining guild has too much power; the freepicks have too much ingenuity turning equipment into weapons to match that power. And ever since the new sampling lasers came down off the orbiting hammers, there has been an outright battle to secure the arrendon deposits in the outer caverns."

"It is war?"

"Close enough." Yemene looked tired. "Two days ago the fighting pushed up into the city itself. Walkspans are smashed; pedpaths are caving in; no one leaves their buildings now except in an emergency. Everyone communicates through the node." She smiled sourly. "The businesspeople practically breathe through the node in their fear of losing what they have to this conflict. Even the religions are broadcasting through the dreamer channels because, except for the temples preaching the prophecy, they can hardly get their worshipers to come out. You cannot go anywhere without seeing some evidence of fighting. If this continues—" She grew sober. "—the miners could destroy much more than a single city. But with negotiation . . ."

Tsia laughed in disbelief. "The child cannot negotiate anything till he is grown."

The woman gave her a cold look. "Of course he can't. But with his birth, we can promise both freepicks and miners a future where each faction can work the ores. We can hold off their hostilities for another two decades. At least until the child is grown and can take over the council." She motioned at her swollen abdomen. "This boy will be able to see into the minds of each side and bring them together in a working peace. No guild esper will do that for us—their talents are locked into Federation work, and they have no stake in Pulan. And we must act now, before the guild and freepicks destroy our land. In eight decades we have not been able to secure a standing agreement. If in the next thirty years we do not achieve some kind of peace between the freepicks and the mining guild, we could lose our industry completely. Our ore shipments are, or were," she acknowledged bitterly, "a quarter of the Risthmus's payment to the Federation for the lease of this planet." She challenged Tsia with her eyes. "You are a guide. Would you allow the loss of this entire world because of war? Because you do not wish to protect the one child who can make the difference?"

"If the stakes are so high," Tsia demanded, "why did Cekulu kidnap you in the first place? Why not wait for some other esper child to be born?"

Cekulu's answer was bitter. "There are not that many high espers born on this planet. Perhaps two in each decade. And the art guild is rich enough to rent space on any planet, no matter who the colonists are. Whether or not we continue here does not matter to their guild. In fact," she said softly, more to herself, "I am half-inclined to think they are themselves behind the mining conflict we now have. Cekulu was too knowledgeable . . ."

"She approached you before," Tsia guessed with sudden insight.

The councilwoman nodded faintly. "She offered me a contract two days after the espers confirmed this child's potential. What she proposed would not have harmed me or the child, but contracts with the art guild have a way of changing after they are imprinted. I turned her down. Pulan is more important than any piece of sculpture, no matter who the art influences." A shadow of pain crossed her face before she hardened her expression. "If it had not been for the mining conflict," she added in a cold voice, "I would never have come within her reach. But there was a chance at negotiation between the freepicks and the miners. I had to try. And, trying, was taken by the artists."

Tsia regarded Yemene thoughtfully. "I still don't understand why an esper's birth would be more important to Cekulu than any other child's birth."

"Don't you see?" Yemene's lips tightened. "Weak espers are nothing. They are not strong enough to be recorded, no matter how sensitive the scanners. I, for example, am a weak esper. I can sense enough from others to make a good councilwoman, but I can give Cekulu only the physical sensations and memories of my pain or my death." Her hand strayed to her belly. "This child . . . In dying, this baby can give a height and depth to Cekulu's sculpture that will burn her art into any human's soul." Her expression turned bleak. "She cares nothing for the prophecy," the woman spit. "She cares nothing for Pulan."

"What was the reading?" Tsia asked softly.

Yemene looked up, her eyes still burning. "They said that the cougar would claw the council free from the rape of its future."

Cougar? Cat feet clawed at Tsia's mind, and she shoved them from her thoughts with difficulty.

"—That a childless mother would take the burning babe from the fires of the smoking warriors. And that, when it finally happened, the water of Risthmus itself would wash the stink of war from the soil." Yemene caught Tsia's frown. "The esper was in trance," the woman snapped. "The language is not important. Only its interpretation. The cat, the childless mother?" She shrugged. "These things make no sense. The burning babe? That—" She stared hard at Tsia. "—could be here. The water of Risthmus would be the subterranean tables blasted by the miners. And the smoking warriors—already we have those in plenty."

"Since the mines were staked," Tsia said slowly, "Pulan has hired more mercs since Risthmus was settled than any other county on the planet. Why didn't you get them to settle this whole problem again?"

Yemene gave her a cold look. "In the past the mercs have been strong enough to hold the county in an uneasy peace. But two weeks ago the freepicks ended up with most of the sampling lasers. A week ago the mining guild struck back with stronger weapons. Since then each day has escalated the violence."

Tsia eyed her speculatively. "Even a miner has to have rights-conditioning to carry a flexor or variable blade. As long as this whole thing is hand to hand, I do not see why you are so worried. Let them kill each other off. Then get more reasonable miners to take their places in the ore sights. That is what you have done in the past. Why change now?"

"Because they no longer limit themselves to hand weapons," the councilwoman said wearily.

"What?"

"They have turned some of the coring lasers into weapons."

"How could one of those be a weapon? A rock puncher has a beam not even a meter long."

Yemene looked haggard. "To fight against the equipment the guild brought in, the freepicks modified their laser amplifiers and lenses. I myself have seen one of the corers that they narrowed and lengthened to a twenty-meter beam. It cut through the interbuilding transport tubes as if they were butter. It will not be enough to stop the guild." She gave Tsia a bleak look. "Two days ago the guild brought in cluster bombs, burton balls, and deep-space salvage gear—like tight-beam breakers and snakes."

Tsia looked at her in horror. Cluster bombs had a blast radius of a hundred meters in light material, thirty meters in dense rock. Burton balls were tiny proximity bombs. A burton ball attached itself to any life-form listed in its target memory, then blew apart its victim. And salvage gear ... Daya, but deep-space snakes could be outfitted with lasers and punchers that would make the coring gear of the freepicks look like clumsy toys.

Any of those weapons not only could destroy the underground springs, it could collapse the main rock shelf of the upper water table into the deeper river tubes. They could drain off half the water table in bare hours. And the tailings from the ores ... Tsia's stomach clenched with realization. The tailings from the existing mines were held for bioreclamation right next to the deposits from which they were created. They were separated from other parts of the mines only by thin walls of rock ...

Tsia looked at Yemene with a tight expression. "The water has run beneath the Sinking Plains for millennia. The entire ecosystem of both the grassland and the strip trees is built on the subterranean rivers. To contaminate or change the water tables could destroy the plains. Why, such an act could wipe out some species completely. We would have to bring them back by genetic reclamation. Do you realize what this means?" Tsia paced from one side of the room to the other. "Pulan could cease to exist. All land leases would be lost. In fact, if the biome is too heavily damaged, the land leases for the entire planet might be revoked by the Federation. How could the miners be so rock-brained as not to see that? They would not be simply fined for damaging a biome. They would be turned into ghosts. Stripped of everything." As she herself was a ghost, a tiny voice said in her head. The cat feet scratched. She rubbed her temples irritably. "Why aren't you using the node sensors to find them? To stop them before they do such harm?"

"Because two days ago the subterranean links were knocked out." A spasm of pain crossed Yemene's face and was as quickly gone. "Our nodies have no way to monitor the mines now," she added bitterly. "The miners and freepicks could be doing anything down there, and we would not know anything about it till the guides in the Sinking Plains picked up the effects. In my absence, the council will continue to negotiate, but ..."

"You are not confident."

The woman sighed wearily. "The Pulanese council is like any other government by committee. Without a strong leader, it degenerates into political infighting. One endless series of maneuvers between members. Which ones align with the freepicks? Which ones align with the guild? Each one will be working to achieve his own personal power and empire. Already they will have laid so many traps for each other that even if I came back yesterday, I could not sort it out before half our land is destroyed." She rubbed her lower back. "Our nodies are good, but even they need a good web of sensors to find human beings in solid rock. And the miners' ghost lines are as complex as any we have seen in the past. Each time our nodies trace the ghosts down to individual ID dots, the miners and freepicks activate a new set of ghost lines. In three days we have not been able to pinpoint the coring lasers whose beams were extended. The guild is blasting every freepick stake they can find. The freepicks keep moving their rock crunchers through the transport tubes, burning out the guild holdings as they go."

"Do the freepicks believe in the prophecy?"

Yemene nodded curtly. "Of course." She frowned at Tsia's expression. "Even if they do not truly believe, the child's birth is the best negotiating tool they have for keeping the ore stakes they have left. The guild weapons are too good. Even if the freepicks band together, they do not have the credit to buy the arsenal they need to fight back. So they have to work with me, with the council, to make peace now based on the threat of future compromises."

"How far do they support you?" Tsia tried to keep the eagerness out of her voice. "Would they have petitioned the mercs for a kidnap grant to come take you back to Pulan?"

"They have no need to do so." Yemene glanced at the door of the suite as if hoping Cekulu would overhear. "Ever since we found out about the coring lasers, we put plans in place for dealing with terrorism. Taking out the council leaders who support a mixed enterprise would be the miners' top priority. Taking out the woman carrying the next leader of Pulan would be their first step. I was not taken without notice."

"Taken by the miners and sold to the artists? Or taken by the miners with the help of the art guild itself?"

The woman smiled without humor. "If Ceklulu is behind the funding and fighting of the miners, my mercs will reach her more quickly than she thinks." The woman glanced at her belly. Her face grew hard again. "We have fifty minutes left of the time

Cekulu gave us," she said as she looked up at Tsia. "I suggest we do something with it besides talk."

Caught by the idea of escape, Tsia began to pace again. "Like what?" she asked, only half listening.

"Teach me this firedance. Show me the guide moves for the fire so that I can try to keep my baby alive."

Tsia stopped her pacing and frowned at the other woman. "The firedance is not a social game. You do not just learn it. Not in a day or week or year."

"I haven't got a week or day. I have one hour."

Tsia started to shake her head.

"One hour," Yemene repeated, "till my baby burns."

Tsia felt her anger rise. "It takes years to learn the techniques in the coal classes before you can be trusted in the flames. Sometimes it takes a decade or more." She herself should know, she thought bitterly. She had spent almost two decades there.

Yemene glared at her stubbornly. "As I said, you do not have a decade. You have an hour."

"You do not understand," Tsia snarled. "Even if, by some miracle, you learned the techniques for the dance, you would never be able to do more than walk on cold-flame coals. There are years of preparatory viruses you have to take before you can accept the guide virus that makes you sweat."

The woman's face was steady, but there was a desperation in her eyes that was hard for Tsia to ignore. "What preparatory viruses? What do they do that cannot be taught to me here?"

Tsia started to pace again. "They modify the body—immune system, nervous system, mitochondria—to accept the guide virus. After the preps, the guide virus makes the final system changes that open the biogate and create the sweat. There is no way to give you even one of the prep viruses. They are vectored into the genes of each guide individually—they are not transferrable without med equipment. And even if we had all the viruses here, they must be taken in sequence. Any one of them could be fought off by your body. If your body rejected even one, the guide virus would not take. Yemene—" She spread her hands. "—I am sorry."

The woman stared at her.

"As for the firedance itself . . ." Tsia tried objectively to study the weight of the woman and the way she would move. "Even if I guide you through the ice mist, you will be burned," she said flatly. "There is no way to avoid at least some of the warmer currents."

"Can you not anticipate them so that when I get there, they are cooler?"

"I will be trying to do exactly that," Tsia returned sharply, "but every time you shift your body, the convection currents from the ice will change, too. Ditto for me. Every move I make will shift the air currents again in the ring."

"Room."

"What?"

"It will be an ice room, not a fire ring."

"What does it matter?" Tsia snarled. "You will burn anyway."

Yemene clamped her mouth shut.

Tsia started pacing again. "And when your skin begins to blaze, will you scream?"

"Probably," the woman said in a short, sarcastic voice.

"No."

"What do you mean, no?" Yemene demanded in turn.

"Screaming will change the currents of the air as much as if you blew on them. If you start to burn, you *must* stay silent and control your breathing. Otherwise I will not be able to tell where the air will shift next."

"And will I be allowed to slap the fire out?" the woman demanded furiously.

"Again, no. Let me do that."

The pregnant woman's face flushed with her anger. "You want me to stand still and burn until you find the time to pat it out?"

Tsia nodded curtly. "Exactly that."

"You are insane."

"Not as much as you will be if you don't do as I say."

"It would be easier," Yemene snapped, "to teach me the firedance than to expect me to stand still while I am burned alive."

"If you want your child to survive as much as you say you do, you will move only as I say to move and stay silent till I put out the flames."

"And you will willingly put yourself in the colder mists to keep me from the heat? You will do this even though you yourself will be seared by the cold itself?"

"Damn you." Tsia clenched her fists. "Yes, I will."

Yemene's face was cold and hard. "And I am to believe that you, an arrogant, inexperienced, atavistic—"

"Watch your language."

"—godless guide, has the guts to burn yourself for me?"

The two women stared at each other.

"You cannot even pace this room without trembling."

Tsia brought her fists to her temples. There was a yowling in her head, and the blankness of the plugs against her brain forced her to believe it was her own gate that screamed. She reached along the biogate that sucked at her senses and felt the desert cats stretching and hunting in the shadows of sandy canyons. She cut her own skin with her nails.

She looked at Yemene, and the woman stared back. Tsia's ice-blue eyes were cold. "I tremble not because of fear," she said slowly, carefully, "but because I tremble."

The woman's face grayed, and she stepped back, her hands protectively across her belly. "You are sick."

Tsia shook her head. "No. I am just . . . Just . . ." She did not complete the thought. Instead, she turned back to her pacing, leaving Yemene to sit and stare bleakly in silence.

15

Cekulu stood back in satisfaction, regarding the room with a practiced eye. "Yemene is over in the chem room?"

Kern nodded.

"Don't dip her yet. The fire will bring on the birth, and this is a dry run. In fact," she said thoughtfully, "let's keep her out of it completely until Tsia is ready for the real thing. We will have an hour for practice, then three hours to prepare the Pulanese woman, then anywhere from one to five hours—if Yemene lasts that long—for the dance."

Kern gestured at Tsia. "Are we running with the full compound now or just the practice mist?"

Tsia stood naked in the room, the blue-white floors and walls stretching around her. Faint patterns on the floors reflected the places where ice spires would grow and crumble, whip and snap away into vapor like the light of a fire. The molecular manipulator was in Cekulu's hands, and she gave the disk a pat before glancing at Tsia. "Full compound. She will need to feel it to get used to thinking of it as fire. Besides," Cekulu said, eying Tsia critically, "the fluid will be drawn in through her pores. When it interacts with her nerves, it will burn then, not up on the skin. She won't be scarred so that it shows, and we don't have much time for her to get used to either room or acid."

Tsia looked at her steadily as Kern left the room. "If you burn my nerves to numbness," she said more calmly than she felt, "I won't be able to feel the temperature differences of either vapor or fire."

Cekulu shrugged. "The effects are not permanent—they wear off faster than an n-rod—and the acid in the fluid neutralizes quickly. You will be able to feel the burn lessen as soon as you move away from the colder mists."

Kern returned with a block to which was attached a pair of metal pincers and another pair of coiled tentacles. He set the block down on the small platform at which Cekulu still worked on the mole. The round, tapered manipulator was a bronze disk in the side of the blue metaplas pattern generator Cekulu used. The silver of the pincers looked cold and deadly next to the other equipment. "Put your head here," Kern directed Tsia, pointing to the space between the pincers.

Tsia stared at the head vise and shook her head. She took an involuntary step back. The memory of the day on the dikes when she was taken by the traders rose in her mind. Suddenly all she could see was Hesse standing over her. Hesse saying, "Trust me, everything's fine . . ."

"Do not worry," Cekulu soothed. "The pincers remove the plugs in your temple sockets. You have to have a link so that you can work the mole and so that I can record your memories and imagery."

Tsia stared. Her heart pounded in a slow heavy rhythm. A link? They were giving her access to the nodes?

Cekulu shook her head, reading Tsia's thoughts from her face. "The room is shielded, kai-al nyeka. Your link will not reach through these walls. The only thing you can control is this." She held up the mole disk.

Tsia eyed it as she would have eyed a watergen if she were dying of thirst. She could not help the sharpness of her gaze. A link outside the room would give her access to the nodes. "Full access?" Her voice was almost a whisper.

Cekulu nodded. "To the mole, yes, but only within this room," she repeated. "You cannot reach all the way to the nodes."

Kern waited with the long curved pincers in his hands. Tsia touched her temple plugs hesitantly. To have them out . . . She moved slowly forward.

The short man positioned her head between the metal arms, and they closed about her head. She shivered. The gentle touch of the tentacle arms lifted the skin flaps from the plugs so that the metaplas plugs were exposed. Then the cold touch of the pincers transferred itself through the plugs to the bone around her brain. She stood it without flinching. There was a slight whirring noise. The plugs were withdrawn. Cold air—what seemed cold to her— touched her where the microscopic network of temple links spread inside her skull. She gasped.

And then the pincers were gone from around her head, and the tentacles coiled neatly back. Kern watched her in satisfaction. "Must feel good after a year."

She had eyes only for the mole Cekulu held. The woman stretched it out, and Tsia almost grabbed it from her hands.

"Easy," Kern said sharply.

Cekulu shook her head at him. "Let her have it."

With trembling hands, Tsia took the disk. She tapped the sides, activating the link, and reached with her mind in ordered patterns that seemed half-forgotten. Activation codes swept back. In a rush of incoherence Tsia snapped commands at the mole. ID dots, locations, communication to Ciordan—pent-up orders she had been waiting a year to send—all of them blanked at the mole, leaving her to stare at the tapered disk in her hand.

Cekulu smiled gently. "There is no link beyond the mole *nyeka*. It is only for this room. Self-contained power. Self-contained patterns for the ice. Except for your access code, the line to the node stops right at the shielding of these walls."

Tsia gave a tiny, jerky nod.

"The mole accepts commands to manipulate material only," Cekulu went on. Her voice was steady, soothing, and Tsia realized that Cekulu was teaching her how to use the tool. "In this room it will manipulate the ice structures dynamically. For example, it will change the shapes and heights of the spires."

Tsia looked up in surprise.

The artist nodded. "You can change them into any shape your mind knows as fire."

"If I can send the commands to change the shapes of the spires—" Tsia's voice was not quite even, and she steadied it carefully. "—then I can put the bulk of the spires as far from me as I want and keep the cold controlled."

Cekulu shook her head. "You will feel the chill of the ice on your skin, but you will also feel the acid in the fluid compound. Your mind will translate the heat of the acid into the sensations of fire. The mole will pick that up." She gestured at the swirling designs on the floor. "As it reads your fire images, it will create ice spires to match your memory images of what the flames would be shaped like. Since your firedance earlier, your images of fire are close and strong. The mole will dig them out more quickly than any artificial images you try to create in your head."

"What about the vapor?"

"The mist matches the heat waves you imagine. The mole melts the spires automatically. Then it shifts them to create the convection currents you expect."

"So I have no real control over this at all."

Cekulu hesitated almost imperceptibly. "No."

Unless she could control both memory and imagination. Cat feet skittered; she shuddered. She could not even control her gate. How could she control her mind? She looked at the floor designs to hide the despair in her expression. "I am a ghost," she said in a low voice. "Through what access are my commands accepted by this mole?"

"One of the dormant artist links."

"Dormant?"

Kern collapsed the last of the equipment into the now-compact stand. "The art guild maintains many dormant links," he explained. "Any artist can rent them for a project. Cekulu usually needs only one, but this time we rented two—one for you and one for Yemene. The links are limited to specific types of equipment. Unlimited links," he added with a grin, "cost more credit than even Cekulu makes."

"It is not the type of link that is important." Cekulu handed her gear to Kern to pack up. "It is the way the mole reacts to the link commands that determines its function. Within this room the mole will accept all commands you give it. This is critical for you to understand. You must think through the mole for every move you make. That is the only way to match the ice to your mental images of fire." She gave Tsia another look, as if to check her for unseen flaws. "We have only a few hours to go over this," she cautioned, "and I want you to get a feel for the manipulator. Your link is active? Good." She took a sip from the watergen tube at her side, then offered it to Tsia. "One more drink?"

Tsia shook her head. She had had enough, and this was ice, not fire. She would not need the reserves of water a firedance would demand. And her thoughts were not on the ice but on Cekulu's words. The mole would accept all her commands? Any material manipulation? Could she somehow use that to help Yemene?

Cekulu tossed the watergen to Kern. Then the artist leaned toward Tsia and tapped the manipulator disk in Tsia's hands. Instinctively, Tsia's grip tightened. The artist smiled indulgently. Pointing to one of the designs on which Tsia stood, she suggested, "Try it out. Move around. The mole will shift the room in the patterns as it reads the sweat from your body."

Tsia looked at her skin. It was dry. "I need the fire to begin to sweat," she said. "I can't dance without the sweat."

"You'll have fire in a few hours," Cekulu promised. "Right

now, just imagine the flames. The sweat will come when you feel the acid burn."

The woman's words chilled Tsia to the bone, and she stood in place, staring at the disk she had palmed. Kern and Cekulu moved toward the door. Tsia tensed to leap through with them, but Kern shook his finger at her. "Don't even think about it," he scolded gently. "The field lets only specific biofields through. After you entered, we excluded your field from the door's recognition patterns."

Tsia held up the disk in her hand. "What about this?"

Cekulu shrugged. "Carry it or put it down wherever you want. I will edit it out of the final sequences or change it into a set of floating images or memories that chase or lead you through the dance." Cekulu let her gaze travel critically around the room again. "Dance high," she said with a smile. Tsia stiffened at the traditional words. Then the door shimmered shut, became opaque, and began to swirl with the same patterns that swept across the floor.

With the mole clenched in her fist, Tsia looked around the room carefully. A manipulator that would create spires . . . To help Yemene or help herself? For the first time in over a year she was alone. No lessons, no one else to consider, no guilt to push her to act.

She stretched, reveling in the cat feet that skidded across the inside of her skull, rejoicing in the lightness of her limbs. To be free, weightless, leaping . . .

She had an hour. No more. The thought sobered her abruptly. She was not free; she was simply alone. And for the sake of the councilwoman and her child Tsia must think beyond, not just react to the lack of the manacles.

She stared around the room. White it was, like the cell from which she had come. Identical in shape, in height. Shielded walls, embedded sensors . . . She could feel the tiny tingling of the fields as if they were visible.

What if she made the mole think the walls were ice instead of shielded metaplas? Would it then re-form those surfaces, too? The ceiling she could never reach. Not unless she climbed the spires that would be made by the mole. Spires of ice that would burn her as she touched them. If that burn was anything like the n-rods used by the guards, she had no hope of working through it. She stared up thoughtfully. High and domed, the roof of the room was patterned exactly like the walls and floor, or else it reflected what was below.

The white-blue light in the room became too bright for her eyes, and Tsia winced. Bare on the frigid floor, her feet became cold, then colder, even though she shifted from one to the other. Then she squinted down sharply. The smoothness of the floor had given way to ridges that pressed on the soles of her feet. She moved away from the sharp bumps, and spires reached suddenly up, soaring slowly, then faster into the room. They re-formed as they went, as if the ice were liquid, not solid. To her left a thin cloud of vapor melted off a spire and wafted up.

Tsia turned in place, eyeing the room in wonder. It was stunning. It was beautiful . . . White, ice white soaring and whipping like cloth in the wind. Like light against light. Like magic.

Beside her, behind her, other spires and vapors stretched. Cold air bit at her nose. An air current brushed across her legs, then her back. Her skin began to feel hot, and the sweat, unbidden, came to her neck and arms.

And then she screamed. Her arms began to burn, and she moved instinctively, ducking and twisting away from the warm air farther into the cold. The acid flared more strongly on her skin, and she stifled a shriek, forcing herself to move against her instincts, away from the cold she had been trained to seek and into the relative heat of the room. Instantly, the pain lessened. Her eyes sought the ice that crunched beneath her bare feet, and she leapt into a blast of cold vapor. The burn set into her thighs, then splashed across her stomach. She gasped and jumped, and the vapor curled after her like a snake. Ice crackled out from the walls. The burn increased. She forced her eyes closed.

Now she danced in earnest. Cold air brushed her shoulders, and she twisted before the fire set in. She could feel this as heat if she tried.

Leap, twist, sweep, side jump . . . Ice burst up from the floor and snapped behind her toward the ceiling. A shower of ice sparks blasted off its surface, landing and growing into tiny licks of ice amid the other spires. Leap, duck, kick, side jump . . . Cat feet skittered; the moves returned. Her mind provided the fire. She clenched the mole to her hand. Its metaplas presence kept the sweat from her palm. If she had tried to carry metal in a fire, she would have burned on contact with it. Here, where her sweat itself was the danger, the metal kept the acid from her skin. Spin, crescent kick, diving roll, duck . . .

Cold, chilly air in her lungs; hot, burning fire on her skin. She knew she leapt between the spires of ice; she knew it was liquid, not heat that burned her flesh. But her eyes were closed, and as

Cekulu had said, her mind knew only one thing: pain. Pain that translated as the heat of a flame. She tried to tell her body not to sweat; with the vapors licking and searing her pores, the virus did not allow it. She tried to control the mole through her link, but she did not understand its process. One part of her mind beat useless commands at the limited line of the link; the other desperately danced in the flames—the air waves of the ice. Twice she tried to image a different shape of fire to the mole. Both times the forced images made her stumble, seeing one and feeling another, burning herself instead.

The mole was a manipulator—it was a tool, she snarled in desperation at her mind. If she could control her memories, she could use this, too. Leap, kick, kick higher, twist . . . A tool in her hands that would let her create the fire she danced instead of react to it. A tool that, if she could use it, would crack this floor like the plate of ice that it was. The mists swirled and curled behind her, following the vacuum in her wake. Spires reached and tried to brush against her knees. They swayed impossibly to the sides, wavered as they stretched toward the roof. Tsia glared at the images in her mind. Race, twist, sweep and roll . . .

Her breathing was coming quickly when she stumbled. She fell against a spire, stifling the curse that shrieked to her lips as the acid pressed through her pores. Her breath gasped. There was a trembling in her limbs that she could not justify. The floor seemed to shake. She slipped once more. And then she realized that for once it was not her own body that shivered. Beneath her feet the building trembled. Fractures that formed in the ice were remelted instantly into smoothly molded spires. But if the building was shaking . . .

Mercs—she almost shouted the hope that surged in her guts. They were here, searching for Yemene in this structure. Cekulu had not been able to keep them from breaking in. The art guild had not hired enough troops to stop them. Desperately, Tsia concentrated on the ice. If they were here . . . If she could get out of this room . . .

There *had* to be some way to control the play of the mole. A cougar yowled in her head, and the cat feet clawed across her hope. Damn you, she shouted silently at the cats. Let me be! I have to think. I have to concentrate—

She leapt between two protrusions that flickered and dissipated into mist. In midjump she built a pattern of fire in her head and held it. When the vapor curled away, she loosed the image in her mind and stepped in the wake of the mist. No acid touched her skin, and she lost her image, the mole hesitating only an instant before compensating with a new formation of ice. Gods, she had almost done it!

She jumped back, twisted, and made a new memory. Now! The cold mist touched her arm; she fired the commands at the mole. The vapor disappeared. Ice subsided beneath her bare feet. She danced toward one of the walls, where the mist curled up.

Another image in her head, held between the racing paws that skidded across her mind. Another image waiting for a space in the ice. When the gap came, she loosed the commands at the mole. Exultation filled her. The mole took them in. Her feet felt suddenly dry; the ice was gone from beneath her soles. She dared not open her eyes. What if Cekulu was watching? The thought split her concentration, and the mole recompensated. Burning crystals formed beneath her feet. She leapt to the side, twisted from the ice that curled down, and formed another memory. She must think . . .

The metaplas bonds . . . Floor or ceiling—which would be easier to re-form? Working on the walls would be futile—they would be well sealed. The room shook, and Tsia scrunched her eyes shut, refusing to look. If the mercs were attacking, why had Cekulu and Kern not stopped the dance? Because, she told herself, they would not care whether she danced till she dropped in the ice and burned her nerves to numbness. They needed her only until Yemene died, and if the mercs showed up, Cekulu would be worried about the Pulanese woman, not the guide. No one would be watching.

The mist swirled. Ice swayed. She forced her mind to focus. Cold, cool, let the fire burn out. Quiet down the cat feet. She chanted the images silently, like a prayer. Chill its flames and steal the warmth from its coals . . . Her fingers clenched the mole so tightly, its edges cut her hand. Smooth, cold, no fire, she thought. No flame, no heat. No heat, no coals.

This time the mole matched her thoughts exactly. Memory flowed. Images of watching the edge of the fireline on Black Pony Slough . . . Images where the heat was sapped by the air and the ground became bare of the light. Memories of a bonfire in the sand where a tide line swept the shore.

Rigidly, she held her images, ignoring the sudden burn across her ankles. It was no burn, she told herself. It was the salty touch of the sea on a demonfish sting. There was no sweat on her legs, just the cold wash of the ocean's steady waves. She stepped lightly, then danced to the side. The mists curled and stung on her skin, but it was just the salt, she imaged. Only the salt of the sea that was whipped up and dried on her legs by a winter wind. Cooler, slower, the vapors rose and hung in the air like someone's breath. Thinning, they barely caressed Tsia's skin. A breeze, she told herself, imaging the sand of the dunes near the shore. Just sand in the pores of her skin. No heat. No sweat. And then the chilly wave across her shoulders subsided into simple air. The floor below was smooth.

Air currents felt distant. The room rumbled. Now the cold bit at less of her nose, and Tsia dared to open her eyes. The ice spires were almost down to the floor. Small bumps and swells marked the walls and designs that swirled as she watched. Away from the touch of the chemical mist, Tsia's body began to lose its glow of sweat, the red, flushed patches where the fluids had burned beneath her skin.

She held the mole tightly, keeping one part of her mind in control. If it manipulated ice, she asked herself, could it manipulate other material? She had a full link to this mole, and this floor—it was merely metaplas. All commands, Cekulu had said. If the mole had not been programmed only for the ice compound, it could change metaplas, too.

A rumbling overhead caught her attention, and she looked swiftly up. The grumbling came again, and she glared at the floor, willing it to change. The mole did not respond. She got on her knees, slapping the mole against the floor and pressing there as she stared at the surface. She stretched somehow through her gate, letting herself feel the way her biofield reacted to the swirling designs. The layer of Cekulu's art—it was thin on the metaplas surface. If she could reach beyond that . . .

She clenched the mole and tried to think. And suddenly the pattern was so simple, she cursed herself. This room—it was like a terrain map. Like a surface scan of a slough. It was more detailed simply because it was small, but there was no difference between the chemical patterns in this floor and the water patterns on the coast. Eddies and races, tide pools and waves—these were the patterns of the floor. No wonder she had had trouble controlling it—it was more like water than fire.

She grinned, her teeth sharp and white. After almost forty years on the coast, water was one thing she understood. Patterns of waves and currents filled her mind, and the mole responded instantly. The floor swirled and became flat and still. The swirls retreated away from the spot in which she crouched. The building shook—how close were the mercs by now? There was no sound to tell—and then bare patches of metaplas became apparent beneath the ice white of the sculpture's mask.

Tsia could not control her exultation. She threw back her head and screamed her hard defiance. Deafeningly, a cougar answered, its voice like a woman in terror. The timbre of the cry cut through her joy, and, her eyes alight, she tamped down hard on the gate. Useless? She laughed out loud. Yes, a useless gate, but at least it shared her joy. Where was Cullen? Her family? The guild? They were gone; they thought her dead. Only the gate was there to fill her. Only the gate was real.

In her hands the mole ate into the metaplas like a dull knife pushing through cheese. Flooring surged and shifted, bulging up by her ankles. Tsia's eyes narrowed in a wild gleam as the metaplas thinned. Beside her the material became thin spires, like the ice before it. It could not simply move the material away, she realized—Cekulu had programmed it only for firelike shapes. She faltered in her concentration, and the spires locked, hard and unmoving. This time, when the trembling came, it was heavy in the floor that now dipped down by her feet. Was the merc force closer? Or, she thought with a sudden quickening of her breath, was the floor that thin? She clenched the mole even harder.

Metaplas flowed. And then, as the metal spires rose and twisted around her, the floor suddenly evaporated.

"What the hell are you doing!"

Crouched, Tsia whipped around. Behind her, Kern skidded into the room. Link wires hung loosely around his neck, and one hand held some sort of scanner. Shock reflected on his tanned, smooth face. The mole's work froze the instant she was distracted. The hole in the floor was only a ragged foot wide.

Kern stared. Coiled around Tsia were spires of blue-gray metaplas that stretched like strange vines suspended in air. Some part of his brain recognized that the effect was because of the metaplas. The flooring had a higher molecular density than the ice compound; its spires would be much thinner than the shapes of the twisted ice.

Tsia, surrounded by the twisted bars, clenched the mole more tightly and imaged furiously. The space below was dark and inviting.

"You—" Kern saw the dangerous gleam in Tsia's eyes. He turned and ran from the room.

Tsia refused to think. He would be back in a second. Another spire wound slowly out from the hole as it widened. Hurry . . . Think, damn you! she cursed herself. Kern staggered back into the

room as the floor shook again. The thin coils trembled. Tsia gripped one of them to steady her feet and refused to look. The hole was almost wide enough, and she was very slender. She could sense Kern racing forward. Her perception of his biofield was like another pair of eyes in back. He was now behind her—
  She lunged to her feet with a snarl.

Kern backpedaled. Tsia's face was like that of an animal. Her lips were bared, her eyes were hard and hungry, and her fingers stretched like claws. He gripped the n-rod tightly and stepped forward with resolution. Slowly, Tsia grinned. Kern's breath caught in his throat. The hole at Tsia's feet widened just a fraction. She hissed just once, then stepped through and fell into darkness.

16

She landed with a shock. Her ankles and knees gave way, tumbling her body forward into an instinctive roll. She fetched up hard against a wall and lay for an instant, half on her shoulders, half on one arm, the breath shocked from her lungs, until she squirmed down off her back and scrambled to her feet.

Above, Kern's face blocked the pool of light left on the floor. Then he was gone. Tsia crouched, her chest heaving. After the bright, white light of the ice room, she could not see even her hands in this gloom. She stared at the tiny pool of light. There was a noise in her head that threatened to deafen her, and it was not the cats. She shook herself twice before she recognized it for what it was.

"Daya," she whispered. "The link—"

She reached out. The link responded, letting her stretch along the lines of data to the nodes. Active, she thought—it was enabled once it was outside that room.

Active for how long?

Kern.

He was probably already tracing her through the artist ID. Slowly at first, still shocked by the dull noise that invaded her brain and drowned out the noise of the cats, Tsia snapped commands through the mole out to the node. First the mole, she thought, then the ID of the link itself would have to change. If she was to keep them, both of them would have to become hers alone. The mole, merely a tool, would be easy to acquire; it was already tuned to her mind. All she would have to do was deny it any outside access. The stolen artist link, she thought, would take more time to figure out. But with the mole, even if Kern shut her stolen link out of the node, she could still escape. She could use the mole to break through the doors between her and the outside air.

She thought frantically, her orders racing through the mole's access, while the cat feet raced through her brain, separating slowly from the noise of the node. She clenched the mole hard. She did not have to create a new access pattern for the tool—she had one ready. She had not spent all her time staring blindly out the window. It took only seconds to fix her new pattern in place for the mole. It locked in; the node lines shifted. Now, as long as her temple sockets were not plugged again, the mole would accept her images and hers alone, whether or not she was linked beyond it to the node.

Quickly, her mind fell back into its old command patterns. It was as if she had been gone from the node a bare week, not the year and more that she had known its absence. Some part of her mind registered the need to move, to put distance between her and Kern, who must be even now on his way to retrieve her. She accessed the room lights and turned them on, stifling the surge of elation that swept her with that simple act. She noted the apartment with that same divided attention, one eye locating the door to the bedroom at the same instant her feet began to move. Clothes—there were plenty here. They belonged to a man—a large one—but that was of little concern. The baggy trousers and tunic would disguise her further from Kern's seeking eyes. The link, however, was a different matter. Seconds only had passed, but Kern would know her borrowed ID dot. When he called up the building overlay in his head, he could tag her like a hot spring in a snowfield.

She pulled the trousers up and fastened them quickly. No boots in this room would fit her; she almost laughed when she jerked a pair from beneath the front room table and tossed them aside in the same motion. Though she was slender, she was not small, but even she would look like a child in this man's shoes. She grabbed a belt in spite of its length and knotted it quickly so that it hung down in front.

The link, her mind urged as she yanked a tunic over her head. How could she modify a dormant link? How could she take an ID dot from the artist guild and make it only her own? She halted, her hands in the act of stuffing the tunic into her pants. The art guild held power. It was one of the strongest guilds in the Federation. How much freedom, she thought suddenly, did that guild have for defining its links? The thought spun out, imaged into the node, and as the answer came back, she clenched the fabric at her waist so tightly that the silk threads almost tore.

The art guild had open links. Limited, yes, but open. Open to any field, any science, any human who was not a ghost. Tsia's hands clenched the fabric of her shirt. This dormant link—it gave her access to any field on Risthmus. She could access any guild for which she could pass the authorization tests. "Daya," she whispered. Ecologist codes, guide codes flashed in her head. She swallowed. She stuffed the rest of the tunic into her trousers, then imaged year-old codes to the net, followed by a request for colonization. The node automatically reoriented the link from the art guild to colonist status. Tsia's hand ran, trembling, through the short hair on her head. With that one act, she was out of the guild. But was she safe?

A line, she thought. She had to lay a line of ghosts. Only some kind of decoy in the node would protect the colonist link from being traced by Kern. She was at the outer door before she thought. In her memory—it had to be there, the way to set a tight line of ghosts. Daya, how long ago had Jak Volen taught her that? His tall, tanned image rose in her head, and she hesitated at the shimmering door. Jak ... She had been twenty-one when she had worked the traces with him for his classes. A good line, he said, was like the tracks of a reaver, twisted and knotted so that one could not tell if one was going forward on the trace or back on the line. False time dots, double images ... Jak had always laid a damn good line.

She could not think about him now, not till she was free of Noirelle, out of reach of Cekulu and Kern. It had been only a minute since she had dropped into the room; it felt, in the tension, like hours. Kern must be almost here.

She stumbled as the floor shook around her. What in all the hells of space were the mercs doing to the place? For the first time she wished that metaplas walls were not so acoustically silent. Then she imaged into the net and caught an overlay of the Noirelle floor plan. The storm of images that flowed was nearly blinding to one so long separated from the nodes. Tsia swayed, reached out, and caught the edge of the doorway just before she fell against the wall.

It was several seconds before she could focus her own thoughts to narrow the overlay to the building in which she stood. It took another second to orient herself so that she could open the door. Then, when she stepped out, she was almost bowled over by the crowd that swept through the halls.

"Look out—"

"Get out of the way—"

"—evacuating the north wing now," someone shouted down the hall. "Get out to the skimmer pads—"

"Watch that gravtrain—"

Bodies surged. A woman in dark clothing shoved urgently through the crush, sending a heavy man slamming into Tsia. The corner of his package dug into her ribs, and the man cursed violently, regaining his balance with difficulty. "Goddamn medtech," he snarled, yanking the package back from Tsia's side and breaking into an awkward run. Forcing herself to move, Tsia ran after him. His fleshy shoulders left a tiny wake in the crowd, into which she darted. She kept one eye on his back, the other on the floor plan in her head.

Around her, people rushed and cursed, bumped and swore at each other in their haste. Weapons were everywhere. Variable blades, flex swords, and rasers hung from every belt but hers. Half were in the hands of the art guild mercs, dark-clad figures who shouldered through the crowd and forced everyone to flinch. Tsia eyed their weapons warily. She could not get near one of their weapons without coming to their attention. But the other people in the hall were not as much aware ... At the first corridor crossway she deliberately crashed into a thin man, sending him against the opposite corner and yelling her apology at him as she slipped his flexor from his belt. He did not even notice.

She linked to the weapon and made it hers, wiping his ID dot from its cell and replacing it with her new colonist pattern. The line, her brain reminded her. She had to stretch the ghosts out to keep Kern—and the node, once the man notified it of her illegal access—off her back. First a terrain, she thought, the vision of the night desert rising in her mind. She imaged herself running across the pedpaths, running for the landing pad. The codes for a skimmer flight, the launch codes she had once known from the slough, filled her mind. She barely noticed the halls around her, realizing ironically as she imaged her ghosts that all the memorization of her route to Cekulu's rooms was wasted effort in this crush. She merely kept her eye on the fat man's back and focused instead on transferring her ghost dot along the node until it had been through so many launch codes and changed so many times that she herself lost count.

When the fat man ahead of her burst outside, she was right on his heels. Coming out of the hallway, through the jewellike field of the door, she was blinded by the sudden darkness of Noirelle. All around, biofields surged and choked her with the nearness of their persons. She almost barreled into the group of dark-clad men and women who raced inside. One of them knocked her against the wall. Another trod on her bare feet so that she cried out. Then they were gone, charging into the hall.

Tsia clung to the wall, where one of the curving ledges cut into her ribs. Cat feet in her head made her own feet itch, and the scent of monkeybrush and sage clogged her nose. The fat man was gone, lost in the sharp-edged shadows created by the rays of light from the sides of the buildings. Before her, the skimmers were backlit against the landing pad, and behind their sleek shapes seven, maybe eight transports squatted in the dark. The shadowed hulks of the heavy aircars made the narrow, wedge-shaped skimmers look like pencils. None of the laser tubes were visible on the skimmers; the pilots, she thought with satisfaction, had definitely been caught with their pants down. Even as Tsia watched, one of the transports lifted, crewless, and hovered for a silent, breath-catching instant before it shot erratically across the compound and crashed into one of the black buildings. Thin streams of smoke began to leak from the transport's splintered sides. Instantly, the streaks were sprayed by the covering crash foam. If there had been anyone inside, he would be solidly cocooned until the medtechs cut him free. Tsia's heart sank. If the Pulanese mercs were in control of the aircars, Tsia would be as unable to use the skimmers as any of the Noirelle crews.

She scurried along the building, looking for a clear path across the garden plazas beside the landing pad. She had to dodge the crews that threw themselves at the skimmers and hunched beneath them, weapons in hand, as they waited for an attack. Not one of them boarded the ships, and Tsia did not blame them. With the cracked shapes of two more skimmers caught on one of the arching black spans, there was little incentive to try flying a ship out from under the Pulanese mercs' control. But even as she watched, distorts sprang up around the skimmers and transports, and the lines of the ships blurred and disappeared beneath rippling waves of bent light. She could smell the displacement of air as the odor of melted metaplas was rechanneled around the light benders.

Those benders would not hide the compound hulls from the mercs for long, she thought dryly. She was right. As the last skimmer disappeared, a brilliant light flared across the ship's distort bubble. The fire line sizzled, following the bender field down to the ground, where it burned out, leaving the skimmer as unprotected as before. A second distort was already cutting out.

Tsia did not wait to see more. In the flickering, wavering light she began to run. The mole was still gripped in her hand; the flexor she had stolen was in the other. Her bare feet slapped hard against the metaplas walks. Ahead of her a woman hauled a man by the arm, taking his weight as he limped beside her. Another—a medtech—was kneeling over a body in the path, setting the skin pads on the open wounds and linking to the scanners in his hands. Tsia jumped the body, ignoring the medtech's curse as she put her shadow across his hands. The open space was crawling with figures. No one fought—instead, they were waiting, watching the fields around them crackle and discharge. Waiting for what? Tsia barely felt the question in her mind before she made it to the corner of the next building and hung, breathless, on its slick surface.

The dark heat of the night was stifling. The scent of sweat and fear, dust and ash, mixed in her nose with the animal smells of the stables. The sound of tearing metal screamed in her ears. A group of darkly dressed figures raced along the side of the building where she clung. She flinched back into the shadow. They passed her without a glance. She breathed again. What was she doing here? Where could she go? The skimmers were under merc control; the gates, under the guild's. If she got out of the complex, as Cekulu had said, there was no place for her to run where the sun would not bake her brains before the art guild caught her again. Unless she could find the Pulanese mercs . . . Surely they would take her with them—with Yemene to her city—when they escaped. She would have helped Yemene. The councilwoman would vouch for her.

But the other woman was in the building she had left, back across the landing area, back in Cekulu's rooms. "Goddamn rat-infested reaver dung." Tsia's curse was low and vehement as she realized her location. She whirled and started back across the plaza. Overhead, the shriek of tearing metaplas sounded suddenly, and she looked up to see the narrow bulk of a skimmer scrape along one of the black walkway spans. A surge of adrenaline hit her legs. She did not even see herself cross the open space. All she knew was that by the time the skimmer hit the ground, she was at the other door.

It shimmered open, and she fell inside, right into Kern's arms. His n-rod clattered against the far wall of the corridor. *"Heyta,"* he snarled, grabbing her wrist. The chains in his hand clipped around her left arm before she could even pull back. Something burst through her gate, and Tsia screamed and kicked him, dropping the mole in her fury. They staggered through a door that opened beside them. Tsia's left fist caught Kern on the jaw; the hook of her flexor tangled in the loose fetters he threw up to defend himself. They both crashed to the floor. He grabbed the hilt of her flexor just as she yanked it free of the chains. Catching the handle, he wrenched it out of her grasp and snapped the other metaplas clip around her right wrist as she went after the weapon. She became an animal, snarling and biting and kicking. Something hit her in the gut, the chest, the face. She did not notice: her hands were around Kern's neck. Something slammed into her legs, her knees. She ignored it. Her face was rigid in its wildness. She dug her fingers into Kern's neck until the choking sounds stopped and his mouth went slack. Then she leapt off, grabbing the flexor from the floor and hacking at her chains in a blind panic until they broke off close to the manacles.

The building shook again, and she dragged Kern to his knees, shaking him to his feet and forcing him through the door. She did not get two steps. The fighters who burst into the hall slammed her back against the wall. Tsia turned her face from them, willing them to ignore her. When they did, cursing and running on past, she looked after them in surprise. It was not until her eye caught the purple stripe along the sand-toned silk of her tunic that she realized why. Purple and sand . . . They thought she was a medtech.

More figures whipped through the corridor. Their biofields in Tsia's senses were like sharp visions compared to the dull physical sense of sight. She did not even hear their voices now. Instead, she dodged between them and grabbed at the tapered bronze disk of the mole. Snatching it up, she thrust it into her pocket. In the same motion she snapped up the n-rod from where it lay in the corner and slid it into one of her belt loops. Then she ducked under Kern's arm and drew it across her shoulder. He was her link to safety. She had to keep him alive. In seconds she had urged him to a stumbling run.

Through the length of the hall, across an intersection filled suddenly with running people. Through a door, a lift, another hall . . . She forced the short man through the building, murmuring in his ears that he was on his way to the medlabs. Every few feet she slammed her hand into the back of his head, keeping him groggy as she propelled him forward. The smell of sweat was bitter in her nose, and she breathed raggedly through her mouth.

No one paid attention to their pace; the faces of the people they passed were concerned about their own safety while the building shook beneath their feet. It seemed hours before she reached Cekulu's rooms, but even as her legs burned with the effort of pulling Kern's weight, Tsia knew that barely a minute had passed. How long since she had left the ice ring? Five minutes? More?

A thought struck her like a fist, and she became suddenly still. Leaning against the wall, Kern swayed. How, Tsia asked herself, had he known which direction she had gone? She had changed her link from artist to colonist, then set at least two dozen ghosts on her trail. Had he traced all those so quickly? All the lines, every single ghost she had thrown behind her ID dot?

She gripped his neck in her free hand, glaring at him with her ice-blue eyes. "How did you find me, Kern?" she whispered savagely. "How did you know where I was?"

The man's head rolled slackly. He groaned, and she throttled his neck harder. "Trace . . ." he managed. He chuckled, then choked with her grip. "*Heyta* . . . You will be a ghost forever." He coughed raggedly, and Tsia twisted her fingers into his shoulders until he cringed. "The first thing—we did—" Even with her forearm on his throat, he managed a vicious smile. "—was put—a trace in—your arm."

"You snake-tongued ball of slime," she whispered. She let go of his neck, and as he sank to his knees, she punched him with all her strength. His head cracked back. His body crumpled at her feet.

Raggedly, she ripped her sleeve back. She saw nothing. She ran her hand along her wrist, digging her fingers into the flesh. Nothing. Down into the forearm, toward the elbow. And there it was. A small, hard line, half an inch beneath the skin. She stared at the muscle, heedless of the body at her feet. Then she stooped and searched Kern for his raser. There was none on his body, and she cursed under her breath. She triggered the door and dragged Kern inside.

She ran through the rooms silently. Neither Yemene nor Cekulu was there. The tension caught in Tsia's throat, and she swallowed with difficulty. She could not deactivate the trace in her arm—she did not know how, nor did she have the time to figure it out. A raser—she could use a laser knife to cut it out. To hell with the scar—it would heal, and it was either the mark of the knife or the metal of the chains. Tsia tried not to flinch from the cold manacles around her wrists. There had to be some sort of raser in this apartment. The flexor would not flick into a short enough point to control a cut like this.

Tsia's jumbled thoughts stopped abruptly. If Kern had been looking for Tsia, what had Cekulu been doing? Was the artist on her way back here now? Had she already seen that Tsia's trace was back in the ice room suite?

Sudden panic made Tsia clumsy. In her haste to search the

worktables, she knocked sculptures, holocubes, everything off to the floor. She ripped through the drawers in the desk at the other end of the room, then stripped the drawers in the closets. No knife, no raser. Where, in all the hells of this place, were Cekulu's tools? She was a sculptor; she had to have rasers to work with—rasers and all the other sampling knives for melting her materials. Where would she keep them? Not here, in the large room, or in the prep room, either. Tsia glared at the open doors that led to the other areas. She caught her breath. The ice room—there had been a series of subtle cupboards in the foyer over there.

Tsia ran back through the suite. Catching Kern by his arms, she dragged his body into the side room where she had first showered. She left him there, his head on the scrub block, while she ran through the suite to the sculpture hall. The ice room door was open. She gave it barely a glance, her fingers already searching the thick walls for the catch to the hidden cupboards. The hole she had left in the ice room was like a sucker mouth, ragged and gaping in the white swirling floor and drawing her eyes like a magnet. The twists of metaplas that coiled up from the hole had turned white again, covered by the dynamic mask of the room as it crawled across the surfaces.

Time—how much time had passed? Her fingers were nervous, and her breath came in gasps. The hard line in her arm seemed like a pipe now that she knew it was there. Where was Cekulu?

The noise of the door shimmering open sounded in the outer room. Tsia whirled. Holding her breath, she backed along the wall, away from the open portal. She gripped the flex sword tightly.

"Through there." Cekulu's voice was hard and tight. "You know the way. Hurry up. I have no time for your reluctance."

Tsia edged around toward the door, reaching the wall just as Yemene was pushed into the room. Cekulu followed, her jaw tight and her violet eyes hard. With her other arm the artist dragged a white-robed figure that Tsia could not help but recognize. A cry of betrayal wrenched itself from her lips.

Cekulu spun, the grace of her movement spoiled by another shudder of the building. In her hands the twisted figure of Vashanna swayed in place. Yemene, one hand on her belly, backed against the wall for support.

"So." Cekulu watched her with narrowed eyes, the lines around them tightening. "You came back to me, after all."

"Vashanna," Tsia choked out, pointing at the silent, burn-blasted figure. "Why do you have her here?"

"Because I thought I no longer had you," the artist snarled. "I have the room, the mother, the babe, and the dancer. There is no more time to wait."

Tsia raised the flexor, snapping the bar into a narrow point. "The mercs are already here. They will stop you."

"Not before she burns."

"Then I will do it instead." Tsia glared at her, crouching instinctively lower.

"Don't even try to threaten me, *heyta*."

"I don't make threats." Tsia launched herself. Cekulu flung up her hands, and pain rippled through Tsia's body, causing her arms and legs to convulse. The sword dropped to the floor. Tsia screamed. She forced her body forward. She hit the artist in the chest, knocking the woman to the floor. Someone was shouting. Her hands found Cekulu's throat, and her fingers tore at the flesh. Red fluid coated her fingers; limp flesh clogged her nails. When Vashanna hauled her off the body, the artist's throat was torn and crushed, yet Tsia struggled wildly to tear it more.

"Tsia—" Vashanna wrenched at her arms. *"Nyeka,"* she snapped. "She is dead. You cannot hurt her anymore."

Tsia, her chest heaving, jerked free, then stumbled back. She held her fingers, red and stained, before her, as if she denied their act by her own distance. But when she stepped on the flexor, lying inactive on the floor, she grabbed it in her shaking hands and snapped it on.

Vashanna spoke in her ear, but she could not understand the words. She wiped at her face, staggering against the wall when the floor shuddered again. Yemene, one hand on her swollen belly, watched Tsia without expression. They stood so for a long moment. Then the door in the outer room blasted open. Three men and a woman burst inside.

"Yemene," one ordered curtly. The pregnant woman moved forward quickly, stumbling in her haste. One of the mercs slapped a disk on either side of Yemene's head. Another slung a dark jacket around her shoulders. The others covered Tsia and Vashanna with their weapons.

"Wait." Tsia took a step forward.

The mercs regarded her warningly. The two with weapons shifted to place themselves between her and the councilwoman.

"Wait—"

Taking Yemene with them, they backed out of the room. In an instant they had disappeared through the broken door.

"Wait!"

Vashanna caught Tsia's arm. "You think they will listen?" Her words stopped Tsia in midstride. "You think they will take you with them? You're a ghost. You don't even exist in their world."

Tsia stared after the group.

"A ghost, *heyta*," Vashanna repeated. "There is no place on this world you can go to escape that."

Tsia jerked free. "I have beaten the r-con. I have beaten the mole. I have a link of my own now. And I am neither ghost nor slave to stay with you. As soon as I get this trace out of my arm—"

Vashanna followed her as she backed away. "If you are no longer a ghost, can you fly a skimmer? Can you access the gates of the base? Can you call your family and tell them you are back from the dead before the art guild finds you again and puts you back in chains?" She grabbed Tsia's wrists and stared at the metal rings that clenched her flesh. "Look at you. You have already been caught once. How much longer till you are caught again?"

"I have a link."

"And what good does it do now that you have killed Cekulu?" Vashanna shook her viciously. "You were listed as dead, not kidnapped. The courts do not know you exist. Rights-conditioned or not, without a legal ID dot you aren't even sanctioned to protect yourself, let alone kill for your freedom. How will you face the art guild now? How will you face the guides?"

Tsia whispered, "What are you saying?"

"You know what they do to guides in your position?" Vashanna demanded harshly. "Are you ready to be stripped of your virus? To be blinded now that you have opened your gate?"

Fear caught at Tsia's breath. The cat feet in her skull skittered to a halt. To lose this—this second vision? To see Vashanna only as a visual presence and not as something more, some essence through her gate? To be blind to the life she could now feel like a wind in her mind? Daya, even a useless gate was still a gate. "They would—they could not do that . . ." she stammered.

"They will. Your link—your *stolen* link—is not even legal on the node. Your very existence now is a crime."

"You are just saying this to get me to stay, to be a willing slave like you."

"Would you rather be an unwilling slave? The pain of that is more intense."

"I don't care about pain," Tsia burst out. "I care about freedom, about the wind, the sea. The grass against my legs. The heron screaming in the sky. The cougar snarling on the heights."

Vashanna nodded to herself. "You are a slave to your virus."

"Damn you—"

"There are no restrictions on your life? No chains attached? You are as free now as you were before you were kidnapped?"

"Are your chains visible?" Tsia snapped back. "You wear no fetters around your wrists. You have a link to the node. If you stay here now, you stay because you want this life."

The other woman met her eyes steadily with a dull black gaze. "I no longer have a life," she answered flatly. "I chafe for no futile illusion."

Tsia wrenched away. "Freedom is futile?" she demanded harshly. "Life itself is to be discarded? Listen to yourself. You have been here so long that you have convinced yourself that slavery is good for you. You have a fantasy for a life. What better *heyta* than you, the one who puts her chains on willingly? And what better master than the one that you need? Cekulu here is as much a part of your life as your freedom was before."

Vashanna looked at her for a long moment. When she turned away, Tsia stepped forward.

"Vashanna," she pleaded hoarsely, "come with me. You were once a guide; they never took away your gate. Please . . ." She held out her hand, her blood-red fingers pleading to Vashanna's scar-hunched form. "We will find a way back. We can get to Ciordan, I promise, even if I have to give my life to do it."

"I," Vashanna said quietly, "am not worth that much."

Tsia stared at the other woman's back. The ridges that warped Vashanna's shoulders were pressed against the tightness of her cloth. "You are the one who sets your worth—not Cekulu, not me."

The woman did not look back. "Then I am worth nothing outside of Noirelle."

Tsia cursed violently. "You cannot throw away your worth simply because you no longer want it. Worth is not the same as will."

Vashanna turned to face Tsia again, her scarred expression calm. In the tortured flesh of her face the skin across her perfectly straight nose was white. "I have a life here. I serve a function. What I had before means nothing."

Tsia stared at her uncomprehendingly. Then, with a hopeless oath, she turned from Vashanna and dropped to Cekulu's form. Her eyes were blurred as she fumbled with the fasteners to Cekulu's pockets. Without a word, she wiped the tears raggedly. What did it matter now if she cried? Vashanna did not see them. Vashanna was a ghost.

There were raser tools in Cekulu's pockets, and Tsia, with her trembling hands, tore them free. It took only seconds to change their ID dots to her own. As she took each one from the artist, she thrust it into her own pants pockets. The last tool was a raserhook, and that one she kept out.

She held the raserhook out to Vashanna. "Help me," she pleaded softly.

Slowly Vashanna turned around. She glanced at the tool and shook her burn-scarred head. Her voice, when she spoke, was calm. "I cannot."

Tsia stared at her. "Daya damn you," she whispered finally.

Vashanna smiled then, a strange, twisted smile. Her brown eyes held no light. "She already did," she returned softly. She turned and walked from the room.

Tsia stared after her for a long minute. Then she imaged the generic med commands to her brain to dull the senses of her arm. Damn Vashanna. Damn her for staying here. She dashed the tears from her eyes with her sleeve. Damn her for her willing chains. And Daya damn herself, she thought, for leaving Vashanna to face them.

She gripped the raser tightly and held it over her forearm. Her left hand clenched a table leg. Her right hand trembled. She gritted her teeth. She pressed down. She could not help the cry that burst from her lips. In spite of the med commands, the burn of the raser was a bite of hell on her flesh. Blood, deep red blood, welled out beneath her thumb. She gripped the raser more tightly. Closing her eyes, she shoved the energy blade down. She sobbed as it sliced through her flesh. Then the hook tucked in below the trace and caught. Her left fist was white on the table leg. Her right hand shook so badly that she could do no more than wrench the raserhook out of her arm. It dragged the trace with it. And then the macabre, clawed cable was on the floor where she flung it.

Shaking, Tsia stared at the trace. Then she staggered to her feet and ripped a medpak from the e-panel in the front room. It took only seconds to tear a generic skin graft from the medpak and slap it crudely on her arm; the graft began to burn as it fused to her flesh and sealed the wound. The dead blood beneath the graft would have to stay; she had no time to clean it. It would delay the healing and make the scar more obvious, but Tsia had little choice. She looked again at the artist's body. Then she jammed the raserhook into her belt, grabbed the flex sword, and ran.

17

A minute and she was down the hall, turning into the corridor she had taken before. Another minute and she skidded to a halt at the intersection to the lift; rubble from the upper stories had crashed into the hall. There were hoarse voices: a med team worked frantically to free the few people still alive beneath it. Tsia turned and ran left—that was north, she was sure of it. The mercs already had Yemene; they could be gone from the building before Tsia ever found them again, and if that was true, there would be no hope of escape except on foot.

She brushed past a group of frightened people. Behind her, the building rumbled. Someone screamed. She did not look back. Lights flickered and went to emergency power, intermittent and shockingly bright after the indirect light of the regular halls. Ahead, a door shimmered open. Five mercs, shouting orders to each other, briefly packed the hall. Tsia threw herself into the shadow of another doorway, avoiding their brutal stride. One of them glanced at her cowering figure, then turned after the others.

Tsia waited scant seconds till they were out of sight. Another rumble shook the floor beneath her. Then the hall went dark. Lights flickered once, searing her eyes, then shut down again. There were yells and shouts to her left. Tsia held herself silent. She sensed no one beside her, no one anywhere near. Taking a breath, she peeled herself from the walls and ran, one hand trailing the wall and the other gripping the flexor with deathlike fierceness. She crossed an intersection cautiously, then bolted as she saw the lights flickering back on in sequence. A group of fast-moving men and women came into view, their boots slapping the metaplas floors harshly as they ran.

She was near the outer walls; she could see the floor plan as clearly in her mind as if she were staring at a map. There was only one more set of suites between her and the outside. The lights flickered toward her. The mercs jogged closer. Art guild men? Or Pulanese? No Pulanese-hired merc would be so calm . . . Tsia ducked into a room and locked the shimmering door behind her, killing its access before she took in the space she had entered. In her haste and bound by the darkness, she tripped over a loose chunk of metaplas, then a shadow whose dead arms clutched at her ankles.

"Daya!" she gasped. She kicked free in horror and slammed back against the wall. The lights were as dead as the man. She sucked air, then fled toward the back room of the suite. The node said there was another door there, which led to an outer corridor. She caught her breath at the portal, then waited tensely as it shimmered open. There was fighting in this hall, the flashes of the variable swords cutting through the intermittent dark. But there was also another door. She darted to it, snapping her access command to the link. It shimmered open, and she flung herself inside, her flex sword ready. The room was silent.

A window against the far wall let in the purple light of the sky, and Tsia padded warily now toward it. Her breath came shortly, and her eyes darted from one side of the shadowed room to the other. And then the door to her left burst open, and a dark figure exploded through the opening.

For an instant Tsia froze. The man had not seen her, but he would realize in a second that he was not alone. She did not wait. She flung herself on him as he whirled to lock the access for the shimmering door. Some sound, some whisper of cloth, must have warned him. The hulking figure spun, warding off her blow and forcing her to jump lightly aside and cut again.

His strength was tremendous. The blow he returned made her dive to avoid the full thrust of it. She snapped her flex sword into a longer blade and slashed back, her bare feet silent on the floor. The man hesitated, peering through the shifting light. It was enough. She stabbed fiercely into his shadow. He blocked and slammed his own flexor into a bar that turned her blow like a hammer. She danced down and away, slashing at his knees when he turned after her. He was between her and the window now, and the door was beginning to glow.

Tsia risked a desperate glance—were the controls holding?— and found herself flung clear back against one of the walls by the sheer speed and power of the merc's unexpected lunge. She gasped, her elbow numbed by the blow. She caught her flexor in her other hand, scarcely able to slash back at the shadow that drove in after her. That she even caught his jerkin was pure chance, but she knew by his grunt of surprise that she had cut him. She dove again. In the moonlight the silver flash of the manacles on her wrists followed the dull glint of her blade like a whisper. Behind the man, the door glowed further. She could not afford to be seen ... The window—by Daya, if she could just make it out the window ...

But the man was there before her, trapping her against the wall for the second time and forcing her to dodge. She slipped—and suddenly found her throat touched by an edge of steel that felt like ice. Her shoulder was crushed in the vise of his grip, her head thrust back to expose her soft white throat. She made no sound. She did not notice the pain of his grip. Her world had narrowed to that icily glaring blade.

"Damn you," she breathed, her green eyes glittering in the sparse light of night. "If I go, I will take you with me."

The man raised his arm fractionally as if to finish his aborted blow, and she tensed. The glow of the door filled the room with a sallow yellow light. The shouting she could hear outside was nothing compared to the slamming of her heart against her ribs. The dulled blue blade hung in her eyes for hours. Then the sword slammed down on the black wall next to her clenched hand instead.

She stared dumbly at the dark eyes that watched her back. She barely noticed the metaplas slivers that had spattered her arm. Not quite believing, she watched with eyes that were hunted and wary.

He dropped his sword to his side and stepped back. He made a subtle sign.

Tsia responded before she thought. It was the identification sign of the rights-conditioned that Jak had taught her so long ago in Ciordan. She froze, realizing what she had given away.

But the man grinned. *"Nyeka?"*

She pushed herself away from the wall. *"Kai-al nyeka,"* she said flatly.

"Not Korshani?"

The translation of his words came slowly to Tsia, and her eyes unfocused briefly as she relearned that link. "No," she snarled. "Ciordani."

"Come." His voice was so deep that it was almost a growl, and Tsia, after grabbing her sword from the floor, ran after the man to the window. She almost laughed at her shadow: The man's back was so broad that her wiry form was like a blade of grass next to a tree.

The merc deactivated the window and leaned out to look down. Far below, the gardens were a patchwork of light and dark. With a mutter, he began feeling the walls around the window. Frowning, Tsia tried to peer around him and see what was causing him to wait, but as she caught a glimpse of the distance they were above the ground, she shivered and stepped back. She would have taken her chances with the height and dived out. She would have died for her haste.

The door glowed behind them. Tsia looked over the merc's shoulder. There was a thin, curving ledge along the wall, part of the design of the building. The man glanced at the ledge, then at her. Tsia had no such hesitation. She tucked her flexor into her belt, then slung one leg over the windowsill and leaned out.

The silk of her tunic was torn, she realized, as her back touched his; the heat of his body burned briefly through her thoughts. But his callused hand steadied her with surprising gentleness. When she shifted out of the opening, her fingers sought the carved design of the wall naturally. Her fingertips fit easily into the tiny details of curving desert grass. As she pulled herself out, her bare feet felt sure on the ledge. She did not look at the stakes pointing up from far below.

The merc eased out beside her, his flex sword shaped like a bar and slung across his back in his harness. Moving ahead, Tsia brushed gritty sand carefully from the stone with her toes as she slid along the wall.

Beside her the man's harsh breath was an echo of her own. A tremor shook the walls. Below a sudden series of screams and shrieks rose up. Metal sheared somewhere, and the wind rose in a howl that almost drowned the cat feet in her head. Tsia laughed, a little wildly. She could swear she heard the ringing sound of horse hooves on the garden streets. The stables must have provided a good diversion.

She edged past another clump of carved stone grasses. Tall grass, running grass, fox grass, she identified absently with her fingers as the ledge curved down, following the side of the building as it dropped closer to the ground. Her hands found the delicate carved shape of monkeybrush, and with a murmur of surprise she gripped a water drain hidden within the stony shrub. The drain stretched up above to the roof; it faded into the wall below the ledge. Where she clung to it, it was round, like a tube; below, it curved smoothly into the wall so that even if her hands had found it, they could not have gripped it at all.

The building shook again, more violently, and Tsia waited till it subsided before swinging past the drain. Her breath was easy now in her throat. The sky, the desert—they were so close . . . She passed a window, then followed the ledge down again. They were not so far above the ground any longer; she could see the tips of the garden spikes clearly.

The next stretch of wall was long and was split only by the ledges that curved up and down along its face. Her bare feet clung, half-sticky, half-slippery, to the stone as her sweat mixed with the windblown sand. She could hear the merc's boots scraping behind her. A moment later Tsia swung around that tubelike drain and was close to the end of the staked ground below. Just a few more ledges down and she could risk a jump, even from this height; the safety of the outer garden beckoned.

She looked back. The merc, with his heavy frame and larger feet, was desperately careful to keep his balance on the stone. He followed two meters behind. The sheen of sweat defined harsh shadows on his face. Far below the razor-sharp spikes reached up. The man glanced up, gave Tsia a faint grin, and slid his foot along the ledge. A third rumble shook the building. The merc's fingers dug into the grass design. Tsia clutched the drain, her face buried in her arms as she clung to the sweat-slick walls.

The rumbling stopped. She heard the merc swear. She turned her head, and froze. He was hanging by his fingers alone. His boots had slipped from the slick, curved ledge until he dangled motionlessly, the wind stinging the sweat that ran across his straining arms. His fingers, as she watched in horror, were slipping out of the stone design. Below, the spikes of the garden fence were glinting. The merc glared at her once, a strange, fierce look. Then his fingers slid off the stone.

Tsia did not think. She locked her fingers around the drain and swung her body like a rope. Her feet caught him on the ribs. He grabbed her calves, and his fingers dug in, sliding down to her ankles, gripping like steel rods driving through her flesh. Then they both slammed into the wall like a handful of putty. Tsia stifled her gasp. Were her arms tearing out of their sockets? Were her knees stretched out of their joints? She slid down the drain until the manacles around her wrists were caught against the ledge. They jammed there, cutting into her twisted fists. The man whose weight would tear her hips off dangled carefully, unmoving again, thirty meters above the darkened spears.

Slowly, cautiously, he shifted, and Tsia clenched her lips to stifle her cry. It was a slow, tearing agony that pulled her ankles and knees apart. Her hands were slipping. Her fingers could not hold on. Now it was the metaplas bracelets that locked her to the drain. Something thick dripped onto her face, and she looked up to see blood welling from her skin where the manacles had cut through both palms.

Her shoulders were ripping; her elbows stretched even though she tried to keep them bent and tight; her fingers seemed to scream. In her head, the abyss of the biogate called, and Tsia cried out into it. She was answered by a surge of power that almost blinded her. For an instant she did not feel the merc's fingers in her flesh. Then the pain swept back.

Below her the merc's boots could get no purchase on the smooth, curved sides of the drain. Instead, he used his fingers to pull himself up her calves, grind into the joints of her knees, and dig into her hip like steel bores driving deep wells in soft sand. He stretched his hand to the ledge and tried to lever himself up. The sweat from his arms made him slip. Tsia could not help the cry that tore from her throat as one hand grabbed her legs again. The merc murmured something softly. It might have been apology or curse. Finally, reaching up to her wrist, his large hand closed over hers. He reached above to the drainpipe and then, his weight gone from her arms, went quickly hand over hand up the tube until he stood again on the ledge.

Tsia hung mutely. There was no more strength in her body. The manacles, locked between the drain and the ledge, trapped her hands behind the pipe while her arms refused to bend, the muscles overstretched and shaking. She was stuck like a fly in a web. She would die here, she thought, her face pressed against the cold stone. Even now the merc was moving to the side, moving away. As before, she would be left behind. Left to be squashed by a skimmer that was directed by this very merc's men. She would hang here like a piece of laundry and watch the ship come closer and closer, watch it waver through the air until its hull smashed her against the wall and she died, bare meters from freedom. She laughed. The low sound was more of a sob. Then a huge hand plucked her from the stone like a weed from thin soil, hauling her up by her arm so that she could cling to the pipe beside him. He guided her fingers to the carved grasses above, taking his hands away only when he was sure she had the strength to grip them. She twisted her head, looking at him mutely. His eyes were black and unreadable in the dark.

"Okay?" His voice was soft, the node translating the word automatically in her head.

She nodded slowly. She did not trust herself to speak. The merc slid his booted feet quickly along the ledge. His fingers left sweat on the stone. Behind him Tsia forced her hands to clench and relax, wiping the blood from her wrists on her tunic and drying her fingers so that she could go on.

Single figures crossed the plaza below, some running, some guiding grav platforms, some staggering along as if in shock. None of them looked up. The crackling noise of a broken skimmer seemed to come from one side of the building, then the other, and it took Tsia several seconds to realize that only the sound itself had changed. Now that they had traversed almost the entire side of the wall, the echoes bounced differently off the opposing structures, but the flashes from the disintegrating distorts and the fighters' variable swords showed that the action was still behind her.

With one eye on the figures below, Tsia slid along behind the merc, following him along the ledge until it curved into an intersection with another protruding ridge of stone. There, the two ledges made a wide X on the building, the two tails of the X continuing down another three or four meters before they curved back up. At the corner of the building the outer garden stretched across a small plaza. On the other side of the square the stone of the plaza gave way to a series of short structures bermed into the sand. Desert shrubs before them made fuzzy shadows on the ground; soft leaves did not reflect the light. Behind this living backdrop the outer wall rose, black and glistening in the pale light of the moons.

The two wall walkers edged farther along. Now only ten meters separated them from the soil. Tsia blinked, then rubbed her cheeks on her shoulders. The sweat that freely ran down the sides of her face was blinding her as much as the flashes of light that came from the other side of the building. Another rumble shook the stone. Grimly, Tsia and the merc crept on. Another meter down, and then there was soft earth below. Tsia did not wait for another tremor to lose her grip. As soon as she moved above the monkeybrush, she let go of the stone grass and fell lightly down to the sand. Above, the surprised grunt from the merc made her smile. With the grace of a cat she tucked, hit, rolled, and came to her feet unhurt.

A second later the heavy man landed beside her, his feet leaving dents in the sand that the wind would have to mend. Silently, Tsia crouched, her wary eyes taking in the plaza at a glance. Several people ran across from one of the bermed buildings; they paid no attention to the pair at the plaza.

Raking his gaze across the square, the merc motioned for Tsia to follow him. She nodded, and he pointed to the far wall. In an instant they were running. Past shrubs and dry desert flowers, past the pedpaths that split the plaza into its diamond-shaped designs. There were shouts, and Tsia's gait quickened, but the merc's did not, and as he jogged in front of her surely and steadily, she forced herself to hold to his pace by will alone. A group of men and women crossed their path behind them, and to their left a skimmer shuddered to the ground and covered itself with crash foam. The air smelled of dust and ash.

When they reached the bermed buildings, the merc halted so abruptly that Tsia almost collided with his back. Instantly, he drew her close into his shadow. Nervously, trembling against his side, she stood as silently as he. He smelled of warmth and sweat. He smelled of dirt and sand and something else . . . The cat feet skittered through Tsia's skull, and she writhed, unable to help the sensation. The merc felt the shudder through her arms and clenched her body tightly, pulling her against him so that she was almost smothered in the thickness of his chest. The dark, the night, the chill that filled the air—Tsia felt wild and nearly free. It was all she could do to stand within his arms until the tremor passed.

Beside her the merc tensed. She struggled to lift her head, but the strength of his arms was undeniable. Two men ran past them, followed by another thin figure. A moment passed. Then the merc let her go. She stepped back. He touched her arm, and as she hesitated, he grasped her again and dragged her with him along the side of the building.

She did not think to struggle. North, she thought incoherently. North to the wall, to the mountains, to home. She began to run, and he released her again, listening to the nearly silent pad of her footsteps as she chased him like a shadow. Seconds later he made a short, chopping motion, and she brought up short, back peddling in her haste. He felt along the wall and touched something. A door panel, hidden in the glistening blackness, opened with a hum. Tsia was through and running almost before his heels passed the threshold.

Inside the low, bermed structure the hallway was silent and dark. The merc did not hesitate. He ran without sound, unerringly slowing and turning as he came to the intersections he wanted. Behind him Tsia's hyperesthetic senses focused on his biofield until it felt lit and brilliant. She could feel his presence, hear his breathing, and smell the tang of his flex sword. She felt the second presence just as the merc grunted. He did something, and a body fell with a faint thud. And then they were both fighting, the shapes coming at them steadily from the absence of light.

Tsia made a strange animal sound. Then her flexor found her hand, and she whipped into a crouch, the flash of a variable blade closing above her head. She stabbed low, felt the body jerk, and ripped the tip of her blade free. Her senses were sharp and clear; the merc was a meter behind her; there were others—four? Perhaps five or six. The body in front of her lost its life, and she stumbled over it, unable to read death and losing the sense of its presence. Something slammed into her ribs, and she crumpled. A foot stepped on her calf. She snapped the flexor into a rounded hook and swung wildly as she rolled. She caught two ankles and jerked. The woman fell with a cry.

Tsia flicked her wrist and swung the sword as a stick back across. She caught the woman on the temple. Then she rolled and stabbed indiscriminately at the shapes that came out of the dark. She slammed into someone's hip, and as that man lost his footing, his variable sword flashed past Tsia's face. She rammed her stick into the man's guts, ignoring his stunned gasp. She dropped him.

The merc she had followed was gone, and in the dark Tsia panicked. She scrambled to her feet. Where? Daya—there, to her right. She could hear the harsh breathing, feel the desperate thrumming of feet against the floor. She flung herself toward the sounds. In her hands the flexor shortened to become a bar, and she slammed it down onto the head of a man whose scent was dry and sharp with fear. His grip on the merc loosened; the merc grunted in surprise. Then he stepped back and dropped the unconscious man to the floor. Tsia staggered back. Her breath was ragged again. The merc was still, listening.

Then, satisfied, he said softly, "*Nyeka*, come."

They ran.

It took mere seconds to traverse the rest of the building. When they reached the other side, the merc hesitated only an instant at the outer door. It triggered, Tsia fled through, and the merc turned and burned out the controls with a pad he held in his hand. Tsia ran a meter, halted, and, aware suddenly of the merc's absence, turned and watched with panicked impatience. The outer wall was in sight, just across that stretch of sand. Come on, she screamed at him silently. The man glanced at her and grinned. In the moonlight his teeth were white and strong. When he straightened, he strode confidently toward the outer wall. Tsia fairly danced beside him, her impatience held back only by the man's soft murmur. "A minute, *nyeka*, nothing more."

She jerked at every sound, half whirled at the scream of metaplas that struck across the square. The merc paid no attention. One hand was on his flex sword; his other hand brought from one of his pockets a small metal disk, which he thrust at Tsia. "Link to it," he said shortly. "Make it yours."

What was it? A tool? A trace jammer? A vision of Hesse rose in her mind, an image of the temple plugs. She stared at the thing in his hand, unable to take it.

The merc frowned. *"Feyl hukha,"* he said somewhat sharply.

"Hurry," she translated. Still she hesitated. With an impatient sound, the man jammed his flex sword in his belt and grabbed her arm. She jerked back. "No!"

He ripped the front neck of her tunic and hauled her against him to quiet her struggles. Panicked, Tsia wrenched at his arms, forgetting the skills Jak had taught her as the merc thrust his hand inside her shirt.

"No . . ." she screamed. His hands were like steel. And then the disk was hard against the base of her neck, its heat like a tiny fire on her skin. She froze.

"Avya, heye," he soothed. *"Seva, nyeka."*

Avya—Seva—loved one? Safety? Tsia stood panting, her hands locked around the merc's thick wrists. His hand pressed the disk to her flesh, and she could feel it in her link now, picking up her heartbeat, catching up her breathing.

The merc nodded. "Feel it. Link to it. It will let you pass the outer gate."

His words finally translated over her panic. Link to it . . . Outer gate . . . Trembling, she reached through her temple jack to the disk and found its access just as she had done before with the mole. Make it hers . . . There was no ID dot in the link of the merc's disk—it was blank. She hesitated, blocking its generic signals from her mind, then gave it her own created dot. While the merc watched her, his hands relentless as he pressed it against her neck, it hummed once, then fell silent. The merc loosened his grip. As the disk fell away from her chest, he caught it and handed it to her.

"Keep it close, *nyeka.*"

She held it without moving.

The merc still watched her closely. "Come," he commanded. His black gaze was appraising, weighing, and Tsia felt her eyes narrow and her lips pull back from her teeth.

She did not move.

"Heyta or *nyeka?"* His words were a derisive challenge.

She stared at him for an instant, balanced on the balls of her feet. She rocked slightly with the wind, her close-cropped hair defining the tight lines of her face. "I am a guide," she returned harshly. "Not a *heyta*. I am *kai-al nyeka*." She shoved the dark metal disk into the pocket that held her mole. Her eyes were an icy blue.

He nodded curtly. "Then come."

He broke away from the shadows of the black building and ran toward the outer wall. The open space between the building and the wall was bare of everything but the design of the diamond lines that cut across the stone. Crossing and shearing away, the lines shone dully beneath the two moons. Something tingled in her skin, and Tsia stared at the lines. She could swear that they shifted, that a light pulse went through the pattern like a hawk on the wing. The merc glanced back. *"Feyl,"* he snapped.

And then the ground around him burst into light. Short lasers lanced up from the lines in the stone. They bent toward the merc, touched his silhouette, and curved away. Tsia almost halted.

"Run," he snarled.

Light shot up in front of her, and Tsia could not stop. She thought she screamed like a cat as she fell through the lasers, but her ears registered no sound. Then she was racing faster, flinching from the lasers, throwing herself through the lines of light. Beams cut the air around her body. Burnt air clogged her nose. Ahead, the merc threw himself across another fire line, and his shadow was lit like a demon in the flames. A diamond shot up before her, and she gasped, but the lasers curved away from her body as if she were repugnant to them. She ran, blinded by the light, guided only by the sense of the merc before her. And then those hands, those massive hands, grabbed her by her waist and one leg and, ignoring her cry of pain, threw her up in the air.

She caught the edge of the wall by chance. Her hands slid along the slick, tingling energy net until she kicked her left leg up over the edge and hung on the top, gasping for breath. She dragged herself over, then crouched, staring at the sky, the plains of the desert that stretched out to the north. She had no eyes for the ground immediately below. There were no structures between her and the northern horizon, no black walls, no spans of darkened stone. Just open sky and sand.

Behind her the merc's boots scrabbled briefly, quietly, and then his hand slapped the top of the wall. He fairly lunged over with momentum. He did not wait for Tsia. Instead, he plunged on to the other side, ignoring the energy net that hugged the top and outer side of the walls. With a grunt, he landed in the sand. Tsia dragged her gaze from the mountains and forced herself from her statue stance. Then, with a wild cry, she leapt like a cougar jumping down from a cliff and dropped beside the merc.

He grinned at her and, breaking into a run, motioned for her to follow him. "Stay close," he said urgently. "Follow exactly."

A laser shot out from the wall, arcing toward, then over his shoulders. The merc did not falter. Tsia choked off her breath as the next one felt out her figure. The heat of its passing singed the cloth of her tunic. Her skin broke out in a thick sweat. She could smell the burn in the air. The merc dodged suddenly farther from the wall, and Tsia followed. The ground erupted just as she stepped from the bulge, and Tsia cried out, a sound more like a yowl than a startled scream. The merc reached back and yanked her away. Still, the vibration shook her bones.

"Breaker," the merc muttered in her ear as he dragged her along.

They ran, dodged, and stopped finally where the short beams of light could no longer reach them. Tsia crouched beside the merc and fingered the tiny disk he had given her. It had redirected the lasers, as if she were a desert animal, not a human target. The merc grunted softly, and Tsia followed his gaze to a clump of dark shadows that smelled of human scent. Warily, the man crept forward.

Of a sudden, he took a quick step and clubbed down with the blunt tip of his flex sword. The man he left behind did not even groan. The merc looked back. *"Chukjha sha hia,"* he whispered, pushing her down against the sand.

Wait here silently. She crouched where he had put her, ignoring the translation from the node. The sense of his tension was enough to keep her quiet.

Beside her, the corpse stank of sweat. She tried not to breathe, tried to keep the thickness of the scent from her lungs. Her free hand drove itself into the sand, using the grit to clean the feel of the body from her flesh where she touched it.

She watched tensely as the merc dodged forward several meters, only to stop between two clumps of brush where a second man lay dying. She knew he was weak; she could feel his life as a thin struggle, leaching her thoughts through her gate.

The merc crouched and murmured something, to which the writhing figure replied in a groan. Then the writhing slowly stopped. The merc placed his hand on the man's chest and pressed. Tsia's hand unconsciously groped to her throat. But the merc kept his hand on the shivering chest until the body lay still. When he rose, he touched the man's forehead and lips with two fingers, then stripped a disk like hers from the dead man's chest. He gestured for Tsia to join him. She hesitated, then forced herself to run across. The merc yanked the boots from the man, then pulled the socks from his legs. He thrust them at Tsia. Then he took a tiny tube from his harness, pointed it at the body, and released a stud. A dark cloud sought out the flesh of the body, and the dead man began to hiss and burn. No smoke arose from the ashes. A few seconds later, when it was done, there was only a fading stain on the sand.

Swallowing her nausea, Tsia sat abruptly on the sand, sliding the warm, sweaty socks over her feet. Gritty and thick with blood, they covered her smooth skin like the scales of a dead snake. She could not stop her shuddering. Then the merc grasped her shoulder with one hand, and the heat of his grip eased the shivers until she could put on the boots. The instant the second boot was up her calf, the merc hauled her to her feet.

"This way," he breathed.

But Tsia hesitated, suddenly aware of an animal scent. An energy, not like that of the cats. "Horses?" she whispered, startled.

"Yes. Hurry." The merc pulled her after him toward the three animals that stood by nervously, their hooves stamping the ground and their ears twitching against the sky.

Then his whisper cut off abruptly. The hand that shoved Tsia back as quickly as it had dragged forward was not gentle, and she staggered in midstride to fall to one knee against a rock. In front of them, swinging up on the horses, three figures kicked the beasts into a charge. The merc leaped forward. Tsia lunged back to her feet and dove after him.

These could not be his men—these were art guild mercs! Tsia skidded in the sand and threw herself to the side. The hooves of the first horse barely missed her. Snorting and plunging, the creature whirled and gathered itself to leap forward again. Ahead of Tsia, the merc leapt at the second rider and hung, one hand on the saddle horn. His flex sword hacked at the rider's legs and waist. Wrenching back, cursing viciously, the rider frantically warded off his blows. The third rider burst out of the darkness and wheeled, slamming his mount into the merc's body.

The first rider lunged back. Tsia tore her eyes away from the downed merc. She felt rather than saw the horse lean into its stride. Her heart jammed in her throat. Instantly, she whipped her weapon into a hooked stick and threw herself at the first rider's legs. The man chopped down as if he were holding an ax. His blade missed. Tsia's did not. She caught the hook in the man's boot top and jerked him so hard that he lost his seat and then his grip. She barely had time to flick her flexor back to a stick, disengaging it from his boot top as she fell back. She hit the ground hard.

The spotted bay bucked briefly, then sidestepped. In a flash, Tsia rolled back to her feet. Before her, the soldier regained his seat and hauled the beast around, spurring the mare to run her down. She leapt up, stumbled slightly, and slashed again, this time cutting the cinch of the horse's saddle.

The man yelled as the saddle slid back and down. Grasping instinctively at the leather, he fell off behind the bay's haunch and hit the sand with a thick *whumph*. As his horse leapt away from the tangle, Tsia caught its mane and swung up, her leg sliding easily over its warm, sweaty back. Her slight weight was nothing to the beast. It snorted and pranced, throwing its head high and rearing up at her unfamiliar touch.

"Down," she yelled, clenching instinctively with her knees. She leaned precariously forward to snatch a rein. Frantically, she pulled the horse in a tight left circle, sliding forward to reach for the other line while the creature tossed its head and fought the tiny signals of the bit on the sides of its mouth. "Easy," she cried urgently. "Whoa." The right rein was just beyond her reach. She kicked the bay to shift it to the side just as the downed man, chasing her, cut at the beast. The bay snorted. In a panic, it sidestepped, only to be hauled back around by the left rein. The man's flex sword, shaped as a double spike, caught Tsia on her boot-protected calf and plunged into her thigh. She jerked back with a hoarse cry. The spike slid free. Tsia kicked out.

Too late, the man threw up his arm to ward her off. The mare, wheeling in a panic, knocked him down. Tsia hauled the creature around again. The man below scrambled away, then flicked his flexor into a whip-tailed point. In the dark the point was like a barb-winged bat aimed at her throat. Tsia could only duck and throw up her own flexor in a flat, clublike shape. The cold metaplas edge of the dart snapped on her club, then slid across her arm. For an instant the jagged dart caught on her manacle. With a yell of triumph, the man yanked. Tsia jerked her wrist free, but it was too late. She slid off the plunging mount in a twisting fall, throwing herself back from the bay's hooves as she landed.

The rein burned through her hands, but she did not let it go. As the bay lunged backward, she clenched the rein in one hand, parrying the man's straight slash desperately. Her sword came up short. The man, realizing her range, grinned. Frantically, Tsia twisted and flicked her wrist in a single movement. Her blade became a tiny, narrow spike, spinning its thin length forward. It drove itself into his chest. The man's black eyes stared at her in shock. Slowly, inexorably, while the horse dragged Tsia backward, her flexor shrank out of his chest and compressed back to a stick. The man fell to his knees. His black, accusing eyes followed her face. His mouth moved soundlessly. And then he fell facedown in the soil.

Tsia watched him fall, then turned and grabbed up the other rein of the horse. She flung herself onto its back and clenched it with trembling knees. She could not help crying out again as the puncture in her thigh was compressed by her muscles. Fresh blood washed down her leg, and her right hand gripped her thigh hard, the hilt of her flexor pressed against the wound to help stop the blood. Behind her, the merc was now mounted on one of the horses, but his arms were locked in a struggle with the last dark rider. Both men leaned away from their horses, the tall beasts lunging and slamming together as their riders forced them to close. The man on the roan had a raser; the merc on the black held a spike. Each one held the other's weapon from his own throat. With every motion of their horses, their bodies shifted.

Tsia did not think. Instead, she whirled and charged. The merc saw her coming and shoved suddenly against the other man. Startled, the other rider pulled the merc forward, half out of his saddle. Tsia's flexor, slippery in her grasp, slammed into the dark rider's kidneys as she passed. In sudden, excruciating pain, the man arched back. He did not fall; his hands were still wrapped around the merc's wrists. The mercenary could not shake him free. The dark man grinned as he dragged the merc farther out of the black's saddle. Beneath the merc's body, the two horses' plunging, nervous hooves churned the weakened soil. Tsia whirled and forced the spotted bay back. The man's roan sidestepped just as she charged, and her mare jammed against its shoulders. It was enough. The merc moved. The dark rider coughed. And then the man's body let go of the mercenary's wrists and dropped slowly beneath the horses' stamping hooves.

Tsia let the bay lunge away. The mare reared, and with a stifled cry at the pain, Tsia gripped hard with her knees to keep from sliding off its sweat-slick back. It plunged down, then tried to buck, but she had the reins hard. It could not get its head down far enough to dump her. "Easy," she kept soothing. "It's all right now. You are fine. Easy, girl. Down." The horse snorted, then sidestepped again, and it was all she could do to calm it. Behind her, the merc had his own troubles. The black he rode was jittery, and although he had caught the reins of the roan, the roan pulled at him in a panic. It was a minute before he calmed them enough to speak to Tsia.

Then, wiping his hands on his leggings, he hauled both beasts around. "From now on out don't use your link," he commanded harshly. "Not for anything. All our lives depend on it." Bracing one leg against the saddle horn, he leaned down and nabbed the water bags from the tangled gear left on the sand. A moment later he yanked another hisser tube from behind his own saddle and aimed it at the mess. The clump of leather and metaplas sizzled and melted into another shapeless shadow, then dissolved into the sand.

"Now go," he snapped. "That way."

She needed no other urging. The bay, still nervous, lunged into a gallop, and Tsia leaned into the mare, the hairs whipping her face. Free . . . Her gate swallowed her fear and sucked at her trembling eagerness. Cat feet in her mind seemed to race beside the horse. She was free . . .

Behind her the merc pulled the roan into a canter with the black. With lengthening strides, the two horses caught up with her leaning, eager form. Then the black, the roan, and the spotted bay raced down, away from the road, toward the hills of the desert beyond.

18

ᥫᩣᥩᩣ

The trail they took from the stronghold cut first through rocky sand, then between the dry grass dunes. Grass gave way to rock; stone gave way to rising, ragged heights. Dark canyons appeared out of nowhere and disappeared again into the cold air of the night. The merc, when she looked at him without stretching through her biogate, seemed to fade into the shadows of first one cliff and then another.

North they traveled. Without the overlay of a map in her mind's eye, Tsia could not tell which hidden canyons ended sharply in the rocks and which ran all the way through. But she did not read the node for the map. Overlay access was like any other access to the node; it would provide a trace that the art guild could follow. Following the merc quietly, Tsia relied instead on the memory of the rocky dunes she had gotten out of her view from Noirelle. The sense of the cats guided her, too; it was stronger now than it had been in the black, glistening city. When she stretched, she could almost feel the familiar paths that the felines took over the rocks. The only disadvantage of that, she realized as they turned again from a trail she sensed through the gate, was that the horses could not follow the cats.

The horses' hooves thudded dully; dust clung to their feet. In the absence of Orpheus, the larger moon, the constellations shone brilliantly across the cold waves of land. The overcast sky had burned off that afternoon; looking north, Tsia could no longer feel the heaviness of the pending storm except as a distant breath of pressure. Only the dry air of Korshan lifted from the ground. No dew fell on the tufts of fox grass that stood brittle guard over rounded digger mounds. Leaning down from the horse for a moment, Tsia tasted only the grit that rose and dusted the trail ahead of them, then wiped their tracks behind.

A flock of bats passed overhead, screaming at the riders. A second flock circled once around the pair, then swept after the others. Tsia stretched a second time through her gate and felt the life of the cloud like a swarm of insects in her head. For a moment she was puzzled. But the link to her biogate had grown with every month she had spent in Noirelle. The presence of people had been sharp when they were near her; why not now the presence of animals? Perhaps, she thought slowly, even if her link to the cats was useless in itself, she had learned to reach beyond it to other forms of life.

Her lips curled back from her teeth at the thought. If the guides found out she had used the gate at all, what would be her fate? She was hardly likely to find out, she told herself bitterly. She had broken contract when she was kidnapped. She had stolen a link from another guild. She was responsible for the torture of a child. And she had killed—not once but seven, no, eight times. If she returned to the guides, she could easily end up as she had been in Noirelle: in chains, a ghost, a *heyta*.

Daya help her if Vashanna was right. If she could be punished for Cekulu's death, she could be punished, then, for Hesse's. And the traders she had killed who had been with him. And the use of her gate? Daya, but even as she had cursed it, she had used the power of the cats to help her fight, to help her flee when she escaped with the merc. What if the guides condemned that, too, as a breach of the Landing Pact? What if they stripped her from the guild? Killed the virus in her body? Closed her gate forever?

Cat feet padded across her thoughts, and she shivered with a cold fear that turned into a viciously sharp bout of the shakes. She clenched her hands on the reins. She had told Yemene that she was not sick, but was that really true? She had begun to realize that these tremors came when the gate called strongly, when she opened her thoughts to the sense of the cats.

Gods, she thought in sudden dread, what if she had caught some sort of fever? Daya would not be so cruel. To give her freedom only to let her die of an ague? There were many diseases on colonized worlds . . . Tsia felt the watchful eyes of a sandcat tracking her horse from a crevice between two stones, and her stomach briefly surged. She quelled the nausea and felt faintly relieved. As the tremors had begun to grow, the nausea had started to lessen, so that now she felt as if she could almost enjoy the sense of the felines. Abruptly, she clamped her lips shut, as if that would stop her thought from being heard. To enjoy, to explore a gate with the cats? With the Landing Pact in place? That was a dangerous idea.

She tried to close her gate, staring into the dark for the crouching shape of the sandcat that watched them pass. No, she told it silently, wondering if it would read her determination. This horse is mine, not yours.

Then she relaxed. It was curious, not hungry, she realized. She peered again at the stone cliff. Although she knew the feline was there, she could see nothing with her eyes. And, she acknowledged, she was afraid to stretch farther to feel it more through her gate. Its presence was strong and focused. She tried to feel it without the tawny sense of powerful animal freedom that raced like shadows across her brain, but the claws in her head seemed to scratch and tickle at the insides of her eyes. When the second shiver hit her, Tsia felt as if she should leap from the roan and run after the cat instead of the merc.

If this was a crippled gate, she thought with a sudden feral grin, Daya help the other guides!

Her slender fingers curled around the reins like claws, and she licked her lips. She was a stubborn woman, not a brave one. Did she have the guts to face the judgment of the guild? Or, she thought harshly as the sandcat stretched and brought tension to her own muscles, would she hide from the guild and be a slave to her dreams for the rest of her life?

"Slavery," she spit beneath her breath. "Has this gate given me nothing else?"

Pulling her jacket close, she rubbed a hand on her opposite shoulder. The jacket—a blunter—had been stored in the saddlebags of the horse she now rode. It was light but warm, and its dull fabric gave her protection from both the wind and the sensors of the art guild nodies. Unable to use the node translations, she could not ask the merc why he was not worried about the node sensors—or the skimmers that crossed the sky above them. But he ignored the skimmers and the threat of the node, and Tsia, trusting him, did also.

The small blunter disk he had given her was sealed in the outer pocket on her chest, outside the blunter's fabric shield. In Noirelle, the blunter disk had warped the plaza beams away from her body; perhaps, she speculated tiredly, it did the same here with the sensors. "Link to it," he had said back there. "Make it your own." She had done that, as she had done with the mole she still kept in her trousers. So was the mole a tool or a slave? she asked herself facetiously. Ah, she was too tired to be thinking.

Trying to ignore the shivers that still crossed her skin, she forced the manacles on her wrists up inside the blunter's sleeves. She did not mind the clothes or jacket, but the boots on her feet made her cringe. The desert night was cold, but it was not that which made her flesh crawl with goose bumps. It was the dead man's socks that gave her chills.

She shifted in the saddle and caught her breath at the shaft of pain that shot abruptly through her right leg. Uncomfortably, carefully, she shifted back to her original position. Those first two kilometers, before she had changed from the bareback bay to the saddled roan, had been the worst. Beneath the skin graft she had slapped on her forearm in Noirelle, the cut where she removed the trace had not stopped stinging. Now it pulsed sharply as she handled the reins. At least that was a minor irritation. Within minutes of mounting up her legs had begun to ache from the strain of gripping the creature's sides.

It had not been easy to force her wounded thigh to press into the horse's flanks; the bruise on her calf and the puncture wound in her quad made the limb almost immobile. Every time she used knee pressure instead of the reins to turn the horse, she hissed her breath out between clenched teeth. At least, she thought grimly, the wound was on the outside of her leg. With the finger marks left from the merc's hands where he had used her as a ladder, her legs were probably more colorful now than an angry man's language. No more so, though, than her trousers. The pants were sturdy but not a weatherweave. By the time she had switched mounts, her pants had been completely grimed with the red-brown dirt from the bay. And, she thought as she blew her breath out forcefully, the bay's gift of dirt was matched only by the stink of sweat that was not hers.

The dirt and sweat of the roan gelding she now rode were not much different from the dirt and sweat of the mare, but at least the saddle made the ride more comfortable. Like a malleable soft instead of a rigid chair, all it had to do was feel her weight and seat to shape itself into the form she needed. Still, if her thigh and calf had not been too sore to stand her weight, she would have stood up in the stirrups.

Ahead of her, mindless of the dry night's chill, the merc rode without inviting her to speak. She kept his silence unquestioningly. Without the node's translation, she would understand only part of what he said, anyway. He spoke Korshani roughly, and the other language he preferred was similar enough to tease her ears but full of images so that half the words she thought she understood made no sense. They could have spoken Standard if they were linked, but there was no way to communicate the images and chorded music of Standard with simple human hands and tongues.

She stared absently at the figure riding ahead. In the night she could feel him as well as if she were riding behind him in his saddle and running her hands over his hard-muscled arms. She could sense the horses beneath the two of them like mountains of pulsing, steady life. She could hear the night cats pacing the rocks around them, the rustling snakes burrowed in the sand . . .

She rubbed her eyes, and the manacle scraped her cheek. So what if she had escaped from the art guild, from Cekulu, from Kern? What place did she have here, with this man—this merc? He must know her link was stolen. When he found out how she had gotten it . . . That she had killed in cold blood . . . Tsia shivered. The mercs had a righteous guild. Sanctioned violence, bought with credit or trade or the justice of the courts. A just cause—what had Jak said three years ago?—when billed to the courts, was always worthy of a fight; all other causes, he had said, were lost.

She shut Jak out of her thoughts and followed the merc with her lips compressed against the throbbing of her body. Each breath brought an ache she was only now getting used to; she knew her ribs were bruised. Each cut on her arms had welled and scabbed, and the scabs broke each time she moved. She had wrapped her thigh with cloth from her saddlebag, but she had ignored her wrists in the mercenary's haste. Now she wished she had not been so careless. With the wind rising in gusts from the sand, the grit had buried itself in the bloody marks left by her manacles. Every time the metaplas rings rubbed against her skin, she clenched her teeth. She could not even image the med commands from the node. No traces, he had said. No links. No med commands, no maps, no translation lines, no nothing.

Ahead, the merc drew up, listening, and Tsia pulled her mount to a stop. Why, she wondered dully, were they riding these beasts in the first place? Why not take a skimmer out of Noirelle? If the merc could mask a human presence from the node, then surely he could mask a ship?

If she had had her overlay on, she and the merc would have shown up clearly as dots on the desert sand. The horses would have been the faint green of a biological; the two humans would have been in orange. The color codes of the guides . . .

Wind chapped her eyes, and feeling the sudden tightness on her cheeks, Tsia cursed herself violently. Daya damn her maundering. Of what earthly use was crying? She was thirty-nine. If she was to cry, let it at least be for something important: the death she had left behind her, the loss of her home, the cry of the cat on the stone . . . Not because she remembered a color code she had once had the right to use.

At the mercenary's gesture she dismounted sharply and moved forward to the roan's nose just before the gust of wind-sharpened sand momentarily obscured the night. She shielded her head behind her arm. The ragged cloth she held over the roan's restless, snorting muzzle warmed with the creature's breath.

"It's all right," she murmured, holding its head against her chest where she could protect its eyes and nose. "Easy, boy. It will be gone in a minute."

They had ridden for close to five hours. Not once had the merc hesitated in choosing his canyons and circling the towering dunes. Tsia had assumed that his overlay was protected, that it had a path laid out, just as the trails on the coast used to show up as lines in her head. The thought that he was using no map did not occur to her.

Reflectively, Tsia watched him wipe out his horse's nostrils. His hulking shadow and solid form were huge compared to her own slender, pale shape. Even the horses were larger than those she was used to back home. Stiffly, she quelled the thought of Ciordan. There were better things here to think about: the shadow trail, for instance, that they followed. The sky, with its brilliant wash of stars. The sandcat crouched up there on the stone. She rubbed the bone of the big roan's jaw, murmuring to him when he tossed his head in pleasure and arched it against her hand. This horse, while a full hand shorter than the merc's mount, was still a good seventeen hands high, tall enough that she had to leap to gain a seat on its back. Thank Daya it had not been as broad; if she had been riding the merc's black, her legs would have reached only halfway down its ribs.

"You like that, huh?" she said softly, raking her broken nails across the roan's rock-hard neck. There were guides who spent their whole lives living with these creatures—she could almost understand it. Like a fierce bobcat or a hunting windhummer, the horses were filled with power. The warmth of this one's neck and the soft kiss of his nibbling lips made her smile. Would she ever touch a cougar or a tam like this? Close enough to smell its breath?

She lost her smile abruptly. Nearly two decades of dreaming, of training, of work, and she had linked to a gate that could not be used, lost her ties to the guild, and become a ghost to Ciordan. What had Vashanna said? What she was, what she had been before, was nothing. That was true and not true. If she had not been a slave before, she was a slave now to her past. Tsia dug her fingers into the horse's neck, scratching with a vengeance.

Looking back, the merc motioned sharply. With her lips set in stubborn lines, Tsia tucked her reins under a rock. Her eyes noted only absently the narrow, spiky leaves of the plant that hung above it. She did not need her nose to tell her that they were stopping for something other than a water break. The ground here was dry. At least she herself did not have to worry about drinking. There were two bota bags on each saddle and, beside them, when the botas gave out, a watergen straw.

Awkwardly, she slid down the small cliff, stifling a grunt as her right calf refused to hold her weight. She wrinkled her nose: She smelled like horse, sweat, and human blood. Her stomach gave a familiar twist. It was a long moment before she could follow the mercenary to the patch of growth he indicated on the rocks.

When he spoke, it was in Korshani, with an accent like her own. "See?" he said as he lifted one of the tiny, thick rubbery leaves. The edge of his flat-bladed metaplas knife did not harm the greenery as his raser would have, but the leaf still curled at his touch. Tsia nodded, curious. She did not recognize the plant, but she had grown so used to the absence of a link that she did not even try to access the biolistings for ID. Instead, she watched as the man carefully cut half the leaves away from the thick, scaly central stem. He held each leaf out as he cut it, dropping it into her obediently waiting hand.

As the leaves touched her skin, they balled up, rolling across her palm. Tsia's eyes widened. The man's teeth flashed in a grin, though he did not look up until he had finished cutting the plant. Then he pulled a pouch from his belt and opened it.

Tsia, glancing at his hands, froze in horror. "No!" she choked out. The merc looked up as she scrambled back, the taste of fear like chalk in her throat. Powder— Hesse had used gold powder just like that to drug her into obedience. She threw the rubbery leaves on the ground and snapped out the flexor, backing away to her horse.

"It's all right." The mercenary grabbed for the fallen leaves. "Wait!" He dropped to his knees, searching in the nebulous moonlight for the tiny green balls that sank into the sand or rolled around on dusty rock. *"Chiangche hyug!"* he swore in frustration.

Demon dung and fighter spit. Tsia poised for flight. The merc paid no attention to her. Instead, he crawled on the sand, digging quickly through the loose soil for the tiny green balls. Tsia backed up against a rock shelf and stood there warily.

Before her the merc sifted steadily but quickly through the sand for the leaves, while on the soil the greenery uncurled and wriggled away. Tsia's lips quirked in a faint smile. He looked like a reaver searching for a cache of sweetroot whose placement he could not remember. Her smile turned into a grin. The merc looked up, his face momentarily darkening. Then he looked back at himself. He began to chuckle.

He said something in his own language and gestured at the plant.

Did he mean it was good for her? "I don't think so," she returned. She kept her sword up.

His black, unreadable eyes noted the tremble in her slender hands. "Watch," he said quietly. He gathered the tiny balls of rubbery green into one palm, then stood and held them out.

"No," she said stubbornly.

"Gepakka yurn," he said again, softly. "Take this." He stepped forward and offered the leaves again. He waited patiently. Finally he reached down to her weapon and pulled its tip against his chest. Then, watching her steadily, he tapped her other hand.

She could read nothing in his eyes. Her hand trembled.

He ignored her shivers, looking instead into her eyes. He waited.

She lowered the flexor abruptly. She did not look down as she snapped the weapon into a stick and thrust it into her belt with a curse. Still holding his gaze, she stuck out her hand and accepted the plant. When she had the rolling leaves in her palms once more, the merc reached again for his pouch and slowly, carefully, pulled a pinch of the powder and held it to his nose. "See?"

Her eyes were still wary. He motioned for her to open and close her palms quickly, then dropped the dust on top of the plants as they were briefly exposed.

"Wha—" Tsia almost dropped the leaves. Before her eyes the movement across her palms increased until the leaves felt like bugs crawling across her skin. With one hand steady on her shoulder, the merc used his other hand to reach into another pouch and bring out a small tube. Motioning again, he told her to rub her hands together, smashing the leaves and powder as hard as she could. In seconds the strange movement of the leaves stopped. When he pulled her hands apart, the leaves had partially dissolved, and Tsia's eyes widened in surprise. He dropped some of the milky white liquid from the jar onto the paste that had developed and told her to rub them together again. When he was satisfied, he bade her wipe the substance on her wrists.

She did so reluctantly, unable to understand why she trusted this man. Then her eyes widened in surprise. "The throbbing—it's gone!"

The man nodded. "Here." He knelt and pulled the torn cloth of her trousers away from the puncture in her thigh, not allowing her salve-smeared hands to waste any ointment on the cloth.

She applied the salve hesitantly. In minutes the pain was gone. As the drug entered her system, the numbness spread, and she grew light-headed, her ice-blue eyes large and catlike in the dark. Her pupils dilated, and her breathing became slow and easy.

Ignoring the effect the medicine had on his patient, the merc helped her take off her blunter, smiling faintly as she shivered in the cold. When he found the cuts across her bicep and the skin graft on her arm, he pointed to each in turn, waiting patiently until she covered each one with the salve.

As she shrugged back into her jacket, she looked up. She hesitated. "Thank you," she said finally. "I—I am Tsia."

"Tsia?" he repeated. He chuckled suddenly, shaking his head at her questioning frown. "*Ar* Ramok," he returned simply.

Ramok. She mouthed the name, tasting it on her tongue. With the pain gone from her thigh and only the bruises on her ribs and calf bothering her now, she relaxed slowly. Appreciatively, Ramok eyed her slender length. She smiled, then boldly she reached out to touch the thin red line on his strong, muscle-ridged neck. Back at Noirelle her flexor had sliced his collar and cut a clean red line into his weather-tanned skin. He had been lucky or, rather, he had been faster than she had thought possible; her strike had made only a shallow mark. Another half inch and she would have taken out his carotid. She ran her hands along the skin, massaging the last of the salve over that red line.

Ramok's laughing, black-hued eyes caught her gaze, holding her motionless until his hands wrapped around her wrists and drew her slowly to his chest. He was no longer laughing.

With a supple twist Tsia freed her arms. He did not recapture them, and Tsia leaned in, sliding them both around his neck.

Ramok chuckled without humor. One of his hands rubbed her lower back till she groaned; the other pulled her head back and ran his fingers through the short, thick hair, while he wondered at its softness on his calloused skin. Until her hot tongue touched his ear. With a muffled oath, he ducked his head and bit her shoulder. She gasped. Then he stood still, murmuring into her ear as he held her and stroked her hair until a blast of wind ended the embrace.

The gust rose again and drove the sand against them both,

forcing Ramok to close his eyes and tilt Tsia's face into his chest to protect her. "Tsia," he said gently. "Tsia, look." He disentangled one of her hands and pointed at her wrist where the medicine had entered her bloodstream. "*Nah imma cray a'man.* Understand?"

She shook her head, her large haunted eyes hypnotized by his gaze. With infinite patience Ramok disengaged her other hand, turned her, and pushed her toward her horse. When she twisted back and looked at him with those wide cat eyes, he shuddered from the ache in his groin. Knowing she was drugged did not reduce his need. Her body was like silk in his hands. He followed her stiffly.

The rest of that ride was only a dim memory for Tsia. Blurred and blank, she rode the horse instinctively, her hips settling into the saddle as if she had been born there. Until Ramok pulled her to a stop, she did not seem to be able to focus on anything. The drug and her exhaustion dulled her senses, and it took several seconds to see the tiny lick of light that appeared where the mercenary pointed. A second time the light winked on, then off again, and Ramok grunted with satisfaction.

Tsia let her eyes flick from the light to the merc. She had not touched a man like that in over two years or been held herself with such gentleness and need. The combination was almost as painful as the desire she felt for the fire. She watched him covertly, but Ramok's attention was still forward, his sharp gaze eyeing the space between them and the light. Frustrated, Tsia rubbed a hand across her dry, irritated eyes. Then she winced because the motion ground the grit farther into her face. Her skin felt clammed up with cold sweat. No wonder he did not want to make love. She pushed aside the pangs of hunger that gnawed at her stomach and longed for nothing more than to crawl into a deep, cool river and let it wash her over and under for hours till she woke to a clean dawn. Cold water, she corrected the thought. Not just cool. Ice-cold to quench the heat that tortured her thoughts.

A flash of movement almost as dark as the shadow it hid in caught the corner of her eye. Ramok scanned the dunes, but Tsia focused through her biogate. The life energy she felt was weak with the distance, but she could sense it. She pointed slowly, careful of her movements, her right hand gripping the flexor in readiness. She needed no cold water now; the lick of fear that came with the light had killed her desire as quickly as it had come.

Ramok nodded, then spurred his horse forward again. Trotting after him warily, Tsia did not take her hand from her weapon.

"*Ar* Ramok," the man called softly.

"Ramok!" The voice from the dark was hushed and tense, but its pleasure could not be missed. He added something of which Tsia caught only the word *wilia*: "councilwoman." So, she thought with relief, Yemene had been brought here, too. The councilwoman could vouch for her to Ramok, make sure the mercs took Tsia back with them to Pulan.

As they passed the perimeter guard, Tsia's eyes were drawn to the two tiny flashes on the quiet man's handset. Her eyes narrowed. She had been duly noted and coded into the camp. She could not leave now, not without Ramok knowing.

The soft sound of laughter on her lips surprised her. Whether she wanted to leave or not, she had nowhere else to go. Ramok glanced back at her wry mirth, and Tsia, sobering, shrugged eloquently. He hesitated, then turned forward again, but the flash of his eyes told her that he understood.

As they rode into a wide space between two rounded hills, Tsia's mount tossed its head and nickered to other beasts that stood in the night. Murmuring gently, she patted the roan gelding's neck. He was not nervous; the gesture was more for Tsia's reassurance than for his. There were jitters in her stomach that did not come from her virus, and the leftover drugs in her blood were making her feel drawn and tired.

The camp was not large, she realized; there were perhaps only sixteen or seventeen people there. She could see them well despite the night. They must have just set up the ground perimeter through which she had come; there was still movement along the edges of the camp. No lights broke the predawn shadows, and almost no sound came to her ears. She could almost smell Yemene in the quiet, but she could not see the woman. If the councilwoman or others spoke, it was in whispers that barely carried over the cold and steady wind.

At last Ramok pulled up on the black and motioned for her to dismount. She did so, sagging from the gelding's mane before her legs started working again. The bruise on her calf made her muscles cramp so that she stumbled; with a wince, she dug a rag from her saddlebag and began to rub down her mount. Ramok was already doing the same. He grinned his approval when he saw the sureness of her hands. Then, digging into a bag next to a rock, he tossed her a small, hard bundle, which held an old-fashioned picket rope. Tsia nodded her understanding tiredly. A few minutes later she staked the horse, removed its gear, and watered the beast with a flexbowl and her bota bag.

At last she hobbled stiffly to the place indicated by the merc:

a narrow slot between two humps of sand where Ramok had already tossed the e-roll from his saddle. Tsia untied the sleeping bundle from her own saddle and rolled it out beside his. Then she sank gratefully to the sand, glancing around only to make sure she knew who was sleeping nearby. She barely waited for the bag to puff out before she crawled onto the bottom layer. Shivering, she tugged the top cover over her chest. She let her head fall back on the fender of her saddle. Ramok, setting his gear for the night, stood over her with his hands on his hips for a long moment. As he watched her, his face softened. He nodded to her. Then, his eyes glancing to his right, he turned and strode away.

Tsia stared after him until the shadows stole him from her sight. Sleep refused to come. The ache of her inner thighs was beginning to be a soreness she could not ignore. She breathed twice, then shifted to her stomach, but her ribs protested against this treatment. When she fidgeted onto her side, it was her calf that was not comfortable. Then the manacles on her wrists rang together, and Tsia cursed at the abrupt noise. When she tossed again, cold air and sand filtered into the e-roll, but that did not bother her half as much as the sudden sensation of tiny legs on her shoulder. She jerked back from the beetle and shook it off in disgust.

On the edge of her consciousness sandcats crawled, disturbed by the appearance of so many men in their hunting ground. The irritation of their unease further sparked her sleeplessness, and she snarled at the gate that clogged her mind. In the desert the cats were becoming a constant rushing sound that made her twist and turn at every watchful set of eyes. She tried to shut them out, but they crept back in, eyeing her, smelling her scent on the wind.

The sand was like fur under her fingers, and she made a sound like a sob. Her throat was tight. A void of grief seemed to latch on to her chest. The blackness rose in her sight, blinding her to the stars, to the dull shadow shapes, to the smell of the horses in their midst. If this gate got much stronger, how would she survive? The guide virus had brought her to the art guild in chains. She thought she had broken those fetters, but she had been wrong. Now her gate bound her so tightly that she could not even think.

She touched the scar on her cheek. What was she now? A slave? A thief? A murderer? If she stayed with Ramok, would she see the lands that he had seen? Travel the skies in his skimmers? Live the fear and excitement that he, with his mercs, did now? She dropped her hands to rub the manacles on her wrists. Would she be anything more than a ghost in his ranks?

The cat feet scratched at the insides of her burning eyes, and she closed them against the sense of her gate. At least, she told herself dully, she would have a way across the desert.

When Tsia snapped awake, the flexor was in her hand and her breathing was stilled as she listened.

"*Esha*, Tsia," A bundle dropped softly beside her, and a huge shape squatted near her saddle. "*Ar* Ramok."

She fingered the weapon back to a stick and sat up, grabbing her blunter and stuffing her arms into it as soon as the cold predawn air hit her skin.

Ramok pushed the package toward her. "Clothes," he said, his thick accent holding the consonants. "Boots and food."

At his urging, she pulled the bundle apart. Quietly, she laid out the goods: a sand-colored jumpsuit, same material as her blunter. A small roll that unfolded to become a pair of socks; the boots looked the right size. There was a shade—the sweep of dull cloth that not only protected one's head from the sun but used a tiny energy net to cool the air inside the cloth—a flat knife, a recharger for her flexor, a medpak, a darkeye, and a pouch of slimchims. The darkeye with its rounded, lusterless contacts intrigued her, but the scent of the slimchims made her mouth water, and she reached for that pouch first. Half the nausea in her stomach was hunger, not virus, she realized as she popped one of the wafers between her teeth.

In another bundle there were several pieces of metaplas that could be formed like a flexor into forked, curved, and straightened shapes. She ignored them in favor of examining the e-wrap she found. It was similar to the emergency type used for temperature extremes, but its colors shifted like a chameleon in her hands, and there were tiny power strips melded into its seams. She repacked the sheet carefully. There were other items—standard, though expensive, survival gear. They went into her saddlebags easily.

Tsia knew that Ramok was watching her intently from where he sat, but she ignored him. However, when she started to remove her blunter and change to the new set of clothes, he leaned over and stopped her. Carefully, he took the small bronze blunter disk he had given her back in Noirelle. Checking to make sure it was still matched to her heartbeat, he opened her collar, then pressed the disk to her neck as he helped her out of the jacket. This time Tsia's hand stopped him.

As she took the disk from his fingers, he grinned. She touched the small, flat circle to her skin herself, then began to struggle, one-armed, out of the jacket. Ramok's hand on her collar helped her, but his smile faded as he noted the manacles still on her wrists. He fingered the metaplas rings with a frown. She shrugged them out of his hands. Then she reached for the medpak and, ignoring her shivers, began to stretch out a skinroll for the gash in her upper arm and the puncture in her leg.

Ramok helped her pull on the rest of her clothes, the fabric sealing itself at his touch. Beneath the uniform the tall man's hands were hot on her skin, and she felt even colder when he withdrew them. He did not seem to notice. A moment later he sealed the disk back in the blunter pouch, then helped her put on the weapon harness that hugged her hips and stretched down along her thighs.

Tsia examined the harness curiously. With its energy packs stitched into the straps and the blunter fabric over everything, the harness was untraceable by the node, she realized. As long as the clothes reflected the node sensors, the nodies would have nothing to identify her as a human, rather than a random, biological. She glanced up at Ramok with raised eyebrows. He nodded.

As she stripped the soiled socks from her calves, she had to stifle her disgust. Ramok chuckled.

She gave him an exasperated look. "What's so funny?"

He shook his head, but all he said was "Tsia," and laughed again. "Here," he said, getting to his feet. He held out the raser and the flat, metal knife that had fallen to the sand, and she took them wordlessly, tucking them into the harness. She attached the flexor last.

"Heea," she returned, holding out the dirty socks. *"Gepaka yurn."* If she had caught enough of his accent to understand it, the words meant "take this."

Ramok glanced at her in surprise, then grinned. "Good," he said. *"Parce."*

Around them camp had begun to break, and in the heavy darkness Tsia could see no more than gray faces, shapes, and moving shadows, though the force of life through her gate was unnerving. The cats that had prowled the edges of the camp retreated at the noise, and Tsia reached for their senses. Warm puffs of breath seemed to hang in front of her nose.

When Ramok's hand brushed against her, she started. *"Esha,* Tsia," he murmured, taking the socks without even glancing at their filth. "I will not harm you."

She shook her head. She was jumpy, not afraid. The crawling sensation in her head had surged, and she wanted to clench her fists to her temples. Ramok watched the way her eyes flickered from one shadow to the next. Thoughtfully, he handed her the darkeye. She shook her head, but he insisted, and reluctantly she opened the casing. She had worn darkeyes before—they were handy for night work in the slough, though the trade-off from color sense to motion could take some getting used to. Ramok was waiting, so she wiped her fingers on her trousers and lifted out one of the contacts. It slid onto her left eye naturally.

She blinked. Colors shifted and disappeared. Gray shadows took their place like a fog. Motion was sharp but flat. As was natural, she strained to see through the darkeye, and nothing happened. The cat feet in her head skidded to a halt. Unaware that she had opened her biogate, she stretched in that indefinable way for her sight. Cats' eyes darkened with the sharp gray fog. Suncats growled, and sandcats shook their heads. Tsia gasped. The claws of the tams pawed at their faces. Through her gate, Tsia felt the blindness bring on panic. No! she cried out silently. Not my eyes! Her paws—her hands tore at her eyes, ripping the darkeye from her socket. Frantically, she tried to fling it as far as she could, but Ramok moved like a cat himself, grabbing her arms.

"No," she cried out, struggling wildly against his grip. Her heart beat like a drum. The cats snarled in her head, and she cried out again silently. She could not touch the cats—the Landing Pact forbade it. Gods, what had she done? She tried to shut herself off from the gate, and the tremors shook her violently. Cat feet slunk across her mind.

"*Esha*, Tsia," he snapped in a low voice. "*Avya . . .*" He wrapped his forearms around her and clenched his hand around her fist. She could not rid herself of the darkeye; his fingers would not let hers uncurl. "*Esha, avya; seva . . .*" Gently, lover-loved one; you are safe, his voice soothed. His arms were locked around her as solidly as if she were standing in the grip of an r-con.

She struggled again halfheartedly, then gave in, sinking against his torso with a ragged breath. Her heart still beat too fast. Daya, she sobbed silently at the cats. Don't listen to me! Don't hear me! She clenched her fists. A second, a minute, an infinite snarling in her head, and finally, with a clawing at the inner part of her skull, the sense of the cats subsided.

She thought back, frightened. What had happened? The darkeye—it was as if it had blinded, not enhanced, her sight. It was as if she had poked her finger into a cougar's eye and the cougar had then reacted. A tremor clutched at her bones, and she quelled it tightly. The virus . . . Her gate . . . Damn it, would it steal her very sanity?

Ramok reached slowly to take the darkeye from her hand. When he released her, she did not look at him. Instead, she gathered up the discarded casing and handed it to him silently. She did not notice as she turned away to pack the rest of her gear that Ramok's gaze on her was thoughtful.

By the time Tsia had unstaked her roan and saddled the horse again, dawn had appeared as a blue-gray light in the east. The rustling of the camp was quiet, and Tsia picked out the low words of different mercs with difficulty. In her nose the smell of the horses was overpowering, and Ramok's sharp scent was welcome when he led his horse to hers.

"Follow me," he said quietly, turning to lead his horse away. Silently she walked after him, hissing as the true stiffness of her muscles began to make itself known. At least she would warm up the muscles if she was moving.

Ramok noted her stiffness with an unsympathetic grin as he led her through clumps of mercs to a tall, thin man who leaned against a rock near the edge of the camp. Ramok made a gesture, and the man took the black horse's reins. The lanky, narrow-faced merc eyed Tsia silently as he reached for the reins of her roan. Then Ramok led her between the rocks to a small clear area filled with the stench of sweat and horse, leather and blood. Here he pointed. "Choose," he said curtly.

Tsia looked soberly at the bodies huddled on the ground. Circling the twisted forms were saddles, small piles of gear, and other items dark against the sand. In the pale, blue-orange dawn she forced herself to examine the equipment quickly. She gathered all three water bags she saw, a cooking cube—its thermally sealed box would fit easily into her half-full saddlebags—and a toilet kit. Ramok raised his eyes at the number of water bags, but Tsia ignored him and carried them out of the clearing to attach to her saddle.

Satisfied with her choices, Ramok made a motion at the other merc, and the lanky man nodded. A moment later Tsia heard the hissing and caught the bittersweet smell that marked the disintegration of the bodies and gear. This time she did not look back. When Ramok offered his hand to help her into the saddle, she leapt lightly up.

She followed him and his horse to the edge of the camp, where he motioned for her to wait. Then he turned and left. Within minutes she was joined by several men and women. A few of them dismounted and rechecked their gear, and Tsia, watching their care, slipped down from the saddle and did the same. One light-haired man beside her straightened from resetting his cinch and made a low comment. Several mercs snick-ered. Tsia, not knowing what he had said, felt awkward and un-certain and made a pretense of checking the loops in her water bags. But a moment later, when the man turned from his horse, his hand moved to circle her waist.

She had been too long away from other people. As a woman to her left began to comment acidly to the man, Tsia's fingers closed around the hilt of the metal knife, not the raser, and the sound that broke from her throat was not a human noise—it was the snarl of a cougar. Her knife whipped flat side down across the thin bones in the man's straying hands.

"Chiangche!" The man stumbled back and clutched his bruised hand to his chest. He cursed at her viciously. Demon dung, space-spawned liver worms . . . To the left, a woman chuckled. The man glared back at her and made a comment that set the others laugh-ing. The red-haired woman smiled coldly at the bone-bruised merc, patting the pair of rasers on her harness. Silently, she challenged him to back his comment. The man shook his head, mounted, and muttered under his breath. Before she turned away, the red-haired woman regarded Tsia for a long moment, measuring her with a look that took in more than her short, thick hair and lean body.

Tsia stared back. She knew the woman now: The redhead was one of the three mercs who had taken Yemene away from Kern back in the black city. One of the mercs who had left her to Vashanna's words. A merc, she realized with a suddenly cold heart, who had seen her with Cekulu's body. Tsia's face grew still. The redhead observed her a moment more, then reined her horse around and cantered out of the group.

When Ramok rode back by and gestured for Tsia to follow him, it was with relief that she tapped the roan in the flanks and fell in behind him. Ahead, the sand was orange-red along a thin line to the east. Only a few stars still shone in the sky. Time seemed to be suspended in the sound of snorting horses. No gear creaked; no voices broke the night. In Tsia's head even the cat feet were silent. Not until Ramok led away at a loose gallop did time turn the world again and let the sun break over the rock-ragged horizon.

19

※※※

There was no wind in the early morning gloom, and a heavy coat of dust lay over the gritty soil. Rock heights, layered in the colors of dawn, plunged into mountains of dead grass that clustered at their stony feet. Shadows created false and rocky dunes across the land. Tenaciously, red sage and monkeybrush grew from the soil and gave the rocky dirt the look of a diseased Earth until the light broke their dusty branches out of the shadows and gave the dry shrubbery life of its own.

The sky blended to yellow, then blue as dawn passed into day. The air dried instantly when the sun hit it. As the coolness of night lost itself in a drying vista of desert, Tsia pulled on her headgear in imitation of the others. She had never used a headgear shade like this in the sloughs. One usually needed heat more than cooling in Ciordan.

Tsia stole glances at her companions. With the light, their features were clear for the first time since she had ridden into their camp. Ramok, riding ahead of her, was older than she had thought at first. Perhaps as old as his sixties. It was the median age for a merc leader; few of them lived to see the 280 that was average for a colonist. Ramok, like others his age, was muscled, toned, and weathered by the wind of a dozen worlds. The tiny crow's-feet around his eyes were the only sign of his years. No gray hairs speckled his black hair. Only scars marred his skin.

Tsia eyed the skin on her own hands. If she stayed in the desert much longer, her skin would begin to fracture and weather like the flesh of the tall man who rode to her right. She glanced sideways. The man on her right had a face that was dark and handsome, though scarred like hers across one cheek, and his skin was weathered as if the time he had spent in the merc guild had been etched on his very bones. If she judged him by his skin, he was younger than Ramok by perhaps a decade; if she looked, however, at his cold, still eyes, he could be older than Orpheus, the first moon. He rode a black and white horse with two white stockings. The horse was built for speed and stamina, and the man, Aron, sat in the saddle as if carved into its seat.

To her left rode a man on a light-stepping dappled gray. Although his horse was as tall as Aron's, the man himself was as small and wiry as Aron was large. This second man, Wren, was that indeterminate age between 100 and 140, when the body was still strong and thick but the skin began to wrinkle and the hair to thin. His face was sharp, split by a thin hooked nose that pulled his expression down and made him look like a hawk. He moved quickly, twisting to notice things as rapidly as Tsia did instinctively through her gate. When he removed his darkeyes for a moment, his pale gray gaze darted from one invisible desert motion to the next, exploring each with his penetrating glance. When Tsia told him her name, he chuckled to himself, but his eyes were cold as he appraised her, and she shivered under his regard.

An hour passed. A sandcat lazed on the top of a rock and watched the mercs with deceptively hooded eyes. A desert hare, wary of the hawk overhead, darted across a patch of bare ground. Idly, Tsia watched it run. The hawk had sighted it; the hare gained speed. It was heading for a clump of rocks, but the hawk was already beginning its dive. The sandcat, watching the hunt through Tsia's gate, sharpened its gaze. Unconsciously, Tsia tightened her knees on the roan, and the horse quickened its pace. The hare flung itself toward the rocks. And then the ground erupted under its feet. A nest of sandsnakes struck up like arcing whips. They impacted the rabbit across its chest and legs, then engulfed it in a boiling froth of fangs and tails, dragging it down into the loose soil. In a moment not even the feet of the hare showed. Tsia clamped her lips shut and stared ahead.

Sandstone canyons edged up in her sight until she rode like an ant within them. Their layers made smooth lines of the ancient sea deposits that indicated their origin. Here and there a cluster of round protrusions was exposed, some having fallen out to leave empty, egglike caves as large as Tsia's head or as small as her thumbnail. She leaned close and scraped her flexor across one of the protrusions; it was as hard as granite compared to the sandstone in which it was embedded.

Fossils poked their bones out of the rock, but Tsia eyed them with a wrinkled nose. The itching in her skull made her want to rip off her shade and frantically scratch her hair; the scent of the horses was making her struggle for each breath. She stared at the fossils, daring them to speak.

"They are alien pets."

Startled by Aron's voice, Tsia glanced at him.

He nodded. "Record on Hyde III. Broadcast last winter. Details one of the ancient Ixia grazing strains." His words were almost clipped in accent, and Tsia frowned, wondering where she had heard that lilting curtness before. "Records match some of these bones perfectly," he added. " 'Course, that was over two billion years ago."

Tsia looked at him curiously. "The noise—we can speak out loud here?"

He gave her the same appraising glance to which Wren had subjected her, but this time Tsia stared back. "Long as the horses move," he answered, "we can speak. Quietly. The nodes ignore a certain amount of sound. It thinks we are part of the herd. Normal noise to it."

She was puzzled. "But won't the movement of this herd be too regular for the node to ignore, anyway?"

He shook his head. "We're heading for Bonnell's Bay. Watering hole on the regular horse trails. No other tinaja—a rock-protected water tank—natural, not man-made—" he added, "in this direction." His clipped voice lilted oddly as he shrugged. "Horses always travel this way to go east along the rift. Between the noise they would make going there and the wind that's rising now, our words will not make a difference."

Tsia rubbed her upper arm absently, wishing the itch of the healing slash would finally be relieved. "Last night—because the horses were supposed to be sleeping, no one made much noise in the camp?"

He nodded. "Until we get to the bay, it will be the same every time we stop. Deserts are quieter than forests."

Tsia returned his nod wryly. Soon the sky would turn white with the inevitable rise of the sun, and the cool, trapped air in the canyons would start to burn away. At least Ramok hugged the bottoms of the ravines rather than the more exposed trails. The man on her other side, Wren, said it was to keep down the bouncing light of mirages. The artists' nodies, he said, would look for anything, no matter how tiny, that told where Ramok's men had gone. Not even a mirage would be allowed to escape their scrutiny. Tsia did not feel more comfortable knowing that. A group this size, she thought, left obvious human marks no matter how many horses they rode and how hard-packed the trail.

Dust ground its way into her pores while the sun obligingly opened her skin with its heat. Within an hour Tsia's body felt like one massive sand pack. Grit dug its way under her blunter and then under the jumpsuit where it stung her cuts with sweat. Runnels of perspiration made tracks down her body as if she danced in the flames themselves. She felt as if she were showering in her own odors and drowning in the smell.

It was Wren who helped her pass the time. Tactfully noting her discomfort, he began to teach her phrases and words in the mercenaries' tongue. Korshani and Merishkan were similar even in form, and the phrases came easily to Tsia, though the idioms were difficult. They could even hold a conversation of sorts, though only a quarter of it was in Merishkan, the mercenary's language.

"How long were you in Korshan?" Wren asked in his sharp, dry voice.

"Fifteen months. A month before that in transit." She looked across the saddle at him. "How do you know Korshani?"

"I worked in the mines for a time," he answered with a small, tight grin. His teeth looked like tiny daggers in his sun-darkened face. "I was a *Jinga*."

"Did someone buy you out?"

"*Ki pastiddi.*" He shrugged. "I escaped."

Tsia digested that for a moment.

"It is true," he said. He showed her his wrist where the slave bracelets had been welded on and welded off again in freedom. He had curiously large hands for so small a frame, and they gave his arms the look of brutal clubs. "In the mines," he said, "they don't believe the ghost chains come off, even in death."

Absently, she rubbed her own wrists where the shackles still clung, hidden beneath her jacket.

Wren eyed her speculatively. "And you," he asked, "you were *heyta*, too?"

Tsia fingered the manacles under her jacket sleeves.

"It burns, doesn't it?" His voice was soft. "The feel of steel on your arms."

Tsia met his eyes slowly. "Not as much as the fire in my blood."

Wren chuckled. "The blunter should hide that metal from the nodes, but you had better get it removed when we reach Bonnell's Bay. A little more metal there won't hurt, and if you miss the feel of the manacles," he said, smiling at Tsia's involuntary blanch, "you can always buy another set in Pulan."

"Pulan ..." Tsia changed the subject, turning to look back

along the line of riders. "Yemene is with us? She is here in the line?"

"*Bussa ke bussa.*" The man gestured with his large, scarred hands. "Look behind you. She rides like the rest of us."

Tsia hooked her leg around the saddle horn as she looked behind. If she squinted and knew what she was looking for, through the dust she could just see a clump of men riding tightly around an awkward figure. She frowned. "The woman is close to labor, Wren. She should not be riding. Not in her condition and especially not in this heat."

He shrugged. "If she wants to reach Pulan alive, she has little choice in the matter."

"She might go into labor."

"Then she will give birth in the saddle. We cannot stop for her to bring forth her child in a comfortable bed on the sand."

Tsia stared at him for a moment, but the man did not retract his words. With a frown, she tightened her knees and, her face set, trotted up to where Ramok rode. "Ramok," she said, breaking into his thoughts and gesturing behind them. "Yemene of Pulan?"

The mercenary leader glanced at Tsia and nodded slightly.

"Yemene is close to birthing," Tsia said carefully, mixing Korshani with imageless Standard and the words of Merishkan that Wren had taught her. "If she continues riding in her condition, the baby will be born soon."

Ramok did not answer for a moment, and she was not sure he understood what she said, but then he turned and called back to Wren. The smaller man broke off the trail to canter back along the line.

Ramok pointed with his chin at a ridge just visible on the sand-mounded horizon. Tsia followed his gesture. The broken line of the ridge seemed like a mirage in the shimmering heat.

"How far away is it?" she asked.

"Three days," Aron's deep voice returned from behind. He trotted his horse to join them. "Three days there," he said in Korshani. "Then, once we reach the mines, a few hours to get through to Levian, the city that sits on top of the mines."

Ramok nodded at Aron's words—Ramok understood the gist of Korshani, even if he could not speak it well—and Tsia followed his nod to glance at Aron. The man who joined them was nearly as large in the shoulders as Ramok, with the same quickness as the mercenary leader. He had the same look of iron in his scarred and weathered muscles and the same cold, quiet danger to his gaze. But where Ramok's grin still touched his eyes, Aron's never did.

"The longer we are here . . ." Tsia hesitated, glancing from one man to the other. "Doesn't it give the artists more time to find us?"

Aron chuckled. "Is it the art guild you are worried about?"

"Aren't you?"

He shook his head.

"Then what," she persisted, "is it that worries you?"

Aron's mount sidestepped a snake hole in the soil, and he soothed the horse absently. He glanced across the dry sand and rocks. "Every contract has its greatest risk," he answered finally. "Here it is water. Only that."

Tsia licked her lips involuntarily, and Ramok followed the motion with his sharp black eyes. Her voice, speaking to Aron, was cool and distant, but it was warmer when she turned to him. He rubbed his chin thoughtfully. He was taking a chance by letting her control her own use of the node, by not plugging her temple link himself. But she was rights-conditioned; there was no mistaking the sign she had returned or the way she had moved with the flexor. She had been in the chains of a *heyta*, but ghost or not, she was no criminal. There was something familiar in her manner, in the way she moved and spoke, that made him feel he could trust her. Even—he smiled faintly—as she had trusted him.

He glanced at her face, his gaze flicking over her ice-blue eyes, the lightning-bolt scar on her cheek, and the stubborn set of her chin. She had wanted out of Noirelle badly enough to kill for it— there had been a desperation in her fighting when she had faced him in that room. A fierceness in her eyes when she had stared at him, knowing she would die yet refusing to give in. He admired that. And she *had* risked herself to keep him safe when he had slipped on that ledge; she had helped him again in the structures. Aron and Wren might question his motives, but he could not have left her behind. If not for this one slim woman, he himself would have been hissing on the sand. Tsia . . . He grinned. He wondered if she knew the meaning of her name in Merishkan.

Tsia caught his gaze and smiled uncertainly back. She could almost read his face now; last night it had been the shadows and the darkeyes that had hidden the expressions in his gaze. She licked her lip again, then glanced at Aron. "If you are worried about water, is there enough for all of us on this route?"

"Maybe." Aron dropped back subtly so that Tsia was forced to rein in and leave Ramok's side if she wanted to ask him questions.

"Then why the horses? Surely it would be safer to take skimmers from here. It would be only an hour by skimmer to Pulan, and water would not be an issue. By now the guild would not expect—"

"You can be sure," Aron said, cutting her off curtly, "that the guild expects just that. By now they have figured out that we have either already reached Pulan or gone to ground near Noirelle. It will take their nodies time to trace our ghost lines. But when they do, they will realize the lines are not recent. They were set in place years ago. The guild will know then that we are still in the desert."

Tsia frowned. "What do you mean, ghosts that are not recent?"

"When you buy a merc, you buy his ghosts as well." Aron smiled faintly at her expression. "You can rent a hundred traces put in place ten years ago for a job you will do tomorrow. It is one of the edges that help guarantee a client's satisfaction."

"And the artists won't be able to trace them if the lines are that old?"

"It is inevitable that they will follow some. As time goes by, their nodies will find out that it is a man named Ramok who led this party. They will research Ramok's history like a reaver after a root. And then they will stop thinking in terms of ghosts and start thinking like Ramok. That is one of the disadvantages of working against the art guild. They are more creative in thinking like their opponents."

"They will find us."

Aron chuckled, and Ramok, ahead by several horse lengths, glanced back. "The art guild," he returned disparagingly, "could not find us if they had spotters on every dune. They are working through their nodies, not their own people. And nodies use their links for everything. It is their one weakness, and it is the weapon we use against them. Most nodies cannot imagine that anyone would willingly drop out of the node. When they cannot find a real trace, they will think we are hiding near Noirelle, waiting for the guild to give up on us so we can come back in. As for the artists? They themselves are arrogant. They will not expect a merc to be so flexible or creative as to drop out of the node, either. They, too, will expect us to go to ground near Noirelle and wait for their guard to go down."

"So that we can steal the skimmers they will have fixed by then and fly back to Pulan in their own ships?"

Aron nodded in cold satisfaction. "In their arrogance, they will search the land around the black city for days."

"But why won't they expect us to actually ride across the desert?"

He shrugged. "For a merc to take days to cross land that in a skimmer would take only an hour? The concept is inconceivable. Even we—" He gestured at the line of riders. "—had to be convinced." He grinned, and the puckered scar on his cheek stretched oddly. "It turns out it is a good idea. No one rides far this time of year. The water holes are mostly dry. Even the high tanks—the rock basins in the mountains—will give out in a dry year. This one has been one of the driest. Only guides and occasional climbers come out here. Only two groups this side of the rift right now. Neither one can use Bonnell's Bay. We locked the reservations for our own group. Used nine of our open links for hiker passes."

Tsia thought about that. "If we must be that careful, then we cannot use the watergens."

"Uh uh. Nodies will push the sensors to high-res scans. Straws draw power. Water bags draw nothing. A good nodie could find a straw. She could never read the material of a bota bag."

A sandcat stopped his washing to watch their progress, but only Tsia saw him. "Even if we don't use the links," she said, "the node will still register us as human biologicals. Why doesn't that give us away?"

"That blunter disk." Aron jerked his chin at her chest. "That is your protection. It matches your heartbeat and temperature to the horse you ride. Node scan picks up the radiant field. When it looks at you, node sees only one thing: a roan horse making its way toward a water hole."

"But I did not stay with the horse all night," Tsia protested.

"You wore the disk at all times, nor were you far from your horse."

Tsia thought back.

"The node assumes a certain amount of reflection from the terrain," the merc explained. "A double signal that is faint—it could be an echo. That is how the node classifies you. An echo. Works best in rocky terrain. That is why we don't stop in the sand."

"But the skimmers—won't they see us?" She glanced meaningfully at a slender white shape that cruised over the desert to the south.

"Skimmers are piloted by nodies. They use sensors for their eyes, not windows. They will see exactly what the node sees. No more. Only a skimmer on visual would see a human here."

Tsia reached forward and patted the horse's neck. "I am curious, Aron," she said. "How did you reach Noirelle unnoticed?"

Aron smiled slowly, as if surprising himself by doing it. "Trade secret."

Tsia looked at him thoughtfully.

He shrugged. "If you become a merc, you will find out. If not, you will never need to know."

Tsia glanced at Ramok's broad back and changed the subject. "Did he," she asked, gesturing with her chin, "arrange for a horse sling for the councilwoman?"

He shrugged. "He sent Wren to find Ma. She will tell him if the woman can ride or not."

Remembering that sharp voice she had heard last night, Tsia frowned. "Ma? A mother is a merc?"

The black-haired man regarded her sardonically. "Used to be a mother. Now she is a merc. Are you surprised? She can fight. She can lay a mean ghost line. She can keep order with a look where even Ramok has to raise his voice. The mercs have simple requirements: If you can fight, you are welcome. If you can't, you are killed."

Tsia's hand went to her flexor defiantly. "I can fight," she said quietly.

"If you could not," he answered curtly, "Ramok would not have brought you along."

Tsia met his eyes with a shuttered gaze, wondering if he was mocking her. He watched her steadily.

"How many people in this group?" she asked.

"Eighteen." He gave her a shrewd look. "You will meet the rest of them soon enough." She frowned at him, and he smiled faintly. "There is a greeting ritual among the mercs that I doubt even you will escape."

Tsia digested this. When she spoke again, she changed the subject. "Do most of you speak Korshani?"

Aron glanced at her slyly. Her change of subject was not lost on him, nor was the involuntary gesture she made toward her weapon. Definitely rights-conditioned. The merc who challenged her unknowingly could find himself in an interesting position. "A few," he answered finally. "Merishkan is the guild tongue. You should pick it up quickly. You have already learned Korshani."

"How do you know Korshani so well?"

He chuckled mirthlessly. "Diplomacy has its advantages."

"You were a diplomat?"

"I was a fool." The man's voice was suddenly cold.

Embarrassed, Tsia looked away. They rode after that without speaking.

It was not until Ramok pulled to the side, waiting for them to catch up, that Aron spoke again, and then it was to translate. "We will stop there," Ramok told them, pointing to a set of broken sandstone pillars. "We will stay in the shade through noon, then move on." He flashed a smile at Tsia and pulled his horse around so that it stamped the sand impatiently. "How do you feel today, little Tsia?"

She frowned at his grin, making out enough of his words to understand the gist of what he said before Aron's low voice translated the words to Korshani. "Fine," she retorted, "except for the handprints you left on my body."

The big man winked at her and trotted off, while Aron gave her a strange look, suddenly distant. "Are you his *heyita*?" he asked quietly.

Heyita? "Bedmate" or "concubine-slave," she translated the term. Her eyes lost their humor. "I am my own woman," she said flatly. "Not his or any man's slave."

"I did not mean slave."

"I know what you meant."

Aron nodded. "Make sure that Red understands that."

"Red?"

"She noticed you last night. She thinks herself Ramok's bedmate." He shrugged. "Takes enough others to the sand when she's of a mind to do so."

"I did not sleep with Ramok last night."

"Does it matter?" He appraised her lean, taut-muscled body. "Ramok has been riding eyes on you all morning."

"Riding eyes?"

"You are new. You aren't a merc. You could be a ghost, someone he picked up on the way. Or an *avya* for whom he feels a bond. Ramok is riding eyes on you to make sure you are not challenged or—" He flicked his glance to a rider down the line. "—explored while you are here. Since he brought you here, he is keeping you safe. Until he lets us know what he will do with you. Although," he added, "I think he is riding eyes on you more as pleasure for his sight than duty for his conscience."

She snorted. "I am marked, Aron. I have no beauty for anyone to see." Her tone stung bitterly, and she involuntarily raised a hand to her cheek, the ragged scar thin like a white snake that crawled across her skin.

Aron regarded her silently for a moment. "Ramok must not think so."

"Ramok met me in the dark."

Whatever else he had intended was cut off as Wren and another rider trotted up. They rode downwind, so that the sand they raised in passing blew away from the rest of the line, and Tsia was grate-

ful for the respite from the dust of more hooves. She found her
eyes watching the second rider curiously.

Big and husky, the woman called Ma towered over most of the
other mercs. Only a little of that height came from the tall, line-
back dun that she rode. Her face was calm and tanned; she did
not smile at Ramok's greeting. They spoke briefly, and then the
woman turned to ride back to her place in the line, while Wren
reined in beside Tsia again. As Ma passed Tsia, the woman gave
her that same merc appraisal she had received before, but with
eyes as cold and black and clear as a piece of space.

"*Ki araka ke, ar* Tsia," Tsia said carefully, touching her heart,
then holding her hand out in the greeting Wren had taught her.

The heavy woman looked at Tsia as if inspecting a plate of
food for nits, then carefully spit at the ground. The spittle made
a neat, round blob of insolence. The woman clucked to the dun
and rode on.

Wren grinned slyly. "That is Ma," he said with an appreciative
look at the disappearing woman.

"Cold woman to be a mother," Tsia muttered.

"Cold?" Wren shrugged. "She is M5. She has worked over
forty planets. Has more experience than anyone here except me.
Or maybe Spade."

Tsia rested her hand on the weapon that slapped her side with
the roan's motion. "I will be sure to remember that," she muttered.

Wren smiled faintly. "Don't worry. It won't be Ma who greets
you."

Tsia glanced at him sharply; she could not tell if he was mocking her or not. "What do you mean?"

"Ramok's been riding eyes on you. That means you're under
his pro—"

"I know what the idiom means," she interrupted sharply. "I
meant, what greeting?"

Wren grinned. "It is just an interesting ritual that introduces a
newcomer to our customs. Red seems to have acquired a vested
interest in the ritual since last night. You'll be fine," he reassured
her wryly. "Just think of it as a little game."

Tsia looked at him coldly. "I don't play games."

He grinned more widely. "That's what makes the ritual so interesting."

20

Dusty hours dragged into early afternoon before they reached the relative shelter of the sandstone pillars. Skimmers floated silently to the south, scanning closer and closer as the merc line advanced. Earlier, when the airships had swept overhead, Ramok had pulled the line into the shelter of ragged canyons that were heavily shaded by ancient water-cut overhangs. The echoes from their blunter disks, he said, would be even more effective there.

They stayed among the rocks for an hour. Tsia, feeling the cats prowl the edge of her consciousness, paced the ledge on which she waited. There was a cougar's lair just over the cliff on which she prowled, and she could feel the creature's unease at their presence. Eyes watching from the rocks. Tawny hide pressed against the stone . . . It was with relief when they moved back to the trail.

At noon, when they stopped again, the shade of the pillars was cooler than the exposed air, but Tsia could not stop sweating. The tremors returned, this time for several minutes without respite, and she bit her teeth together hard. If she had not done so, they would have chattered like a chill. She had to clench her fists to hide the shaking of her hands; she could not wipe the sweat from under her headgear shade until the shakes released their hold.

Bringing her hand back from her forehead, she glanced at her botas uneasily. Two were already empty, and only one of those had gone to her horse. How many days would they spend in this heat? And why had her body not compensated? She could walk the firepit easily; why was she not comfortable here?

In disgust, she wiped her sweaty hand on her jumpsuit before swinging stiffly down, then suppressed the groan that was becoming her only comment on the ride. As her feet landed lightly in

213

sand, the blood began to circulate in her buttocks again. It was with gritted teeth that she acknowledged Wren's amused grin.

For a moment she watched the other mercs dismount and stake their horses along the shade. When she followed suit, Wren gave her a glance of approval, then strode off to talk with Ramok. The mercs left their horses saddled, though they watered them carefully, then they dropped into the shadows and flung themselves down to sleep.

Tsia's legs were already stiffening, but she did not want to sit. Instead, she checked the field bits where they touched the sides of her horse's mouth—sometimes the field-generating tabs could give a horse a sensitive spot that needed salve—but the inner contacts of the tabs were clean, and the roan's lips were clear of rawness. Satisfied, she carefully wiped its eyes of the crusted sand that had accumulated, rubbing the back of its jaw to calm it as she did so. When she uncinched her gear, the roan stood quietly. She saw no burrs, no desert lice, no beetle sores on its back. It had not been likely, not with the treated underside of the saddle—nothing but the best for Pulan's mercs—but, uncertain what else to do with her time, she checked anyway.

When she was satisfied, she rinsed the caked sand from the beast's nostrils and then brushed his neck and mane, moving her hands back along its ribs to its flanks. Even dusty, the roan was beautiful. Its body and legs had the reddish tint of the sandstone streaks. Its hide was spotted with white along its rump. Its shoulders were powerful, its neck thick, and its head wedge-shaped and strong, not narrow like some of the ancient breeds. It was built not for speed but for stamina and strength—more of a mountain horse than a desert breed, she realized, the kind that could drive its way through deep snows and heavy mud where the smaller, lighter horses would bog down. That it did so well in the heat was a tribute to its breeding. She ran her hand down its legs and checked its hooves. She trailed her hand along its rump as she moved behind it, and the horse, though it stamped, did not kick. When she finished, she reset the saddle and cinched it up. Then she offered it more water.

"You like that, huh?" she murmured, using the last moisture in the rag to clean the eggs of the sandflies from around its eyes. She had never considered that there were as many insects afflicting the horses of the desert as there were in the sloughs.

"You treat him well," Ramok said in a mix of Standard and Korshani behind her. Tsia whirled and the horse jerked back and snorted, and the big man chuckled. "*Esha*, Tsia. Rest *ehinde*—a while in the shade. After this, we ride till we reach Swan Rocks."

She nodded shortly, trying to relax. When he left, she gathered her small pack from the saddle and made her way to one of the rock ledges, where she could sit in comparative shade. She could not help meeting the eyes of the auburn-haired woman again. Red—was that not what Wren had called her?—seemed to challenge Tsia from where she stood, and Tsia met her gaze deliberately before spreading her e-roll in the shadows.

She had nodded off when sudden movement made her start. Her hand found her flexor instinctively, but she relaxed when she saw that what had brought the other mercs to their feet was only one of the men, waving and gleefully holding up a snake, fat and round and very dead. It had lazed too long in the sun on a ledge above the mercenary's head. Now it would be his lunch. Seeing the others look up at him, the lucky man waved toward the rocks, and in minutes the hunt was on. Sand-colored men and women swarmed over the formations in search of their luncheon prey, while others set out their cooking kits.

Curious, Tsia watched the mercs grab pieces of flex metaplas from their saddlebags. Snapping the pieces out, they created forked sticks that would hold a snake's head to the ground. They could have snapped their flex swords into forked shapes, but then they could not have used the weapons against the snakes. All weapons read the scannet IDs that identified the life-forms in an area; no weapons activated against a nonhuman biological—not even a venomous one. Weapons worked only on people. The reason the mercs could use the flexplas on the snakes was that the flexplas pieces were shelter tools, not weapons.

With their flat knives and flexplas, the mercs took to the rocks, and Tsia, with an eye toward the hot stones overhead, followed suit. If she wanted anything other than slimchims in her churning stomach, she would have to get it on her own.

Going a different direction from the others, Tsia slipped past the horses and around the cliff to an isolated rock formation. Noiselessly, she made her way through the sand, her boots leaving only small, shapeless depressions to mark her path. When she reached the low rocks, the sun glistened off their surfaces in shimmering waves, heat worse than that which was rising from the bright and burning sand. She found herself grinning as the heat brought more sweat to her skin, found her feet moving more gracefully, as if she were almost dancing to the stones. She shoved her sleeves up over the manacles and bared her arms to the sun.

She climbed over the first couple of rocks quietly, making little sound. She could sense the life force of the desert like music in her blood. So many creatures in this heat—she could not identify them through the gate, only feel the force of their presence. Her eyes caught a glimpse of a darker stripe on a stone, and she moved left to see a fat snake sunning itself. Cautiously, she raised her flexplas stick. And froze.

Just in front of her, at thigh height, was a thick, coiled rope of red-splotched brown. Oh, stupid woman, she cursed herself as her heart seemed to stop. The eyes of the snake were on her legs, and it was now as motionless as the stone around her. It would be an instant only before it struck. And this was a lethal festal snake. She held her breath, and the cat feet in her brain seemed to be frozen, too, as if the cats crouched with her on the rock. Her hands, for the first time in months, were without even the shade of a tremor in their muscles.

The snake she had intended to catch flicked its tongue and mocked her. The flexplas fork was poised to fall. Below, the weathercloth of her jumpsuit would not stop the festal's fangs from plunging through the fabric; festal fangs were serrated and raser-sharp, the better to plunge through the hard scales of the diamond-red lizard backs. Not even her blunter would protect her from those teeth.

Tsia eyed the snakes with a cold knot of fear. Her hand was tensed. She could catch the top snake with the stick, but the second one would bite her. She did not have her flat knife in her hand—she had used her fist for climbing. She could neither grab it nor call for help—both movement and sound vibrations would irritate the snake to strike. In her right hand, the flexplas was motionless; in the sun, the manacles on her wrists became burningly hot.

With a slow, measured breath, Tsia judged her distance. Then, with the speed of a sandcat, she jerked her body to the side and snapped her left wrist down in front of her guts. The coiled snake struck home in a blindingly fast flash. Its teeth bit down on steel. Exultant, Tsia jammed the manacle against the rock to keep its fangs trapped while she ground its head against the stone. At her shoulders, the other snake writhed beneath the forked tip.

Carefully, she crushed the festal to death, her eyes glinting with a feral depth while her nostrils flared with the hot, bitter scent of torn flesh. Her tongue flicked along her lips. Only when the festal snake moved no more did she realize that her lips were pulled back from her teeth.

Abruptly, she distanced herself from her gate and wiped her face of expression. She studied her position. Her left hand still held the festal against the lower rock; her right hand held the flexplas. Cautiously, trying not to allow the higher snake to move from under the pressed-down fork, she shifted her body until she could step with her right leg on the fork and hold it in place there, at chest height. As soon as the snake was secured, she grabbed her flat knife from her harness. A second later the viper's head was off.

The long tail wriggled and snapped in a frenzy, and in Tsia's head the cat feet seemed to pace back and forth over her brain. Not until the snake became still did the padding claws subside to the depths of her gate. Silently, she grinned her thanks at the presence of the cats. For once they had seemed to help her—speeding her reflexes—instead of hinder her with their distracting power. She felt a surge of animal joy at the thought. Was this the meaning of the gate? The partnership that other guides could feel? A pair of tams snarled deep in her mind, and she met their mental growl with one of her own.

And then froze. Gods, what was she doing? Frantically, she withdrew from the gate, closing it down and backing mentally away. She was a guide, even if the guild no longer knew her. She was bound by the Landing Pact the same as the others. To deliberately seek out the cats . . .

"Daya . . ." she whispered. "Their call is so strong." She shuddered. It was with a sense of guilty dread that she snagged the festal viper by its crushed jaws and detached it from her manacle. Slowly, she got to her feet.

"*Parce,*" an admiring voice said behind her.

She became still for an instant. Then, without taking her eyes from the festal, she milked the poison from its mouth by stroking its fangs against the edge of the flexplas, just as she had once milked the surfsnakes in Ciordan. When she had emptied the venom sac, she cut the festal's head from its body with a quick movement. Only then did she look up.

The young man who eyed her was perched on a rock to her side, his loose cloth hood thrown back to expose cold, curious blue eyes and a hard, angled face burned dark by the sun. There were three snakes of his own stuck limply through the thigh loops of his harness. He could not have been more than twenty.

She met his eyes with curiosity—the mercs seemed to take all ages. "*Ki araka che, ar* Tsia," she said in greeting, kicking the snake heads down into the sand, where the beetles would find them at dusk.

"*Ki araka che,*" he returned. "*Ar* Moki." His eyes traveled over her body, then regarded the pair of serpents on the rocks. When he jumped lightly down from the rock and strode away, she looked after him with an oddly wary expression. He was an unusually silent climber: She had not sensed his approach at all.

Thoughtfully, Tsia wiped the festal poison from her manacle. With her wrist raw, she could not risk a drop of the venom working its way into her blood. Daya only knew how the virus would make her body react. She might heal quickly now and reject most med commands and drugs, but she had still been sensitive to the use of the numbing gold powder.

Using the knife, she slit the snakes open and cleaned them out, scraping the meager guts from their insides and burying the slimy refuse in the sand. When she had cleaned the blade and stuck it back in her harness, she looped the corpses in her hand, then made her way back to the shade.

There were a dozen cooking cubes lying out on the rocks by the time she returned. Ramok, Wren, and Aron were not there to keep her company; they were in the group that surrounded the pregnant councilwoman. Uncertainly, Tsia returned her flexplas tube to her pack and set out her own cooking cube where the sun was harsh and direct. Inside the cube, she laid the snakes so that the thin scales were inside the coil of meat. Then she moved back to squat in the shade while the smell of roasting meat made her mouth water. Beneath the sun the expandable cube soaked up the rays and focused them inside, cooking the food without flame. She did not worry about the node sensors detecting the heat. The cooking cube, like other merc gear, hid its focused heat with a blunter shield. Excess energy was radiated away, the emissions matching the expected radiance of the rocks beneath the cube.

Waiting quietly, Tsia rolled her shoulders and then rubbed at her wrists. A woman and man across from her laughed suddenly, and a third stout, round-faced merc stood, running his hand through his blond hair and winking at Tsia as if she would be interested in his attention. She ignored him, and the man's face shuttered, but he did not advance on her. Instead, he said something about Tsia to the woman next to him, who chuckled, then leaned forward to check her own cooking cube.

As soon as a snake was done enough for Tsia's taste, she speared one of the sizzling bodies with her knife. It was juicy meat, and she licked every drop of hot grease before it could fall and disappear in the sand. She left the second, larger snake to continue cooking while she moved back into the shade.

A few moments later a huge man stepped over to the circle of cooking cubes, and she looked up. She had thought that Ramok and Aron were big men, but this merc would tower over both of them like a tree over saplings. His face was dark and brooding, with heavy bones that looked almost hewn out of his seamed and weathered face. The shade he wore hid his hair, but his eyebrows were as black and heavy as the rest of him, sprinkled with gray so that they lightened the amber color of his eyes. He had a strangely light-footed walk—almost a glide—like a firedancer, Tsia thought with sudden amusement.

The tall man glanced around the cooking circle, then squatted and lifted the corner of the shade over Tsia's cube, eyeing the snake within. One of the women said Tsia's name and pointed at her. The man did not hide his chuckle. Tsia regarded him coolly. When he raised his heavy eyebrow and indicated the snake, she nodded slowly. With a flick of his knife, he spitted the hot meat and straightened up, then saw that Tsia still had half a viper by her side. He gestured at that piece.

"No," she said flatly, not bothering to stop chewing to answer his question. "This one is mine."

She spoke a mixture of Korshani and Merishkan, but her meaning was clear, and the huge merc stood in a fluid movement. When he stepped toward her, the others watched with anticipation.

Tsia tilted her head to look up at him, recognizing the sweet scent of the guides on his skin. She grinned, and slowly, the merc's eyes glinted with humor; but when he reached down, her knife casually touched his wrist on the underside, where his veins pulsed darkly against his bare, tanned skin. He looked at the hidden knife, then, amber eyes unreadable, withdrew his hand carefully. In spite of her easy smile, Tsia's ice-blue eyes were very still and her hand, for only the second time in weeks, was rock-steady.

Without taking his eyes off her, the merc took a bite of the juicy flesh of the snake in his hand, and, straightening, said softly, "*Yur* Tsia *a'*Ramok *pash a'ruk.*" Then, without a backward glance, he turned and made his catlike way to the next group of cooking cubes, to repeat his foraging there.

"You handled that well," Aron said.

Tsia glanced up as the other man squatted down. "What did he say?"

"I did not catch it."

"Something about me and Ramok *pash a'ruk*," she repeated.

The man beside her chuckled. "He said that the touch of Ramok's feather was sharp."

"Feather?"

"*'Tsia'* means 'feather' in Merishkan."

Her face flushed. "Is that why everyone laughs when they say my name?"

"There are worse names, Little Feather," he said softly, touching her arm and trailing his fingers down her flesh until she shrugged away from him. "You remind me of my sister," he said easily.

"Then," she said sharply, "keep on being reminded." She got to her feet and moved away, her walk made stiffer by muscles that had sat too long unmoving. Behind her, Aron chuckled. She did not glance back until she reached her horse, and when she did, she saw that Ramok had appeared in the shade with Aron. The two faced each other in a tense tableau until Aron slapped Ramok's shoulder and the taller merc laughed. They walked off together.

She muttered, checking the saddle cinch with irritation. The shackles slid on her wrist, and she glared at them. Wren must know who could either pick the lock for her or seam-unseal the weld. She dared not use the mole. She had used it only that once, and she did not know what would happen if it was directed toward her skin. Besides, she could not get the metaplas matrix of the manacles unless she linked again to the node. No variable sword could cut through metaplas—varswords were made only for flesh and bone. And her flexor, though it had broken through the chains with repeated hacking, would never cut through the fetters without slicing off her hands.

Lost in thought, Tsia stood by the roan and scratched its neck, smelling its thick odor until Ramok gave the signal to mount up. She would have swung into a place near the end of the line, but Ramok called for her to follow him at the front. She had to ignore the speculative looks of those by whom she rode but paused to greet Yemene quietly as she passed. The woman's face was wan and dusty, the lines around her mouth and eyes deep with grime and exhaustion. Tsia supposed she ought to feel grateful for riding with Ramok near the head of the line. The dirt would be less pervasive at the front than in the rear, where the hooves would cast it up into a mouth-drying, low-hung cloud of grit. But on display and on edge, she merely nodded to Yemene and ignored Aron's greeting when she passed him, her ire rising as he chuckled again.

The midday hours passed sluggishly. Tsia dozed in the saddle, then jerked awake at the hunting cries of a pair of spotted tams. She was wide-eyed, and her gaze darted across the dusty rocks, but there was nothing there to see. The tams were back in the canyon they had just passed. Only she had heard their cries.

By the time evening began to cool the air, Tsia was tired, sore, and restless. She was still following Ramok, whose huge shadow careened across the darkening ground as his horse scrambled in the loose soil. Behind them sixteen other riders crested the yellow grass dunes and walked, then trotted between the rocks. The dull thunder of their life force filled her mental ears until she thought herself deaf.

Finally the sun sank. In an hour the heat dissipated with the light until a cold darkness expanded in the sky. Ramok kept on, leading them through the chilling, twisted shapes of the desert, guiding himself by the stars so that they covered six more cold kilometers between dusk and drycamp.

Tsia let him choose the spot where she would sleep again and, after dropping her gear in place, took care of the roan. Alone in the dark except for the skitterings of the night creatures that explored the edges of their camp, she thought she heard the hunting cry of a desert cat, but it melted into her gate as she closed herself against it. In minutes she had dropped into the formless sleep of fatigue, where her dreams were disturbed only by the soft snarling of the cats that crawled through her head. She did not know how much later is was that she registered Ramok's scent in her sleep. She did not even roll over to give him more room until he gently nudged her in the back.

Dawn was nowhere near their camp when Ramok's abrupt movement roused her. When he saw she was already awake, he gestured sharply for her to rise and follow him. He allowed himself only a brief grin when she rolled out of her sandy depression and stifled a groan and a shiver at her stiffness and the chill. He barely waited for her to pull on her boots; as he strode off in the dark, Tsia scrambled after him, shrugging into her blunter as she went.

Heavy as Ramok was, the quickness and quietness of his stride continually amazed her, and she almost smiled. But her expression turned sober as she slipped through the crowd he had reached an instant before and came upon the body that he was examining in the dark. The dead man had been relieving himself just before he had died—that much was clear. His face was already torn by the sandrats that had gathered instantly at the scent of a kill.

With the flat of his metal knife, not his raser, Ramok lifted something from the body and flung it far out on the sand. Then, carefully, he examined the ground. Nodding to himself, he lifted the clothes from around the man's neck and wrists, then pulled down the loosely laced boots to look at the limply twisted ankles. He grunted softly.

"Look." He pointed. On the man's left limb, just above his boot, a bruise was blackening and spreading even as they watched. "Seryal."

Those behind her muttered to themselves, and Tsia, too, felt a chill creep inside her blunter. Ramok had been lucky. The seryal spider he had flipped away could have had a mate still hiding in the dead man's clothes. The merc left the body as it was and motioned curtly for one of the women to come forward. She pointed a hisser at the body; the skin began to sizzle. Tsia was not aware of stumbling away or the shifting of the mercs to get out of her way as she ran. The hissing of the body seemed to fill her ears with the growing snarl of the cats in her head, and the sharp smell of disintegration clogged her nose like burned cheese.

When she finally stopped, she was outside the boundaries of the camp and the shadows of the mercenaries were far behind her. She stood there, her head tilted back to blindly search the sky, her mouth open to suck in the thin air of the night. She closed her eyes and stretched her arms to the stars. A cougar growled a long, low sound, then raised its voice in a scream, and she trembled with its promise. It seemed to take her home not to Ciordan but to a more powerful, primitive place, as the roan could never do. It was not until she felt Ramok approaching that she lowered her hands and silently followed him back to camp.

21

It was a dry, drab morning that followed the night. In hours, the day had become depressingly hot and time morbidly slow. In the brain-roasting waves of heat, the sun crept across the sky. In spite of the temperature, Wren and Aron continued to tutor Tsia in the Merishkan tongue. Her accent was too light, they said. Many of the words she had learned were the same as they were in Korshani, they acknowledged, but her accent was all wrong, too reminiscent of the desert tongue. Or of Ciordan, she realized as she noticed that the problem lay not with the tone in which she spoke Cekulu's language but with the lilt of her own native tongue.

"Be more aggressive with it," Aron advised. "Merishkan is short and rhythmic. If you want to save your lunch from Forrest again, you will have to speak it with confidence."

"Forrest?"

"The ox of a man who took one of your snakes yesterday."

"He was welcome to it," she returned. "I needed only one and did not mean to catch two in the first place."

Aron raised his eyebrow, drawing his dark face into the lines of mocking amusement that she was only now learning to tolerate without offense. "Generosity can be seen as a weakness. Give too often and you might find yourself giving your life to retain what is worth a fight."

On her other side Wren grinned. "Aron is full of philosophy these days," he commented slyly.

The other man smiled, the expression never reaching his eyes. "I tell myself it accompanies me during the day. Keeps my e-roll warm at night."

Wren chuckled. "That's what you get for coming from Arctica. Those ice worlds always leave a man worried about the warmth."

"Are all of you from different planets?"

Aron shrugged. "Most, though about half of this group are from Risthmus. Ramok wanted mercs who knew the terrain by feel and sight, not overlay. Most mercs live on the last planet they served on. They shift after each call. Some of us stay at the guilds. The rest have homes in one place or another."

"I would think the guild would be a dark atmosphere to live in."

Aron raised his eyebrow sardonically. "Of course not. You are driven, challenged, forced to push yourself every day. When you are not fighting, the guild is the best place in the sixty-four worlds to spend your time. There is always something new—techniques, equipment—to learn how to use. Always something alien or new coming in from the rim."

Wren glanced over at Aron. "Did you see that new breaker that Old Heak brought into the Lonestone guild before you shipped out? He picked that up out on the rim."

Aron nodded. "Smoothest piece of action I ever saw."

"They say it uses Dhirrnu technology—warps right through a neutral suit to break the bones within."

"Saw him use it on a shoot suit but not a neutral. Like to see that." Aron glanced at Tsia, then looked out over the trail, his darkeye-enhanced gaze noting even the pattern of grass in the wind. "Heard we got a new dart in, too. Got proximity shields built right into the link. Baken's group used it on Wolf III in the Tallers. Didn't lose a single one to the reachers in the trees."

"Reachers?" Tsia questioned.

"Flesh-hungry life-forms," Aron explained. "Hunt in pairs, sometimes groups of four. Chameleons—like the shapers we have here. Every couple of decades their populations blow up into the millions. Like a cancer. Have to go in and clean them out." He grinned. "Hunters keep the pops down in season, but in the red years it gets bad."

"I worked the Tallers twice," Wren commented. "Spent three years in the Canopy Wars. Then I went back fifty-three years later to fight for Quentin in the Snow Rebellion."

"Good action there," Aron agreed. "Worked with Quentin myself."

Wren smiled faintly. "Last time I saw her, that old woman was still trying to drive the devil to ground. She never got him. That alien was one of the frostiest bugs I've ever tried to trace."

"Figure he's still there?"

"Naw. I think he went rounder within a month of starting the action."

"Rounder?" Tsia interrupted.

"Went into orbit around the planet," Aron explained.

Wren nodded. "I think he set himself on an asteroid in the Wide Belt, then sat back to watch it happen."

"Got the shielding to do it," Aron mused. "Chubs like him blend in damn well. Like to get a foot on their home planet sometime. See some of those facilities they gloat about."

"They've got to have the best distorts in the Federation. We used one on Freedom, and it made all the difference."

The two men fell silent, and Tsia wiped the sweat from her brow. "Was Ramok with you in those places?"

Wren glanced at her out of the corners of his small, birdlike eyes. "Ask the man yourself," he answered slyly. "He is most likely missing your company."

Aron gave him a warning look. "Red sought out Ramok this morning," he said to Tsia. "Found him in your arms. You were both lost to the world."

Tsia gave him an irritated look. "We were only sleeping."

"Aye." There was a wealth of nuance in Wren's word. "The noon break should be interesting, don't you think?"

"Daya take you all and your tainted thoughts," she muttered.

She wiped her forehead irritably. This heat, which should have invigorated her, sapped even her anger. She did not understand it. Fire was a stimulant. When she left the flames, she felt excited, alive. This sun was like a spoiled child: The more it took, the more it wanted. Of Tsia's five water bags, three now were empty, and the fourth one only half-full. "How long before we reach water again?"

"We reach Bonnell's Bay tonight," Wren answered. "The dredger fields there will hide our presence from the node, and we can make as much noise as we want—at least until we leave again."

"Leave?"

He nodded. "We will split up to cross the mountains. There are three landing pads along this stretch of the Cheba Rift, and we will cross the rift using skimmers."

Tsia slapped at a fly on the roan's neck; the red splotch dried instantly on her skin so that she had to scrub her hand on her breeches to scrape off the scaly wings. "The art guild won't have someone waiting for us there?"

Wren chuckled. "Do you fear your former masters, Little Feather?"

"Stop calling me 'Little Feather,'" she said softly, "or I will stuff those words so far up your nose, I will have to read them out of your darkeye next time you try to say something."

Wren's eyes narrowed, and Aron started to laugh. "The Feather shows her teeth," he said with a grin.

Tsia glared at both of them. "May the diggers make your graves on stone," she swore. Then she spurred the roan to a reluctant lope until she caught up with Ramok. The tall merc glanced at her flushed face as she matched his speed. At the look he cast behind him, the other two men dropped quickly back in the dusty line.

"Ramok," Tsia asked, holding out one of her wrists, "is there someone here who can open these for me?"

The man frowned, his black hair dragging across his forehead with the motion before he answered. "Spade," he said, "or Red."

"Spade?" She raised her eyebrows. "Is that a name or a nickname?"

He grinned. "He always carries an e-wrap on him somewhere, and we figure he is going to be buried in one." When he spoke, it was in a curious mixture of Korshani, Merishkan, and Standard that, though it was awkward and lacked the depth and imagery of Standard by itself, was a mixture she could at least somewhat understand.

"We will go to Levian?"

He nodded. "The councilwoman wants her child born in a temple, if possible."

Tsia glanced back along the line. Yemene, on her bay, was out of sight behind a twisted formation of yellow-striped stone, but Tsia could picture the heavy body as clearly as if the woman rode beside her. "Because of the esper forecast?"

He nodded. "We were hired only to protect the birth of the child. We don't care whether it is in a temple or not, so if it is possible, we will deliver the woman there."

Tsia shifted uncomfortably as the cat feet teased her thoughts. "If the miners do not want Yemene returned, won't they fight us at the temples?"

Ramok glanced sideways, but he saw only curiosity in her gaze, not fear. He nodded in answer to her question. "Another *nyeka*," he added softly, "would be welcome."

Sand whirled in the wind, and the sun caught it up in a yellow-red cloud. Welcome ... To fight? To speed across deserts and seas? A cougar cried out in her head, a long, lonely sound. What about her work? she asked herself harshly. What about the judgment of the guild? Ciordan? What could she do for the mercs to be useful to them? Guide them without using her gate? That would be a laugh. Nor could she leave the planet when they had work on other worlds. Ramok's offer, she thought bitterly, was empty of all but his bed.

Ramok urged his horse up the next dry grass dune. He glanced at the set of her face. His comment had unnerved her, and he wondered what she thought she would do when they reached Pulan. A ghost from any guild other than the artists' could always try to go home, but a ghost created by the art guild? No. The artist guild was dark and hungry. It chose its victims carefully and often ate more than once of their flesh. Even Yemene would have to be careful.

He glanced again at Tsia and noted the way she licked her dry lips. "Might as well drink now," he remarked. "Bonnell's Bay is close."

"There is plenty of water there?"

He nodded. "The bay is the only water hole that can handle the size of our party. Once we hit the mountains, the tank levels will be low, and the springs mere trickles, if they are not already dry."

"Will everyone ride to the mountains?"

He shook his head. "One group stays at the bay to verify the water-usage ghosts after we leave. Once they get rid of their horses, they will appear as hikers, not equine biologicals."

"The rest of us travel together?"

"No, but—" Ramok had heard the hesitation in her voice. "Don't worry, Feather. You will stay with me. Unless, of course," he added with a glance back at the two men who trailed them in line, "you prefer to ride with Aron."

Tsia set her jaw. "I prefer no man at all," she returned curtly. "But if I must ride with someone, I prefer to ride with you."

Ramok grinned and leaned over, and she found herself snapped out of her saddle to sit in front of him on his, the reins trailing across to her horse as it snorted and trotted nervously beside the other beast. Tsia stared at him for a frozen second. "Put me down!" she snarled, twisting her wiry body like a cat out of his iron grip. "I did not mean—"

"Sharp teeth," Ramok murmured as he set her back on her own saddle, "but a soft mouth."

Tsia regained her seat in a flash and snapped the reins to break into a loose gallop that the roan protested before giving in. Even a creature such as he, genetically engineered for Risthmus, could not maintain such a pace for long in the heat. Tsia let him drop back to a smooth walk.

She was angry, she realized, not because of Ramok's actions but because she found that she missed the hard strength of a man more than she thought she had. She was trembling again, too, and the wildness that seemed to lurk beneath the surface of her mind was crawling with the feet of the creatures that she sensed. When Ramok had touched her, his hands had been like a cluster bomb breaking a dam; she had wanted to revel in his arms the same way she danced in the fire: uncontained, moving simply to feel the shifts, breathing just to taste the air. Was this merely a reaction to her freedom from the chains?

Wren's words haunted her: ". . . if you miss the feel of the manacles . . ." A cold chill spiked itself into a series of shivers, and she stared at her hands with sudden dread. Was this the virus uncontrolled? Had she become one of those guides whose virus had to be killed to save their bodies? Oh, Daya, was that the cause of her tremors? The chill turned into a lance of cold dread. What if they had to strip away her gate?

The felines scratched at her skull and clawed at her thoughts. In the heat of the evening, the cat feet swarmed. Her sweat came freely to her brow, and she wiped at it automatically. If it was such a useless gate, why did she care if it was closed? She posed the question to her gate, and the presence of the cats surged. She almost cried out with their strength. An animal snarling answered her, deafening her to the man who rode up alongside.

She could no longer imagine life without them. She had to admit that. She had thought that her longing for the fire was strong, but the gate itself was addictive. Even in the short time since she had left Noirelle she had twice reached into the gate to tap the cats for their feelings. Twice breached the Landing Pact simply because she wanted to touch the cats. Twice she had betrayed the guides.

Ramok watched her thoughtfully. "You do not seem to like the idea of staying with me and the mercs."

Mercs? It was the cats that held her thoughts. She dragged her attention back with difficulty. "I could offer you nothing," she answered finally.

"You already offered me my life."

She did not answer, and his eyes narrowed.

"You have a colonist link," he stated quietly, "but you say you *are*—not *were*—*kai-al*. Therefore, you belong to the guide guild here on Risthmus. The link you have now is stolen."

Tsia's face became expressionless at his words, but he continued, his voice steady. "The ghost line you left behind you—if it is not tight . . ." He shrugged. "Anyone—merc or otherwise—could tap in to that, trace your link, and take it away from you again. You will be safer with me," he emphasized, "than almost anywhere else."

Tsia tried to read the emotion behind his words, but in the blinding slant of the late sun, the black gaze, hidden by the darkeyes he wore, gave nothing away. She had freed herself from Cekulu; was she already so conditioned to the chains that she would allow this man to take the artist's place? Her body felt hot, then cold, and her fingers trembled on the reins.

"There are some," he added gently, "who might not wish to help you as I do. Leaving out friendship, respect, and trust—those things, like love, take time—at least there is between us this: I owe you my life; you owe me your freedom. Gratitude is not the best bond, but it is a link through which we can work together. And ghosts," he said, gazing out across the grassy dunes, "do not usually make their way home again without help."

Home? She had broken the Landing Pact. Not once but twice. She could not go home. Not to the guild, not to her family. She tried to smother the sudden wave of grief, but all she managed to do was turn her face to hide her eyes as they filled with tears that spilled out onto her cheeks.

Ramok watched her silently. When her body stopped its trembling, he spoke again, a statement, more than a question: "You cannot return to Ciordan."

Her grip on the reins tightened.

"You are *kai-al*," he said thoughtfully. "I read your link in Noirelle. You have open colonist status. There are a number of guilds that would protect you just to have you on their lists."

Tsia forced her hand to relax, ignoring the shivers that weakened her resolve. "I cannot hide my scent forever, nor my gate, nor the way I need the fire," she returned steadily. "The guides are a tight-knit group, and if I return to my work, they will discover me someday no matter what guild I join."

Ramok gave her a sharp look, and even his darkeye could not hide his startlement. "It is the guides, not the artists, from whom you flee?"

She hesitated, but he saw it.

"Some guilds," he said slowly, "are strong enough to protect the identity of their members. Give them new names, new homes. Guilds," he said, "like mine."

Tsia stared at him. All the rage and impotence that she had felt for the last sixteen months crawled up out of her gut and into her voice when she answered. "I am a biologist—an ecologist—not a merc," she said vehemently. "And I belong on this world, not any other. I need *this* heat, *these* sunbeams, not the rays of another star. I need this wasteland, full of seryal and snakes and sand. I need green watersheds here, in Ciordan, in the Sinking Plains, in the lowlands of the Vulcans, not the trees and shrubs of another planet. I need to see the running grass spread across these plains, feel the shadows of the stillhawks in the dunes." Hear the screams of the cats on the stones. She gestured sharply in her frustration. "You are a merc," she said angrily. "You move from world to world. There is no place for me with you."

"Today," Ramok agreed, "I work on Risthmus. Two years ago, I was on Rogue; and ten years ago, on Aktiki." With sharp eyes he watched a skimmer float across the sky in the northwest, toward the Cheba Rift. He glanced back at Tsia's face. "You saw Forrest. He is *kai-al*, and he is a merc. Our guild is like any other, except that, since they cannot travel between worlds, we have even more need for guides among our people."

She started to protest, but he continued.

"Guides for terrain artists and scouts—like Forrest and Ence. The guides in the merc guild have to be able to fight—no one joins without some skill in that—but you are rights-conditioned and trained already, and a guide's specialty does not have to be weapons. It can be Risthmus itself."

Tsia scowled at him, and Ramok gestured at the hill up which they rode.

"An experienced guide can hide this very hill from the node. Can hide the shadows of the hawks on the wind. Can make the moons disappear. The sensor net has many ways to trace a human being," he added quietly, "but a guide like you, with your sense of life and your experience in the terrain of this world, could beat the net with your ghost lines. You could learn to hide an entire canyon from the node."

Tsia rode quietly for a moment. "I thought traces were active," she said finally. "I thought they were set only for humans, not for terrains and biomes."

Ramok shook his head. "You can set a ghost line for anything. It only requires enough knowledge of the life-form or biome to make it real enough to the node so that it is ignored. Only a biologist or ecologist can do that. Only a guide has that knowledge. Like setting the blunter disks"—he motioned at her chest pocket—"which tell the node you are an echo of a simple biological—a horse."

"But a disk like this was not set in a few hours," she protested. "A ghost that masks both heartbeat and temperature and is sensitive to terrain ... Such a ghost would take a week to set up."

He nodded. "That is why we have Horen with us." He motioned at a merc who rode six back in the line. "He is a naught, but has enough experience to make ghost lines his specialty. His blunter disks are the best in the business. And these"—he tapped his own chest pocket—"were done well enough that the artists have yet to figure out that we are not still hiding outside their walls. If Horen's other ghosts are set as tightly as the echoes on these masks, we will be able to ditch the horses at the rift and ride the skimmers back to Pulan."

Tsia's thoughts mulled over his words. "How—" She stopped. "If Yemene was kidnapped only two days ago, how could you have set up the echo ghosts in time to use them now?"

"Trade secret."

Tsia gave him a sour look. "That's what Aron said."

"Join us," he said softly. "You will no longer have to wonder."

She gave him an unreadable look and urged the roan up the crest of the loose hill. With Ramok, she slid down the other side, then plodded up the next.

It had become a habit for Tsia to ignore the shimmering lakes of color that clung to the rocky, bottomed-out soil. This time the wavering images of shrubs were real: Two small stands of dried needlewood stood rooted in the ground, but their twisted branches were brittle with the lack of water. Tsia noted their dryness and tapped her last bota, reassured only when she heard the faint slosh of water. Needlewood roots were deep, and their underground storage nodules lasted for up to five—sometimes even six—months without moisture. For them to be so dead, the water tables must be down a long way.

Behind her the other mercenaries stretched out in a ragged line. Here, where there was no real trail, they zigzagged along the hills in bunches.

"The soil must cover the stands of needlewood sometimes," she pointed out to Ramok as the horses lunged down the next slope and threw sand in the air with each kicking, sliding hoof.

Ramok nodded. "Monsoons."

"Fever winds," she corrected. "When the fever wind blows, everything that exists today could be covered in an hour."

"Fever wind?"

"They are called that because they blow hot, then cold, like a fever that breaks and begins again." Her own words made her shiver, and she tamped down hard on the shakes that threatened to break out. "How do you know there won't be others at Bonnell's Bay?" she queried.

"There have been no dust clouds to betray any movement other than ours, and there are no buzzards to indicate someone waiting." He motioned at his saddlebags. "I checked the power sources on my trace before you joined me; there was nothing other than the dredges that maintain the springs. And not once today has a skimmer landed to the south, where the bay hides behind that hill."

Tsia peered at the whitened sky and wondered if she would have seen a dust cloud if there had been one. Ramok and the other mercs, who wore the darkeyes day and night to enhance their ability to see motion and heat against the ground, were not bothered by the glaring light of the sun, but Tsia's blue eyes, burned by the sun and dried by the wind, ached constantly. She glanced at Ramok and saw him examining the rounded hills ahead. She felt her gate stretch and realized that she could have told him that there were only rodents hiding in the soil, but he did not ask.

Ten minutes later they topped the next dry hill, and Tsia pulled the roan to a stunned halt. Before her, hidden by dusty ground that crawled up to the very edges of the trees that grew below, was Bonnell's Bay, a valley that stretched out like a massive holotank in the desert. Lush greenery created a canopy that stood thirty meters above the floor of the sheltered valley. Towering trees planted themselves in loose crevasses among the rocks that rose from the valley floor and defined its other side. The twisted roots, exposed where they crawled from one stony crack to another, were brown and tough like the trees. The tree trunks themselves were ridged and shaded by their leaves, carved with tiny rows of steps that circled ever upward on the dusty-white wood. Below the trees, shrubs littered the ground with sparse, rubbery leaves. The thickness of this green expanse was overwhelming. Tsia wiped her hand across her face to hide the sudden pain in her eyes.

Beside her, Ramok sat motionless for a long moment, scanning the growth with an intensity that left her wondering if there was danger after all. Then he nodded to himself. She looked at him askance, and he motioned toward the edge of the dune. "Dredger fields," he explained. "They keep the hills from crawling south into the spring. They kick on whenever the soil shifts too close to the floor. Sometimes, if there are rocks to move, it kicks on for days." He eyed the top of the dune again. "If we passed through the field, it would log our physical shape, not just our heartbeat and heat. But it is not on right now; I would have been able to see the upward shift of sand if it were." He grinned. "When it is on, it is strong. You will see. It will mask any power use we have to make."

"It is not on now?" she peered at the top of the hill. She could see no shift, but her eyes ached and the sense of the cats made her sight half-unfocused.

He shook his head. "Must have gone on this morning—the hill is well back from the trees." He stood up in the saddle and twisted to wave at the mercs who were just cresting the last dry-grass hill. Aron, the first one over, stood in his stirrups and signaled the line behind. The horses rode forward.

While they rode up, Tsia dismounted and walked to the top of the dune. The edge of the wind lifted tiny sails of sand and dust from the hilltop—like an offshore breeze on a coastal dune—and left a smooth, sheer, untouched drop to the valley floor. Beside her the roan tossed his head impatiently. Tsia soothed him, eyeing the downside of the dune with speculation. Ramok was looking back, watching his mercs approach and not watching her, so she stepped experimentally to the edge. In Ciordan one could jump off the sheer sides of the dunes that formed between the beach and the inner lakes. She felt the cat feet skitter across her skull and with a wild laugh tossed the reins around the saddle horn and ran to the edge of the hill.

"*Aiieee!*" she cried, throwing her arms out suddenly and twirling on the soft precipice.

Startled, Ramok twisted in the saddle. Then, before his widened eyes, Tsia flung herself from the crumbling edge and disappeared.

"Tsia!" he shouted. He leapt from his horse and raced to the edge of the sandy cliff.

Tsia was flying. Below her, the slope rushed up and engulfed her legs in a huge slide of shockingly cool sand. Thrusting out, she sprang away from the nearly vertical slope, the yellow cloud from the surface arching after her like water. Up with her body, up away from the dune, she soared in a golden sky. "*Aiieee,*" she shouted again. Her feet skidded into the sand again, and her boots were full of weight. She heard Ramok's shout, but she threw herself off the slope once more. This time she flipped in a neatly tucked roll, straightening out just before she landed near the bottom. She rolled the rest of the way in a tumbling heap of sand and skin. Coming to a stop, she lay breathless and laughing at the furious face of Ramok glaring over the edge above.

"Tsia!" he roared. Aron and Wren reached the crest and pulled to a stop, leaping from their horses at his shout.

"What is it?" "What the hell . . ."

Ramok leaned over the edge as much as he dared. There were three great holes in the burning sand where the *nyeka* had hit, slid, and then leapt out into space again. Now he could see her slender body lying on the floor of the spring's valley, shaking with laughter.

From beside him, Aron chuckled. "Lose your feather so soon, Ramok? It seems she will go to great lengths to evade your embrace."

"You little fool," Ramok yelled at Tsia. "I should beat some sense into you when I get my hands on you . . ." He shook his fist.

She laughed, dusting her pants and hair from the wild fall. "Then come and get me," she taunted in Korshani.

Wren gave Ramok a speculative look, then flicked his glance at Aron. "The feather flies till it is caught by the wind. But who, I ask, is the wind?"

Ramok gave him a sly grin. "Wren," he ordered, settling his weapons securely on his harness, "take the horses." He started running toward the cliff. "Of the rest of you," he shouted over his shoulder, "the last one down has sweep duty." He gave one great leap, then disappeared. His wild yell as he hit, rolled, and gathered speed was lost in the sudden clamor of the others, who swore, glanced at each other, then, as they heard more laughter from below, jumped off their horses and shoved each other to get to the top of the dune.

By the time the last of them had gathered at the crest of the sandy mountain, Ramok and Aron and Tsia had clambered back up the dune to jump again. The wind was filled with the sound of their growls and snarls. With every step, avalanches flowed. For every two meters they climbed back up, half of them slid back four. By the time Wren and two others had followed the horses down to the valley floor, almost everyone—even Ma—had taken a turn, however unwilling, from the top.

It was not until an hour later that Tsia caved in to her exhaustion. She had stripped the sandy bandages from her wounds, leaving the garbage to hiss on the sand with the other merc trash. Her cuts had closed over quickly, and the skin grafts had sealed and hidden the flesh beneath. Had it not been for the virus, she would have had to wear the bandages for nearly a week. She scratched at her head. The sand in her short hair would probably never come out, she told herself sourly, and her clothes were still leaking grains of sand from their seams. She shook out her blunter, then hesitated before putting it back on. Her body alternated between being too cold and being too hot, and every time she took the jacket off, she wanted it back on within seconds. Finally she folded it over her arm, the blunter disk close to her skin in her jumpsuit.

A hundred meters away, while the chill air of night descended, the mercs had started two fires underneath the shelter of a large repulsor tarp. Like a passive blunter, the tarp absorbed the heat and light, storing it in cells that could be tapped later for energy. If they had planned to stay at the spring throughout the day, the tarp would have used that energy, as well as that of the sun, to cool the air beneath it. Curious, Tsia had questioned Aron about the repulsors, and the merc had explained that the dredger fields would mask the repulsors as well as or better than the repulsors masked the flames. The leaping fires, built out of wood provided by the desert guides who stocked the bay for hikers, would not even be noticed by the node.

"But when we leave," she had protested, "the woodpiles will show that some is missing. The guides who work this terrain will see that, even if the artist nodies don't."

Aron had motioned at the largest merc, Forrest, and she saw that next to him, a blond man and a dark-haired woman were at work over a portable holotank. "Horen and Pilo are setting ghosts in the node now," he explained. "A week from today, on their regular schedule, the guides will register the loss of the firewood and replenish it. Until then the pile will scan out as full as it was before we got here, and its scansign will decrease in the node normally, with anyone else's use."

Now, as the fires spread into the stone-edged rings, Tsia felt the cat feet in her skull speed up and the virus urge her toward the flames. She rubbed her wrists absently until she realized what she was doing, then she stared at the manacles in disgust. She could never step in the fire with metal on her skin. It would sear her wrists so that she would bear the scars for life. Small scars were one thing; large scars were areas that could not be protected by the sweat of the flesh around them. One could bear only so many scars before one had to give up the flames. Tsia, her dreams in the past having been on her gate, not the firepit, had not truly considered what that would mean. Now, with the virus calling her to the fire, her skin crawled. She looked up suddenly to see the red-haired woman regarding her with hostility from a stand of the towering trees.

Tsia rose to her feet in a swift, lithe movement. "Red?"

The woman nodded slowly, her eyes black and expressionless.

Tsia held out her wrists. "Ramok said you could free me of these."

Red pointed at Tsia's flex sword, and it took Tsia a moment to realize that the woman wanted the blade in payment.

"No. Something else."

Around them a few of the other mercs had stopped to watch. Red pointed again at the length of steel. *"Ke naga botag, chuk chiha ke buk,"* she said mockingly.

" 'She holds the sword as she holds her fear,' " Wren translated in a low voice behind her. "She is speaking of you," he added unnecessarily.

Tsia's ice-blue eyes narrowed coldly.

"Uze wier taabon k'im," Red continued derisively.

Wren's voice echoed softly, " 'Her will is weak within her.' " He gave her a speculative look. "She speaks like that to them, not you," he explained, "to show that you are not worth being addressed directly."

Tsia's face flushed. Red gestured again at Tsia's sword, this time with a different meaning. Tsia needed no translation to understand this. To the side, several mercs grinned and placed their bets. Another thrust a stick into the fire that grew at his feet.

Tsia looked from Red to the others. "All right. I'll fight you," she said finally. "If you win, you get the sword. If I win, you take these off—both of them."

The red-haired woman nodded with a sharp smile. Watching Tsia with a predatory smirk, she removed the weapon harness from her hips and hefted her flexor in her hand. With each toss it lengthened and sharpened and shifted until slowly, wickedly, it became a triangular blade with each edge serrated and hungrily sheening.

"That's right," Tsia muttered. "Try and scare me." She pulled her own harness off, removed her blunter, and shoved her sleeves up to bare her forearms. When she took up her own flexor, she played no such games. She glanced at Red and, with a predatory smile, abruptly snapped the weapon into a tapering point that sported a hook partway down its length. The suddenly wary look in Red's eyes was rewarding. Tsia smiled grimly in turn. Unless Red had worked a mudcrab den before, the shape of Tsia's flexor was not one she had ever seen. It was not a shape Tsia would have considered as a weapon—not, that is, until Jak Volen had shown her how to use it for things other than hooking crabs.

The two women circled. Red feinted in close. Tsia let her come, refusing to use the hook on her spike to turn Red's light attack. Suddenly Red blitzed forward. The woman did not even get to the front of her lunge before Tsia danced lightly away and snapped the sword across Red's ribs. There was surprise written in the other woman's face.

Red, wiry and tough as a bullwhip, glanced at her own blade. There was no blood on it, and she smiled wolfishly.

"*Bussa je botag*, Red," one of the women called. "Look to the heart of your sword." The others laughed.

Red merely called back with a curse. Twice, as they feinted and lunged, Red almost disarmed Tsia—once by casting sand up from the ground with a parried tip and then by a quick flip of her wrist when they came chest to chest for a second over a fallen log. But each time Tsia evaded and learned.

Both were sweating. They twisted and slashed, but Tsia still did not use the hook. Red drove Tsia back, then was forced back herself. The merc clenched and whipped the suddenly shooting spike of her sword up past Tsia's face. Tsia threw herself back. As Red's blade whirred by, Tsia twisted her wrist. Her own blade hooked the merc's sword, and with a sudden snap it slid, the hook dragging Red's blade with it, down the length of Tsia's sword. The flexor was twisted from Red's hand before the woman could resnap its shape. Tsia danced back, throwing the blade behind her. She grinned. It was a mistake.

Enraged, heedless of the sword, Red threw herself at Tsia, knocking her back. The two women crashed into the mercs who were watching from the side of the fire, and both men and women scattered. Tsia avoided the flames easily, but by the time she rolled to her feet, Red had a flat knife in her hand.

Tsia's eyes grew cold. She met the other's attack straight on, catching Red's lightning-quick hand and twisting till both she and Red were strained like a silent statue. Then, with a soul-chilling expression, Red grinned, her teeth a long row of white broken only by the browning marks of a dead tooth. Red knew she was stronger. Slowly, ever so slowly, she forced Tsia's arm back and down, over the fire.

Then a strange look came into Red's eyes, and she looked down. The heat was beginning to bake her own skin. She tried to pull free, but Tsia, whose unmarked flesh had been licked by the blaze for seconds, had an equally deadly grip on Red's arm. Red found herself locked in a nerve hold almost identical to the one she had forced on the *nyeka*. Orange lights curled around Tsia's elbow. Red gasped. Sweat started from her brow; her black eyes widened in panic. Slowly, her white-knuckled fingers uncurled until the knife dropped from her hand to the coals. The brands scattered their glowing eyes on Tsia's boot until she shifted and they fell off.

"Sleem take you," Red gasped. "*Ki newah.* I give in."

Abruptly, Tsia let go. Red stumbled back, shaking her wrist where it was red and blistering from the flames. Grabbing a water bag from the stack by the fire, she dumped its contents on her reddened wrist, her face white but her eyes blazing as she made her way to a medpak. Quickly she jerked a generic skin flap from the pak and wrapped it around her wrist.

Tsia stooped. Calmly, with all eyes on her, she reached into the fire and picked up the knife, ignoring the sizzling blade. There were no marks on her hands or arm, just the sweat dripping and evaporating from her fire-flushed skin. Tsia took two steps toward Red and offered the blade hilt first, the fire-touched steel resting easily on the back of her bare hand. Her eyes were not mocking, only serious, and Red glared at her, examining Tsia's skin where it was unmarked by blisters. Then one of the men made a comment, and the black-eyed woman grinned slowly. "*Illia sassey, kai-al,*" she said as she hot-fingered the blade into the empty scabbard on her belt. "A pretty trick." She stalked off.

"Wait a minute." Tsia started after her. "We had a deal."

The red-haired woman merely glanced over her shoulder and said, "Spade."

Helplessly, Tsia looked after her. With an oath, she strode to the place where her flex sword had fallen, picked it up, and then caught her harness and slung it over her shoulder. When she turned, the mercs who were still standing around the fire watched her with interest.

"Well," she said scathingly, "did I pass?"

A tall man stepped forward. His shoulders were rangy and broad, but his frame was not heavy; he seemed to hang his body from his shoulders rather than support it with his legs. He gestured for her to come closer.

"Spade?" she asked.

He nodded.

"Then take these off as Red said you would."

He pointed at the fire instead. "Walk in there," he said in a deep Korshani rumble, "then I will take them off."

She smiled, the expression somehow feral in her face. "Remove them first. Then I'll walk in the fire."

He stared evenly at her. Tsia kept her face calm, but her body trembled. The expression on his face unnerved her more than she cared to admit. Like the other mercs, he was wearing darkeyes, so his gaze was flat and unreadable. But his face, his bones, the skin around his eyes—there was no curiosity or anger or even disdain in his expression, just the depthless look of a soul lost and lonely and blind to all but an infinite wasteland of violence.

Finally he shrugged. His thick fingers picked a thin roll of cloth from a pocket inside his jerkin, and from that he pulled a tiny disk similar in shade to the mole she herself had stolen. Eagerly, Tsia shoved her sleeves back from where they had slid down to her wrists.

Kneeling, Spade was almost as tall as she was standing up. She watched him carefully as he slid the disk around the manacle until it seemed to catch. A second later the metal split along an invisible seam, and its weight was gone from her wrist. With a dull thud, the fetter dropped to the ground. Tsia trembled. Her blue eyes flashed with a strange light. No more nerve rods, no more slave chains to weigh her down . . . Her guts twisted, and the cat feet in her skull skittered across her brain. It was an eternity before Spade moved the disk to the second shackle. Almost free . . . . Tsia's shivering was more noticeable now, and the man glanced up, scowling as he met her eyes.

Then the second shackle snapped open, and Tsia threw her head back and screamed her defiance. Ashen-faced, Spade jerked back. Vaulting away from him, Tsia shook her limbs out like a cat coming from the water. The group around the fire fell silent. She stretched and screamed again, then flung herself in the air in a nearly impossible twist of her body, landing as lightly as if she had stepped without moving her feet. "Aiieee . . ." she cried out, shaking her hair and stretching her arms up to the sun.

A thin woman shook her head. "Ramok's feather is crazy."

"Yeah, but who's going to tell Ramok?" returned her neighbor.

And Tsia stalked the fire. She paced the clearing, stepping high as her legs felt lighter and lighter. She went faster and faster till she raced toward the trees. Then she was gone, slipping through the low, rubbery brush like the ghost she had been, and ran on, her boots softly slapping her knees front and back till she reached the hills on the other side of the spring and collapsed, her eyes still bright with a fierceness she had learned only in slavery.

Finally, when she heard nearly silent footsteps, she stirred and slipped away, not wanting to face anyone yet—even Ramok, whom she suspected as being the owner of those quiet steps. Instead, she made her way back to where she had left Spade, calming herself though her steps still pranced in the sand. She knew that Ramok still followed her and knew that he knew she was aware of him, but she did not care.

Spade and the others looked up as she entered the clearing again.

"Build it bigger," she said without preamble, gesturing at the small, bright fire that burned beneath the repulsor tarp.

Wren, who stood beside Spade, grinned. With their rasers, he and two others sliced a fallen tree into manageable chunks. They broke it up with kicks, the softwood bending before it shattered under their boots. With one eye on their progress, Tsia laid weapons in a pile. The other mercs gathered. Aron joined them, but as he saw the firepit, he frowned.

Ramok strode into the clearing just as Spade threw the last armful of wood on the fire. "What do you think you are doing?" he said coldly as Tsia unsealed her jumpsuit. Spade turned slowly. The big man shrugged, but Tsia grinned at Ramok, the wild light still bright in her eyes. She stripped off her boots in a graceful move. "A firedance, Ramok. To pay for my freedom." She pulled the jumpsuit down over her arms. *"Ji kai-al,"* she said. *"Jit nyeka."*

She grinned and in a fluid move stepped out of the suit to leave her slender body bare in the cool, shadowed dusk. The golden color of her skin was broken by purple-black bruises from ankle to waist, and her ribs were one mass of darkened flesh on the right side. She shivered more with anticipation than with cold, and Ramok tightened his lips. As he watched, Tsia shook her head, stretched, and let the sweat begin to flow. She closed her eyes and moved to the fire, and Ramok strode forward.

"No," he said strongly, gripping her arm.

Tsia opened her eyes, but her gaze was only for the fire. Outside the firepit, the heat washed only one side of her body, and she wanted it all around her. "Let go," she said quietly.

"Enough of this," he snapped. "I will not have you burned for the sake of your pride."

Tsia laughed. "I have no pride, Ramok, only desire." She twisted free of his grip and spun on her feet. "Can you not feel it—the flames licking, kissing your skin . . ." She used Korshan, the tongue bringing more image to her words than the crippled language of Standard.

Ramok ignored her. "Your leg, your arms." He pointed at the gashes. "Even a guide must wait for the skin to heal. Your skin grafts are barely fused—they will never sweat enough to keep you cool."

"I don't care."

"I do." He grabbed her arm again and yanked her away from the fire.

Tsia struggled wildly. "I need the flames," she snarled, jerking away. "I need this heat on my skin. I will die without it!" She wrenched free of his grip and flung herself onto the coals. His hands closed on air. He stood, hands still outstretched, till the flames leapt over her legs.

Twice Tsia twirled in the center of the fire. Flames crawled up her calves and whipped around her thighs. The cats yowled in her head. She ducked and twisted, kicking up a dazzling flurry of sparks, then sweeping low and curling under an arc of orange-red gas that stretched out over her head. The fire hissed and crackled. Coals turned beneath her feet. Heat ate at her legs, her waist, her arms, until even she, with the wildness still singing in her blood, felt the burn of it in her wrists. The wound on her thigh felt as if a white-hot spear had burned away the bloody scab. Her cheek throbbed with a lance of its own heat.

Still she danced. There was no home, no Ciordan, no Jak, no guild, no slough. There was nothing but the fire, nothing but herself in the flames. Only she breathed this burning air. Only she felt the grief of the void in the darkness outside this ring of fire. Her voice sang to the coals, coaxing them up, up along her legs while she leapt ever higher to avoid them. Her body glowed, clothed only in sweat and flames. Till finally, in a crumbling shower of sparks, she threw herself from the flames and, tumbling, landed on one knee in the sand.

She drew herself up slowly. The blazing blue of her eyes was still wild and uncontrolled against the orange-red of the fire. Wren, Aron, Yemene—none of them spoke. Someone sighed, broken out of the awe of his reverie.

Then, deliberately, Tsia turned and saluted Spade, whose ashen face was grim. With her limbs still trembling, she stalked to her jumpsuit and boots and gathered them up. After the heat of the fire, the chill of the evening struck her like ice. Only Ramok followed her from the clearing.

"Little fool," Ramok growled finally, reaching a spot well clear of the others. "What possessed you to do such a thing—" He cut off short as she dropped her clothes and ran her hot hand down his chest, one eyebrow cocked in a quizzical look. His breath caught. Tsia, her heart still pounding from the dance, her body glistening with sweet sweat, burned now for a comfort stronger than the fire. She did not think. Instead, she ran her hand along his neck and traced the heat of her skin into his flesh.

Ramok shuddered, then cursed slowly and softly. Tsia lowered her hand, and with a gentle oath Ramok tore off his shirt and gripped her arms. He pulled her roughly against him.

"Avya, nyeka," he said softly. "Now, come."

22

In the chill of late evening Ramok created a detailed line of twigs and rocks on the smoothed sand by the well. His darkeyes allowed him to see the rude map as well as if it were day, and the other mercs picked up his directions easily. "Eller," Ramok directed, "take Pilo and go up Two Moon Pass, then through the south trail to the skimmer pad at Rendering. Remember that here—" He stabbed his finger down. "—and back here, there was water listed before we left Pulan. If you are careful, it will be enough. Pilo—" He gave the woman a nod. "—will set the primary ghost line on your trail."

He motioned at Red, who squatted beside him. She gave him a deliberate look, and Aron rested his hand on her shoulders. Ramok ignored Aron's grin. "Red," he ordered, "you and Aron will have a rough ride through Dubious Way to Puma Peak. We will give you the four extra water bags among us, and Ence will be your guide." He nodded at her surprised look. "You will need Ence more than I will. He will be carrying the ghost lines for everyone except Pilo and Eller, in case they get scanned. Besides," he said, grinning slyly, "you might want a chaperone." Aron gave him a disgusted look, but Red laughed out loud and slapped his shoulder. "Ence," Ramok continued, "if you see skimmers heading over Catmount Ridge, set your ghosts loose and dig in. The nodies do not know how large a party we have, and they should be distracted long enough by your signals to let us cross and get to Levian."

Ramok pointed to a spot farther down the line of twigs and nodded at another man. "Ward, you have the easy route to Nairo. It is long, but there is plenty of water at both ends of the Severed River. You will be carrying your own set of ghost signals and those of my group, too. If Red gets pinned down at Rendering, loose your ghosts in the node and go to ground. Once the art nodies locate your ghosts at Nairo, they will split up their skimmers. That will halve the men harrassing Red."

"Durran," he directed, "you and Twit know the routine. We will set your horses free in the hills. You will stay here, at the bay, until tomorrow. Then hike out to the Far Reaches. Once you are verified by the node, you can take your time catching a skimmer to Pulan." He sat back. "Wren, Forrest, Spade, and the rest are with me. We will ride east to Redeye Ridge, cross at the narrows, and meet Aron and Red—if they get past the skimmers—in two and a half days at the Ishtarin temple." He glanced at the two. "We will expect you at oh eight hundred. If you don't show, we will go on through. It will take us two days to reach the narrows, but the other side is a fast descent." He looked around the group. "Who's on sweep?"

"Twit and I," Durran answered to his right.

He nodded. "Make sure the bay is clean. Hikers sometimes try to override the reservation locks during weak seasons. With this heat, this is the weakest season the bay has had in two years. Stay sharp. I don't want any scans going out to the node."

There was little murmuring as the group broke up. Only Ramok, Wren, and Tsia were left by the bed of coals. Tsia looked longingly at the firepit, but the chill of night was in her skin. She drew her blunter close.

"Ramok," Wren said in a low voice, "the route up Redeye Ridge goes past Catmount Ridge as well."

Ramok nodded.

Wren tilted his head. "Two Moon Pass, Nairo, Dubious Way—even the narrows—those are not close enough to the top of Cheba Rift to be included in the restrictions of the Landing Pact. But Catmount Ridge . . ." He frowned. "The great cats barely tolerate guides and Gea people there; they will not allow a hiker. They are not likely to look on the eight of us as anything but an invasion. And you know how they feel about that—we would be a sitting dinner to them if they wanted to take us out. We have standard arms, and not even a flexor activates against a biological."

Tsia held herself tightly against the surge of growling that leaked through her gate at his words. Catmount Ridge? Daya, they would take her into the mouth of her gate itself. A shudder shook her slender frame, and she clenched her fists in the sand. There would be cougars and tams and even sandcats on the ridge. Sandcats . . . She could have touched the feline she had stood with last night. Had it been curious? Had it sensed her through her gate as she had felt its presence? Would the tams on the ridges feel her, too? Her eyes turned to the north dunes that hid the Dry Mountains from her sight. If these shakes were a warning . . . If her virus was out of control . . . If it would kill her, she acknowledged harshly, before she got back to the guild, then at least she would touch one of the cougars and live what the other guides lived before she died. She set her jaw and stared deliberately at Ramok's map. Two days to the top. Two days, then, to break the Landing Pact and reach out herself to touch the cats. And Daya damn her, she thought, for doing so.

Ramok glanced at Tsia, then at his map. "There is water along Redeye Ridge, Wren," he pointed out. "Even with this heat, there is no reason to go all the way to the springs on Catmount Ridge unless all the other water holes are dry. We should be able to sneak across the narrows without setting foot on the ridge."

"I would rather risk the art guild than the cats of the Cheba Rift."

Tsia rubbed her wrist. I would rather risk the cats, she thought silently in return.

"Forrest," Ramok pointed out, "will tell us if the cats come near. He is sensitive enough to feel almost any life in these hills."

Wren picked up the sticks of the crude map. His massive hands gathered the twigs and smoothed the sand with the delicacy of an artist, and Tsia shuddered at the thought of hands, delicate hands, sculpting ice and fire and flesh. The merc's quick eyes caught the movement, and he eyed her absently. "Even one small tam could be trouble," he commented.

"More trouble than the art nodies' men at the skimmer pads in Pulan?" Ramok shook his head. "This artist, Cekulu, gave credit to the miners at the Adest Strike so they could bring in the high-range weapons and escalate the violence. Force Yemene out in the open for negotiations. Even if Cekulu is dead—" He flicked a glance at Tsia's averted eyes. "—it does not mean her project is killed. An artist's work goes to the guild when she dies. So the guild will have had its nodies standing ready for our appearance. They don't even need mercs. The nodies can direct the miners' weapons against us without even stirring from their guild. And at that point they might be working on visual, not just scan." He pointed to the map. "Any trail other than Redeye Ridge puts us in plain view of all three western mines, and those are miner, not freepick, holdings. We need the concealment. We won't make it into Pulan without it."

Wren glanced across the second fire, where Yemene was

propped uncomfortably against a saddle that leaned in the soil. "Are we going in at the mines themselves? Take the transport tubes to the surface? If we were in the tubes, it would take only minutes to get into Levian."

Ramok shook his head. "Too many tubes are shattered. When we are close enough, we will use the gravlines to get over to Levian. Otherwise, we will steal a skimmer from the miners. If we are not seen coming off the ridge, no one will expect that. Plus, with all the conflict, no one will expect the councilwoman to come back to Pulan in a mining ship."

Wren nodded slowly. "With the ghosts laid along the other part of the rift, we should be fairly safe from anything the art guild can throw."

"That is because," Ramok said, grinning, "even the artists know that no one can make it past Catmount Ridge without the mark of the cats on their throat."

Wren snapped one of the twigs in his long, thick fingers. "We have the largest group. If something goes wrong, what is our backup?"

"If the mines are hot, we steal a skimmer off the ridge and go straight to the city."

Wren tossed the twigs into the firepit. The tiny pieces of wood flared, then crisped to blackened ash. "We'll need Ma."

Ramok hesitated. "The councilwoman is not due to give birth for another three weeks. Ma will stay with Eller. He will need her to get through those canyons above the Severed River. She is the only one who knows them well enough to traverse without an overlay."

"And Horen?"

"He rides with us."

Wren frowned. "Is that wise? You heard what he did on Freedom to those women. With Feather along . . ."

Ramok flicked a glance toward Tsia. "We have to have him," he said flatly. "Everything we do depends on our ghosts in the node, and Horen runs the best ghost line in this quadrant. Without him, we have as little chance of getting through to Pulan as a sandsnake has of boring through rock. Neither Feather nor Yemene will be bothered," Ramok added in a hard voice. "And Nitpicker has worked with Horen before; she cut him on Chaos. He knows she will cut him again if he goes for her here."

Still Wren hesitated.

Ramok saw it. "I will be watching him. And you, also."

The other merc nodded reluctantly. With a sideways glance at

Tsia, he rose and moved to his e-roll. Within minutes he was asleep.

Ramok glanced at Tsia. She was once again clad in the sand-colored jumpsuit and drab blunter jacket. Her short, dark hair was still sandy, he noticed with satisfaction as she ran her hand through its abbreviated length. He reached out to touch her hair, but she shrugged away. He grinned at her skittishness. "What is it?" he asked, reaching for her hair again.

She shivered.

"Feeling the night?"

She shook her head. "There are more creatures hunting in the desert than I would have thought possible," she answered slowly.

"And some," he answered meaningfully, "are hungry."

Shaking off his hands, she got to her feet. Thoughtfully, Ramok watched her walk away. She was jittery even for a *kai-al*, he realized. And the tremors he had felt in her body—they were not caused by fear or nervousness but by something else. He would have to ask Forrest about it or get Durran to run a scan on her. The dredger fields should hide that as well as they hid the repulsor fields of the tarps, and he was beginning to be curious. But Durran and Horen were friends. Better to keep Durran out of the scanline. He got to his feet with a faint frown. If it was a guide problem, Forrest would be the one to ask, anyway. Nothing got away from that merc's eyes.

By the time he found Forrest near the rocks, most of the other mercs were sleeping. Ramok squatted next to the hulking man and greeted him with a silent nod.

"You want to know about your Feather." Forrest's voice was gravelly, as if he did not use it much. His words were more of a statement than a question. Ramok glanced at him, surprised that the big man had spoken first. Forrest nodded. "She cannot wear the darkeyes. Or stand the touch of metal on her skin. She has the shakes like a wind in a skinny tree."

And the wildness, Ramok thought to himself, remembering the fierceness in her hands and eyes when she touched him. "Is this normal for a guide?" he asked. "Or is she sick?"

"She's about forty?"

Ramok nodded.

"Then it's probably both."

"What do you mean?" Ramok eyed Forrest's bulk in the dark.

Forrest watched the stars for a long moment. "Guides go to the virus young. She was probably twenty when she took it in."

"Her age has something to do with this?"

The big man glanced at him. "The virus," he explained, "is killed after a year in the new guide's body. That stops it from mutating her to a point where her body can no longer survive. But sometimes not all the virus in a guide's body dies. In about a tenth of the guides the virus mutates instead, then goes into remission. Then, fifteen, sometimes twenty years later, it comes back and tries to complete its set of changes. Kills the guides sometimes, even before they can get to the guild for help." He glanced across the spring. "Fevers, chills, tremors—they are sure signs of second stage. Your Feather, Ramok, has it bad."

Ramok hesitated. "How bad is bad?" he asked finally.

Forrest's silence was his answer.

"Bad enough to be fatal?" Ramok pressed.

The big man nodded slowly.

"Durran's carrying our self-contained med equipment," Ramok said finally. "Could you use the SCAME—halt the progress of this virus until we get to Pulan?"

Forrest stirred. "No SCAME has the med codes you need. Only the guild knows how to build the right pathogen to stop a second-stager."

"You sure?"

Forrest did not have to tell Ramok that the merc could work a trace in the node for the guild codes—Ramok could read the comment as if he were reading Forrest's mind. He dug his hands in the sand and let it slip through his fingers. "I can't search the node without giving away our position," he said quietly.

The deep gravelly tones of Forrest's voice blended with the wind as he answered. "Then you will lose your Feather for sure."

Ramok cursed quietly. "She was not mine to begin with, but dammit, I owe her. Those bruises on her legs—they are from me." Forrest did not move, and Ramok's voice was low. "I would have been hissing on the sand if she had not saved me from a fall off the side of one of the Noirelle buildings. I climbed her body to get back to the ledge we were walking. Later, she took one of their men off my back. I can't leave her here for the art nodies to find; Red says she killed Cekulu, the artist who took Yemene from Pulan in the first place. If they find Tsia here and take her back, the guild will kill her slowly—or let her live so that she wished she had died in the first place."

Forrest did not respond, and Ramok got to his feet. He looked at the other man for a long moment. "Dammit—" His voice halted. He cursed under his breath. Forrest watched him silently. Ramok stared down at the other merc. Then he walked away.

Curtly, Ramok posted sentries on the outlying rocks, then checked the dune where they had roughhoused earlier that evening. The wind had already softened the prints in the sand, and the dredger fields had kicked back on an hour ago, shifting the entire mass and smoothing away the signs of their play. Two skimmers flew overhead while the dredger field was on, and the mercs watched them silently, but neither ship slowed down. They were still on full scan. They disappeared to the north, where the sky was already sharp against the mountain peaks.

Under the repulsor tarp, Tsia leaned on the bole of a tree, her arms wrapped around her knees. She could not find an urge to sleep. Instead, caught by the chill of the night and the warmth of the sand under her buttocks, she thought over the Merishkan words she had learned from Wren. Each time a pattern of words fell into place, she went on to the next, reviewing the language and idioms with the focus she had learned in chains. When Aron stepped out of the trees and joined her, she merely nodded in his direction. She ignored the blond merc Horen, who trailed subtly after the other man.

The fires in the two pits were almost out; the coals that were left made two red eyes in the ground. Tsia regarded them absently as the few mercs around the ring held their conversation. When Forrest's large, gliding frame appeared from out of the trees and approached the small knot of mercs, her attention sharpened. Curiously, she watched him join the others. The tall guide moved as much like an animal as if he danced continually in the flames. There was silence and stealth in his gait, and his muscles rolled as he walked. His eyes barely flickered at the mercs he approached.

Spade, the merc who had removed Tsia's manacles, held up his hand, from which dangled some vipers. "Two snakes," he offered, though he did not set the meat down or bring it within reach of the other man.

Forrest merely looked at them until a second mercenary pulled a pouch from her harness and spilled the contents of her pouch into her palm.

"Ahana jerky," the thin woman said.

Forrest raised his eyebrows, and Wren held out a skin of liquid. "Wind wine," he said. "Half a skin." When Forrest still said nothing, Wren made a rude noise out of his beaklike nose. "Whole skin," he amended.

Forrest nodded then, and the mercs around him chuckled. They laid their offerings in a small pile by the first firepit, the one in which Tsia had danced. Forrest adjusted the snake meat on the edge of the fire, where it would heat with a natural smoky taste. Then he began to stalk around the clearing, uttering short, piercing sounds from his throat.

"What is he doing?" Tsia whispered to Aron.

Aron glanced at her. "Testing the acoustics of the bay. Best throat singer in the merc guild. Inside the Imbetin ring, that is."

Forrest paced the clearing twice in a complicated pattern, then squatted about two meters from the fire, where a jut of stone met the brick of the well. Two tones—one out of the nose, one out of the throat—came from the man. Then a second low sound burst out, noise like a slow word made without tone, except that it resonated like a note. A whistle pierced the word, flaying its strange syllable until it disappeared, and the nasal tone curled up.

Tsia leaned forward. Forrest's voice reverberated, and she could not tell if it was because the rocks he faced echoed his weird tones back in double strength or if his own throat provided the surging noise. There was something about the sound—her ears pricked, and the short hairs on her skin reached for the slight wind. Odd, lilting whistles teased the bass tones of his song, sending shivers down her back until Aron put his arm around her. Irritably, she shrugged it away.

But Forrest's tones were hypnotic. Tsia's world narrowed until her eyes seemed not to see anymore, and the images sent to her brain were of scent and sound, not sight. From behind her now the throat song rose up and to the side. Did her virus cause this confusion? Or was there something in this noise? She stretched to sense the desert cats and found them listening on the dunes. Curious. Hungry. Wanting water. Wanting silence. They waited for the men to leave and listened instead as Forrest sang.

Aron eyed Tsia speculatively. The woman barely noticed. She got to her feet and paced to the edge of the repulsor field, where her eyes were full of the sky and the light of both moons. Her nostrils flared. The song made her teeth tingle and her tongue reverberate, and then it wailed in her ears as a desert cat screamed on a dune. She leapt suddenly, ignoring Aron's startled hands as he reached to sooth her skin. Around her—

The vibrations touched her teeth, then her sternum, while the shrill overtones sent ice cascading down her spine. Her ears were full. She melted into the shrubs, the instincts she read from her gate taking over where her mind could not cope. She fled across the rock-strewn sand by touch, not sight, brushing the rustling branches away and slipping through the valley like a ghost. The sounds vibrated in her thighs. Her mouth opened and closed to make the sound rise and fall curiously inside her skull as it did between the stone ridges that blocked her way. The valley trembled with noise.

Her distance grew. But Forrest was far into his song before Tsia knew that she was no longer running. Her eyes began to see again, and she looked around. She was crouched on a ledge that hugged the sand. Another shape became clear in her peripheral sight: the silent figure of a desert cat perched beside her. On the stone her puzzled companion perked its ears and regarded the scene below with the same feral gaze as she. At her awareness, the sandcat turned its unblinking stare on her, but she greeted it with a sound low in her throat, and the night creature relaxed, its green eyes caught again by the light and the movement of air in the valley.

How long they crouched together, Tsia did not know. Only that the sound clung like a leech to her chest until the cat beside her tensed, shifted, and disappeared and the sounds of a man's nearly silent steps in the sand reached her ears. Instinctively Tsia drew her knife, holding it blade up against her arm to hide its glinting metal.

"Tsia," the shape said in a low voice. "It is I, Ramok."

She hesitated, unable to form an answer.

"Tsia?" he said again.

A long moment passed, then she slid down from the rock, her lithe form shivering with the memory of the weird song.

"Come," Ramok said gently. "You will chill in the night."

23

At dawn Tsia mounted long before the others were ready to ride. She took the roan out on the dunes, then brought him back, then took him up again. After two days in the saddle the bruises on her legs were still sore, but the skin grafts had sealed almost completely. She ignored the bruises. Waiting for the others, she stood in the saddle to see across the yellow soil to the burning desert dawn, then sat down again and paced irritably with the roan.

By the time the groups of twos and threes had left, Ramok's group had moved out toward the main trail, and the last two mercs had taken up their lonely positions in the valley, Tsia was shivering with her need to run. She stripped off the blunter, then jammed it back on. She pranced the roan along the trail, ignoring the other mercs who passed. It was for Ramok that she waited. He bound her to him with the calmness of his hands. He burned the fires cleanly from her skin with his strength. Was she his *heyta* or *heyita*? Slave, lover-enslaved—she did not care. The chains of the artists were gone. Now there was only Ramok and her biogate to bind her to her body. She sang to herself and did not notice that the tones that escaped her lips were not human but the soft yowling of a cat.

When Ramok joined her, she greeted him with a feral smile, more like a predator than a guide. He leaned across from his saddle and gripped her arm so hard that she could feel the bruise beginning, and when he kissed her, it was a savage kiss that left her to stare wide-eyed at his expression. He smiled. For once the humor did not touch his eyes.

She fell in behind him, holding back the roan when it wanted to trot ahead, egged on by her nervousness. When they had gone a few kilometers, they reached the twin Pillars of Salt, named for an ancient legend of a desert apocalypse. Here Ramok turned east. Within two hours they had ridden into the hard-packed earth of the lower hills, heading for Redeye Ridge on the route he had outlined the night before.

No clouds marred the morning sky, though it was already pale with the rising of Risthmus's sun. The yellow-white orb was heavy and sluggish; it seemed to struggle to clamber up the rocks and cliffs, so that every minute was like an hour. Tsia, sweating again, wished she could ride without the blunter, but the last time she had taken it off, Ramok had told her curtly to put it back on.

Since they had split off from the main trail, Ramok had become even more cautious. Including Tsia, there were only seven fighters to guard Yemene's belly. Ramok and Wren, Tsia and Yemene, Forrest and Spade, and two others made up his group. Ramok's black was in the lead, followed by Tsia, then Wren on his speckled gray. Forrest rode a massive hammerheaded buckskin whose eyes held a stubborn glint when the burly guide mounted. Spade rode a long-legged bay.

Tsia spoke to her roan as she rode. Its ears flicked with her voice, and absently she pulled the hairs of its mane out from where they caught under the saddle. Soon she would be up on those stone walls herself, and the roan would pick its surefooted way along the ridge that beckoned high above. Soon she could crouch and scream like a cougar on the heights. She hid a smile. Back in Noirelle Yemene would have had even less confidence that Tsia could control both their feet in the fire if she had seen how Tsia had acted last night on the rocks. Now though, Tsia did not care what the councilwoman thought. She had not spoken to the woman—except a bare greeting—since she had been brought by Ramok to the mercs, and except for the firedance, Yemene had patently ignored her.

Tsia glanced back at the other riders. Spade rode just ahead of the third woman in the group, a merc called Nitpicker. Tsia eyed the woman surreptitiously. The thin woman rode as if she were part of her tall, long-legged Appaloosa, and her gray and white streaked hair matched the horse. More so than any other besides Forrest, this woman seemed a part of the land itself rather than part of the mercenaries' world. She carried an image-guided fibergun on her back, and her weapon harness was heavy with the flat knives, flexors, and breakers that she used. The previous night, after the throat singing was done, several fights had been refereed by Aron under the repulsor tarps. Tsia had been surprised to see Nitpicker beat Ramok in the ring, later to be bested herself by Wren, who in turn gave way again to Ramok.

Tsia shifted uncomfortably. The presence of the cats made her want to leap from the roan and run instead on foot through the dust. By now the grit of the rocky desert had become as much a part of her skin as her own sweat. She glanced back. Yemene must be feeling even worse. Tsia dropped back and pulled alongside the councilwoman, noting how, like Spade, the woman's face never tanned in the sun but remained ashen and only sweated. Yemene glanced at her but did not speak, and Tsia forced herself to talk. "Are you all right?" she asked.

The woman did not turn. "This child will be born in Pulan. That is all that matters."

"The espers said only that the child would become a leader," Tsia returned. "He could be born in any county and still become what you need."

The woman's eyes focused slowly, and she pinched her lips, drawing herself up haughtily. "The child," she retorted, "will be brought forth in Pulan—"

"By the smoking warriors. You said that before." Tsia gestured at the woman's stomach. "If you go into labor here, that prophecy will not do you much good."

The councilwoman glared at her for a long moment, and Tsia, stifling her irritation, rode back to the front. She ignored Forrest's speculative amber gaze and dropped into line again between him and Ramok.

After that there was little to think of except the click and clop of the horses' hooves on stone. Like antique clocks endlessly ticking away, the horses kept their steady pace. Barely half an hour after sunrise the heat had already begun to radiate from the white stone cliffs; it rose from the ground like waves of clear steam that paved their way in sweat. If it had not been for the stretched shade from the cliffs, Tsia was sure that in spite of the cooling headgear they used, they would have been parboiled by midmorning. At least the sun could not reach them half as fiercely in the canyons as it could on the flats. If it had, her face would have been burned far darker than it was.

The air grew thinner as they climbed the narrow passes. Ramok, pulling up for a moment to point at the cliff, said, "Redeye Ridge hits a false summit up there, near the top of that peak. Past that, it is only thirty kilometers to reach the narrows—a single day's journey on these mounts."

Tsia nodded. She studied the bare striped-stone visage with an intense gaze. There would be cats up there: cougars in the thickets, bearcats on the rim.

Ramok glanced back to the west and, with a silent oath, brought his horse to a halt. Behind him the line of mercs abruptly stopped, their gaze following his down to the desert plains. The shadows of the skimmers converging on Bonnell's Bay were clear to see. As Tsia watched, the skimmers whipped down into the valley and disappeared. Minutes passed. They did not rise again.

Ramok eyed the distant spring narrowly. As time wormed by and still no ships reappeared, Tsia grew restless. Finally, Ramok clucked to his horse and urged him forward. "We will push to reach the top of Redeye Ridge tonight," he said over his shoulder. "We will cross the narrows tomorrow. If we are lucky, none of the cats that make this ridge their home will think to try us for supper."

"The bay?" Tsia asked.

Ramok did not look back. "Returning to the bay is no longer an option."

She shivered and reined the roan back onto the trail as the cat feet slunk across her brain. Since they had reached the mountains, she had felt light-headed, and though at first she had thought it was the heat, as the air thinned and the heat dropped off with their altitude, she realized that the sun was not the cause. Ramok's words echoed in her head; the mention of the cats had caused a tingle to run up and down her spine. She had to clench the reins to hide the tremor that gripped her hands. She could feel the cats more clearly here than she could even in the bay. Their feet in the dust, their eyes on the ridge, their kills hidden in shallow, open caves . . . Even the cold threat of the skimmers in the bay did not lessen the impact through her link. Daya, if this was the strength of a useless gate, how engulfing would a normal link be?

Deliberately, she fell back from Ramok to ride by herself, then reined in beside Forrest. The tall merc glanced at her sideways.

"Cat kill," she said softly, pointing with her chin to a spot upslope.

The man squinted.

"There are more cats in the rift," she added, "than any other place on Risthmus except the Red Savanna."

Forrest gave her a sharp look but remained silent.

"In Ciordan," she said almost to herself, "there were only three cats in my watershed: a pair of bearcats and a water tam. There was only one bobcat farther up in the slough. I never thought . . .

I never dreamed I would see this place, where the tams and cougars mixed."

"You won't see it even now. We will stay this side of Catmount Ridge."

She went on as if she had not heard him. "I hiked in the Sinking Plains ten years ago. I can still remember the way the medilions herded their prey." She shivered, then asked abruptly, "Does proximity—or the number of life-forms—make a difference in the strength of your biolink?"

Forrest urged his horse across a wash before he answered. When he did, he answered with a nod, not with words.

"So, hypothetically," she pressed, "if you were linked to . . . the blue pelicans and they were hunting in a flock of hundreds, you would feel them like—"

"Like a wave. Like a presence you could not ignore."

Tsia fell silent. She felt that wave, the pull of the cats. She spurred the roan ahead, and, uneasily, Forrest watched her go. When Wren rode up beside him, he scowled.

"She's nervous as a digger before the trap is sprung," Wren said.

"She does not understand what she is feeling," Forrest said slowly. "She does not seem to know the signs. A guide should know that. A guide is trained to feel."

"Maybe," Wren said thoughtfully, "she is not the kind of guide that you expect."

Forrest glanced at him, his black gaze flickering in the brightness of the light. Wren grinned, the expression making him look like a hawk on the hunt, and the other merc looked away, his eyes following Tsia as she rode forward.

Tsia searched the top of the ridge constantly with her eyes. Even when she stood in the saddle and shaded her heat-bleared gaze with her hand, she could see only unbroken lines of rock. She could not see the cats that prowled her brain.

To her sand-burned eyes, Redeye Ridge was just a thin line below the oddly shaped Catmount Ridge, which thrust across this part of the continent. On the other side of Catmount Ridge was Cheba Rift, hidden by mountains. The rift was almost three thousand kilometers long. At its widest, it was twelve hundred kilometers across; at its narrowest, the valley disappeared and it became a thin trail between two high, rocky peaks. The entire rift, from the desert heat of the Javan plains in the south to the snowy peaks near Ciordan, was haven to all but humans. No colonist ventured within its stone walls except for the Gea or the occasional guide, who once a year checked with the denizens of the rift to make sure their genetics remained adaptive and their ecology was stable. The Gea and guides were tolerated but not exactly welcomed by the cats. Even the Gea wore neutral suits to the valley, cutting off their presence from the predators they studied.

Tsia looked up along the ridge again. She could imagine Catmount Ridge before her. The closer she got, the more the ragged edge drew her. She tried to force her gaze below, but she could not hold it on the distant desert. What had been endless mountains of dried grass and weak and rocky soil was now only low waves of yellow that washed against the rock formations. A sea relieved only by the jutting pillars and singular cliffs of colored stone. From the dry grass dunes the wind rose up in whirling gusts that made dust dance in the heat, while the sun glinted off the white points of light that betrayed the skimmers that crossed the plains.

Up on the ridge trail Tsia guided her horse between fallen boulders that choked the trail. She gasped at the thinness of the oxygen. The wind was only a cool breeze, and it touched her neck like a surprisingly gentle hand. Above her, it raced over the dry peaks in high, trailing currents of air. She wanted to feel those currents, dance along the ridge top. She wanted to leap into the rift that waited on the other side. There was an anticipation, an anxiety building in her guts. It replaced her nausea with its jitters and fed the chills that swept her as she rode.

Her horse kicked a loose stone, and Tsia watched it bounce and clatter away. The rocky slope was like a steep stair. The thickets within the crevices were thick with dried, dead brush. Out near the trail, nothing seemed to grow more than a finger's width from the stone it clung to, though there were dead tree stumps hard as basalt that told of ancient lushness. It was strange to see the fossilized forest when the tracks of cats and snakes were so fresh. Twice Tsia thought she saw fresher prints of humans, but her eyes were bleary with the angle of the sun, and she ignored them.

Few of the mercs talked, but the noise broadcast by the line made her wince: Hooves rang against stone and echoed off the ridge, saddles creaked incessantly, horses snorted, and rocks sprang away from the trail in loud rattles as they climbed. Every time a skimmer sped across the plains, the line grew tense. The threat of the Cheba Rift tams seemed distant compared to the visible threat of the art guild's scans. But even with the blinding white of the skimmers both east and west of their position, Tsia found her eyes remaining on Catmount Ridge above.

"The cats in Cheba Rift—they are the cats of First Drop, not the animals of Risthmus," Jak Volen's voice echoed in her head. "They have the strength and cunning of the old ones and the presence and intelligence of Gea. There are thousands of cats in that cleft. If we landed inside, they would tear us to pieces, then suck the marrow from our bones."

"Couldn't we set down near the top of the valley?" she had asked him once.

The look he had given her had been answer enough. "Even the ridge falls within their domain."

". . . domain." Wren's voice broke her concentration. The merc had taken Forrest's place in the line, and Tsia stared at him until she realized what he had said. "There—" He pointed. "See that dark line along the top of the peak?"

She nodded.

"That's the edge of the inner valley. It stays green all year round, watered by springs in this area, though farther north it is watered half by snowfall from the mountains. The entrance," he said, gesturing to the east, "is guarded by a line of stone cats the size of corncows, and in each claw they hold fresh meat. You think that is eerie? Ask Spade sometime why he shivers at the sound of a cat."

"Scaring the *kai-al nyeka*, Wren?" Ramok interrupted. His eyes were cold.

The small man's gaze shuttered. "Just telling her where we are going." He reined back, and Ramok wheeled his horse to the fore again.

Tsia frowned. At the spring, when Spade had removed the manacles from her wrists, he had seemed to start from the snarl she had released. She did not need to look at the ridge again to see the image Wren had left in her mind: the line of stone cats stalked her thoughts as, from the ridge, they followed the line of mercs.

At the third day spring Ramok called a halt and told the mercs to water their mounts. Tsia had only two water bags now; her extras had gone with the mercs who rode to set the ghost lines. Two botas was one more than any other merc in the line, but already most of her water was gone. She eyed the dry wash with longing. It would do no good to dig here for water; even the needletrees were dead and dry.

Behind her the other mercs squatted in the shade of stones and sat beneath one leaning wall of rock. Gradually, the dust settled down around them. While the horses drank from the expanded flexbowls that the mercs filled with water, Tsia glanced at

Yemene, then to Ramok, who looked out over the desert. She followed the line of his broad shoulders to the rock, then to the slope above. Then she froze. She was not aware of dropping the reins of the roan in the dust, of leaping to the top of the stone beside the path, where she crouched, staring at the slope.

Movement—she had seen movement; she was sure of it.

"*Esha*, Tsia . . ." Forrest's voice was soft beside her.

She did not look at him. "There—upslope," she breathed. "By the rounded rock."

Forrest followed her gaze. He nodded slowly. "Something watches us," he agreed softly.

"Can you not feel him? It is human."

Forrest's hand on her arm held her in place. "Wait here."

Ramok turned and motioned sharply for the mercs to take cover. In an instant none of them remained on the trail. Even Yemene, hauled into the protection of a boulder, was no longer in the open. Ramok, below the outcropping on which Forrest and Tsia crouched, eyed them narrowly. Forrest made a subtle gesture. Ramok's flat gaze flickered up the cliff. Then Nitpicker, the slender, tanned woman from the back, rose and quietly faded along the trail.

Tsia shifted under Forrest's hand. The merc did not loosen his grip, and she twisted again. "*Esha*, Tsia," he said softly. "It is already taken care of."

She shook her head. She could feel the man up on the slope. His presence was a thick shadow among the cat feet in her skull. With a tremor, she tried to shrug away, but Forrest held her fast. He murmured something, and she tried to focus on his words, but the shivers hit, and she crouched unmoving until he drew her down off the rock. Then she found herself beside Wren, the clublike hand of the small merc wrapped around her bicep in the way that Forrest's hand had been before.

Tsia twisted absently against Wren's grip, ignoring his sharp glance. Her roan was brought forward by Spade, who moved to lift her to the saddle, but as Wren let go of her arm, she leapt up before Spade could take her arm. Expressionlessly, the dark-eyed merc watched her mount. Then he stepped back, but he handed the reins to Wren instead of to Tsia.

A minute passed. Then another. Tsia could still feel the human above them. The other mercs tightened their gear. Then a low call floated down from above. Nitpicker's arm waved, and Ramok, vaulting over the boulders, made his way up quickly. When the two mercs came back down, they picked their way more carefully between the boulders that studded the soil, and Ramok had a body draped over his shoulder.

Tsia did not have to look at the body to know it belonged to the man who had watched from above. She could smell him before they dropped to the path. The nausea in her stomach surged briefly, then subsided, replaced by jitters that would not cease. As Nitpicker jumped down to join Ramok on the trail, Tsia watched the lithe play of muscles across the other woman's back. The merc did not seem to care that Tsia watched her; she caught Tsia's eye with disinterest and turned to resetting the fiberdart of her gun. She indicated the body that Ramok deposited gently on the trail.

"He is a guide, for sure," Nitpicker said. "Look at his hair. Except for the color, it is a perfect match for yours, Forrest." She grinned at Forrest's raised eyebrow. "Got the same receding hairline, too."

Tsia looked carefully at the unconscious guide. He was dressed in sand-colored shorts and a faded purple-gray shirt. His legs were weathered and wiry and, like hers, hairless. His eyes, when his lids were lifted by Ramok, were blue, like Tsia's, and his lips were thin and grim even in his unconsciousness. The lines in his face and hands had deepened and then webbed so that she knew he was, like her grandmother, well over two hundred. And all across his tanned and weathered skin were star-shaped indentations that had scarred white.

Ramok straightened from looking at the pockmarks. "He is first-gen," he said thoughtfully. "And a dropper. Starry-night plague only hit the ones who came down on First Drop; it mutated by the time everyone else came dirtside eighty years later."

Horen, the blond merc, scrutinized the man from a distance. "What is he doing out here?"

"He is no hiker," Ramok observed. "Look at his clothing, his gear. He is a working guide."

"Yeah," Horen agreed, "but he did not register on contract before we left Pulan. I memorized all the guide links before we left; there was no node listing for this man to work the ridge this week."

Beside him, Nitpicker adjusted her weapon harness on her hips and resettled the fibergun across her back. "Guides have never been known for having regular schedules," she commented.

Ramok stooped and checked the old man's pulse. "We will take him along," he decided. "If we get to the skimmer pads without problems, we will cut him loose there. It won't make any difference if he calls the miners then."

The presence of the cats in her gate sharpened suddenly, as if their mental shapes perked their ears, and Tsia frowned.

Ramok caught her expression. "What?" he asked quietly.

She shrugged uneasily. "Nothing," she said finally. "Just that . . ."

She leaned down and reached for the reins, and Wren, looking to Ramok first for confirmation, gave them up slowly. And all hell broke loose. The old guide threw himself to his feet and slid out from under Ramok's startled grasp. With a fluid movement, the old man grabbed a flexor and slashed the bota bag on Wren's unmounted horse. Water gushed from the bag. Horen swore, and Yemene screamed. Spade threw himself forward. The old man dodged beneath Horen's horse and cut another bag, and the dappled bay sidestepped into Tsia's mount. The roan reared. Wren staggered away from the flying hooves while Tsia fought with the reins, and the old man slashed the third and fourth botas.

Forrest slid between the rearing mounts, grabbing reins and forcing the horses to stay on the trail. The old man cut; Ramok grabbed a horse from backing off the overhang of the trail. Wren snapped his flexor out and slashed at the old man's arm. Impossibly, the man dodged away, sliding beneath Horen's cut and spearing yet another bota as he went. More water splashed free. Yemene had backed away on the trail, her hands across her belly and her eyes wide. The man's stolen flexor flashed again. Spade threw himself between the councilwoman and the old man, and then Nitpicker's fiber dart caught the man in the throat, and he made one more weak cut before Wren landed on his shoulders and they both crashed to the ground.

Nitpicker retrieved her dart and watched Wren secure the old man, then looked at Ramok with a grim expression. "I hit him straight the first time."

"It's because he's a guide." Ramok stared down. "Their bodies are resistant to drugs." He raised his gaze to the horses. Only two of their bota bags had not been cut, and one of those—Tsia's— had been empty, anyway. Nine bota bags, he thought, and only one to see them through the narrows. He stared at the wet spots in the trail. The summer mud would be gone in ten minutes, and soon they would be without water.

The old man was not unconscious for more than a minute, but by the time he came to, his wrists were touch-tied and any movement he made stuck more of his skin together. His temple links were not plugged, but they had been jammed by one of Horen's bronze-colored disks. As soon as Horen linked the disk to the man's ID dot, the merc ghosts took over, and the node listened to the merc images instead of the old man.

Tsia, still mounted, regarded the old guide expressionlessly. His blue eyes had opened a moment earlier and had turned first to Nitpicker, then to Ramok, then examined the group until his gaze returned to Tsia and Forrest.

Ramok squatted beside his wrinkled body and waited until the old man turned his head to acknowledge him. "We are mercs," Ramok said without preamble. "If you work this ridge, you know of the conflict between the freepicks and the miners in Pulan." The old man gave no indication one way or the other, so Ramok continued. "We are taking that woman—" He nodded toward Yemene. "—back to Pulan. We silenced you so that the node would not recognize us as more than biologicals. If we are caught, the woman and the child she bears will die." The old man merely looked at him. "We will keep you with us until we reach Pulan," Ramok explained. "We will set you free near the mines. You can request retribution through the merc guild. It is logged on that man's disk—" He indicated Horen. "—and will be fully logged in the node once we reach Pulan." He straightened. "Wren, Nitpicker," he directed, "you two are lightest. Draw straws."

Spade snapped off two dry grass stems from between a rock and shortened one of the brittle blades. Wren drew the long straw. Nitpicker made a face. Wren chuckled as he tossed his straw back between the rocks. "You tag 'em, you bag 'em," he said to the woman. She shot him a sour look as she began rearranging her saddlebags to make room for the old man. In the meantime, Forrest and Horen made their way up to the old man's perch. They found no gear, and when they returned, Ramok spoke to the man again. "Would you tell us where your gear is stashed?"

Though he watched Ramok steadily, the old man did not answer, and the merc raised his thick eyebrow. "Your food? Your e-roll?" Still there was no answer, and Ramok shrugged. "You might wish you had told us of the e-roll." He got to his feet. "Since you slashed our botas, there will be nothing to drink for any of us except the councilwoman."

The man's eyes flicked to the watergen straws against the saddle, and Ramok smiled without humor. "Watergens leave traces in a sensor net. To use those would bring the artists down on us faster than a hawk on its prey. You guessed that before you used the flexor."

The gray-haired man never answered, but his eyes glinted.

He was mounted behind Nitpicker, and the woman moved forward in the line till she cantered her Appaloosa between Horen and Spade. Tsia rode behind Ramok, in front of Forrest. Wren, staying with Yemene, brought up the rear. They headed out, the horses eager to move up the trail and the riders wary. Tsia could not help taking one more look at the desert as they wound into a cleft that cut off the view. The plains rolled across the dry-grass desert and seemed to engulf the black, shimmering city that she could almost see on the horizon. She stared for a long moment, her neck twisted to look behind her, then she spurred the roan and caught up with Ramok.

One hour and three skimmers later Tsia's hands itched to drink from her bota. She touched the loop from which it hung, then withdrew her hand abruptly. The thirst that parched her lips made them crack, and she wished she had thought to borrow some lip salve from Nitpicker. Then the shakes hit her so that she gripped the saddle horn to stay on the roan. When they subsided, she found her left hand clenched on the bota loop. She stared at it for a moment. Then, lifting the bag quickly, she reined to the side of the trail and handed the bag to Forrest as he caught up. He gave her a careful look, but she ignored it. A moment later she was back on the path.

By midafternoon the sun struck them full force from the west. The rocks bounced the light back like an oven wall, and not even Wren was immune to the sweat that stuck to their skins and dried into a tight, gritty layer of discomfort.

When they reached the false summit, Ramok let them dismount so that Yemene could ease her aching back and legs. The old gray-haired guide did not speak even when he was handed carefully down from the horse. Instead, he eyed Tsia, then leaned against a rock and closed his eyes as if he were sleeping.

Ramok, motioning for Spade to watch the old man, tucked a slimchim in his mouth and offered one to Tsia before lifting his horse's hooves to check again for stones.

Tsia chewed and swallowed the bland slimchim with a scowl, and the expression pulled at the scar on her cheek. Her tongue flicked to moisten her lips, even though she knew it would do no good; the wind-chapped skin was only a prelude to the thirst she would feel by nightfall.

Behind her Wren popped a black seed in his mouth and spit out the husk. To his side, Horen watched Tsia silently. Tsia barely no-

ticed. Her eyes were drawn up to the rocks, to the thin clumps of
needletrees and drywood that grew out of the gullies. Above, the
wash stretched up to a flattened slab that jutted from the side of
the rock. It would have been a waterfall in spring, but in the heat
of summer it was merely a shaded overhang in which the
sandsnakes nested.

Tsia eyed the wash. There was a spot higher in the rocks from
which she could see the plains again if she looked from that vantage point. Hesitating only an instant, she tucked the reins of the
roan under a rock, then climbed into the gully. Within minutes she
had left the rest of the mercs behind. The wind, a mere breeze on
the trail, became a strong breath against her skin. Feeling it, she
shoved the head shade back on her shoulders. Instantly, the wind
dried the sweat on her scalp and made the skin under her hair
prickle. She scrambled over the boulders and, avoiding the nest of
snakes, climbed onto the overhang.

The desert plains wavered in the distance. She could see the
black city better now; for the moment, the light bounced its reflection above the other waves of heat. Behind her, the thicket of
brush grew into a dense tangle, and the scent of dry soil and
dusty, sweet sage filled her nose. She only glanced at the brush;
her eyes were drawn to the plains instead, where a skimmer
floated up to the base of the Dry Mountains. Becoming still, Tsia
held her breath as she watched the ship. It nosed into the canyons,
floated out, then moved along the cliffs. The mercs below made
almost no noise, and Tsia stepped back until it seemed as if she
were alone on the ridge. There was no sound but the wind, no
heartbeat but her own.

Silently, she stood with her arms wrapped around herself until
she felt the tightness across her cheeks. She blinked to clear the
tears, then froze. Behind her something watched. Her biogate
seemed to open wide, and she felt the cat's eyes peer into her
brain. She took a breath. The presence was not just in her brain—
the yellow gaze of a cougar was boring into her back.

Slowly, warily, she turned.

There was nothing there. The thicket was silent except for the
brushing of the wind in the brittle twigs of sage. There was only
the shadow cast by a strangely pitched stone in the light. She had
been sure . . . She stretched through the gate and felt the cougar's
gaze fade.

There were tracks, and they were fresh. Kneeling, Tsia bent and
sniffed the dirt. The musky scent of the cat still clung to the
pressed-down soil, and she breathed more deeply, sucking the

odor into her lungs and holding it till she felt faint. Unbidden, her hand pressed into the soil. She brought her fingers to her cheeks and rubbed the scent into her skin, heedless of the dust that smeared across her face. To be so close . . .

Oh, gods, she would break the Landing Pact again. She knew it. The cats did not avoid her, and she could not close them out. When she got back to Ciordan, when the guild found out she had touched them—even called the cats through her gate—they would strip her of the virus. Her gate—her useless gate—was too strong for her to deny. Daya, she snarled in her mind, no wonder there had been pity on their faces when they saw the link to which her virus had resonated. They were guides. They had known how it would call her. How it would force her to respond. They had known the whole time that they would have to strip it away and leave her blind to the cats once she started intruding in their lives. Oh, Daya, she cried out, that was what she was doing. Intruding. She could not stop reaching for the comfort of their presence.

Comfort? She rocked herself silently, the laughter bitter on her lips. The presence of the tawny animal power had been a torture to her in Noirelle. Now, with the high thickets and cliffs around her, it was a siren song in her brain. Vashanna, she thought harshly, had been right all along. She, Tsia, *was* a slave. She could not escape the chains that bound her to the cats.

She said nothing to Ramok when she returned. Only Forrest cast his glance back along the stones where she had stood. A few minutes later they were gone, riding along the trail, and only the moving shadows in the rocks spoke of the watchers on the heights.

As the horses climbed and the horizon lowered and time carved its way into evening, Tsia's thirst grew until it ate at her flesh the way the sun seemed to eat the paleness of her skin. It took all her will not to beg for the bota she had handed to Forrest. Her hands clutched at the place where the water bag had hung, and she rubbed the roan's neck fiercely, as if the motion would rub out her thirst. The other mercs were as silent as she. The trek and the constant threat of the skimmers had leached away their humor.

The biogate pulled, and the cats in her mind seemed to snarl, and Tsia knew there could be no freedom from the gate. To be a guide had been her dream. Now it was her nightmare. The cougars she felt, the tams—they knew her through her gate. They watched her, not the mercs. They wanted her, pulled her, and taunted her with their nearness when she tried to shut them out. She could feel their muscles as if they rubbed and swatted at her skin. She could feel the saliva on their tongues as they licked across their forearms.

Unable to help herself, she stretched along the gate and licked her own lips, and the saliva that softened them startled her. Saliva? Had the cats sent her that . . . sense . . . through the gate? A cougar yowled softly, and she shivered. Her eyes sought out Forrest's bulky shape. Desperately she wanted to ask him, but she was afraid he would find out what she was doing. That she was linked with the cats. That she was listening to them, sending to them, reaching for them even when the Landing Pact forbade it. With an anguished mental cry she drew back within herself and locked her eyes stiffly on the trail.

The dust hung over them like a heavy cloud of wool, irritating their eyes and making them sweat even more as it clogged their pores and stuck their fingers together like glue on the reins. Even when they rode into the canyons, there was no shade on this trail. The horses snorted constantly.

Ramok rode back and forth along the line. He had checked each hour with Yemene, and as he passed Tsia this time, he reined in so that he was even with the pregnant woman. But when he asked the same question he had before, the woman motioned angrily for him to leave her.

"I have told you no four times," she snapped. "I will not give birth before we reach Pulan. Do you intend to plague me to death with your questions or guide me back to Pulan in one piece?"

Ramok eyed her expressionlessly. "One piece is better than two."

"The child will be born in Pulan, not in these goddessforsaken hills." Yemene set her mouth. "The reading by the espers will not be cheated by your incompetence."

Now Ramok smiled, but the expression did not reach his eyes. "Think of this as a vacation," he suggested softly. "Then you can rest assured it will end all too soon." He turned his mount and made his way back to the front of the line. Tiredly, Tsia had dropped back behind both Forrest and Wren, and it was up beside the smaller merc that Ramok now reined in.

"The councilwoman is in good humor today," Wren commented wryly.

"Her humor is as foul as the tailings from the western mines."

The other man chuckled. "But she has metal enough to snap at your Feather."

"Hah. Tsia's tongue is sharp enough on its own to carve designs in stone," Ramok retorted.

"You've experienced the depths of her ways already?" Wren was openly teasing now, and Ramok grinned. Both men stilled for an instant as a skimmer appeared over the ridges to the east; then Ramok, his eyes still on the sky, answered. "Not all, my friend, not all," he returned. "But she is a woman and will have myriad ways of telling me that."

"Best tell her to ride farther up, then."

Ramok glanced back sharply and saw that Tsia was riding back, just ahead of the blond-haired merc. Even from where Ramok sat he could see the lust gathering in Horen's eyes. He pulled up. "Tsia," he ordered sharply, "ride with me."

Tsia stiffened slowly at his tone. She urged the roan forward, but her ice-blue eyes glittered. "You have need of something?" she said acidly as she passed Wren and trotted her mount up beside Ramok's.

Ramok frowned, but behind her, Wren spoke first. "Ramok was just saying how he wanted to show you Redeye Ridge before the dust from the rest of the line obscures the view. You must not have heard him call the first time."

She gave Wren a hard look. "No."

Ramok cleared his throat. "The first crest in the ridge is only a kilometer from here. We should find fresh water at the spring near its top."

She regarded him silently, but Ramok smiled, and she followed him without comment. The tremors in her hands were almost constant now, and Wren glanced at them before reining back to ride beside Forrest. Neither man said a word.

The path up the ridge became rigorously steep, and they were forced to ride single file. What Ramok called a trail was little more than occasional flat stretches between rockfalls, and Tsia let her eyes imagine the dry canyon thickets softened with soft, wavering grass. As they rode, the sun sank across the plains and the canyons began to fill with shadows. Wind curled the dust into eddies, so that the shadows seemed to move and dance in the darkened heat. There was a keening note to the wind. Tsia cocked her head to hear it better, and Ramok nodded to her.

"It is coming through the vents," he explained, "along the top of the ridge." He pointed, and she could almost see the dark holes in the stone.

She followed his eyes with a frown while unconsciously rubbing her temples. The keening was more like the snarling of cats in her head than the constant moan of the wind. Cats, tams, cougars . . . She tightened her lips. Her gate sucked at the sounds. A pack of tams crawled along the ridge and watched the riders pass. Three cougars on the heights pierced the dust with their glowing yellow eyes.

"Daya," she whispered. To run beside them . . . To dig her fingers into tawny fur . . . The shakes took her suddenly, and she had to cling to the saddle to keep from falling. To touch the cats was forbidden, she snarled at herself harshly. If she could not remember that, then she *should* return home and let the guild strip this addiction from her soul. Let them kill the gate before it swallowed the rest of her reason. Let them chain her down from her dreams.

But it was the cats themselves that called her, a tiny voice whispering inside her head.

She ignored it.

Could the guild condemn her when her own gate called? the voice went on. The cat feet slunk across her brain, pushing her thoughts with their presence.

Go away, she screamed at the feet. How can I reason this out when you don't let me think? When you don't stop this scratching at my head? She clenched her fists against her temples until the animal power subsided and the cat feet settled down against the inside of her skull. It was a long, dry moment before she dropped her hands again to the reins.

When they reached the top of the ridge, the sun had already lain down behind the ridge. Its light streamed across the sky in an orange-blue wash, and the stars had begun to come out in the east. When she dismounted, Tsia tilted her head back and stared at the sky. North—she was going north. She was going home. Home to Ciordan, to the guild, where they would kill the gate within her and lock her forever from its tawny touch.

The image of the white cell walls of Noirelle rose in her mind. Was being locked out, her tiny voice asked, as bad as being chained in? If she lost her gate, could she stand the silence in her mind? Could she bear the loss of those snarling songs, the sense of the hunt in her nose?

She forced herself to uncinch the roan and stake him out in the small clearing, where he nibbled eagerly at the dry grass. She stared at the heights. She could hardly swallow; her mouth was puckered dry like a withered prune. She wanted to touch the saliva of the cats again, to feel its wetness sooth her tongue. She backed off from her gate abruptly and turned instead toward Ramok.

"What is it?" she asked as she noted his frown. Her voice came out like a ragged croak, and he barely spared her a glance as he continued to peer up the cliffs.

"There should be a spring here," he muttered. He vaulted a massive rock and reached back to help her over. "There is the runoff, but it is dry as deadwood in a three-year drought."

She took his hand and jumped up lightly, squinting up the steep slope, but she saw only the same tangle of dried shrubs and the inch-thick layer of dust that lay across all the rocks. Any tracks of water that used to run through the cleft had been cleared away months earlier by the relentless sun.

"You did not come through here on your way to the art guild stronghold?"

"We took skimmers in."

She glanced at his nearly-empty water bag. "You were counting on this water hole."

"As much as a merc can count on anything he does not carry himself." He eyed the brittle shrubs within the cleft. "We could dig down to its source," he mused.

Tsia reached out and snapped a twig off the bush. There was no tenacious wick in its center, and she sniffed the branch for any scent of sap. She shook her head. "These have deep roots," she explained. "They reach down in cracks between layers of rock to get to water up to nine meters below. But these shrubs are completely dead. Their water nodules must not have contained enough water to sustain them." She looked down the dusty drop-off. "The source for this spring has dried up or rerouted itself under the rocks." She could see no sign of water reemerging below. No taint of green touched the orange-yellow dust, and the rocks looked as dead as a tombstone. The only life she could see was the night lizards skittering across the rocks like the cat feet that crawled in her skull.

Beside her, Ramok scanned the hill. "Wait here," he said finally.

"Are you going up?"

He nodded and hitched his weapon harness more to the side. Watching him, Tsia hitched her own harness as he did.

"What are you doing?" Ramok glanced down from where he crouched on a jutting rock.

Tsia was already following him up, her feet making no sound on the smooth stone. She grinned and pulled herself over onto the ledge, reaching up for his hand. With a resigned shrug, he lifted her over a second stone to stand beside him.

As they worked their way up the cleft, Tsia examined the peb-

bles that still lay in the cleft. They were rounded, not as sharp as
they had been out on the exposed cliff, and in the shadows were
the remains of moss and tiny flowers, dried and shriveled in their
dusty grave. Near the top the merc and the guide scaled a small
chimney. Tsia went first, and Ramok followed below, where he
could help her if she faltered. After he showed her how to place
her feet on either side of the walls, she braced herself with her
hands as he did, so she could walk up as if she were stepping on
two ladders facing each other. She laughed and, like a spider,
scuttled up the cliff till she paused, the sweat beading on her
hands and the thin air tiring her quickly.

Below her, Ramok grunted. "As you were—do not stop," he
corrected. "You will not be able to get going again."

She nodded. When she looked down, she saw first Ramok's
huge shoulders, then the shadows of his legs beneath him. The
broken stone of the trail seemed suddenly very far away.

"Keep going," Ramok ordered again.

She tried to obey, but her hands would not move. Her chest
heaved with exertion and an emotion she would have called fear
had it not been so paralyzing. There was a yowling in her head,
and she could not seem to find the strength to lift her hands
again—Daya, but her grip was slipping . . . She was going to
fall . . . Her eyes turned into cat slits, and her fingers suddenly became claws digging into the dust.

Ramok quickened his climb. "*Esha, avya,*" he soothed urgently. "Just stay there." He reached up and found a place in the
columns where he could lean out and around her body. Her face
was a mask, her lips wrinkled back from her teeth as if she would
growl at him, but he swung his body out and jammed his booted
foot into a notch dug away by the wind. Then his shoulders
tucked her tightly into the stone channel. Her eyes were still
locked on the dust far below. She did not notice the strain in
Ramok's muscles as he clung to the rock around her. His fingers
dug and twisted into tiny cracks while his feet braced the rest of
his weight away from the cliff. He tugged at her hand. "Tsia," he
ordered, "put your arms around my neck."

She yowled and clung tighter to the rock.

"Dammit, woman, let go." His strength finally ripped her desperate clench off the chimney, and she fell, her wrist caught in
Ramok's steel grip. Ramok thrust with all his might against the
rock to keep from being thrown out by the force of his yank. Tsia
twisted in midair and latched on to Ramok's neck, her thighs

clinging to his body and her wild eyes staring out over his shoulder at the vast expanse of air that swept away from them both.

"*Eshe*, Tsia," he muttered, cramming himself back into the chimney. "*Eshe, avya.*" He did not have to warn her to hold tight; the death grip she had on his neck would have killed a lesser man. Did she know what she was doing to his breathing? He could feel her heartbeat, quick and pounding where her neck touched his.

He cursed under his breath. It was another five meters to the top of the chimney, and when he got there, he was going to shake the sense back into her. But as he reached the top, his breath came harshly and he paused for a grip. Tsia did not wait. She leapt from him to the cliff top in one lithe movement.

She crouched, shivering, then ran along the top of the cliff while Ramok dragged his body over the edge and squatted. He shook his arms out vigorously. Their strained muscles were hard and pumped. He glared after the *nyeka*, but she was still heading toward the other edge of the cliff. "Tsia," he said sharply. "Get back here."

Startled, she turned, and he could have sworn he saw her blue eyes glitter with wildness before he blinked. Then she looked past him and growled. Ramok was up on his feet in an instant. Instinctively, he grabbed Tsia, thrusting her behind him as he grabbed his flexor and snapped it to active. But as he lifted the weapon, its weight became unbalanced in his hand. He knew then what they faced.

In the slanting light of sunset the cougar crouched on the rock as if it were part of the rays and regarded them with a malevolent gaze as yellow as Tsia's were blue. Tsia slipped by the merc with a feral gleam in her eyes; he had to lunge to catch her before she darted right into the cat's waiting fangs. She halted, locked in place by the iron grip on her arm. But even his tightening grip did not stop the snarling in her throat that was as low as that from the cat they faced. The cat's tail flicked. Its muscles tensed to spring. The merc tightened his grip further. He could throw Tsia out of the way and wrestle the cat himself if he had to. But Tsia hissed and flexed her hands as if they were claws. The cat shifted. Then it was gone.

Ramok did not loosen his grip. Tsia stared after the cat. She could almost hear its breathing fade between the stones. A few more seconds and the wind dissipated the scent of the cat until only its already dust-filled tracks left evidence of its warning. With the iron grip binding her arm, she began to struggle silently.

"Stay quiet," he ordered in an almost inaudible whisper. He let her go only when he saw the sanity return to her eyes, then made his way silently and stealthily to where the beast had appeared. Warily he poked his flexor into the shadows, but there was no further trace.

Behind him, Tsia rubbed her arm absently. She pointed toward the other edge of the cliff top. "There is water down there," she said in a low voice.

Ramok crossed the ground to look where she had indicated. His shoulders twitched as if he felt the eyes of a cat on his back, but when he turned, he saw nothing. No movement, no heat. A shape in the rocks tugged at his memory, and he realized that they were on the edge of Catmount Ridge. He pointed at the sculpture, and Tsia flicked her gaze toward it, nodding absently at the stone-carved puma caught in midcrouch on the rocky ledge. Her eyes were drawn back to the valley.

"Look at the life," Tsia whispered. She licked her dry lips. "Look at all the green."

Ramok crouched beside her carefully.

Tsia breathed in a lungful of odor and exultation. Below her the rock cliff slid down and waded into a sea of dusk-shadowed growth that could only be described as a temperate forest. Where Bonnell's Bay had felt lush after the desert, Cheba Rift was ten times as thick in trees and summer greenery. From her height it looked like one giant patch of two-toned moss that stretched from cliff to distant cliff and ended only when it butted up against the closed mountain pass of the narrows. Tsia licked her lips as an updraft from the rift caught her nose. Echoes reached them from the surrounding cliffs.

Ramok glanced around. "Look here—we stand on a leopard's forehead. And there, to our right, a bearcat's face."

"I want to go down."

"No."

"*I* would be safe," she said flatly.

He glanced at her. "We will not find water here," he returned flatly. "If we ride on, we should come to a tinaja said to hold water even in the dry years."

Sliding and scraping their way back down, the two regained the trail with nothing more than a banged elbow for Ramok. "The spring is dry," he said in answer to Wren's raised eyebrow. "There is another water hole up ahead. Four kilometers."

Wren nodded. He turned his horse and moved back while Horen brought up the rest of the line. Tsia mounted in a quick, sharp movement, gathering the reins and slapping the dust from her blunter. She glanced back over the other riders until Horen met her gaze with a penetrating stare. She stilled, then looked away.

They had not traveled three kilometers when the councilwoman pulled off to the side and urged her mount up to Tsia's horse. Ramok glanced back and slowed. "What is it?" he asked.

Yemene gave him a haughty look. "I must stop again."

"It is only one more kilometer to our night camp," he growled, "and you have stopped twice this last hour already."

"The baby has dropped and is pushing against my pelvis and bladder," she snapped back. "I cannot help my needs. Pregnancy does not make for an easy ride."

"Nor for a pleasant temper," he returned under his breath.

"I wish to speak to the . . . *Jinga*." She indicated Tsia.

Ramok gave her a dark look but signaled for the others to stop. He pulled back to give them the privacy Yemene desired. "Take a break," he told the others. "You've got ten minutes."

"What is it?" Tsia asked curtly, adding as the councilwoman hesitated, "He is out of earshot."

"I—I need your help."

Tsia looked at the other woman steadily. It must have taken a great deal for her to ask for help; Tsia had begun to think that Yemene's pride was stronger than her body.

"I need to—to relieve myself, but at the last break someone watched me where I went."

Tsia gave her a sharp look. "Did you tell Ramok?"

"I do not discuss my hygiene with a common mercenary."

In spite of herself, Tsia laughed. "You think I am any better than they? I traded a slave's chains for a merc's blade. Am I still good enough to help you?"

Yemene looked at her coldly. "You are a guide, not a killer for hire, no matter what guild you follow."

Tsia met the councilwoman's eyes with her own glittering blue gaze. "So now you ask this lowly, inexperienced, arrogant, atavistic, godless guide—" She threw the words back at Yemene. "—to help you against an unseen foe when there are six armed mercs ready to die at your command."

"It was one of those six," Yemene retorted, "who followed me before."

"And how am I to protect you from whomever that may be?"

"With your flexor, as you would yourself."

The councilwoman's calm assurance made Tsia want to reach out and scratch her face. Instead, without a word, she swung off her horse and tossed its reins around the nearest shrub, motioning for Yemene to dismount. The woman was awkward, and Tsia had to steady her until she caught the saddle horn with one grasping hand and lowered herself to the ground.

"Take my arm," Tsia said. "In the dark, you will probably fall off the trail without it."

"I need no help to walk."

"As you wish."

But a moment later the woman stumbled, falling against a rock as her ankle turned on a loose root that was hidden in shadow.

"Take my arm," Tsia offered again.

"Don't patronize me, *Jinga*."

Tsia stilled at the use of the term. "I am no *Jinga*, Yemene. Nor am I your *heyta* to command."

Yemene bristled.

"And," Tsia added scathingly, "if you do not accept the help you ask for, then you deserve every bruise you get. Think what would happen if you fell on that belly you are so proud of. Now take my arm. It is dark, and we are already away from the trail. No one can see."

Furious, the woman glared at her.

"Take my arm," Tsia warned, "or I will call Forrest or Ramok or Spade and have one of them carry you."

"You would not dare."

Tsia smiled slowly. "Wouldn't I? I never could resist a dare, and I have more than enough breath to call all six of the mercs."

The black-haired woman shoved herself away from the wall and took the proffered arm. She refused to meet Tsia's gaze. But she clutched Tsia's arm tightly a moment later when she stumbled again in the trailing roots of some shrubs. Only Tsia's strength and braced stance kept her from landing on her knees.

"Thank you," the woman muttered, smoothing her robe over her belly.

"Are you always this gracious to those who help you?"

"This child will be the greatest leader Pulan will ever have," Yemene retorted. "You should be proud to help."

"I would be," Tsia returned sourly, "if I helped a true leader and not one who, if he is anything like his mother, will be no more than a spoiled brat who abuses his position."

The sound of a ringing slap echoed on the cliff as the woman's hand struck Tsia's face. Like a cat's paw, Tsia's own hand slapped her back. The woman stood stunned.

"You struck me."

"You struck me," Tsia snapped back. The night shadows fell across her face, leaving her blue eyes to glitter in the rising moonlight.

Yemene clenched and unclenched her hands. When she finally spoke, it was in a low voice. "Why do you say I misuse the power vested in me?"

Tsia's answer was curt. "You have no respect for anyone other than yourself."

Yemene looked at her silently.

"You think, because you met me in chains, that I am still a slave. And you think, because I was Cekulu's servant, I will be yours as well. For the past two days you have ignored me until you wanted something; now you order me around as if you had an r-con on my brain."

"I am under stress," the woman muttered finally.

Tsia laughed out loud. "That is your excuse?" Yemene glowered at her, and Tsia took the woman's arm again. "Do you think that the greater your need for someone, the more justification you have for simply taking that person and using her, with no regard for the person herself?"

Yemene shrugged off her hand, but Tsia gripped her hard by the elbow, forcing her to accept her assistance. "Is that what you think?" Tsia persisted.

Yemene stared at the ground in front of her. "What is the difference," she asked in a quiet voice, "between my using your presence to keep my baby safe and your using Cekulu's death to find your own brand of safety?"

Tsia's hands tightened involuntarily till Yemene gasped. With a snarl, Tsia released her. They did not speak again until they reached a private spot half-sheltered by the rocks and hidden by the tall, dried brush.

Yemene was about to speak again when Tsia stiffened. "Be still. There is someone behind us," she said in a low voice.

She stretched along her senses. It was not Forrest . . . Not Ramok . . . She would have heard less than she had if it had been either of those. Nor could it be Nitpicker. That one was silent as a ghost. Unconsciously Tsia stretched farther, feeling faintly the energy of the human who watched. She scanned the path, then the clearing again. Cat feet skittered. A yellow tail switched out of sight behind a rock, and a pair of yellow eyes glared from a shadow. Her hand tightened on Yemene's arm. "Be still," she whispered. "Be very, very still."

Yemene stood petrified. Tsia growled in her throat, and an answering snarl came from the rocks in front, to the side, and behind. She rumbled, and the hair on the nape of her neck stood out. Before her, she stared at the sandy-colored beast. It was massive—a single paw was the size of Tsia's entire head, and its fangs were long and sharp like knives. Yemene, looking from the cougar to Tsia and back, was ashen.

The cougar crouched lower, and Tsia hissed. She could hear this creature in her head. Sense it. Through her gate, she could feel it guide her to the place where the human watched the women and the yearlings watched the man. And then the air went taut to the breaking point as four tams, their yellow-white stripes and stocky bodies flattened out on the rocks, crept forward. Their hind legs were tensed to spring, and their short, thick tails flicked in the air with their concentration. Wide paws flexed on the stones. The cougar greeted the tams with a mental snap; the tams, intent on the women, ignored the cougar completely.

Tsia eyed the cats and snarled again. In her head, their hostility was deafening. Her lips bared her teeth as she crouched to match the felines. This time the answering rumbles were less. When Tsia yowled low in her head, her lips silent to her ears, the sound echoed into her gate and seemed to disappear. Yemene was hers, Tsia snarled silently at the cats that crawled through her mind. No more for taking than that yearling she saw to her right. She marked no territory. She would not bring the cub forth in their thickets.

Did they hear? The hair on the tams' knobs seemed to settle. The muscles of the cougar stayed tense to her sight. Frozen behind her, Yemene could not close her eyes, could not move, could do nothing but pray that the mercs had not missed the noise that signaled the end of their lives.

Then, incredibly, Tsia said, "Relieve yourself." She relaxed imperceptibly into her crouch. Her muscles were ready, tensed to pounce, but she knew the cats would not leap.

To Tsia's surprise, the councilwoman did as she was told, squatting as awkwardly as she had gotten off her horse. One of the tams stalked pointedly past Tsia and disappeared into the pale shrub on the other side of the niche, and then another cat followed. Holding herself up by the rocks, the councilwoman let her lips move in silent prayer. There was a sudden, cut-off cry from the rocks to their right, and the pregnant woman froze. But the cats were gone.

"*Seva*, Yemene," Tsia said quietly. "You are safe."

"Safe." Yemene straightened. She pulled her loose robe down

over her buttocks and allowed Tsia to help her forward. She seemed stunned. It was Tsia who pulled the spray from her toilet case and used it on her stool to dissolve the fecal matter into the soil.

Yemene cleared her throat. "The . . . cry?"

Tsia gave her an unreadable look. "As you said, there was someone following us."

The woman hesitated only a moment before taking Tsia's arm to get back to the trail. "Thank you," she said faintly.

They were silent as they edged between the boulders and crossed the uneven ground. When they reached the trail again, the woman turned to her again. "What did you say to the cougar—to the tams?"

Tsia glanced at her, then halted. Her blue eyes were uncertain. "I—I don't know." She gazed back at the rocks. "I think I told them you were my daughter."

Yemene stared. "You what?"

"They wanted to know who intruded on their ridges. I . . . became a cat. You were with me. They allowed us to remain."

"And the man's cry we heard?"

"I told them they could mark the one who hunted us."

"Kill?"

"Mark only."

Yemene nodded. She did not speak again until they had nearly reached the horses. "I thought at first you were a tool of the art guild," she said in a low voice. "I thought that you never truly left Cekulu's service at all but came with Ramok only to be close enough to kill me. Or that you worked for the miners and wanted my child dead at any cost. I was wrong," she said softly. "*Nyeka*, forgive me."

Tsia gazed at her. "Do you know that is the first time you have called me anything but a slave?"

Yemene inclined her head, acknowledging the rebuke. "You did not believe that the reading was about this child."

"I'm not sure that I do even now. Esper readings are too easily averted."

"Not this one." Yemene looked at Tsia's ice-blue eyes. They burned with a bright gleam in the light of the moon. " 'And the cougar,' " she quoted, " 'shall claw the council free from the rape of its future . . .' "

Tsia's gaze shuttered. The cat feet that had poured through her gate seemed to dance and settle in her brain, and she could not see for a moment. Neither one spoke when they returned to the trail.

24

Forrest watched with speculation as the two women made their way back. He stood near the old man, and both noted the quick, nervous stride of the *nyeka*, the tremble that shook her hands when she reached for her horse's reins. Not even the dark could hide the hunted expression on her face.

"Second stage," the old man said suddenly.

Forrest's eyes flicked.

"She's a second-stager, isn't she?" The old man shifted his shoulders, his hands still touch-tied behind him. "You going to let her go down?"

Forrest turned his head slowly. The old man grinned without humor, the expression a challenge in the gray dusk shadows.

"No node access, no links—that means no guild, either," he persisted. "So she shakes herself to pieces. You don't get her to a guild soon, she's going to lose it completely." He noted the way Forrest's gaze flicked toward Ramok. "You tell him you better get her some help or you'll have to leave her hissing in the sand." He smiled, the wrinkled skin of his face pulling into a thin expression that belied his next words. "Hate to see what the guild will do to you for passing a stager like that. You being a guide and all." The gray-haired man chuckled. He did not speak again, and Forrest tossed him back up on Nitpicker's horse. The old man was still chuckling when Nitpicker swung up and reined back into her place in the line.

When she had returned, Tsia had gone directly to Ramok, intending to speak to him of the merc who had followed Yemene. But he was talking with Wren, and, unwilling to speak in front of the other merc, she halted and pulled herself into the roan's saddle instead.

Absently, she wiped her hands on her jumpsuit. With the evening and altitude, it was cooler, but the sweat still clung to her fingers, and the soft, watered green she had seen in the rift haunted the cat feet in her mind while her hands along her pants cloth scraped grit into her skin like sandpaper. She soothed the roan, murmuring to him and leaning forward to run her hands along his neck. He was hot and dusty, and her fingers came back grimed with more of the reddish-brown dirt she had just wiped off. She gave the horse a feral smile. Her once-sand-colored clothes were now almost the same dirty shade as the roan. Even the drab color of the blunter jacket had been lightened by the dust and dirt. In the darkening shadows she could fade like a cat into any stone she sat beside. She stared along the gray-yellow trail. The wind lifted. Her eyes burned.

"Redeye Ridge was named for a reason," Wren muttered as he swung up to his own saddle and fell in beside Tsia. His disproportionately huge hands held the reins of his horse loosely while his keen eyes searched the hills for movement. In the last hours of evening he had not seen a lizard, a snake, or a massflea, but he could swear that there had been a cougar watching them from above. Here and there a forgotten skeleton lay disarrayed in the dust, its bones cracked and white. With the coming night, the bones looked as if they would clothe themselves in shadow and rise to run the ridge again. Tsia shivered, looking at an elongated skull that was attached to a spine too curved to be human.

"This area was never settled," Wren commented. "There are still plenty of remnants of Pre-Drop alive in the hills. Things that were never explored or even seen by the First Droppers. If the old man—" He indicated the hostage who rode with them. "—were more inclined to talk, we could ask him about the bones." He made a surreptitious sign. "He is old enough that he could have been here when some of them were made."

Tsia, licking dry lips, did not take him up on his wry gambit.

It was almost dark when the trail wound onto a flat spot between two tapering rock cliffs. Ramok swung down and strode ahead, leaving his horse to stand stamping in the path. Tsia moved to dismount also, but Wren reached across and stayed her. "Wait."

Ramok was back in five minutes. "The tanks are dry," he said shortly. "We will ride to the next spring." He shook his arm suddenly, and a black seryal dropped from his sleeve. It scuttled toward his leg, but he stomped quickly, grinding the brittle legs to death under his boot. He saw Tsia's startled disgust in her eyes. "Not all water is guarded by cats, Little Feather." He mounted and motioned for the line to move again. He did not look back.

Water. The water carried by Forrest in the last bota bag was hot and stale, but even that was something to dream about. She swallowed, dragging her dry tongue out of her sticky throat. Her hands trembled when she looked at the saddlebag that contained her watergen. It took all her will to ride back beside Forrest and, indicating the saddlebag with a stiff nod, say, "Take it."

The man's amber eyes were strangely shuttered as he leaned over and, lifting the flap with one massive finger, plucked the water straw from the bag. Tsia clenched her fists on the reins. For an instant Forrest's hand covered hers. *"Eshe,"* he said softly. His hand withdrew, and the heat of it seemed to take her shivering with him. Startled, Tsia glanced up, but the big merc watched her with an unreadable expression.

In the east Orpheus had risen above Catmount Ridge. Its light turned the trail into swatches of dry gray and black through which the horses moved like momentary harlequins. The second moon, Eurydice, trailed behind and was obscured for a moment by a low-sweeping skimmer that looked like the hand of Hades on the moon's visage. Though all eyes were on the ship, Ramok did not allow the pace to slack. He did not halt the line until they were halfway between Redeye and Catmount ridges.

When they stopped, Tsia was too dulled to realize at first that this was more than a place to check another spring. Not until Ramok reached up to her waist and removed her from the saddle did she stir. "We camp here," Ramok said as her hands clutched his arms. When he released her, she reached up and touched his neck. His muscles tensed. She gazed at his black eyes and drew her fingers down across his trachea so that he shuddered. She licked her lips. His skin was gritty like the fur of a cat. She stroked his neck again.

Ramok had to force himself to turn away and drag his bedroll from his saddle. Only when he was sure that Tsia had turned to her own gear did he look at her again. She had placed her e-roll beneath a web of the coaba branches as if she sought a thicket in which to rest.

Forrest moved up beside him. His voice, when he spoke, was low. "The cats will come tonight."

"We will keep close watch."

"Better to keep wards than watch." At the dark voice, both looked up. Spade stood there, his brown hair and black eyes pools of shadow in his pale, moonlit face. "It's not from without the camp we have to watch but from within."

Spade's eyes flicked to Tsia, who, hearing his words, straightened from unrolling her bed. To her side, Wren noted the wary poise of her muscles. Ramok eyed Spade thoughtfully. "Say what you mean, Spade."

Spade stood his ground. "That *kai-al* you brought with us will betray us."

Ramok regarded him for a moment. "You are tired, Spade. In the ten years we have worked together you have never been unsettled by a simple *nyeka* before."

"She"—Spade spat the word—"is not a simple *nyeka*. She is a danger."

"How," Ramok returned quietly, "will she betray us?"

Tsia moved up to stand beside Ramok. She did not miss the subtle way Spade shifted to put himself farther from her reach, but his eyes were on her face as he spoke.

"She knows the cry of the cougar like she was born to it," the man accused harshly. "And I myself saw her with a sandcat at Bonnell's Bay. It sat with her and never touched her with its claws." He jerked his thumb over his shoulder. "And a few hours ago Horen came back from his relief with the marks of a cat across his arm. It was the only time Feather and Horen left the camp at the same time."

Tsia's eyes flickered to the blond merc only to find that he was eyeing her sardonically. So. It had been Horen, not Spade, who had spied on the councilwoman, preyed on her like a tam stalking a grouse. She wondered why she had not recognized his scent, then realized that she had read only his energy, not his odor, through her gate. Wren's words echoed in her head: ". . . what he did to those women on Freedom . . . what he did on Chaos . . ." She eyed Horen with her jaw set, and slowly the man grinned. Tsia's neck prickled. She thrust her hands in her pockets, hiding them where they clenched as if they ended in claws.

Ramok gestured coldly at Spade. "Feather is a guide," he said flatly. "It does not matter which animals she sits with or how she deals with Horen. Like Forrest, she will always be more of a help than a hazard."

Stubbornly, his eyes hostile, Spade shook his head. "We are too near the rift. Forrest is experienced; he is under control. She is not. Her affinity for the bioenergies will betray us to the cats, and we will not be able to defend ourselves in any way. Our weapons are useless against biologicals."

"Ramok," Tsia began.

He hushed her. The rest of the group had gathered behind Spade, and Tsia felt the heat of tension warm her blood. Ramok barely glanced at her; his attention was on Spade. "She," he said, indicating Tsia with a jerk of his chin, "could not betray us any more than Forrest could—or that old man there." Ramok pointed at their hostage. Spade shifted his weight from one foot to the other while Wren scratched absently at his ribs.

"Ramok," she tried again.

"Hush," he said aside. To Spade and the rest he said, "As a guide, she can feel the cats like any other life-form. That is what she is trained to do. And that link is what the cats—though they now consciously reject humans as their guides—are engineered to respond to. Her senses will help us stay ahead of the nodies, not push us into the mouths of pumas."

Spade glared back. "Ask her what her link is, Ramok. See what she says."

Forrest watched Tsia's lips tighten. He said nothing, and Ramok nodded at her. *"Nyeka,"* he said softly, "will you tell us?"

She stared at them for a long moment. Finally she choked the words out. "My link," she said harshly, "is the felines."

Spade spit and put his hand on his flexor. Ramok did not seem to move, but suddenly he was between Tsia and the other merc, and Forrest, his hands on Tsia's arms, drew her back against his hard body. She jerked against his grip, but he held her tightly, ready to thrust her behind him, while his eyes never moved from Spade.

"Thirty years ago," Spade said slowly, deliberately, "I saw a *kai-al* like this one. He claimed to be linked to the cats like this Feather of yours. One time he called a tam to us to lead us through a stretch of forest that had become overgrown by stinging cores. Only four tams came instead." He paused. "They tore him apart. Two of us made it out of that forest alive. The other three were killed by the tams. My sister," he said softly, "was one of the ones who died."

Ramok listened impassively. Spade did not take his hand from his hilt, and the merc leader eyed him steadily. "There is an easy way to find out if she is a danger, Spade."

"How?"

Ramok grinned mirthlessly. "We will put her to the test. She will call through her biogate, and the tams or cougars will answer, and we will see if their claws cross our throats. If they do, we will know that they would never have let us cross the narrows in the first place. If they leave us be . . ." He shrugged. "We will know we have a ward stronger than a set of neutral suits and one that cannot be traced by the node."

To the side, the old man chuckled. "You got a guide in second stage," he said, "and you want her to call her gate. You got less brains among the eight of you than a pinhead in its larval phase."

Horen cuffed the man on the back of his head, and the old guide fell silent, though he did not hide the flash of his eyes. Tsia's jaw was tight and angry. "Ramok," she said sharply.

He glanced back. "Hush," he returned softly.

Speculatively, Nitpicker eyed them both. She dug her foot in the soil, turning it over absently. "You are going to risk the whole mission on an *avya* you found in the sand?"

Wren stirred. "A man—or woman's—bedmate," he said softly, "is his own business."

Spade barely glanced at the smaller merc. "Not if she gets the rest of us killed."

Yemene glared at him. "She kept a cougar from attacking me—" she started.

"She is calling the cats here unconsciously even now," Spade accused.

The old man cut in again. "The *kai-al* is untrained. You can see it in every move of her body—"

"She knows what she is doing," snapped Yemene.

A sandcat yowled distantly on the heights above them, and Horen whirled, his hand pressed to his temple. His ghost lines were ready; he could have them spread in the node as fast as he linked. No one else moved. Then Spade stepped forward aggressively. "Your Feather," he said viciously, "will have us torn apart—"

"Enough!" Ramok's hand shot out and stopped Spade in midstride. A skimmer passed by overhead, and the group froze in a tableau of unuttered oaths. Ramok glared at the mercs. "We are overreacting." The softness of his voice belied his anger. "Yes, there are cougars and tams on the ridge. But think about this: They are getting water from somewhere. If Feather's gate is linked to the cats, she can find out where the water is and bring it back to us."

Spade did not back off. "We would be better off risking the use of the watergens than we would be trusting her."

Wren gave him a disgusted look. "A single surge in a watergen would bring the nodies down on us like lightning."

Ramok nodded shortly. "I have staked my life on this *nyeka* twice and was not wrong either time. She stays here, and as long as she is here, she will remain safe." His eyes glared at Spade. "If you have a problem with that, find some other place to sleep."

The sandcat growled behind him, closer than it had been before, but Ramok ignored it, his black-hued eyes boring into Spade's angry gaze.

Forrest dropped Tsia's arms, and, trembling, she rubbed her flesh where his fingers had left bruises. He stepped back, went to his bedroll, and spread it out in the soil near Tsia's bed. Wren was next, moving quietly to his horse and unlashing his gear. One by one the other mercs followed suit until only Spade and Ramok and Tsia were left. With an oath, the brown-haired merc spun on the balls of his feet and stalked to his horse. Ramok watched him go, then turned and pushed Tsia toward her bedding.

She sank slowly to her e-roll, then drew her knees up to her chin. Her eyes glittered with suppressed anger and fear. "Spade would have killed me," she said bitterly.

Ramok said nothing.

She looked beyond him to the rocks, where she could feel the tams gathering. In the thin air she could almost see the yellow-white creatures watching and waiting, settled on their haunches as they eyed the isolated camp. "My gate is getting stronger," she whispered.

"I know."

"I—I am drawn to them."

"*Esha*, Tsia. I know."

"I have been too long from Ciordan," she said more to herself than to the merc. "This rift," she shuddered, "will suck me in."

Ramok touched her shoulders, then massaged the tightness he found in her muscles. She trembled in his hands. "*Esha, avya,*" he murmured. "You are safe."

Something in his soothing voice struck a chill in her, and she twisted to look up at his face. He kissed her forehead, then gently pushed her head back around. She fell asleep with his strong hands on her shoulders, petting and soothing her as if she were one of the cats herself.

25

⤶⤷⤶

Tsia opened her eyes to silence. None of the mercs were snoring, and the cats that surrounded the camp were quiet. There was something in the air . . .

She lay still for a moment, looking up at the web of branches and tasting nothing but sweat, horses, and dust in the dry, dry chill. To her right Spade's bay was nervous, and its long stockinged legs pawed at the ground, while Wren's speckled gray snorted softly. The dust from the shuffling hooves dug its way into her nostrils so that even the heat of her e-roll was clogged with the scent of the land.

In the dark the motionless cold clung to her face like a shroud. A cloud of nightgnats hung over Horen's unprotected neck, and the sound of their faint buzzing was like a saw in Tsia's ears. She shifted her weight to turn over. In the instant before she moved, a tawny shadow flickered at the edge of her sight. Tsia froze. Then, in a single, fluid movement, she rolled from her bedding and crouched between the feline—a tam, she realized—and Wren's still form. The feline froze, its forehead knob bristling. Glaring at her, its amber eyes glowed in the faded light of the moon. From its mouth came a low, subsonic growl.

Tsia did not take her eyes from the cat. Between its ears the hair on the cat's rounded, bony tuft stood on end. Its amber gaze was unblinking. Tsia edged forward, and she heard Wren's almost silent hiss as his breath let out. He had not been asleep; he had been waiting, watching the tam as it had stalked him. His flexor was inactive, lying beside his bedroll, but his massive fists were loosely clenched on his flat knife, and his breathing was slow and steady. As Tsia crossed in front of him, Wren did not relax. Instead, his cold eyes watched her as warily as she watched the pale form of the tam.

Tsia shifted in an infinitesimally slow circle as the tam slunk

285

around her on the perimeter of the sleepers. Her eyes were slits. She could feel the life of the tam in the pulse of her heart. Around the camp, on the rocks above the mercs, others crouched and watched. Three, then four of the cats hid in the shadows. Their eyes, blinking, caught glints of light. Slowly the tam picked its way along the sandy ground. Tsia stepped lightly forward. A skimmer flowed by overhead. The pale cat crouched lower, and its tail flicked. Then it was gone. Tsia blinked. The tracks of the tam were still and silent in the dust, and its presence faded in her mind, but the smell of it still clogged her nose, and the yowling in the distance kept a shiver crawling up and down her spine. Around the camp, the other tams shifted away. It was not until Forrest's hand touched her arm that she started.

"*Esha*, Tsia," he said softly. The gravel of his voice blended into the shivering cry of the tams to the east. She looked at him, her unfocused eyes confused, and he pointed at her bedding.

They will not return tonight. He could have spoken the words, they rang in her ears so loudly. Tsia's body ran cold, then hot. Forrest gave her a brooding look she could not read, then led her back to her bed. Ramok, awake but watching silently, nodded at the other merc. She hesitated at the e-roll and glanced back at Wren. He said nothing. Instead, he simply turned over and went back to sleep.

Dawn was an endless series of wind gusts that blew down from the ridges above. Each one forced the mercs to close their eyes against the whipping dust; each time they opened their eyes again, they saw the sky as a lighter gray. They had mounted an hour after the tam had entered the camp. No one except Wren and Forrest had slept past that point anyway, and Ramok decided that the two could nod off as well in the saddle as out of it. He had had to help Tsia with her saddle; the trembling in her hands had grown so that she could barely cinch the gear. She mislaid the bit twice before she settled the tiny contacts correctly against the roan's soft mouth.

Forrest, watching silently, said nothing, but he followed Ramok as he rode ahead on the trail, leaving the rest of the mercs to wait for his signal.

When he spoke, Ramok's voice was harsh. "If I call the guild to get her, the nodies would see the trace in a second. Yemene would be killed within minutes of the call, and the art guild would find Tsia before the guide guild even registered her scan." He stared at the predawn gloom that hung over the trail. "I cannot leave her here. Like us, she cannot stay with the roan forever; someone will eventually see her, and then her echo will be blown. Even if she rode as far away as possible, the distance would be no more than minutes in a skimmer. She would have to use a watergen sooner or later, and the second she does, the nodies will pinpoint her image down to the way she ruffles her hair. And," he added bitterly, "she cannot survive the ride back down to the bay without water."

Forrest, the harsh planes of his face shadowed darkly, was silent for a moment. He looked out over the desert. Patches of darker soil made black pools between the dry hills, and his eyes searched each one, seeking movement, seeking the glint that would betray a skimmer from Noirelle. He glanced back at Ramok. "She has become important to you."

The other man nodded slowly. "Twice she kept me from hissing on the sand. I owe her *derori ka'eo*—the freedom victory." He used the old words instead of Merishkan, and his voice was hard as he said them. "I owe her release from her chains."

Forrest turned his head to shield it from a wind gust. He breathed in deeply. There was a dusty dryness to a summer dawn that was the same all over Risthmus. The flavor of the air was not crisp but blunted with the thickness of scents that whirled in its wake. His lungs held the air and let it out a little at a time, tasting his exhalation as he did. One could not free a guide from the gate. Did Ramok not understand that once a gate took hold, it never let go? Even when one's link clogged one's mind, it offered a freedom of the senses, of perception, that could never be given up. He had seen guides who had tried not to use their gates. They were fools. Within hours of making such rash promises, they had reached through their links again, tasting the energy of the world as a child grasped at life.

Ramok looked up at the brush-clouded ridge, then out over the valley. The shadow of a skimmer crossed the plains. Blackhawk 3200, he thought absently, noting the shape of its nose in relation to the tiny lines that, in the distance, indicated its side vents. He looked at Forrest. "If I keep her," he said flatly, "I give her another day of life outside of the art guild. If I leave her, I give her no chance at all."

"She will," Forrest said softly, "be dead by the end of the day any way, or by tomorrow morning."

Ramok clenched his hands on the reins. "Then," he said harshly, "she will die with me."

He kicked the black in the flanks, and the horse, startled, jumped onto the trail and cantered around the corner. Forrest waited till the other mercs caught up, then dropped behind Tsia as he had the evening before.

Dawn came in softly with the wind. The sky was hazy with dust, and the heat of morning grew quickly. The mercs were used to high altitude, but Tsia and Yemene were not; both women breathed more deeply than they had the day before. The last of their water had been doled out that morning: some to the Pulanese leader, some to the horses. Now there was only dust.

The old man was quiet on the ride. First Wren, then Nitpicker took him behind on their saddles. He seemed to feel no discomfort, and Tsia glanced back at him often. He watched her with the same unreadable gaze of the other mercs, his blue eyes observing her from behind when she refused to turn.

Two hours past dawn it was difficult for Tsia to focus her thoughts; the thirst that dried her mouth and the cat feet that skittered through her skull gave her shivers that would not abate. Twice her trembling turned into violent shakes. The second time Forrest spurred quickly forward and took the reins from her clenched hands. She found herself in his saddle, held in place by his arms. When the tremors subsided, he lifted her without comment back across to her saddle. She stared at him, but he still said nothing. His amber eyes looked like the eyes of a tam.

At noon the heat boiled her sluggish thoughts and baked her brains to apathy. Not even the two skimmers that floated along the range made her lift her head. By midafternoon the horses were dragging. Their body temperatures soared as their engineered metabolisms tried to keep the heat difference between the air and their bodies to a minimum. Tsia could no longer stand to touch the roan. When she was cold, his neck felt as if it burned beneath her fingers. When the heat hit her, his hair seemed icy and chilled.

The sun grew bigger, its white shape bloating while it ate its way down to the jagged horizon before getting stuck on the cliffs. Tsia could taste the clouds to the west, but she could not see them. They seemed to taunt her with their promise of rain.

Another hour of lunging and scrambling over rock falls. Another hour of dodging unexpected holes. Four times they passed mounds of dust and torn dirt where cougars had scraped the dirt together to stake their territory with the scent of their urine. Once they rode by an old kill scene where cubs had worked at the carcass of a deer, trampling and tearing the thicket around the corpse and strewing small piles of bones across the entire canyon.

They rode through a long, low brush-clogged pass to climb steeply toward a narrow ravine. Halfway up, rounded tracks were driven into the dried mud, showing where a cougar had leapt from one side of the rocks to the other. The paw marks were as large as Tsia's hand.

The afternoon passed with the same dry heat as before; then the dry and dusty evening dragged on. Yemene's face was flushed over an ashen complexion; Wren's tight-boned face was burned. Spade was pale as usual, his skin chapped and peeling as his sweat sucked his flesh dry even under his shade. Nitpicker spit seeds along the trail, sharing them with the other mercs when one dropped back for a handful. Even Ramok found his thirst distracting. As his mouth grew dry and his eyeballs hard and his body dehydrated further, it took more and more effort to keep his eye on the line; to watch Spade, who rode with his broad, rangy shoulders hunched; to tell Horen, who dragged farther and farther back, to ride closer to the rest of the line. All their lips were chapped and pale, as if there were not enough moisture left in their veins to keep their lips red.

Of them all, only Forrest and the old man seemed unaffected by their thirst. Behind Wren, on the dappled gray, the old man merely examined the mercs as he took his ride, smiling grimly to himself at the signs of their discomfort. Forrest, with his clear, amber eyes and his broad shoulders, sat his huge buckskin horse with the same silent grace he had before. He kept pace with Tsia, eyed the sky when the skimmers snaked by in the distance, and kept his thoughts to himself.

By dusk the body of the narrows was in sight. Above them by several kilometers, it beckoned with its promise of Pulan while the last light of the sun, long since gone from the trail and hidden behind the heavy bank of clouds that hung on the other side of the pass, burned faintly on the top of Catmount Ridge. The horses plodded steadily on, and Ramok's face was grim.

When the fourth skimmer floated up toward the pass and disappeared behind the ridge, Ramok pulled them to a halt. The warmth of the air was fading, and the nightgnats had already formed disgusting clouds around their heads. With every breath, the gnats flew into their eyes and mouths. Tsia's mouth was so parched, she could no longer murmur to the roan to soothe him. The gelding stamped his feet slowly, and Tsia eyed their camp with burning eyes.

As she dismounted, the others followed suit with lackluster motions. Yemene could not get down from her horse; it took both Ramok and Spade to catch her awkward weight as she slid from the saddle.

"Stake the horses together," Ramok ordered hoarsely. "We cannot afford to lose any to the tams."

Horen dragged the touch-tied old man from behind Wren so that the wiry merc could dismount more easily. On the other side of the horses Spade joined Nitpicker to watch the skies for signs of the last skimmer that had gone down in the narrows. They chewed only slimchims for dinner, and the moist cakes made their thirst painfully obvious.

Trembling and nauseous, Tsia merely sank onto her bedroll. She did not even bother to pull up the cover as she curled into a ball. It was Ramok who did that, regarding her silently with a bitter, determined look. When he lay down, it was where he could keep one hand on her back as she slept.

Soft sounds crept into Tsia's ears, dragging her out of her sleep. Uneasily, she opened her eyes. Someone was watching her. Someone close . . . Ramok had rolled on his side to sleep, and she sat up slowly, her eyes seeking the shadows. There were cats there—she could smell them. The thick, musky scent of the tams, the sharper scent of the cougar. They were on opposite sides of the camp, waiting now as they had waited the night before. Tsia glanced toward Horen, who was on guard. He met her blue gaze and smiled slowly. She felt the cat feet in her head become still. The merc beckoned, and she shook her head. He grinned and glanced toward the rocks. A tam appeared, but Horen did not notice even when the horses snorted and nervously stamped their feet.

Abruptly, Tsia stood, and Ramok woke at her movement. Immediately, his eyes went to her, then flicked to the outskirt of the bedding area. He took in the tam, then glanced at Horen with a narrowed gaze. "Nitpicker," he said softly. As if she had been waiting for his signal, the woman opened her eyes and rolled from her bedding in a single movement. She gathered her weapons from the saddle against which they leaned and, without a word, took Horen's place on watch. The blond merc shrugged at her and, with a lingering look at Tsia, lay down and closed his eyes.

Ramok reached out and touched Tsia's leg, and she jumped as if shot. *"Seva?"* he asked quietly.

Were they safe? She hesitated. "I don't know." She moved toward the rock where the tam still crouched. Behind her, Ramok and Nitpicker watched silently. When she was within two meters, the tam seemed to slide backward without moving its legs, then disappear. Tsia looked at the rocks to the sides. There was room there, just room enough for the cat to slink through to another vantage. She could smell its scent in the air. Through her gate, the cat feet padded and pressed across her thoughts, confusing her sense of their animal force. She stretched into the gate. Tams ran in packs, like prides. Where there was one tam, there could be half a dozen.

Minutes passed. Tsia stayed on her feet, crouching, then stalking through the camp. She growled at the shadows, her voice echoing her mind and forcing the cats to give way. They shifted like the wind, coming first from one side, then another between the rocks. Nitpicker, her eyes on both Tsia and the rocks, moved from one watch point, staying out of the *kai-al*'s way as Tsia paced from one side to the other. An hour later her watch gave way to Wren's.

The tams crept closer. Their scent was thick in the air on all sides of the camp, and Tsia could not keep from shuddering at the smell. They seemed to surge forward when she turned away; when she spun around, they sucked back into the shadows. Her throat rasped when she growled. All around her the smell of the tams was like a low fog, punctuated by the stamping of the horses. All through her head the sense of them was like a wave surging against the boundaries of her skull, smashing at her reason. She did not think; she felt. She did not block them; she threw herself into her gate. Their movements were a reflection of the images in her mind. Her own muscles tensed and copied their shapes.

She whirled suddenly, countering a move by another tam. Her hissing broke raggedly as the rasp of her throat caught and choked her. It was becoming harder to drag her mind out of the feral gutter. The predawn grew gray, and Tsia rubbed her dry tongue against her teeth. Her feet tripped her with exhaustion, and her eyes burned as she forced them to stay open. Dry eyes. Dry and red as her sun-seared skin. Light was painful, yet each blink was torture with its sweet second of rest from the dust and the dry, dry air.

The horses snorted constantly. Forrest and Wren slept; Horen tossed fitfully. Ramok and Spade were dozing in a half-awake state that let them listen to the cats and decide the level of danger before they rose. Of them all, the one person who should have slept deeply—Yemene—was the most wide awake. Her ashen face paled regularly, and when Tsia looked at her, the woman's hands clenched her bedroll, but she made no sound. And all the while the cats paced and growled outside of Tsia's reach.

The cats came in a wave now, shifting closer like the wind ripples in a field of grass, and Tsia snapped more quickly at the eyes that gazed hungrily toward the figures behind her. As the gray light struggled over the rocks, one tam stretched its foot off a rock, and Tsia pounced. There was a yowl; the sudden din of snarls brought everyone out of his bed and to his feet.

Tsia screamed at them, her voice hoarse and harsh. The cry of the cougar that leapt from her throat halted the yellow-white tams in midstride. The surge of creatures sank back, and Tsia poised, one hand raised slightly above the other, her fingers flexed and clawlike, her lips curled back and her nose wrinkled with a feral fury. For an instant the tableau held. A pair of green eyes glinted in the shadows, then slunk away. A seryal crawled from its hiding place in the rocks and scuttled across Spade's bedding. Cautiously, his eyes on the cats, Spade reached out with his boot to shove the spider off his e-roll. The air erupted.

"Get down!" Tsia snarled. She had felt the motion through her gate even before the cats had tensed. Spade flung himself back with a gasp. The cougar leapt. Ramok lunged forward and grabbed Spade, wrenching his body down as the cougar's paws ripped by. Then, hurtling like an arrow through the gloom, Tsia's wiry figure slammed into the cat's flank and turned in midjump. They landed against the rocks, and the screech of the cougar was deafening in the surrounding roars.

Ramok shouted, "Get back!"

The cougar screamed and wrenched away. Tsia shoved its forelegs apart before they could grip and tear at her back. Dust clogged her mouth. She felt herself airborne, and then her back slammed against a rock, her head snapping back. The hot breath of the cat blasted her face, and she twisted, thrusting up, inside the cougar's reach. Its back claws were long and sharp and were kicking down even now . . . She jammed her feet against its thighs. A hot stench burst in her face. Was it she or the cat that screamed this time? There was fur in her mouth. Or was it in her gate? She did not know. She slammed across a flat boulder, and her ribs—the pain that shot through her senses sharpened her thoughts momentarily. A massive paw caught in her blunter and flung her across the dust, tearing the jacket across the back. She screamed, the sound of the cougar breaking from her dry throat, and at that instant the gray light of the sun flooded across the rocks. The cougar leapt away. Tsia flung herself after it. And it seemed that, from under the mercenaries' feet, a dozen tams lunged after the *nyeka*.

And then there were only hanging clouds of dust where the earth trailed in the air after the feet of the leaping cats.

"Wren, Horen—control the horses," Ramok shouted. "Nitpicker, get that old man!" The mercs scrambled. Yemene, clutching her belly awkwardly, shrank back against the cliff. Ramok stared into the thick night. "Forrest," he said urgently, "where is she? Can you see her? Can you feel her?"

Forrest scanned the gray pockets of rock with unerring amber eyes. "Nothing." His voice was low and graveled with his own thirst. "Nothing. She has gone into the rift."

Ramok gripped his arm. "I cannot go after her."

"I know." Forrest plucked the flat knife from Ramok's harness and tucked it in his own. He stared deep into Ramok's black eyes, feeling the strength of the life that pulsed in the man. When he spoke, he used the old words that bound a man in honor. "*Ke avya paka'ka chi*—she gave you your tomorrow, your life." He leaned down to one of the piles of gear and caught up three water bags, the one good and the two that were torn. "Even as a ghost in the hands of the artists," he said softly, "she has been true to the guides."

Ramok's voice was harsh. "She is alone."

"She has a gate to the cats. She cannot be alone with them—even if they kill her." Forrest stuffed the botas into his harness. He looked at the other merc. "But your Feather deserves more than that." He tossed his shading headgear at Spade, then launched himself at the rocks over which Tsia had sprung. For an instant he hung against the gray-lit sky, then he was gone.

Behind him the old man stepped toward the rocks until Ramok's arm across his chest stopped him. The prisoner glanced at Ramok, then stepped back. His expression was thoughtful, nothing more.

Ramok's face was set as he turned to Nitpicker. "Access your link. Close the echoes for Forrest and Tsia," he ordered curtly. "Horen, lay in a ghost line to Gea links. They are the only ones allowed in the rift, so tapping into their dots is the only shot we have at keeping Forrest and Feather masked. The art nodies will see their traces—they cannot help but spot them with the number of skimmers they have scanning this ridge—but they should accept the Gea dots for a few hours. Make it tight," he added tersely. "By the time they figure out that the webs are false, we must be through the narrows. If they catch us up on the ridge, we will have little chance of getting through to Pulan."

Throwing his saddle on his bay, Spade looked over at Ramok. "What about Forrest?" he asked, pulling the cinch through and tightening it with a short movement. "He is not linked with the cats. They would kill him as soon as they would put claw to an elk."

"He is a guide, and Feather will protect him," Ramok snapped, the tension in his voice belying his belief in his own assertion. He ran toward his own horse. "Mount up," he commanded. "Mount up. We ride!"

26

A hundred meters away Forrest paused only to take a breath before jumping and catching hold of the rocks above him. Before him, fresh tracks were thick on the ground. If Tsia was still ahead of the cats, she could be no more than a quarter kilometer ahead, running through the forest that reeked of moisture in its hidden roots. He closed his mind to the thought of water on his tongue and, his amber eyes expressionless, hauled himself up onto another broken column, where his fingers slipped on the slickness of cat hair caught in a crack. The sweet scent of Tsia's sweat came to his nose. He breathed deeply, searching for another sign of her passage. The air was dusty and dry, and only the faint scent of the cats lay behind.

Forrest increased his stride. Being linked did not mean that the cats would accept her. Since the Landing Pact, more than half the guides who linked to the cats had been killed by the animals of their own gate. He reached through his gate to feel the life in the valley. It was hot and pulsing with power. Faintly, to his right, the hair-raising scream of a cougar rose above the canopy. It was smothered instantly by the screams of two other, younger beasts. With his jaw set, he tried to judge the distance he felt between them—if there was still time to catch Tsia and get her out before the cougars turned against her. Then he plunged through the growth toward the noise.

Ahead of him, Tsia ran exultantly beside a cougar. She clung to its deep fur and scrambled up where it leapt; she snarled back at its irritated growls when she pulled its hide like a cub. It cuffed her, claws in, across the face, but she grabbed an out-hung root and swung up beside it. For an instant her knees weakened and threatened to drop her in the dust. Then sight flooded back as she caught her feet on the rocks again and, with a snarl of incoherent animal joy, raced on.

Two tams passed her, their fangs like white knives. A young cougar paused and glared to the side, and she pounced past it up onto the last outcropping before the top of the ridge. She reached up—and slammed against the ground as the second young cougar jumped up and nailed her. Her temper flared. She yowled through her gate and bit the creature's ear in a lunge. The young female twisted. And then they were running again. Behind her, in the dust, two drops of blood congealed.

The green cliffs hid a narrow path; the cats took it at a run. Tsia slid once, misjudging the distance from one rock to the next, but the patch of moss that tore from under her feet dropped her over the edge and down five meters, back into the head of the line behind the first two tams that had leapt down into the valley. She scrambled up, slapping at the young cougar behind her that sought to pass. The others did not pause. Within seconds they disappeared into the dark-shadowed depths of the valley floor.

As they entered the forest, the tams dropped out of the pack and loped north on a trail through the ferns. Tsia called out to them through her gate, but they were hungry, and there were deer in the lower meadows. The sense of them faded until they joined the din that clogged her head.

She ran through clouds of gnats that hung between the trees. One flew into her eye and blinded her for a moment, and she stretched through her gate to see. A sudden sense of being lower to the trail hit her hard. She blinked and ducked, running in a crouch with one arm up; the low, sharp branches of the thickets seemed to seek her out in the gloom and strike at her like snakes.

The bittersweet scent of a shadow-line peach caught in her nose just before she ran into the low, thick tree, and she grabbed a yellow fruit on the run. Some distant part of her mind noted its color; water ran beneath the tree or it would not have fruited out. With a wild laugh, she stuffed part of the peach in her mouth, licking the juice from her lips and smearing her sticky hand on her jumpsuit. She did not slack her stride as she ripped out the pit of the unbitten half and then stuffed the rest of the fruit in her mouth. The sugar of its juices soaked instantly into her tongue.

Two of the cougars sailed over a deadfall. Tsia leapt after them, landing in the edges of the dark mass and tangling for an instant till she thrashed her way out. The third cougar passed her with a taunting swat on her shoulder, tumbling her down in the dust. She came up with a hiss. Heart pounding, she raced after the three, catching up as they ducked through a copse of pinnut trees whose bark was shredded with claw marks. A moment later they burst out into a sudden sea of grass.

Tsia loped beside the cougars while the waving, golden grass heads slapped her legs and made her laugh out loud at their sensation. Thickets of dense brush surrounded jutting rocks and dotted the meadow, and black dots of barberries formed clumps of color like unexpected holes in the ground. To her left, the forest closed in on the meadow and rose into great dark trunks and the dim shadows of musty ferns. The right side of the valley narrowed sharply into a stark canyon that beckoned toward the top of the rift. The meadow itself was not lit; the sun had not yet cleared the cliff top, and its half-light made the ridge across the long clearing look as if it were burning, while the rock walls were still dark with the gloom of dawn. A stream edged the west side of the meadow. Beyond it, through another hundred kilometers of forest, the carved stone cliffs on the other side of the Cheba Rift rose up. As if they mocked the dawn, dark clouds hovered at the edge of those cliffs. The wind that blew across Tsia's face was cold with the storm she had sensed before.

Tsia changed direction toward the gray, shimmering surface of the stream. The three cougars that paced her shifted at her sides. Their shoulders rolled with their lope; their long whiskers brushed through the grass. The yearlings came too close to Tsia's flashing legs, and the mother cougar snarled; Tsia threw up her arms and screamed in imitation of their cry. She reveled in her senses. Her lungs seemed to breathe not just in her own chest but in the chests of the cougars that paced her to the side. She cried out again, and the low growls of the cougars were like a harmony to her ears. She saw them more in her mind than with her eyes. She felt their feet pounding in her brain more than she heard the pad of their paws on the dirt.

Useless!? Her gate was everything she had dreamed. Every sense in her body was sharp. Every thought was crystal clear with the intent she felt in the cats. They called her, pulled her, forced her to run. She could feel them and, through them, feel the force of their instincts honing her own. She leapt high, threw out her arms, and screamed her defiance of the guild, the guides—even the Landing Pact itself. In her head the maw of her gate seemed to open and swallow her up with a snarl.

Had she expected some sort of human intelligence? There was a sharpness to the energy of the cats, a sense that they could read her thoughts and feelings, but they had not been engineered to be humans in feline skins; they were still predators, wild and territorial. Even if they read her, they projected not coherent thoughts but a sensual power and focus, a curiosity about her intent, and a hedonistic exultation in the recognition of their own scent in the soil.

Breathless, she reached the stream and plunged in, heedless of her clothes and ignoring the green-gray shadows that darted away in the depths. The cold gray water shocked her. With a gasp, she threw herself beneath its surface. Her mouth ached with thirst; her skin cried out for cleansing. She rolled underwater, coming up full seconds later to laugh at the eyes of the beast that crouched on the bank and lapped at the water. Diving and surfacing again, she drank deeply, desperately, then pulled herself to the bank and collapsed, half on the soil, half still in the stream.

One of the smaller cougars got up and padded forward, lowering its nose to her face. Its yellow-green eyes were slanted, its face was streamlined yet powerful with clumsy youth, and the black stripe that defined its nose curled down from its eyes with a quizzical look. Its cold nose butted hers for an instant, then its tongue scraped her cheek. The roughness stroked up over her eye. Rising on one elbow, Tsia twisted and stretched. She met the yearling's forehead with her own and slowly rubbed her face against him until his short, smooth hair was soaked in her scent. A rumble rose in his throat.

The older cougar slowly bared its teeth. Reluctantly, the younger cat drew back and padded obediently to the side, where it dropped to the ground. Reaching out, the large cougar batted Tsia's torn blunter experimentally. The cat's paw was larger than Tsia's face, and as the paw swung again, Tsia jerked back, her teeth in a feral grin. She snarled silently through her gate. Slowly, the cat settled down in the grass. Tsia pulled herself up beside the feline and stretched, rolling her neck and arching her back. The cougar batted at her again, and this time Tsia's arm slid past the blow and slapped the cat back on its shoulder.

The cougar snarled softly. Instinctively, the skin on the back of Tsia's neck prickled, as if she had fur that could rise. Her scarred cheek twitched. Her mind hesitated, caught in the grip of the gate, and she growled. Unblinking yellow eyes stared back and challenged her right to the grass.

Uneasily, Tsia's ice-blue gaze flicked from one cat to the other. The yearlings crouched with eagerness in every line of their bodies. Was she a toy to teach these cubs to hunt? The larger cougar snarled again, and the rising and falling of its tones made Tsia clap her fists against her temples. The hostility of the cat was a palpable thing; its territoriality was clear. If she stayed in the rift, she must move on—find her own places to hunt, her own thickets to sleep in and mark, her own cliffs on which to climb and stretch herself in the sun. If she stayed here, in this meadow, she would fight. Or she would be hunted and killed.

Tsia stared at the glowing yellow eyes. If she stayed? Were these cougars stepping outside their own Landing Pact to allow her to live in the rift? So that she could feel the animal power forever? So that she could run with these cats as the First Droppers had two hundred years earlier?

The older cat seemed to sense her questions and, with a snarl, launched itself forward in an aborted lunge. Hissing, she dropped to a crouch two meters away in the grass.

Tsia half stretched out her hand, trying to sense the emotions that governed the creature before her. In an instant she was swamped with the desire to run, the urge to fight. The younger cougars sat back and watched, the tips of their tails twitching in the grass.

There was a breathless hesitation in her gate. Tsia's muscles tensed. The older cat sprang. There was a flash of tawny shoulders, and Tsia was tumbled with a savage swipe of the massive cougar's paw. She rolled to her feet and leapt back, but the older cat dodged away. In a fluid motion, she stripped off the torn blunter and threw it to the side. The silent game changed. The tumbling became more fierce. Abruptly, Tsia swatted the larger cougar and threw herself aside as it twisted in midair. The cat landed in front of her and flung her roughly into the grass. This time Tsia came up more slowly, favoring one side.

On the edge of the meadow Forrest stood up. Neither cougars nor Tsia noticed him. He moved out from the trees, then ran toward the three figures.

Tsia was flung again to the ground, and this time she did not rise from her knees. She hung there, one hand clenched to her ribs, one leg sprawled to the side as the older cougar paced around her in a tight circle. Her mind was clogged with the scent of this cat; her ears were deaf with its snarls.

One of the younger cougars noticed the man running across the meadow. The yearling yowled. The older cat froze. Tsia's eyes never left the older beast. All three cats flattened their tawny forms in the grass. Tsia's wild, glinting eyes shifted from the cougars and stared at Forrest as if he were a ghost. She could smell him through her link; she could sense his strong male energy as if it flooded her gate with the sense of the cats. She threw back her head and yowled. The older cougar moved at the same time Forrest did. Deliberately, Forrest drew the two flat knives from his harness. He stared at the cougar, his amber eyes boring into golden yellow. The cat flexed its claws and hissed. Its neck seemed to lengthen, and its muscles rippled as it shifted its weight along its legs. Tsia felt her lips curl back from his teeth. The cougar seemed to give Forrest a scornful look. Then it melted into the grass.

The younger cats slunk away, and the wind in the meadow hid their passage. Tsia still crouched with the feral gleam in her eyes. Her cheeks were pale beneath their sunburn, and her white teeth were slightly parted. Slowly, Forrest squatted down and watched her in silence.

The edge of the sun flared over the crest of the cliff, and light began to wash the treetops. Neither Forrest nor Tsia moved. A herd of slender, double-horned johnnies bounded into the grass on the far side of the meadow, where they grazed with a careful eye toward the stream. Three purple hares edged out from their burrows. Forrest picked a green stem from the clump of grass by his knees and began to chew on it. He ached for the water in the stream, but he did not move from Tsia's view. Long minutes passed for both of them. Tsia's eyes began to lose their wildness. The din of her gate seemed to lessen. Cat feet slunk back and stopped their scratching at her skull. With a ragged breath, she drew her legs under her and eyed the merc with a wary but human gaze.

Forrest watched her closely. He shifted, saw her tense in reaction, and said softly, "*Eshe*, Tsia." She hesitated. Carefully, he unclipped the bota bags from his harness and, his eye still watching her responses, moved cautiously through the grass to the stream. There he cupped the water in his hands and drank, first sparingly, then deeply. His parched tongue and cheeks seemed to suck the moisture from his mouth before he could swallow, and his stomach twisted at the chill of the water. He let the moisture run through his hands, then stepped down into the stream and dunked himself as Tsia had done before.

Tsia, still crouched, watched the muscles that rippled across his shoulders beneath the shirt that clung to his back. A shudder shook her slender frame. She rubbed at her temple, trying to stem the flood of sensation that swept through her gate. The exultation that hit her first—that she had finally touched the cats, dug her fingers into fur, and tasted the scent of their breath—filled her with a wild joy that her gate was not cold and dead as she had been led to believe. It sucked at her and called her and gave her senses such depth that she could not let it go.

The realization brought a chill to her skin. The dread she had felt, the unease that had plagued her for a month ... It was not that the gate was strong, it was that she feared now to lose it, even in its hedonistic torture of her senses. And now her dread was worse. She had not just reached through her gate; she had spoken with the cats, negotiated a space in their territory. If she returned home, returned to the guild, they would have no choice but to strip her of this gate and annihilate her senses. Blind her to everything she had yearned for and finally knew as part of her very soul.

Forrest's shoulders rippled as he splashed water over his head again, and Tsia regarded him for a long moment. A grim realization solidified beneath her dread. If she stayed with the mercs, she would die. It had to be true. The way Forrest had looked at her ... The way Ramok had touched her when she shivered ... They knew.

So, she thought, her gate would after all give her everything. Even death.

Forrest's muscled back was still turned to her as he dunked himself again, and Tsia brushed absently at the grass that clung to her jumpsuit. Then she stripped the weapon harness from her body and dropped it on her blunter. If her gate would give her everything, then she would give it the same. She would live through it completely before she died. The challenge, the senses, the animal energy that swept through her mind ... That was not enough for a—a one-year guide. She smiled to herself at the term and kicked off her boots. Her body writhed with the stretch of the cougar that watched from the woods. Hungrily, she stared at the rippling scars on Forrest's back. Then she stripped off her jumpsuit and threw it aside.

When she slid into the water beside him, Forrest became still. Like a snake, his eyes followed her movements, noting the finger bruises on her legs, the skin grafts on one arm and thigh. Her slender body did not have the soft roundness of youth but the lean shapeliness of a woman who had yet to bear children. Her ribs had begun to shift from purple to a yellow-green, and the scar on her cheek was pale against her tanned skin. Her hair, short, shining, and already dry from her earlier dunking, lifted slightly in the breeze. Around her eyes the tiny lines were white where she had squinted into the sun. And her eyes were blue—ice-blue—against the clarity of the stream.

She stooped into the water and let it run across her body. She looked at him deliberately. "You feel this," she said quietly. "You feel me."

Forrest nodded slowly. When he looked at her, the burning energy of her presence was in his gate like a star crammed in a doorway. It was bright—too bright—for a guide. There was too much power there for a human to hold.

She held out her hand, and her fingers were curled like a claw. She flexed the fist, her eyes drawn to it as if fascinated with the motion. Water rippled at her waist, hiding the bruises on her legs. When she looked up at him again, there was a challenge in her gaze that sharpened her eyes till they seemed to blaze out in her face. "Make love with me," she said softly.

A sudden tightening in his groin startled him. He took half a step forward, rising into the shallows, then hesitated. But Ramok had called her his *avya*—the one he felt strongly for—not his *ava*, his intimate one. And Ramok had said he felt gratitude and loyalty—protectiveness—not love.

The hunger grew in his loins, and Forrest looked deeply into Tsia's eyes. He could feel the desperation, the fear, the determination in her heart, and the exultation of her gate. A hedonistic power flowed from her link into his.

They stepped together at the same time. Their bodies were slick with water. His weapon harness scraped across her skin, and he wrenched it off with a twist, throwing it up on the bank. They did not kiss. Instead, they stared at each other, amber eyes boring into blue, while his hands ran along her taut shoulders, down her slender arms to her hands. She twined her fingers around his, then raised them to his chest and pressed them inside his collar, against his muscles. This time, when he released her grip, he ran his hot touch down from her neck, across her breasts, and onto her smooth, flat stomach. His hands were large and roughly calloused, and they stroked her with a gentleness that made her burn. She made an odd sound. Her fingers trailed down his thighs into the water. Intimately, they teased back up. Amber eyes grew hard. With a sudden movement, he cupped her body in his hands and raised her onto the grassy bank. When she bit him, he shuddered. She bit him again, then softened her mouth, licking dust and salt from his skin. Forrest raised his head and met her gaze for a long, burning moment. Then they coupled like animals, their movements crushing the grass in a frenzy of snarling thrusts.

27

Tsia lay on her side, her head pillowed on Forrest's forearm and her body cushioned by the mat of grass. Soberly, she watched the slow rise and fall of the massive merc's chest. One finger traced the ridges of scars that stretched along the side of his ribs, up under his arms, and across his back. They were strange, precisely edged marks, smooth and clean, each exactly a half inch deep. They cut into his muscles as if they had been plowed in. Only a variable sword could make wounds that perfectly defined, she thought. He must have been very still when they were made; there was not a nick or bobble in the perfect cutting curves. She let her finger trail down the scars into the crushed grass between their bodies. Her voice, when she spoke, was quiet.

"I am dying, aren't I?"

Forrest rolled to his side. He gazed into her eyes for a long moment and saw the stubborn acceptance that she poured unconsciously through her gate. The virus that raged in her body might kill her, but she would not give in to its weakness no matter how the tremors sapped her strength. He traced a shivering pattern on her skin. *"Ava."* He said the word in a low voice, almost to himself. *"Kai-al nyeka."*

He let his hand rest lightly on her neck, her heartbeat quick and erratic under his fingertips. Her skin was flushed. There was a fresh bruise on her side from one of the cougar's blows, and along with the finger marks he himself had left on her hips, she would ache inside for some time. She gazed at him with eyes that seemed strangely wise and pained beneath their brightness.

"It is time to go," he said quietly. He rolled to his feet, bringing her lightly to hers. When he handed her the clothing she had dropped on the ground, she dressed in silence. She tugged on her boots, then gathered up her torn blunter and fingered it thought-

302

fully. Her blunter disk was still sealed in the chest pocket; in her other pockets she had lost only one of the sculpting tools she had stolen from the artist's body. She did not see it in the grass; it had probably been trampled under the growth by the cougars.

She glanced at Forrest, and he hitched his harness around his hips. The torn water bags slapped softly against his thighs. The sound was sharp, and her mind seemed clear, for once, and her thoughts more focused. The din of the cats was a soft, constant sound; the cat feet seemed lazy, not irritated, in the way they padded across her thoughts. "We are taking water back?" she asked.

Forrest nodded in answer to her question.

She nodded at the botas. "Have you fixed them yet?"

"No. I will carry them upside down to hold the water in. It will not be much, but it will be enough for Yemene and the old man."

Tsia fingered the thin, tapered disk of the mole. "We could try fixing them first."

Forrest shook his head. "Flexan—" He fingered one of the botas. "—is thermally sound, but it does not repair well."

She hesitated, then drew the mole from her pocket and turned it over in her hands. She felt no more fear of the art guilt. What could they do to her now? Kill her? She almost smiled at the thought. "I have a mole," she offered. "Self-contained power and imaging systems. I unlinked it in Noirelle." She tossed it to the merc. "It is set for an ice-based structure, but I used it on metaplas to escape. It might work on the flexan; the material is similar to metaplas."

The big man eyed her thoughtfully. Portable moles were expensive. Only a few specialized fabrication and service sites used them. And artists, he amended his thoughts. He examined the small disk carefully. "Self-contained power . . . That might still register on the node."

She nodded. "Could our biomasks—the blunter disks that make us seem like biological echoes—could they cover that?"

Still examining the disk, he shook his head. "They were deactivated. Ramok had us listed as Gea the instant we dropped into the rift. Our scansigns are now human."

Tsia raised her eyebrows. "Can he do that without using a link?"

"Horen is a genius with the ghost lines, but Nitpicker can work a trace beam like a master." He handed the mole back. "She would have activated the Gea web on a tight single-pulse signal to one of the mersats—we have our own orbiting net," he explained. "Only a high-res scan aimed directly at her would pick that one pulse out of all the other noise."

Tsia took the disk back and fingered it absently. "If we are listed as Gea, we can use our links?"

He nodded.

"Will our Gea traces justify the use of a mole?"

"Doesn't really matter. Gea use a lot of links, a lot of tools. A Gea who did no scans or traces while he was here would be more suspect than one who activated all the sensors in the net." He fell silent, thinking. "You are a biologist? You still have access to the biocodes for the felines?"

"All biocodes," she answered slowly. She shrugged at the glint of surprise that touched his eyes. "I have two Gea degrees. I have worked half a dozen contracts with them in the past." She glanced at the mole. "You want me to open a scan to a cat—as if I were on Gea contract—and activate the mole as if I were sucking power for the scan?"

He nodded. "Biocodes cannot be transferred link to link, so I cannot activate a scan for you. But while you do that, I can access the materials link and use the mole to meld the botas back together."

She rubbed her temple absently. "You cannot use this mole. I severed its access lines and left only my own link open. You have to go back to the manufacturer to renew access to a piece of equipment like this."

"If you have to do both the scans and the mole, we will have to wait till we are up on the ridge before we activate either one. If our traces are not clean, the nodies will split our signals out of the Gea net within seconds. It would not take long after that for them to wash our signals clean. And I don't know how closely Horen will be watching the lines and structuring new webs to cover our signals." He glanced at the cliffs. "We will have to be close enough to the rim that if the nodies wash out our traces, our echo masks can be reactivated to cover us."

She pointed to the high, jagged edge of the narrows. "Follow the stream up to its headwaters? We can keep to the east and meet Ramok up there."

He nodded. The wild brightness to her eyes belied the clarity of her thoughts, and he touched her face, sliding his hands down to her neck, where he could feel her pulse racing beneath her skin. He turned without comment to the water.

They drank again, then followed the stream south across the meadow. At first Forrest held their pace to a walk, but Tsia, feeling the eyes of the cougars and of a distant pack of tams on their backs, pushed them to a jog. Their voices in her head were a constant growl. She longed to throw herself in the grass and writhe in the scent of the tams. The sense of their urine in the dirt, their bellies touching the ground as they crouched, and their eyes unwavering from their prey so filled her mind that she almost fled across the grass.

At the end of the meadow the shadowed waves of yellow-green growth petered out, and they drank again from the creek. It flowed onto the meadow by way of a short, narrow waterfall that plunged out of the barren rocks. Eyeing the boulders, Forrest and Tsia settled their harnesses and began resolutely to climb.

Tsia's limbs no longer shook. There was a lightness in her legs that let her leap where Forrest hauled himself up. Her eyes, sensitive to the light, no longer ached and burned but longed for the heat to soothe them, and her skin, cold again and sweating, lusted for flames to burn off its gritty oils. Her breath was quick but even, and Forrest did not have to slow his pace to keep her on his heels. Her descent into the dark rift meadow had taken perhaps ten minutes; the climb out would take an hour.

The waterfall ended above in a thin, swift creek that cut back into a higher canyon. There the rocks gave way to soft, dusty summer soil, and the bed of pebbles and stones faded to a thin cover of dried grass and short, brittle flowers. They drank there and then, half a kilometer later, drank again as they followed the thin creek farther back.

Within a kilometer the stream turned abruptly west into a narrow wash tangled with a thicket of pinnut trees and shrubs. Forrest squatted and rested his legs, regarding the sharp bend thoughtfully. In a ragged thrust of reddened stone the narrows rose directly above them. The rotten rock itself was sheer, but the stone walls to the east and west were crumbled and layered like stairs.

They could go east and take a chance that they would find water again with which to fill the botas, or they could follow the stream west instead. If they went west, they would be trying to catch up to Ramok once they reached the ridge. If they continued east, they could be fairly certain of meeting the merc on the other side of the narrows. In the rift, the path from one side of the narrows to the next was steep but short and direct; up on the ridges, it wound around the rock formations in a slow and tortuous trail. What took an hour to cover here would, above, take Ramok three. Going east, they should reach the crest just as Ramok was entering the pass. Forrest eyed the ridge again, noting the heavy clouds that seemed darker than before. When he rose, he turned to the east.

Halfway up, his faith was borne out by a spring that gushed from between two rocks and bounced away toward the rift floor. They could hear the spring as they climbed, but they could not see it, and at first it seemed as if its sound were an echo from another narrow canyon. It was not until they scrambled up onto a tiny wash no wider than four meters that they saw the spring itself flowing and bouncing from between two rocks. The knife-edged walls that rose on either side of the spring precluded animals climbing down to it but not from approaching the way they did. But there were no tracks except those of small rodents in the soil before the spring. For such a thick and bubbly spring, the stream that wended away was thin and shallow. But it was water, and Tsia felt the thirst rise again in her flesh. She moved forward lightly. She stopped. Something about this wash—

She half turned, leapt, and then Forrest's iron arm caught her as the ground crumbled away. She twisted, clinging to him like a cat as he hauled her back onto a visibly thick ledge of rock. They stared at the crack that had split the soil. As they watched, the shelf of rock groaned, then broke off from Tsia's footprints and fell away into a cavern below, leaving only a black maw to gape open with broken, jagged teeth. Inside the hole faint, hollow sounds of water washed and fell in a darkness that had been absolute only a moment before. Forrest eyed the hole, then, tapping the flat with his foot, crouched, then edged down onto his belly in the soil.

"Forrest . . ." Tsia whispered.

He glanced back over his shoulder. "*Ke seva*, Tsia," he said soothingly. "It is safe for me." He wormed his way forward, one hand thumping the soil as if it were a melon to be tested for ripeness. He froze once at a cracking sound, but as nothing fell away, he moved forward again.

When his eyes reached the opening, he could see down into the hole where the stone maw seemed to swallow his view in its darkness. The morning light shone into the cavern in a single dim shaft, only to splinter into a thousand sparkling beams as it reflected from the cavern's shining walls. He reached carefully forward and touched the edge of the opening. It was thin as his finger. It did not taper out to the thickness of his hand until it reached where his knees were resting. When the bead of sweat from his forehead slid down his nose, Forrest did not shift to wipe it until he had edged back far enough to sit up again safely. He glanced at Tsia and gestured at the hole. The sardonic challenge in his dark amber eyes was clear.

She glanced at him then at the opening. Like the abyss of her gate, it called to her curiosity. Slowly, realizing the analogy to the cats, she grinned. The feral expression made her ice-blue eyes seem diamond-hard. "I never could resist a dare," she admitted. A moment later she had bellied out as he had done, taken her look, and then inched back. Her pale face told him she had realized the same thing as he: Only the paper-thin integrity of the rock had held her above the depthless cavern below.

They made their way around the raw opening and back into the cliffs, moving east. At this end of the valley the cliffs, spotted with thick, dry shrubs, seemed deserted. There were urine mounds and scratch marks of cougars, toed-in tracks of toads, and droppings from the chi-chi birds on the brush, but the dust did not hold scents well, and the creatures hid. There was no sound besides themselves and the whistling wind for their ears.

They disturbed only two more cats: one simply faded from their path, and the other yowled until Tsia snapped at it and chased it from sight. She no longer fought her biogate; it was as if she had a second wind in the strength she used to control it. The energies of the life in the cliffs filled her but did not overwhelm. She could sense the soil, the grasses, the patient thirst of the rock lizard that hid in the shadows and waited for the storm . . . There was an animal power in the air itself. She reveled in it, stretching her arms when Forrest was not looking and twisting to look and sniff at the creatures that hid in the rocks.

When they were two hundred meters from the top of the narrows, they came across a tiny waterfall that fell over a ledge above their route. The pool at the bottom of the fall was shallow and clear. Quietly, to the right, the water poured out of it in a smooth, gray, glistening flow that swept down a shadowed channel and twisted out of sight. There were tracks of a male cougar—she could tell by the size of its print—in the dust and sign that a family of cerys used the pool for bathing their wrinkled, hairless lizard skins. Forrest stopped and drank deeply, then washed his face and neck. Tsia moved up to do the same, when she felt the male cougar watching them. She moved slowly, tilting her head so she could see the cat on the ledge of the waterfall. She growled in a low voice. Forrest looked up, saw the cat, and with narrowed eyes signaled her to keep the cat in place. Carefully, wasting no motion, he pulled the torn water bags from his harness.

Above them the cougar did not relax until Tsia reached to touch it through her gate. Then she pulled the mole from her pocket and, for the first time since she had left Noirelle, imaged a command to the node. The biocode shot back with the authorization for a scan, and she closed her eyes with its forgotten speed, tuning the node's resolution to the cougar. At the same time she felt the fabric of one of the botas pushed into her hands.

Beside her, Forrest imaged his own set of commands to the node. Knowing how Horen worked, he hooked into the traces that identified his dot and Tsia's, then spun them out into a series of activated tests that exploded into a widely fractured web. Ghost codes he had set himself years earlier were called in, pulling the web this way and that, linking to bioscans that raced along the node until they petered out as if finally disabled. Patterns of old webs meshed with the new one, obscuring the sharpness of the images Tsia made with the mole.

As she worked, Tsia made no sound except to growl occasionally at the cougar that observed them from above. She placed the mole on the first bota where it had been sliced, then began a search of the structural images stored in the node. She had studied organic structures, not inorganic ones, and she tapped the wrong image line before its monitor realized what she wanted and shunted her to the flexan fabrics. When the flexan pattern structured itself for her view, she imaged it to the mole and activated its manipulation circuits. Instantly, the patch of flexan beneath the mole melted, flowed, dripped onto the rock, and hardened into a glassy mess.

With dismay, Tsia frantically halted the mole. She and Forrest stared at the shining pile. She felt more than saw the cougar's curiosity make it stretch its neck to watch her and flare its nostrils at the unfamiliar scent of melted flexan.

Tsia rearranged the half-melted bota over the mess and tried again. It took six attempts to figure out the technique for layering fabric immediately after the flexan stiffened; the botas she finished had odd bulges where she had moved the mole too quickly. But they were serviceable, and there were no seams in the fabric. She handed the bags to Forrest, and he eyed them warily. He pushed one of the bulges out comically, and Tsia smothered a laugh. Then he dipped them in the spring, rinsed them, and filled them to a few inches below their taps. When he slung them over his shoulder, Tsia looked at his massive frame in the blunter, remembered with a sweet hedonistic torture the muscles that rippled along his arms and thighs, and did not offer to carry any of the bags.

Forrest gestured up at the cougar, past the falls. When Tsia growled at the cat, it slunk away, and they again began to climb.

"You think they caught our trace?" Tsia, feeling the sense of the cat fade in her mind, scrambled up the sharp stone boulders after him.

"Uh huh. Could have minutes. Could have half an hour before they wash our traces clear." He reached down and hauled her up to his ledge by her arm. "I laid the ghost line fast, and I probably left a dozen loose threads to connect the Gea trace with your use of the mole." He continued to climb. "The pattern, once they find it, will be a fast trace. There is the line from the horse's bioecho, to the Gea trace, to the mole use . . . It all points to the narrows. But I think we timed it right. We should reach the top of the narrows just about the time they clear our traces." He eyed a rough stretch of ground, then opted to go around it rather than tackle the loose stones that hung on the steep sides of the ridge.

Tsia said nothing more. The break to fix the botas seemed to have sapped the strength she had felt after their union in the meadow. Her lungs seemed so full of air that she could not breathe. Her heart pounded, and there was energy flowing in her limbs, but she did not seem to be able to use it to climb. The color of her skin was strangely flushed over a pale, white pallor. Perhaps it was the lime that colored her skin; they were both as dusty as if they had never bathed in the meadow, and Tsia's sweat was thick with the grime of the already hot rocks.

The short, flat spots along the ridge soon gave way to sharper boulders that had been broken off from out-thrust ledges. The few clumps of monkeybrush that decorated the ragged cliffs gave scant relief to the bland colors of rock. Even the sage was a whitish-green with lime and dust. Far below, the greenery of the rift valley seemed more mirage than reality. But they were near the eastern ridge of the narrows. Soon they would reach Ramok.

Both Tsia and Forrest now sucked the thin air into their lungs. Tsia's muscles ached, and she kept bumping and scraping her bruised ribs on the rocks. Her eyes no longer seemed to burn; she noticed their dryness only when she blinked. She took Forrest's hand often when she paused.

It took twenty minutes to reach the top of the ridge. By the time they crawled over the summit rock, Tsia's sweat was cold, as if it had lain on her skin all night. She began to shiver again, and Forrest took her arm to draw her away from the ledge. Gently but firmly, he propelled her forward until they both crouched over a steep, sweeping slope of stone. At the bottom of the slope was a narrow, wending path—the trail that led back into the narrows—bordered on the other side by a steep rise of rock. And there, on the trail, was a line of horses that stretched tiredly back into the narrows like a snake emerging inch by inch from its burrow.

Forrest stood and waved, then took Tsia's arm and raised hers beside his. The lead figure in the line raised his hand slowly back. Forrest glanced at Tsia to reassure her, then sharpened his gaze. Her skin was strangely clear under the dust. He felt something clench in his gut, and it took him a moment to recognize it as an odd combination of satisfaction—that she would live long enough to join Ramok again—and pain. He puzzled over the growing ache, then touched Tsia's hair, sliding his hand down to her slender neck. She had touched him inside, he realized, touched him as he now touched her racing pulse. Shared her gate with him. Shared with him the sense of her death. *Ava*, he had named her. He rubbed his fingers on her smooth, gritty skin so that she scowled. Slowly, as if his dark, brooding face had forgotten how to make the expression, he smiled.

Tsia looked up at him uncomprehendingly.

"Ava," he said softly. The word escaped his lips like a kiss. He touched her arm. "Come."

28

৶৽৺৻

The two guides made their way gingerly down the rotten slope. With the water bags sloshing across his back, it took all the animal grace Forrest had in order to remain upright; Tsia fared better. Already the morning heat was rising, and Tsia, shivering with the chill that sat on her skin like dew, tried to soak up the sun's rays. Her gate swarmed with the skittering of cat feet. They seemed less strong than when she had been in the meadow, and she no longer tried to ignore them. They were merely the presence of the cougar and the pair of tams that watched her from the ridge.

Her gaze flicked from one side of the pass to the other. To the east she had a clear view of the top of the steep trail down into Pulan. In the distance she could see the pale city of Levian, sitting beneath the heavy clouds that hung above its roofs. The front that she had sensed two days earlier still curled against the Cheba Rift and refused to move away; it cast the county into a shadow that morning did not erase.

To the west, between the rock ridges, glimpses of the Korshani desert stretched to an obscure horizon. Below, on the trail out of the narrows, the horses plodded, heads down. Tsia turned and looked back along the slope. In a low voice Forrest urged her to hurry, and she tried to comply, but her nerves were jangling. There were more than three cats up there now. She nearly missed the baleful glance of a backlash lizard as she dropped her boots over the edge of a rough, wind-carved step in the sandstone. Grit made her slip. She shrugged her shoulders, unrelieved of tension. Her energy began to flow out like a drain, while below the stubborn line of horses wavered and seemed suddenly far away. It took all her concentration to bring them back into focus.

Forrest had halted, looking up at her. She waved him on, then turned and stared back up the slope. Eyes in the light. Yellow eyes tracking her movements, following Forrest. They were there, watching and waiting and moving closer all the time. Tsia's blue eyes narrowed. With a twist, she turned on the face of the slope so that she could stand, albeit awkwardly, and look back up the hill. When she finally saw the dun-colored beast, it was almost a relief.

She took a step, slid painfully to her knees, and ended up on her hands and feet, the pebbles gouging her skin. As the rocks cut her palm, she felt an irritation build up in her guts. She did not wait for the cat to come face to face with her before she began to snarl. Above her the sleek, muscular creature paused, but its tail began to twitch. Hackles rose. Tsia growled louder, and the cougar picked its way down in a slinking creep until it stopped barely a meter away. They stared at each other. Then the cat reached out a paw as if to bat Tsia off the stone. Heat suddenly flooded her hands. Heedless of the claws stretching out toward her face, Tsia stood abruptly up and roared her defiance. The cat hissed. Its eyes narrowed. But it did not move forward again.

Giving it a last snarl, Tsia turned and let herself slide down the slope on her boots. By the time she landed at the bottom, back in the shadows of the cliffs, the chill had contrarily left her skin, and she felt feverish and hot. The calm strength she had felt when they had first left the meadow was gone; now she stood on the balls of her feet, uncertain if she should follow Forrest or wait for Ramok. The cool green shade of the rift called her like her gate. She flexed her feet; even her boots seemed to be burning.

She watched as Ramok met Forrest quickly. Forrest tossed a bota to him, threw one to Nitpicker, then carried the third to the councilwoman himself. Nitpicker slid off her spotted horse and pulled a flexbowl from her saddle gear, taking only a small drink herself before watering the horses. Finally Tsia moved toward her roan, and the horse raised its head dully as she caught its bridle. With the flexbowl from her saddlebags she took her turn watering her mount, murmuring and soothing it as it drank greedily.

In the meantime Ramok had pulled the old man from behind Wren and steadied the touch-tied prisoner against the ground. He held the water bag to the man's lips, letting him take as much as he wanted. Then he took a swig himself and passed the bag on to Wren, who then helped Nitpicker with the horses. The old man, ignored for the moment, gave a thoughtful look to Forrest, then Tsia.

Ramok, helping Forrest steady the councilwoman in her saddle, subtly indicated Tsia. "You found her on the ridge?" he asked in a low voice.

Forrest took his eyes away from Yemene. "Down in the valley," he answered.

Beside him, Horen regarded Tsia with a strange look in eyes. "Only cats come out of the valley," he said obliquely before pouring more water for his horse. Spade, who had been watching the exchange with narrow eyes, shuddered.

Forrest pointed with his chin at the ridge. "There's a spring twenty minutes away by foot."

Ramok shook his head. His voice was still hoarse from thirst. "We need speed now even more than water. Yemene has been in labor since before dawn, and the scans in this area went on highres the minute you left."

"Skimmers?" Forrest asked.

"Half a dozen have been overhead, and Red's ghost lines activated an hour ago. Ward's went on in Nairo soon after, but not all the skimmers went after them. There are still three ships cruising this ridge." Wren handed Ramok the bota again, and the merc took a swig, sloshing the water around his mouth before swallowing it in small gulps. "I want to bring one down, but a glimpse of us and they will just log us into the net and burn us out before they bother to land." His eyes went to Tsia as he spoke, noting her pale complexion as she stood next to the roan. He lowered his voice. "How is she?"

Forrest followed Ramok's gaze. "Fast, light pulse," he answered flatly. "Fevers and chills. Focused one moment; distant the next." He hesitated. "Ramok," he said with a curious sort of reluctance, "she could bring a skimmer down herself. Her own link does not read as a merc but as a colonist; they would be curious enough about that to land. And if she was by herself, they would be confident enough to open the hatch and come out to take her."

Ramok's shook his head. "She is wearing merc clothes, merc boots. They will assume she is one of us and kill her anyway."

Forrest regarded him for a moment without comment. "Feather saved you in Noirelle," he said finally, his voice harsh and unyielding. "You brought her away from the artists and as far as you could toward safety. But you cannot give her life when she cannot hold on to that herself."

Ramok's eyes flicked to Tsia.

"She is dying. We both know that. And you owe her nothing more than *ma'ke ka'eo*—the death victory," Forrest added, using the old words again. His amber eyes met Ramok's black gaze with a hard look. "This," he said, "is the time to give her death some meaning."

Ramok looked at Yemene. The councilwoman's hands clenched, and she could not stifle the groan that broke from between her lips.

"All right," he said abruptly. He moved across to Tsia.

When he reached her, he took her hand and stroked his fingers absently over her translucent skin. "We need a skimmer," he said quietly. She glanced up, and he nodded. "There will be one coming over the ridge soon—there have been several since you left earlier. If you are by yourself—If you dared to meet them . . . A single person with the horses . . ."

Tsia said nothing for a moment. She felt the old pull of a challenge, and in her head the cat feet suddenly tugged and pulled at her thoughts. Shut up, she told them savagely. They subsided. She stared at Ramok until his image focused in her physical sight. "They would be willing to land to check me out?" she asked.

He nodded.

She glanced down at her hands, noting the clarity of her skin and the tremble that had come back to shake them. She smiled faintly. "What have I got to lose?" Ramok's face turned grim, but he took her blunter as she shrugged out of it. She redistributed the mole and sculpting tools in her jumpsuit and removed her weapons harness, handing that to Ramok also. He looked down at her for a moment and traced her lips with his thumb.

She met his eyes, then frowned. Something stirred in her gate. Her nose twitched as if she could smell a threat. "Ramok . . ."

Ramok followed her gaze to the west. Over the ridges the blunt nose of a skimmer poked, hovering, then moving forward, pausing, then edging along again. For one long second Ramok watched it, then he snapped, "Nitpicker, Wren—everyone get your gear off the horses." He ran with Tsia's gear to the edge of the cliff, where he threw it against the rocks. "Get under cover!" he ordered, racing to Yemene's side and hauling her down. He staggered under her bloated weight. "That skimmer's on visual," he snapped, "not scan."

Tsia jerked the cinch open and caught her saddle as it slid off the roan. The sense of the cats' eyes watching from the cliff had sharpened with her tension, and she could almost feel the view from the felines' perspective. She shouted at them to leave, but they ignored her, crouching down and blending into the stone shadows until they were invisible.

Snarling at them in her mind, Tsia dragged her saddle and bridle to the side of the cliff and dumped them in a pile. Around her, the other mercs raced to do the same. Then they yanked their e-wraps from their saddlebags and whipped the thin covers over themselves. Spade had his extra wrap out of his pocket and spread over Yemene even before Ramok had gotten his own e-wrap out of his bag. Within seconds the wraps molded themselves into the facade of a cliff, changing color to match the surrounding terrain and taking on the shape of the rocks around them. Tsia blinked. The skimmer nosed out from behind a rock corner, but the line of mercs had become a tiny wall of stone.

Tsia could no longer tell the edges of the e-wraps from the edges of the cliff; she could sense the mercs only by the energy fields she felt through her gate. With a fluid motion she turned and leapt up onto the bare back of the roan, and the cat paws in her head reveled in the feel of her legs against the creature's hide. The horse plodded forward a few steps. She tapped its flanks, and the other horses began to follow.

The skimmer disappeared in another bend of the pass, and Tsia let herself relax into the horse. She rode without hands, her arms listlessly at her sides and her knee pressure telling the roan where to go. Pray Daya the shakes did not take her now, she thought wryly, or she would not be able to even stay on its back.

Behind her the skimmer floated out of the last bend and into full view. It seemed to hover over the tail end of the line of horses, then darted forward to stop just behind Tsia's position. She did not look up. When, with a subtle venting of air, it whipped ahead, then landed in front of her, she did not change direction but let the roan pick its own way toward the wedge-shaped ship. The ship was angled into the pass, clogging the trail and almost touching the steep side on which Ramok and the others hid.

Still Tsia did not raise her head. The sense of the cats grew sharp, and she felt the energy of the humans in front of her like dull spots in her gate. She could not smell or hear the nodies she knew crewed the skimmer craft. She tried to focus instead on their fields and realized that one field was slightly different. A woman? She nodded to herself. The sense of life she got through the gate could make that distinction for her.

Absently, she raised one hand to rub her temple, then, remembering, dropped it back to her side. Without the blunter, the heat of the morning sun struck her body as she rode into a shaft of light, and sweat began to soak her shirt. A few more seconds, and the skimmer door opened and a woman leapt down. Warily, the nodie approached the horses. "Hey, there," she said sharply. "You! Stop the horse."

Tsia did not respond. The woman bit her lip. She glanced back at the skimmer, and two men edged out of the open hatch. Together, the three of them advanced. One held a flexor, and one held a spotstun; the first nodie appeared unarmed. The cat feet skittered in her head, and Tsia subtly used her knees to urge the roan on.

"She's dressed like a merc," one man observed quietly.

"Doesn't link like one," the other man returned in a low voice. "Got a colonist dot for ID."

The first nodie said sarcastically, "They do use ghosts."

They fell silent. The nodie woman stepped in front of the roan so that the horse was forced to turn away or walk over her. Uncertain, the horse came to a halt. As it did so, Tsia let go with her knees, tilted, and slid off the the horse, falling into a limp huddle on the ground. Like a cougar setting a trap, she could feel their scent, their eagerness in her mind.

"Hey—" The woman moved quickly.

The roan sidestepped away, and the other two men closed in around her. Behind them, a piece of the cliff moved forward and slid under the nose of the skimmer. Tsia held herself still. Her gate yawned, and the cougar up on the cliff shifted its crouch forward as if it, not Tsia, hunted these nodies. She felt the woman reach for her and had to tamp down hard on her impulse to swipe at her grip.

"Scansign is off—way off." The woman used a handscan to read Tsia's vitals, then glanced up at the other two. "This is a guide, not a merc."

The first man frowned. "A guide? Here?"

"Uh huh. She is in poor shape, too. One of her viruses must be out of control." The woman stood. "Bet she is the one they are looking for. We will get a double bonus for this—"

Her words cut off abruptly as Horen's flexor, sliding into the shape of a club, hit her sharply across the temple. Instantly, his stick swung back and clipped the other nodie on the back of the head, while Nitpicker dropped the second man with the silent sting of a fiberdart in his neck. The other mercs swept beneath the skimmer and flooded into the hatch. Horen gave Tsia a hand up. Caught in the grip of her gate, she clenched her fists into claws as if to strike him away, and he stepped back with a sardonic grin. Then he turned his back on her, stooped, and touched a small bronze disk to the temples of the downed nodies.

Nitpicker eyed him sharply. "Got their links?"

"Almost." He paused. "All right. They are off the node. I will plug them now to make sure they stay that way."

With a tiny tool he inserted metaplas plugs into the temple sockets of each nodie. Then he ripped off his headgear shade and tossed it and his watergen on the belly of the unconscious woman while Nitpicker turned and ran to the skimmer. Horen made instead for the rocks, where Yemene and the old man waited with Spade. The councilwoman had one hand pressed against her side and one hand on the stone; her face was pale as the moon. Horen grabbed the woman's arm, and she jerked away to fall against the other merc. Spade snarled at Horen, and they traded—the old man with Horen, the Pulanese woman with Spade. Tsia hesitated. Her gate pulled her to the rocks, but Forrest glanced back and caught her eye. She shuddered. Thrusting away the sense of the cats in her mind, she ran stumbling to the ship.

Inside, Ramok and Wren disabled the pilot and stretched him out on the main cabin floor. Forrest went aft to check the back cabins and relief areas, but they were clear, and he returned in seconds. When Horen and Tsia reached the ship at the same time, the skimmer pilot was laid out on the ground by the other nodies, and the blond merc had only to plug the man quickly, then jump up to the skimmer after the old guide, then Tsia, had been hauled in by Spade.

Spade thrust his way through the others to the front of the main cabin. Nitpicker joined him, flinging herself hastily into the malleable pilot's soft. She did not give it time to mold itself to her body before she linked into the console. When she accessed the node, the chair read her images and jerked into shape abruptly.

Before her, the holotank that displayed the terrain and their position went active. Nitpicker imaged in her commands, and Ramok slammed the hatch shut.

"I've got power and nav control," Spade said shortly.

"I'm on the links," Nitpicker responded.

Forrest and Wren powered down the armfuls of e-wraps that Wren had stuffed in the ship. As each lost power, it snapped automatically into a tiny package, and Wren redistributed the wraps to the mercs, placing Spade's extra in one of the few saddlebags they had brought into the skimmer.

Ramok and Tsia helped the councilwoman to a position in front of one of the malleable flexan chairs—the softs—while Horen snapped three more softs out of the walls and stood the old man in front of one of them. The merc's left hand kept tapping his temple jack as he thought, his imaged commands laying ghost webs throughout the node even as his hands automatically set the seats in the cabin.

"Seats up. Body check." Nitpicker's voice was curt. The softs flowed, stretched, and became thick, flat-paneled chairs with hinged sides. "All in," the woman ordered. As one, the mercs sat in the flexan seats. Horen pressed the old man down. "Body check, closing," she said sharply. The sides of the softs closed in over the mercs. Tsia felt the suffocating foam press down for an instant. The cat feet in her head panicked, and she had to force herself to stay. Then the pressure was gone. The sides of the softs folded back, now impressed with the shapes of the individual passengers. Nitpicker's launch access cleared. "Body check completed," she said. "Rise in ten."

Ramok leaned forward and snapped at Forrest, "Get Yemene down flat."

The other merc imaged the controls on the side of the chair nearest the woman, and it reclined so that she could lie back. Her face was rigid, and her fists were clenched. She groaned. Tsia tried to shut out the sound, wondering if Yemene could image her own med commands to her body in her state of pain.

"Plan in," Nitpicker said, confirming the node. "Access on—"

"Gyros on," Spade's voice automatically laid over her tones.

"Main air on, main espee on—"

"Tubes in, vents cleared—"

"Bios away, launch ring cleared—"

"Lifts set—"

"Cabin decoupled. Launch is ready." Spade did not look at Nitpicker as he imaged his commands and checked his console against the access he had in the node. "We verified?"

"Roger that. I am bouncing the launch command through the distort web." Her overlay gave her the air currents, and she set her vectors in motion. "Nodies know we will use the distort, but it will cost them ten minutes to find the right line and sever our control."

Spade nodded. "Air currents mapped. On your mark."

"Mark."

The skimmer lifted up smoothly. The gyros kept the main cabin from shifting as the outer skin of the skimmer flared into tiny slats that would catch the wind and help turn the ship like a sailboat. Nitpicker trimmed the slats and glanced at Spade. "Watch your access. When the nodies cut in, we could lose more than power."

"Put her on manual?"

"Every system we can."

As soon as they lifted, Tsia was out of her seat, restless and pacing the cabin. Without the blunter and weapon harness she felt strangely chilled and light, and she went from one side of the ship to the other, then paced from forward to aft. The fourth time her shadow crossed Wren's scanners, the merc did not even glance up. "Tsia," he said shortly, "if you can't sit still, go aft and give the rest of us a break."

With a silent snarl, she spun and dropped into her soft. From his place at Yemene's side Forrest reached over and touched her on the arm. She flinched away. *"Esha, ava,"* Forrest said softly, almost under his breath.

Yemene groaned. "My water has broken," she managed to say before another convulsion took her.

Ramok gave her a sharp look. "Forrest?"

The other man knelt at the woman's knees and, pulling some medwraps from a kit, gently spread the cloths below the woman's legs and hips. Yemene clutched at the fabric, her fingers digging into the foam of the soft. Ignoring the clench of her hands, Forrest draped a cloth over her legs to give her a sense of privacy, something that the ironic glint in her eyes told him she appreciated. When he greased his finger and ran it around the edge of her vaginal opening, she gasped and stared at him, outraged. He spoke to her in a low voice, and she lay her head back reluctantly as he continued to massage and relax the opening. With a glance at the old man, Wren rose and went aft to use the relief.

Left in his seat, the old guide rolled his shoulders to ease the cramping of his muscles. He glanced at Yemene, then at Tsia, then back to Ramok. He cleared his throat with a guttural sound. "You," he said to Tsia, "I've been thinking, are old enough to be a second-stager."

Tsia flicked her gaze at him and felt the old flush of shame hit her cheeks. Too old to become a guide . . . The cat feet clawed at her brain, and she almost welcomed the sensation. In the distance they were a softer, quieter pressure on her thoughts.

The old man watched the skin around her eyes tighten. "You got the tremors and the chills. Your skin is going clear, but," he said, glancing toward Forrest, "I don't think you have the second-stage virus at all."

Tsia eyed him warily, trying to sort out the terms in which he spoke. First stage? Second stage? The cat feet swelled in her head with the fever heat of the virus, and she tried now to push them back out.

It was Ramok who asked. "What do you mean? What else could it be?"

The old guide hesitated. He watched Tsia closely as she pressed her hands to her temples. "That cat grace of yours is natural, not trained in, isn't it? Raw through the gate?" She nodded imperceptibly, but he felt the motion through his own biolink. "And at dawn you ran to the rift—toward the cats—not away from your gate like any other guide would have done."

Thoughtfully, Forrest eyed the old man. "You think," he said softly, "she is a first-stager, not a second-stager."

The man nodded. Bewildered, Tsia glanced from one to the other. Of course she was a first-stager. How could they not know that?

Because, said the tiny voice inside her head, of her age. Guides took the virus young, when their bodies could mutate more easily.

She opened her mouth, but Ramok was already challenging the old man's words. "If Feather was a first-stager," he said sharply, "she would have not had the virus much longer than a year, and anyone can see she's almost forty. How could she still be a first-stager?"

Beside him, Yemene groaned and clenched her hands. "Because—" she started.

Tsia found her voice. "Because I took the virus a year—sixteen months—ago. I . . . came late to the flames."

Yemene gave a harsh laugh. "Why do you think," she said to Ramok, "I was so scornful of her dancing the flames to keep me safe from that artist?" The contraction strengthened, and she spoke from between clenched teeth. "Your Feather has been in the fire only three times—except for the flames at Bonnell's Bay—since the guide virus took to her body. She told me that herself."

Ramok stared at Tsia. "And you said nothing to me, nothing to any of us, about this?"

Tsia's voice was faint. "No one asked. I did not know it was important."

"And you?" he demanded of Yemene.

"I assumed you knew about her yourself," she returned snappishly. "You and she are, after all, *avya*." She clenched her fists, and her words turned into a cry of pain. The contraction subsided, and she breathed raggedly. The med commands she imaged to her brain barely helped. She could feel the hemorrhaging in her body.

Wren returned, and Ramok rose to go aft to the relief himself. The smaller merc sat down again beside the old guide. Ignoring the merc, the gray-haired man said softly, "A year alone, away from the guild. She's a renegade, a wild gate. And with a link to the cats . . ." He shook his head, his eyes glinting at Tsia. "That close to the Cheba Rift—I bet you did not recognize the lot of us except as a scent in your nose."

She stared at him without answering. He knew what it was like? He felt the gate like a flood across his senses?

Forrest felt the surge of power that leaked from her gate. "*Eshe*, Tsia."

Ramok, returning, glanced at the other man. The old guide caught his eye. "You understand what this means? Your guide's not in second stage. Her virus did not mutate. It was never killed. She's still in first stage. Look at her." He motioned with his chin. "She's practically feral now. You don't have a wild virus. You got you a wild guide. A renegade with an uncontrollable gate."

The virus had not been killed? Tsia caught her breath in sudden realization. They were going to kill her virus? Even with the distance from the rift, her gate seemed to blaze open. Tsia sprang to her feet.

Forrest's hand flashed, and he grabbed, then crushed her wrist with his grip. "As you were," he said harshly. She cried out, writhing against his strength. "Tsia—" His deep, gravelly voice cut across the panic of the cats. "Every guide's virus is killed after a year. You did not know that, but it is true."

Uncomprehendingly, she stared at him.

"Every guide's virus," the old man agreed. "Killing the virus does not destroy the gate, not when it has opened enough to be sustained by the pathways it has made in your brain. Killing the virus only stops the growth of the gate so that it does not become too deep—too wild—for you to reason with."

Stop the growth? Keep the cat feet from clawing her thoughts apart? Tsia clenched her fists. Hot exultation burned through her gate. To feel without being so lost in the power? She pulled against the grip of the merc without being aware of the motion.

Ramok came forward. "You said there was nothing you could do if she was in second stage," he said to Forrest. "But what about now? We have access to the link." He nodded at Horen. "We still have the self-contained med equipment."

The old man glanced at her blazing eyes. "Can't do spit with SCAME," he said. "Virus isn't stopped by some simple sequence stored in that self-contained scanner. It isn't stopped by some med command you send down to her brain from the node, either. Only way to stop it is by injecting her with pathogen—a parasitic one— the antivirus."

Forrest released Tsia slowly. She ignored the white marks on her wrist. In her head, she was beginning to understand. "Where," she asked in a hoarse voice, "can I get the antivirus? Where can I get it outside of the guild?"

The old man looked at her steadily. You touched the cats, didn't

you? Broke the Landing Pact? His silent questions seemed to reverberate in the air between them.

Tsia gave a short, ragged nod.

"You are a ghost," he said softly, "or the guild would already
have stepped in to help you. And if you're on an illegal link . . .
The guild, when they find out, will have to strip you of your
gate." He watched the skin whiten around her eyes. "I've seen it
happen," he said more to himself than to her. "It's a cold, bitter
thing to do." His voice sharpened abruptly. "You're too far locked
into your gate, aren't you? You would rather die than lose it?"

The yowling that undercut the old man's words made it hard to
hear. She forced her fists to relax. "Yes," she agreed quietly. "I
would rather die."

Ramok stepped forward, and his voice, when he spoke, was
hard. "Does she have to?"

Slowly, the old guide rubbed the pockmarks on his cheek.
"Maybe. Maybe not."

Tsia's blue eyes flickered. Ramok nodded to her as if he were
promising her the future of which he had spoken before. "How?"
he asked softly.

The old man shifted uncomfortably, but his eyes were clear as
he answered. "Heard, long time ago, that the parasite was bred
into all the Gea-engineered scout animals. Wolves, herons, por-
poises, cats . . ." He nodded at the sudden glint in Forrest's amber
eyes. "It's in their saliva and sinus fluids. In their blood. In cougars, it's even in the tissue under their claws. In the venom sacs
of the tams. Used to be the way the first guides stopped the
virus—by getting clawed or bit. Four hundred years ago, anyway.
Leastwise, that's what my great-great-grandfather said." He stared
at Tsia's pale skin, at the quick pulse of her heartbeat in her neck.
"It's not an easy way to get the cure. Have to control the gate
while you get your link to slash you." He met Tsia's eyes with a
deliberate challenge. "You're a renegade. You got the guts to hold
yourself out of your gate? You got the guts to live?"

She stared back at him silently. The cats surged in her mind,
and the animal power of their motion flowed into her body from
her link. Determination crystallized. To control the width of her
gate . . . To feel the cougars but not be dragged down by them . . .
To have a future unchained from the certainty of death . . .

Her ice-blue eyes burned. "I have both the will and the control."

He judged the emotion in her eyes, then nodded abruptly.
"Then go back to the cats," he ordered. "If they don't kill you,

they'll help you. Bite, scratch—maul even—doesn't matter what they do. Get that parasite into your blood, into your flesh. Your body will do the rest." He glanced toward Ramok, then looked back. "The parasitic antivirus is not as potent as the pathogen used by the guild. Remember that. The quicker you get to a predator, the faster the parasite can infect you. The longer you wait, the greater the chance that the pathogen won't have time to save you."

Tsia stood for a minute as the hot exultation of her gate spilled into her mind with her knowledge. To live . . . Free of the guild. To go wherever she wanted. To see every cliff and height . . .

Yemene cried out, and Wren glanced at the woman's sweating face, then back to Tsia's swaying form. "These mutations," he said, indicating Tsia with a nod. "These fevers—will she be always as she is now? Unfocused, restless? Wild?"

From the side, Forrest shook his head. Yemene stifled a cry, and the mercs carefully averted their eyes from her straining body as Forrest tried to soothe her. The old man answered for the other merc. "A guide's body rejects the last mutations made to it by the virus when the virus is killed. Your Feather—her body should recover so that it is almost normal. For a guide, that is."

Normal for a guide. Not useless. Not ashamed of her gate. Tsia's blue eyes sharpened. If she lived. Her gaze flashed to Forrest, then Ramok, the grim determination and fright in it hidden beneath the fire of the fever.

Ramok took a step forward. The darkeyes hid his expression as he noted the transparency of her skin and the cold tremor that clung to her hands. Gently, his hand touched her cheek. "I will get you back to the rift." His voice caught for an instant. "You will return to the cats."

She nodded. She was not aware of moving her feet into another round of pacing. Her thoughts were focused through her gate. When the shudder took her, she stumbled against Horen's seat and put out her hand blindly. Automatically, the blond merc caught her before she could fall. She wrenched herself free. His touch, like the chills that spread across her skin, was frightening, and it cut through the background snarls that filled her head. Averting her eyes, she stumbled aft to the back cabin.

Trembling, she sank down on the relief. The two doors between her and Horen did not seem to be enough. His grasp had been like an icy threat that negated everything Ramok promised. His touch was like a glacier weight of fear and dread that included Cekulu's art and Hesse's n-rod and the metaplas chains of the guild. She pressed her hands against the off-white walls of the relief and felt the thrum of the skimmer through the surfaces. Cat feet padded in rhythm with its vibration. Even at this distance, where the presence of the cats was less, they still clouded her mind and pressed at her thoughts as if by their weight alone they could change her into one of them.

She stared at her hands, against the pale walls as the cougars pressed against her mind. She could not hide the translucence of her own skin from her eyes. She could not hide the fever that brought sweat to her forehead even when there was no heat in her bones. How much time did she have? How much time to reach the city, access a skimmer, and return? Hours? A day? She tried to focus her mind, and the cat feet tore through her focus. Ducking her head, she curled her hands into fists and pounded them twice against the room.

If she did not fight for her future, she would die. Right now the fear of the death and the fear of the living were almost the same. She had said she had the will and the control to fight her gate, not the guts. "Daya," she whispered, "give me strength."

A long moment passed in which the struggle between her thoughts and the tams in her mind became sharp. She forced their senses back to the gate, then lost her energy and let them sweep forward again. As if she stood in the slough and protested the tide, all she could do was shove back against the waves. "Daya," she breathed. She raised her head. "I will not give in." Her jaw was tight with the words, and her pulse was hard and fast against the skin of her throat. "I will fight."

The next shudder mocked her resolve and took her as she opened the door to the relief. And then she ran into Horen's rock-hard chest. Her lips parted in shock. Automatically, his arms came around her, catching her body as he eyed her with a hard, eager look. Tsia cast a suddenly desperate look toward the cabin door, but Horen, his fingers digging into her arms, ducked his head to her lips.

"No—" she cried out, wrenching back. Her gate seemed to widen and surge with the panic of a cougar caught in a trap.

Instantly, as he felt her motion, Horen slammed her back at an angle, grinning as her head hit the door frame. She cried out, and he slapped her across her cheek so hard that blood spurted from her nose and spattered onto the wall beside her. For an instant she was dazed. There was a roaring in her mind as if a dozen tams snarled, and her eyes—she could not seem to focus.

With a low laugh Horen snapped her around and slung her almost disdainfully across the cabin. A yowl burst from her lips. She landed in a partial roll, slid across the floor, then slammed into the wall, her head tucked between her arms. The air blasted out of her lungs as her back and shoulders hit. Cougars screamed in her mind; tams clawed at her frozen thoughts. One of her arms was twisted and trapped beneath her. In an instant Horen was on top, throwing his body across her free arm and grabbing her face in his hands. His lips grinned, but his black, expressionless dark-eyes bored into her terrified face.

Fascinated by the frantic pulse beating in her throat, Horen ran his thumbs over her translucent skin, then dug his fingers maliciously into the back of her skull. "Arrogant guide," he breathed. "Reveling in your gate. Do you know what it's like to be a naught?" Brutally, he jammed a knee between Tsia's thighs. "You'll share that with me. You've wanted to do that for days." He twisted, and his knees spread her thighs with ugly intent.

She clawed at him. She tried to scream, but the only sounds torn from her throat were snarls. The cat feet lunged in her head. Horen's tongue spread saliva across her chin as he covered her twisting mouth with his own and forced her head back into the crack between floor and wall. Her eyes were filled with animal panic. The gate— She reached through the gate toward Forrest—

Horen gripped the front of her jumpsuit—

Forrest, she screamed.

—and tore it open.

Ramok, a chilling look on his face, burst through the door, the tingling of the filter field like a shock on his body as he did not wait for it to clear. Horen whipped his head around. With a roar, Ramok launched himself at Horen. The other merc, his eyes cold and hard with lust, lunged up.

They met halfway. Ramok's twisting impact slammed Horen into the wall with a sharp cracking sound. Ramok followed him up, catching him as he tried to turn and slugging him in the gut before throwing him against the opposite wall. With a groan, Horen slid to his knees.

Ramok grabbed Tsia by her arm and hauled her up. Clumsily, her fingers sealed her shirt as he dragged her out of the room and back to the main cabin. She was shaking. Her eyes were wild and blazing. Blood still dripped from her nose, sliding down over her lips, and she wiped ineffectually at it, her breath coming out in a constant tiny snarl.

Roughly, Ramok threw her into her seat, then grabbed a medpak from a wall panel and jerked out a wipe. Furious, he knelt and reached for Tsia's face, but she hit him with shocking force. She stared at him, her eyes raging. The marks of her fingers were white, then red on his skin. Silently, refusing to meet his eyes, she snatched the wipe from his hands and began to rub at her face, scrubbing the feel of saliva and fingers from her skin and flinching from her own touch.

Forrest, by Yemene, looked over to Tsia with his dark, unreadable, gaze, but there was a power in his shoulders that seemed barely contained. She saw Ramok's fury mirrored in Forrest's amber eyes and knew she had reached him—it was why Ramok had come. She wiped at the blood on her face. The muscles on the sides of Forrest's face rippled with his intent, and Ramok gave him a warning glance. Wren's quick look from Ramok to Forrest was thoughtful, and Ramok, still kneeling before Tsia, said, his voice low and steady, "I can't kill him for you, Feather. We need him to set the ghosts for our lines."

She stared at him with a blind hate that twisted her eyes into slants. She felt trapped by his statement, as if she were not free even to demand her own justice. What was she to him? *Avya* or *heyita*? Her biogate flared open with her hostility, and even at this distance the sense of the cats swept in and deafened her with their growls. Instantly, she clamped her hands to her temples. She tried to close her mind to the sounds—tried to shut them out—and suddenly, as if the distance created a darkness through which the cougars could not reach, the din faded. Ramok watched her silently. She took a ragged breath.

"I don't need you to kill him for me." Her voice was tight. She looked up suddenly, and her ice-blue eyes blazed. "I can do that for myself."

Ramok, though his eyes were still hard with his own anger, twisted his lips into a slow smile. "Yemene to Levian first," he said softly. "Then you, back to the Cheba Rift. We close your gate. Then you can fight him if you wish."

He twisted around toward the front of the cabin, looked at the holotank sharply, then got up and strode forward. The floating images of terrain showed the skimmer beneath the clouds and the pale, consolidated city of Levian shifting every few seconds in scale. The double view showed both the long-range view and the up-close scene of the rapidly decreasing distance between skimmer and city. Behind him Yemene groaned, and he asked Nitpicker tersely, "Time to the pad?"

Nitpicker's voice was sharp. "Eleven minutes, thirty-five seconds."

Yemene almost screamed. Forrest murmured to her softly and placed his hands between her thighs. Tsia, remembering Horen's hands on her body, shuddered.

Ramok watched Spade closely. The merc was imaging commands to the node so fast that his half of the holotank seemed to be nothing but flickers. "Everything on manual?" Ramok demanded.

"Negative. Can't get power or links off the node, but we should be able to navigate even if they cut our lines."

"Stay on the links," Ramok commanded. "If the access goes, it will be fast; We'll have to catch the link loss before it compromises the manual overrides. Wren—" He turned back to the main cabin. "Release the old man. It won't be safe for him to be touch-tied once we land."

The quiet orders were punctuated only by Yemene's hoarse cries and Forrest's soothing murmur. The rear cabin door opened, and Horen staggered in. Tsia did not have to look to know he had entered the main cabin; she could feel his presence like a dark force in her gate. Even as closed as she held it, the gate was still active enough for that. She clenched the bloody wipe in her hand to hide the tremor that shook it. There was fear beneath the hate in her eyes.

"*Seva*, Tsia," Forrest said softly.

Behind them Horen leaned against the wall to hold himself up. One hand was held to the back of his skull, and he shook his head unevenly.

Ramok looked back. "Sit down." The cold, vicious tone of his voice left no doubt as to his feelings. "Get on your ghosts. You make any other move and I will burn your knees off myself." He turned to Wren. "What's on the scan?"

Wren did not glance up. "Levian is closed up tight. Businesses are down and waiting. Local skyhook pad is locked down till the conflict settles. All skimmer and dart traffic is locked down, out of the node, except that controlled by the miners and freepicks."

Ramok nodded as if he had expected that. "Where's the heat?"

"Hot spots across every mine. Two—maybe two hundred and twenty—miners near the plaza. With the subsurface scanners out, even the node is guessing how many freepicks are waiting. I'm reading through the ghost lines now . . ." He frowned to himself, his beaked nose drawing his face down even farther into a scowl. "Got a hundred freepicks' echoes in the subsurface tunnels," he continued a minute later. "Maybe another eighty right up under the streets. Looks like both sides are standing off the plaza."

"Art guild status?"

With one hand to his temple, Horen, his face expressionless, imaged into the node and answered Ramok instead. "Hot. There are three art nodies running a scannet so tight a gnat would not get through." He nodded as if to himself, and Tsia tried to ignore his voice. Her skin seemed to shiver at his every word.

"Harder to tell about the others," he continued, ignoring the expression on her face. "Lot of noise on the temple links. Temples are packed. Esper net is hot. Standard guards in the temples—M1 only. No merc contracts on the node except ours." His voice trailed off as he imaged further into the net. "No new men or gear since the skyhook and skimmers shut down. They are using their own men, their own weapons, but there's a hell of a lot of gear on active status."

Yemene groaned, and Tsia stared at the woman's clenched fists. The cloths around her legs were soaked; her skin glistened with sweat. She stifled another scream into a groan. Her flesh tore down from the circular opening, and the top of baby's head was pushed through in a slick mess.

Ramok glanced back only briefly. "Nitpicker." He turned forward again. "Can we make the landing pads at the mines?"

"Negative. All four of them and both public pads are out. We can land in the trade plaza or on top of either temple. Only buildings in the city with flat roofs—everything else is covered in an energy net, is too hot, or too far away."

"The trade plaza sits right between the guild buildings and the council," Wren murmured from behind the merc leader. "Kumuda is only a block from the council building. Istarin is a good half kilometer."

"City's quiet," Horen returned. "No fighting in over a day. Got a temporary cease-fire in effect." His voice was flat and professional, and Tsia ground her teeth to hide the fury that grew as her fear subsided. That he could act so coolly now . . . Concentrating on his net, Horen frowned slightly. "Istarin temple is less crowded than Kumuda. Kumuda has the place packed to the doors. They read an esper in service."

"Art nodies?"

"Scanning sharp. I think they know we are here."

"Wren," Ramok commanded, "check the status of the prophecy—that esper reading. I want to know if it has changed. Anything about the future leadership—it is what the miners have the most stake in."

The small merc frowned, and his beaked nose wrinkled with his dark, concentrated expression. "It is still active. No change from the previous reading. Cougars clawing the rape of the future . . . Smoking warriors, childless mothers, burning babes . . . It's all still here."

Ramok thumped his fingers against his thigh. "Espers tied in with the art guild?"

The blond merc answered. "Negative. Esper guild is clear of everything. But the art nodies have some fingers in the miners' net. Looks like a contract agreement for the use of their equipment."

"Salvage snakes and tight-beam breakers, burton balls and bombs." Tsia was not aware she had spoken until Ramok nodded.

"Miners and freepicks will favor the burton balls," he answered. "Art guild will favor the snakes. A good nodie can run a snake fifty meters away, and they have some specialists." He grinned mirthlessly. "Besides, they prefer a more individualized approach. It's why they don't often hire mercs." He glanced back at Horen and lost his smile. "Sensor report," he ordered.

"Still sharp on the transport tubes, the skimmer pads, and the pedpaths," Haren answered without expression. "Everything—and I mean everything—is locked down. Council wants no traffic in Levian. We'll be lucky to make it down in one piece."

"Ramok?" Nitpicker broke in. "I need a target. We're getting too close to waste trajectory."

"Istarin temple," Ramok decided. "I want this quiet as possible. No telling how the miners will react when they find out Yemene's back. That cease-fire could be waiting for a catalyst to break it, and we will have a tough enough time avoiding the nodies' snakes to worry about the miner's lasing us in the back."

Yemene groaned, then screamed. Forrest grunted. More of the blood-streaked head had just appeared against the circle of vaginal flesh. Tsia averted her eyes, but Forrest snapped her name. "Tsia, I need you."

Tsia forced herself to look. In the wave of senses that swept through her brain, she could almost feel the duality of the birth. Yemene's energy was hot and shallow; the other presence was tiny and bright—like a pinpoint star that hung in her gate.

Cat senses seemed to breathe in the energy and lick at the tiny presence they felt through her mind. Cat feet padded faintly against the gate, stretching and clawing to get through the distance and strength of will that pushed them so tightly from Tsia's thoughts.

Yemene screamed again harshly, and Ramok refused to look. The infant's head, shoved convulsively out of the mother's body, rested in one of Forrest's massive hands, and the merc gestured sharply at Tsia. Reluctantly, she advanced, averting her eyes from Horen's cold, predatory gaze.

Forrest cradled the baby's head and guided its rotation to the left. At his direction, Tsia took a clean wipe and held it against the flush of blood that came out with the baby's shoulder. Yemene almost ripped the flexan of the soft in her clenched fingers. Forrest's hands, infinitely gentle, took the weight of the baby's torso as its lower shoulder delivered. The rest of the baby followed in a rush of two convulsions, sliding into Forrest's fingers so that it rested across the length of his hands. Yemene gasped in abrupt relief. Forrest barely glanced at her. Birth tissue still covered the baby's face, and he wiped it away with his fingers, then held the infant down so that Tsia could sponge out its mouth and nose. The merc did not wait for the umbilical cord to stop pulsing. Instead, using the laser knife from the medkit, he severed and cauterized the cord as fast as he could. Yemene grunted; then, a minute later, the placenta slid out of the birth canal in a bloody lump. Tsia barely caught the discharge in the wipe. She stared at the raw mass with barely concealed disgust. But the infant was in Forrest's arms, covered in a clean wipe that soaked the blood and fluid from its skin.

Wren glanced away from his scanners and raised one eyebrow at Tsia as she held the limp placenta uncertainly, her eyes flicking between the infant and the tissue. There was a strange feeling in her gut. One hand pressed against her abdomen.

The guide guild held her gene samples, she remembered with a pang. She took in a short breath, and the smell of blood and fluid choked her. The cat feet, fainter with the distance, shifted irritably in her mind. Tsia shook her head, as if doing so would deny their twitching nostrils, force the scent of blood and new flesh from her nose. She stared at the kit—the infant in Forrest's grasp. It was so small, so red and wrinkled next to the merc's dark-tanned skin . . . Such tiny little fingers in Forrest's massive hands . . .

With a soothing murmur, Forrest laid the baby on Yemene's bare belly where she could reach it, then took the raw mass of the placenta from Tsia. She remained where she was, fascinated, watching Yemene touch the infant with trembling, sweating hands. A moment later Forrest turned away, and the skimmer shuddered and dipped sharply down.

Tsia staggered and grabbed at the edge of the soft on which Yemene rocked. The cat feet in her head seemed to scrabble among her thoughts. Her eyes went forward, following Ramok's quick order.

"Nitpicker?" Ramok queried sharply.

The woman did not look back. All her attention was on the console and the link she had to the node. "Lost nav control," she returned. "They've got us on the node beam now, and on this approach I won't be able to fight it long enough to get to the Istarin temple. Have to set down on the Kumuda or the trade plaza." Her eyes were narrowed with concentration as she imaged the flight plan into the node.

Horen looked up. "Are you space-crazy?" he snapped. "The trade plaza sits right between the guild buildings and the council seat. The Kumuda is only a block away. The nodies will see us coming in before we even start down."

"We've already started down—" Nitpicker gestured tersely at the holotank. "—and both the Kumuda and the plaza are clear."

Wren glanced at Ramok. "There are three hundred miners and freepicks in that place. And the cease-fire is only temporary. There has to be a better place to land."

"There isn't," Nitpicker snarled over her shoulder. "Kumuda or the plaza?" she snapped at Ramok.

"Kumuda," Ramok returned shortly.

"And the proximity to the guilds?"

He gave her a slow grin. "Even after reading our trail, the nodies won't expect us to drop so close. If Horen's ghosts are tight, we'll have five, maybe six minutes before they figure out where we landed." He gestured at the holotank. "That close to the plaza, minutes could be all we need to get to the council building." He looked around at the mercs. Forrest was still attending the councilwoman. "Forrest, stay with Yemene. The rest of you, set up. Wren, you're point. Nitpicker, you're on the forward scan. Horen, Spade—you're anchor. Tsia, you're with me."

Wren, his clublike hand shutting down his scanners, glanced at Tsia with his black eyes unreadable. His small, birdlike nose twitched once. The other mercs checked their gear and monitored their scans with sharp eyes. Tsia waited uncertainly.

Yemene's white, sweating face looked at Tsia. *"Nyeka,"* she whispered.

Tsia turned and knelt beside her. The infant lay quietly on Yemene's bare belly, its hand clenched into tiny fists, and Tsia marveled at its breathing. But Yemene's voice was weak, and Tsia wrenched her attention to the woman whose words barely reached her ears. "My baby," she breathed.

Tsia's hand was gripped hard in Yemene's fingers. The woman's flesh was thick and clammy on Tsia's clear, pale skin, but her grip was like that of a vulture. "Take care of my little boy . . ."

Tsia's eyes narrowed. "Yemene—" She tried to withdraw her hand, but Yemene had it in a death grip. Behind them the mercs, intent on their preparations for landing, ignored the two women.

"My boy—take him."

Yemene was serious. The cats in Tsia's head surged and snarled at her shock, and in her sight, Yemene's strained face blurred and became the twisted face of Vashanna back in Noirelle. The infant became an older boy. Limp limbs in her hands; the smell of blood . . . Limp hands, tiny hands in the water . . . Her gate was no protection from the guilt that swept her body. If this were her child . . . If she could not have children herself . . .

No! She had just gotten free of the chains of the guild. She would not be chained to another man's destiny—not even through the life of a child. She had to fight for her own life now. "Yemene," she said in a low, tight voice. "You must raise your own child. I cannot keep him for you."

"*Nyeka*, please . . ."

Tsia jerked her hand free. She was a guide, not just a *nyeka*. Not just a fighter. Not just a body to keep between this woman's son and the artists of the guild. Had not the art guild taken everything else from her? Her work? Her family? Perhaps her life itself? The only thing she had left was the hope of her own future. Her jaw set. They would not take that, too.

Yemene saw the denial in her eyes. "The prophecy," she breathed. "You must keep him safe from the fire. He must live to lead Pulan to peace."

"Damn you!" Tsia's whisper was vicious. "Does no one want me for myself? You—Cekulu, Vashanna, Hesse . . . Even with the hope of my future, am I still just a guide with a useless gate? I have no value—only others do? I have no skills for my work—only my firedance has meaning?" She clenched her fists. "I am no longer slave to Cekulu or to your prophecy. I am an ecologist, not a nanny. A guide, not a priest. I will not be forced to dance in the fire of your making."

"I cannot do it," the woman cried out. "You can." Forrest glanced up from slamming the medkit back into its seal on the wall. His expression was hidden in the dark planes of his face.

"My destiny is my own," Tsia hissed. "I dance the fire for myself and for Daya. And if I agree to wear chains again on my soul, they will be of my making not yours. Your son is in danger only if you push him into it. You are his mother. You keep him safe. You keep him yourself."

The skimmer whined around them; the mercs waited tersely, their attention on the holotank in front. With desperate effort, the councilwoman lifted her baby with weak fingers. "Children are sacred to the guides . . ."

Her arms shook. The infant trembled and began to fall. Automatically, moving like a cat to catch the tiny body, Tsia snapped forward, cursing herself even as she did so. Yemene's eyes flickered, then closed.

Tsia stared at the limp, squirming child. If she had been bound by her honor to protect the child before, in Noirelle, she was bound now by her own hands, by her own soul. "Oh, Yemene," she whispered, "why did you do this?"

She looked up, met Horen's black, speculative eyes, and, with a chill, quelled her own despair. Her face set, she turned slowly to her seat. The holotank showed the skimmer clearly; they were going down.

"Nitpicker," she said flatly, "I need a body check. Seat two. For impact."

"Now?" The woman's voice was incredulous.

"Now," Tsia snarled back.

Nitpicker cursed. "Roger that. Seat two, down," she snapped. "All in." She paused as Tsia sat down awkwardly, the baby in her arms. "Body check, closing." She imaged the commands. The foam slabs slid up and over, and Tsia held her breath as the porous slabs reshaped themselves to include the infant in her arms. "Body check complete." Nitpicker snapped. "It's done. All right, everyone, get soft—"

The mercs leaned back in their seats. Tsia held the baby close. She closed down on her gate, expecting the cats to burst through and blind her with panic when the impact foam closed over her face.

"Impact in ten," Spade said calmly. "Nine. Eight."

"Cabin is locked to the hull."

Spade's voice was short, steady. "They've cut our link."

Nitpicker snapped. "We're going down."

Tsia stared forward at the holotank. She clutched the baby tightly. Then the images of the skimmer and the structure's roof rushed together.

29

The skimmer hit. The nose dug into the surface of the roof and folded gently back, collapsing in on itself as it cushioned its impact. Inside, molded flexan pads encircled the mercs. Bodies lurched. With an endless, ear-piercing, metaplas scream, the skimmer's belly scraped forward across stone until it slammed into the power housing on top of the building. The cocoon around Tsia stretched forward. Her fingers clutched the infant. Blood rushed to the front of her body. Her brain and guts pressed forward against her bones and the foam supports that held her in, and, like a bungee, the molded pads soaked up the impact. There was an instant of suspension, a fraction of a second where time and motion were stilled, and then, slowly, smoothly, the cushions eased back into softs. Tsia began to breathe.

As the pads folded themselves away, they split cleanly from the skimmer passengers and reformed into the sides of the chairs. Tsia looked down. The infant in her arms wailed softly, and she crooned to it as the hissing of crash foam flooded the hull.

Ramok had not waited for the flexan to pull back completely. Even as the soft reformed, he leapt up and lunged at the hatch, wrenching the door partway open. He did not have a chance to jump free. The foam was already spinning out over the cracked nose and open hatch like a thousand webs, and as he watched, it thickened and hardened to a shell of solid white.

"Blast-damned, digger-spawned, pile of johnnie droppings," he cursed. "Make ready," he commanded. "They will be here in minutes, and after that they can crack us like an egg or gas us anytime. Spade, monitor the holotank. Horen, stay on your lines."

The mercs checked their weapons automatically. Nitpicker, jumping up from her soft as soon as it retracted, snatched up her set of wafer packs and attached them to her harness. Tsia, impatient to move, forced herself to stay seated and out of the way, clutching the infant and crooning to its tiny ears. Spade nearly tripped over her legs, and she drew them back quickly, then glanced at Yemene.

"Ramok," Tsia cut in haltingly. There was blood pooling at the woman's crotch. It stained the sponges of the wipes that had been set against her vaginal opening, and as he saw the extent of it, Ramok's lips tightened. "Check her," he commanded curtly.

Forrest glanced over and shook his head. "She's dead." He did not have to touch the woman; in his gate, he could feel no life in the birth-weakened body.

The old guide glanced at him, reached over, and placed his fingers against the councilwoman's throat, but her pulse was gone— her blood flowed out from gravity, not from the pumping of her heart. The gray-haired guide looked at Ramok, then at Tsia, who still clutched the infant to her chest. He had heard what Yemene had said to Tsia; now his eyes were grim.

"She did not name the boy," Tsia whispered.

The old guide touched the child gently on its head, then moved to Yemene and pulled the sheet up over her face.

"Horen," Ramok asked curtly, "what's on the node?"

"No skimmers active; no gravpads active." The voice was dry, without inflection. "Could be hiding some of their scansigns in those clouds. Weather is thick enough in the scannet to mask a lot of power use if the ghost lines are set right."

Tsia got to her feet. She held the baby protectively, almost fiercely to her chest. "Ramok," she interrupted.

"What?" he snapped. "What?" he asked more gently.

"We could melt our way out of here."

"Negative. Not even a variable sword works on crash foam. It takes evac or salvage gear to melt this stuff." Salvage gear like the snakes controlled by the artists . . . . He did not have to voice that thought; Tsia could read it in his mind.

He was already turning away when Forrest cut in with his low, gravelly voice: "Feather has a mole."

Ramok halted.

Tsia nodded. "I used it on ice compounds, metaplas, and flexan. The foam—"

"Is a flexan compound." Ramok's eyes narrowed to the bronze-colored disk she pulled awkwardly from her pocket as she shifted the limp, wriggling infant into a cradling position in her left arm. "How fast does it work?"

"Fast."

Wren jerked one of his oversized hands toward the door. "She doesn't have to work through the hull. Hatch is open, even if the foam is already hard."

Ramok nodded at her curtly. "Do it."

Tsia moved to the door and, with the infant still cradled in her arm, set the mole against the webbed, glossy wall of foam. With their flexors drawn and shaped, Wren, Forrest, and Nitpicker waited. Wren was ice-cold and calm; Forrest, dark and brooding but balanced on the balls of his feet. Nitpicker was silent, her eyes unfocused, her flexor in one hand and her fibergun in the other, her attention split between the node and the door.

Feeling them over her shoulder, Tsia pushed the sense of the cats out of her mind and reached for the flexan pattern she had found before in the node. She caught up its details, modified it for the crash foam, and imaged it onto the mole. For an instant the foam before her seemed to shudder. Then it dissolved, melted, and crisped away in a faint cloud of gas that clung to the rest of the foam surfaces and crawled away in the stiff wind. As quickly as it melted, the sensors picked up the movement of air between the skimmer cabin and the outside, and webs sprayed out again. Wren, about to dart through the opening, drew back quickly. One of the strands caught on his shoulder, and the webs flowed in after it. Instinctively, he jerked, then forced himself to stand still.

"Quick!" Nitpicker snapped.

Tsia shifted and caught up the pattern. In a second the solid strand began to soften and melt. Flowing along his arm, it dripped down to the floor, where it rehardened into a slick puddle. Wren grimaced.

"Next time," she muttered. The wall was thin—still building up again—and she fixed her focus on the mole. This time, when it melted into the hole, Wren went through before the white webs began to spray. Nitpicker was next, then Forrest. The opening became thicker as webs built up on its sides. Ramok, barely waiting for the hole to open again, practically threw the old man out. Spade, grabbing up his extra e-wrap, jammed it into his pocket and followed the gray-haired guide. Horen jumped through without a word, and Tsia forced herself not to recoil from the blond merc's presence. Ramok followed Horen closely, and then only Tsia and the infant were left.

Though she was outwardly calm, Tsia's heart beat in her throat. Her hands itched to spread claws and tear at the foam. She had to force herself to hold the mole to the hissing foam. She looked down at the infant, then, with the mole in one hand, created the hole through which she herself jumped. She did not have a chance to land. Not waiting for her to hit the uneven stone roof, Ramok grabbed her arm in midair and hustled her and the baby after the other mercs. As if they gave wings to her boots, Tsia felt the cat feet speeding faintly through her mind with the sense of Ramok's urgency. She sucked in the gritty air and tasted the ash of metaplas. The air made her feel light-headed. Or was it the virus? She shook her head, trying to clear her senses. Behind her the crash foam re-formed itself in a bulge around the door until the skimmer and its potential fluid leaks were sealed completely from the air.

She caught a glimpse of the streets: To her right, above the level of the gray temple roof, the lower walkspans were cracked and melted; a coring laser had burned through their substance. A third walkway hung out above the street below, its other end blasted into nothingness where the building to which it had been connected was raw with a gaping hole. There was no bright sun to glisten off the once-white spans or rain to wash away their stink; the day seemed plain and strangely dull, as if it did not care what happened below its skies.

She glanced back once, as if the skimmer had offered some sort of protection, but the mass of crash foam that now covered the ship made the wreck look like a white tumor on the gray temple top. She felt a shudder begin deep in her muscles. She did not want to follow Horen or any of the other mercs. She wanted to leap down the sides of this temple and run for the safety of the streets. Run to the cliffs. Run back to the Cheba Rift.

Instead, she ran with Ramok toward the power structure on the roof. Feet pounding, the infant's head and body clutched tightly to her breast, she caught a hasty glance of a tall blue-gray structure that rose like a massive square twist. The logo of the mining guild was etched in the stone rim around its top story; the burned-out spans that arched away spoke of the accuracy of the freepicks.

A glance to the other side showed a white building shaped like a double coil that was only half-carved-out. Two stories up from the ground-level pedpaths a hole had been blasted through the white curved wall that faced the temple. The bent metaplas of the wall had flowered out in a ragged design. Inside the hole two figures sat calmly on the torn floor, watching the street below as if they were sitting in a dreamer bar and enjoying the show. The line of carving that flowed along the building's sides beneath them brought a chill to Tsia's skin. She stumbled and barely caught her balance before Ramok could jerk her forward. The art guild. Right next to the miners. She bared her teeth and caught her breath in a hiss. The infant in her arms wailed softly.

Past the old guide, into the power housing, Ramok pulled her with him. Her view of the art guild was cut off. She caught only a glimpse of the cramped dives of the alleys on the northwest edge of the town; they were low and half-hidden by the buildings next door. The cat feet in her head sneaked out of the gate and pressed her to run, to flee to the alleys. She could hide there, hide in the thick of the buildings like the cats that hid in the thick of the woods. And at dusk she could slink from the city and flee to the cliffs . . .

The mercs pressed back onto the gravplate; Tsia hesitated. Then Forrest's huge hand closed over her arm and yanked her in.

Ramok looked back out at the gray-haired man who stayed on the roof. "Horen will unjam your link when we get to safety. Otherwise, the merc guild will do it for you. You are logged and authorized for second-level compensation—MG127."

The old man glanced at Tsia, and she could almost feel him pushing a challenge to her through her gate. "Go back to the cats," he said, his old blue eyes burning into hers. "They'll keep you alive. If you've got the will to live. If you've got the guts."

Ramok stepped back; Nitpicker imaged the portal closed. The gravpad sank down to the next floor. With a subsonic hum it stopped at the maintenance room of the temple, but instead of opening to let them off, it automatically locked a fraction of a second before a shock wave rippled across the lower story and hit the upper lifts. Tsia stumbled against Ramok's arm; Wren grabbed the walls for support. Then the rumble passed, the door flickered open, and they lunged out of the tube.

Wren staggered out of the lift and, with his eyes darting from one side of the room to the other, crossed the room in a flash. Spade stepped out and glanced back at Horen. "Cluster bomb?"

Horen nodded and imaged a set of commands to the node, twisting his query through a dozen webs so that it did not appear to come from his location in the temple. "Cease-fire broke the moment we landed," he reported.

Ramok, already striding across the room after Wren, called back over his shoulder. "Nitpicker, give us the overlay."

Still clutching the baby tightly, Tsia stepped out between the rows upon rows of power cells. There were no filter-field doors on either end of the room; there were black bulkheads instead to block it off from the rest of the building. She tried to reach through the bulkhead doors with her gate, but her mind confused the physical sense of stored power that hung in the room with the mental presence of the mercs.

" 'Picker," Ramok snapped, "you got the plan yet?"

"Affirmative. Overlay on delta three one five," Nitpicker returned. "Lot of power surging subsurface. The coring lasers are hot and active."

"Horen," Ramok ordered, "watch for spikes on the energy scans. Any sign of a tight-beam breaker or a deep-salvage snake?"

"Negative. Negative." Horen shook his head absently, fixing their ghost lines in the node, while the mercs linked in and picked up the mental map through Nitpicker's coordinates. "Some unverified scans coming out of both the mining and art guilds. They've got something, but it's nothing I can clear."

Tsia, imaging into the node, watched her own stolen ID dot spin out and shift and saw herself become a temple worshiper in the node. Her scansign disappeared from the upper level and merged with the mass of the congregation that registered on the floor below; her ID dot became that of a young mother with a year-old child. Her hands closed protectively on the baby. It began to wail, and she ducked her head like a cat and sniffed its face. The tiny infant, wriggling in her grasp, became quiet as she soothed it with a crooning purr. If this were her own child, she would name him . . . If she lived long enough to do so. If she had the guts to live . . . The crooning died in her throat.

She tightened her lips, brushing them against the tiny head, then straightened, balancing again on the balls of her feet. Forrest, Ramok—they would get her back to the rift. She could keep this child safe until then. Daya—her gate—would give her that much strength.

Ramok reached the opposite door and spun to face them. "Listen close," he ordered. "We are one street and the width of the plaza away from the council building. We'll run the block on the pedpaths, then circle the inside perimeter of the square to the other side. We can't go around the guild buildings this far back from the plaza. The longer we take to get there, the greater the chance they will pinpoint us on their scans. We will go right between the guilds. That's where their own scansigns will be burning thick in the net. With Horen's ghost lines we have the best chance of hiding among them, not outside."

Horen met Ramok's eyes. "I might not be able to verify our entrance codes at the council building. Access is locked down, and I can't crack their node lines even with the authorization we got from Yemene."

"Power shift? Miners got into the council?"

"Don't know. But it almost looks—" He glanced at Tsia. "—as if the council doesn't want to know we are here. As if they don't want the kid to get back."

She set her jaw at his taunting expression. Cat senses made her nose too sharp, and she smelled his breath as if he suffocated her with it. Her hands curled protectively around the infant. "If they don't let us in—" she snarled.

"If they don't let us in—" Ramok's face was cold. "—we will just go on through." His gaze swept their group. "Once in," he said curtly, "we deliver the child to Feldon, second in council. With Yemene out, no one else—unless Feldon's dead—has authorization to sign out our contract. You've got his scansign in your link." The mercs nodded. Ramok nodded at the thin woman. "Nitpicker, you're point from here on out. Tau-six formation. Tsia, you're with me. Watch for suckouts," he added sharply. "Some of the mines could be falling through."

Nitpicker moved ahead; Wren and Forrest fell back. Horen and Spade brought up the rear, behind Ramok, who shielded Tsia's body with his own. She no longer had her blunter; they had forgotten it on the ridge. In the city her sand-colored shirt would be an easy visual target for a spec laser; the white medcloth around the baby made it even worse.

They went through the door quickly, reading the scansigns for the building off the node. A wave of scent seemed to suffocate her, and Tsia reeled in the flood of fear and excitement that seemed to emanate from the mercs who surrounded her. She breathed it in and let it fill her mind.

Ramok, reaching back, steadied her automatically. She jerked free. But there was a shudder growing in her slender frame. The nervous energy increased, making the cat feet pace irritably on the other side of her gate. She had to clench her jaw to clamp down on her gate; she used so much force that her teeth ground horribly together. Senses: the eye-quick sense of the hunt, the ear-sharp sense of the prey ... Which was she? The animal power swept through her gate and made her dance irritably behind Ramok. Now he did not have to urge her on: She moved because it was easier than standing still.

Two by two they filtered like ghosts through a long hallway. Within seconds they reached the next gravpad. Nitpicker motioned them to a halt. Without a word, she stepped forward, tucked her flexor in her harness, loosened a breaker disk, and, with the breaker hidden in her hand and the fibergun behind the length of her leg, took the lift down alone.

A minute later Horen grunted that the access below had cleared. They crowded onto the pad. With a nearly silent thrum the gravpad dropped, and the filter door for the lift shimmered opened to reveal Nitpicker standing guard over three temple personnel. One was unconscious, one had a broken arm, and the third, a sullen young woman, sat with her hands on her head and a bruise beginning to darken her pale, high-boned cheeks.

Tsia, holding the infant close, licked her lips. Nitpicker met Ramok's eyes with a shrug. "They resisted." She continued resetting the fibergun and slipped it back in its sheath.

Wren took over the guard, and Horen, following close behind, pulled his disks from his pockets. A second on the node, and he said shortly, "Got the links."

Ramok nodded. "Plug 'em."

With Forrest and Spade each holding down one of the temple workers, Horen inserted into the metaplas plugs into their temples, confirmed their webs, and linked them to his ghost lines. On his way after Nitpicker, Ramok stopped before them only briefly. "You are logged on MG127. Standard compensation. Complaints go to the guild." There was no sympathy on his face as Spade touch-tied the prisoners. In silence, the mercs left the room.

They passed into a hall and broke into a quick-paced jog. Another gravpad, and they came out into one of the wide side halls that led to the main worship chamber. The harmonic tones of singing echoed into the small hall.

". . . water shall wash the war from the soil . . ." The temple rumbled. The singing strengthened. ". . . the smoking warriors, the burning babe . . ."

Nitpicker slowed, and the group dropped its pace to a cautious forward creep.

". . . shall wash the stink of death from the soil. Shall wipe the future away . . ."

The singing vibrated in Tsia's temples, and she screwed up her face against its tones. Her ears seemed to twitch. Halted behind Ramok and pressed against his back by Spade, who moved up behind her, Tsia glanced down at the baby—at its tightly closed eyes. Daya, she thought, suddenly bleak, Vashanna had trusted the life of her child to Tsia, and that boy was dead. The children in the slough had trusted their lives to their teacher and then desperately to Tsia and her brothers and Jak, and now they were dead and entombed in the very mud of this earth. In her arms . . . Oh,

Daya, she held another child in her hands. An infant, like the ones she might never bear herself. A tiny, eyes-closed, trusting child, forced on her by a woman who thought she would bind the child to his esper-read destiny as tightly as Cekulu had bound Tsia with her own guilt. Forced on Tsia by a woman who, with her death, had chained Tsia to the child as surely as if she had touch-tied their skins. Tsia wanted to recoil from the infant; instead, she inhaled his strong-sweet odor and breathed him into her soul.

Ramok pulled her forward again, and she followed him on silent feet. They reached the end of the hall and paused only briefly to note the guard at the entrance arch to the sanctuary. The resonant, lyrical music contrasted oddly with the dark functionality of the guards, and Nitpicker grinned as she pulled her fibergun from her back. "I know that one," she whispered. "Took his training at Lonestone. Thinks he's the toughest thing this side of Chaos." She linked in and locked on the guard, and the fiber spun out, slicing through the man's collar to his neck as he turned. His eyes widened, his hand came halfway up, and he fell to his knees and then his side without more than a muffled thud.

Nitpicker winked at Wren. Abruptly, she stopped smiling. "I lost the link," she snapped to Horen. "He registered down."

Horen shot a glance at her and tried to pick up the web, but it had already spun out. "Too late to fix," he snarled. "Nodies will pick that up in a minute."

Ramok pointed at the narthex. "Go!"

Like a dog pack, they sped through the corner of the narthex to the side exit. When they spilled out onto the street, they did not stop. Tsia's heart pounded in the wind that cut down across the street. Her hands felt numb, and the weight of the baby was part of her chest. Daya, she prayed as she tried to call the cats back through her distance-darkened gate. Daya give me strength.

Outside, the diffused light of the clouded sky hit her like a slap. She winced and closed her eyes. Ramok felt her falter and grabbed her arm, hauling her after him. To their right a low-level blast rumbled down the green and gray patterned street.

Like a wave, the shock traveled along the metaplas, stone, and earthen beds. It staggered the mercs and threw them drunkenly from one side to the other as it passed with a smooth rippling in the ground. In its wake, between the lines of green, the street cracked in the middle. The wide stone paths fractured like a web between the buildings. Almost beneath their feet, a faint beam shot up through one of the cracks. The air seemed to crackle and burn near the light, and as the beam brightened, the ground began to melt away.

"They've read us!" Nitpicker shouted. She jumped away from the cracks. "Get off the paths!"

Panic hit Tsia with the smell of melting stone. She felt the speed from the cat feet in her mind and sprinted wildly, crashing through the growth lines and leaping awkwardly over shrubs as she ran with one arm crushing the infant to her chest. Behind her, the coring laser broke completely through the ground. Its beam sheared the air and hit one of the overhead spans, vaporizing the open arch with a roaring, snapping *whoosh* that seemed to crackle in her ears forever. Cats yowled in her head, and she screamed, unaware of the panicked light in her eyes. The edges of the walkspan dissipated into an exploding cloud of metaplas sand and pebbles. Then the blast of air hit her in the back and blew her against the building across the street.

She twisted instinctively to protect the child. Side-first, she slammed into the structure and staggered to her knees. Her shoulders had taken the brunt of the blast. Forrest hit the wall beside her, and Wren was blown against the bigger merc. Tsia shook her head; her ears were ringing. Then Ramok hauled her into the protected entranceway of the art guild.

She caught her breath raggedly, trying to calm the panic that swept into her mind with the realization of the walls against which she pressed. Cream-colored walls with the gray inlaid stone in a striking star and snake-curved pattern . . . Back to the art guild. Back to chains . . .

No! she shouted through her gate. She struggled against Ramok's iron hand, which held her behind him, against the wall of the guild. The infant in her arms wriggled its tiny hands inside the wrap and opened its mouth to cry as if it, too, would fight the pressure that held them there. A shudder shook her. It was a long instant before she realized that this one was in her body, not in the building. Slowly, her hands clenched away from the child so that she did not crush him, she sank against the wall, her eyes glued to the patterns of stars and snakes.

The design ground itself into her mind. For an instant, with the surge of cat sense swelling her mind, she did not hear the whine of the variable swords around the corner, the rumbling of the subsurface bombs, the shocking blast from the coring laser that vaporized the street, or the quick, harsh breathing of the mercs at her side. She did not see the six pairs of cold, black darkeyes that narrowed and darted and dissected the falling sand

and cracking streets and skimmers and darts that flitted through the air. She saw only this: the white and gray design of stars and snakes that curved across the wall. Stars that promised a freedom she would never see. Stars that promised a future this child would never have.

The street rumbled again, the wind blew cold and then hot with the fire of the coring laser, and another intersection of pedpaths began to melt away. "I name you," she whispered to the boy. "I, the Feather from the fire—" Her lips made a twisted, bitter smile "—name you Star. I defy the guild. I defy the chains of your destiny. I name you Hu'te. I name you Star."

The baby snuggled deeper against her body. He made no sound. Another rumble shook the ground, and Tsia snapped the medwipe over the baby's face to shelter it from the cloud of dust that blasted against her face and stung her lips and whipped her short hair back from her scalp.

The coring laser broke through the street a second time, its beam at a slant as it bit overhead into the edge of the building beneath which the seven figures crouched. Ramok held his arm across Tsia's chest, trapping her against the building's entrance, and, her eyes flashing and wild, she stared over his thick arm as dust and sand floated down. Her feet itched to run; her body was tense with the heart-pounding sense of the cats that flooded through her gate.

Across the street the temple guards pressed up inside the beveled doors while their reflections were distorted in the angled panes. They stared at the mercs as Tsia stared at them but did not come out into the street. They pointed at her; they gestured at the child. The music that escaped the low, broad building echoed eerily between the broken spans that arched across the street. Now only the whooshing blast from the laser that hungered for metal, not mere stone, punctuated the temple singing.

No skimmers or darts dodged the laser's beam between the spans; no traffic of any kind broke across the streets. Wren eyed the rubble with quick, sharp eyes. " 'Let the humans hide,' " he quoted wryly, " 'so the machines can do the killing.' "

Ramok grinned. Above them a corner of the curved building blew out, raining debris down on the pedpaths. Still none of the mercs moved. The baby began to wriggle.

"Why do we wait?" Tsia whispered sharply.

Ramok did not take his eyes from the sky. "Darts," he returned shortly.

The coring laser faded to a subsurface beam, and a second later two needlelike air riders flashed past the building entrance. They came to a spinning halt near the ground holes, then fired their mounted spec lasers into the smoking stone maw. Neither rider glanced toward the mercs. "Stinger-9000. On scan, not visual," Ramok added. He waited another second, and a skimmer sliced across the street, then shot straight up toward the roof of another structure. The stingers followed.

"Clear," Horen reported curtly.

"To the right. Go!" Ramok directed.

Nitpicker darted out into the rubble, disappearing in the clouds of dust that gusted up with the wind. Wren and Forrest followed, the small merc like a spider scuttling across the loose sand, the massive one gliding through. Ramok and Tsia were on their heels like glue. Spade waited scant seconds with Horen while the last merc reset their ghost line, then the two men raced after the others. They rounded the building and dodged into the sunken side entrance to the art guild, but as they barreled into the space, Spade cursed and lunged on through the group, then wrenched at the door. He dragged a young man from behind it and glared at him so that the youth cringed with horror.

"He's trade, not guild," Horen said, verifying the young man's link. "Drop him."

The youth's eyes went to Tsia and to the baby in her arms. "Mercs—warriors!" He gasped. "Smoking warriors—and the babe!"

Spade shoved him back inside the side door, then tore a finger welder off one strip of his harness and ran it down the lock in a fiery line. Tsia stared at the white face of the youth who was pressed against the now-smoking crystal door. Then Ramok yanked her around and shoved her toward the next building. She flinched as two skimmers hummed overhead.

"Run!" Ramok commanded. Like wasps changing direction for a kill, the skimmers zipped to the right and sped away into the plaza, to disappear around the corner of the mining guild. Tsia felt their hum ring in her ears and bones, and the shudders it triggered made her feet clumsy on the street. Cats padded in her head and confused her thoughts. Her nose smelled people, sweat, then fire and ash. The new scent of the baby clogged her nostrils; the odor of melted metaplas filled her mouth. She swallowed, gagged, then spit out the taste. The rubble that still rolled in the dust absorbed the moisture as if it had never been.

Four freepicks staggered around the corner, glared at the mercs, then ran on. The mercs ignored them. One of the freepicks halted in midstride a meter away and whipped around. One side of his face was bruised and bleeding, but his eyes were wide and excited. "The child?" he demanded harshly as the mercs continued running. He took a step after them.

"Get out of here!" Ramok thundered over his shoulder.

The ground rumbled, and the freepick staggered. Ramok grabbed Tsia to steady her, and dust clouded the air. Muffled by the wrap, the baby wailed.

The freepick stared at them. "The smoking warriors!" he accused in exultation. "The burning babe! Hey!" he shouted at his companions. He turned and raced after them. "Hey!"

Her breathing harsh, Tsia shoved herself away from Ramok. A hundred meters away, to her right, shrill cries broke out, and another coring laser broke through the plaza stone in the middle of the open space between the guilds. For a second, the blue-white beam burned air, then it tilted, wavered, and fell over, biting across the square as, below the surface, its mount was blasted by a heavy cluster bomb. The rippling that swept the pedpaths was concentrated. Tsia's free hand gripped Ramok blindly; her other arm curled around the infant. Her eyes were wide as she watched the laser burn its perfect path below the surface, vaporizing rock and subsurface supports in a smoking, lengthening underground tube that ate its way toward the art building.

Ramok cursed under his breath. "Go! 'Picker, you got the locks. Horen," he ordered over his shoulder, "—make it look good. We want them to think we're going in for an attack, not around toward the council. Haul in the traces. I want all attention on the inside of this building."

Tsia's legs felt numb, but her heart was pounding fast, and she followed on Ramok's heels. The mole in her pocket hung heavily; the baby's weight dragged at her arms, and there was fear in her mouth: a thick, choking fear that tasted like burned paper and smelled of dusty ash. In her head the cat feet paced and leapt back and forth through her gate, speeding, then slowing her feet as she read their animal power and pushed it into her fevered limbs, then tried to shut them out of her mind. She ran full-tilt toward the walls of the mining guild and twisted only at the last second to slam her back against the dubious protection of its stone. Spade and Horen threw themselves against the wall beside her, and Forrest, with a single blow of his flexor, smashed through the lock panel at the gate of the guild. In an instant Nitpicker linked herself in.

"She's got a match," Tsia whispered urgently, noting the flame-throwing tube on her back. "Why doesn't she burn her way in?"

Spade searched the skies for signs of other skimmers. "Using a match on a filter field causes a fire flare, then opaques the door on automatic reflex." His words were hurried, absent; his eyes darted down the street. "Fire backblast isn't bad—blunter will take it—but it's five minutes to burn your way through a door that's been opaqued. Hell of a lot less time to link in and close down the security locks."

In the square of the plaza a woman poked her head over the smoking rim of the laser's perfect hole, looked warily around, caught a glimpse of the mercs, then ducked back out of sight.

" 'Picker?" Horen breathed.

"Almost—"

"I can't hold off the node when the visuals read us clear."

"Got it." The doors shivered, their subsonic hum dying out as the woman jerked back. "Forrest?"

The big merc stepped forward and wrenched at the tiny gap in the doors.

Horen hissed, "Make it fast, Forrest. We've got to get inside to get clean access—" His voice cut off abruptly. He cursed. An instant later two dozen freepicks poured out of the hole in the plaza like ants boiling from their hill. Tsia felt the force of their charge like a blast of mental wind in her face.

"Ramok," Horen said urgently, "we've got to shag ass *now*!"

"As you were," Ramok snapped. For an instant his darkeyes pierced the facades surrounding the square, ignoring the freepicks who split and raced toward the mining guild and the council building.

Tsia's eyes followed the freepicks, but in her biogate she sensed something else—something like a thundercloud hanging overhead. Hunching her shoulders around the infant, she raised her free hand and pointed at the front of the council building across the square. "There . . ."

Horen and Ramok followed her finger. Horen searched into the node as Ramok and Wren stiffened.

"The perimeter's a trap," Horen hissed. " 'Picker, close the access."

"As you were!" Ramok ordered harshly. "Forrest, rag on it!"

As if his words had broken open the very buildings, the facades of the council tower and the mining guild seemed to shift out from their supports. Barely ten meters away armed figures cast off their e-wraps and surged into the plaza against the freepicks. The two nearest miners caught sight of the mercs; one's eyes widened in surprise. Without thinking, the miners lunged toward the corner; Ramok jumped forward first. He spun the lead man, stomped the back of his knee, then caught the woman and threw her bodily into the street. The man spun on his knee, and Ramok slammed his elbow into the guilder's head. The miner dropped without another sound.

Tsia, poised on the balls of her feet, darted her gaze from one side to the other. Energy—there was too much force in the air. The cat feet scratched and clawed at her thoughts, tensing and rippling her muscles to force her to run, but Spade grabbed her arm and ruthlessly held her in place.

From behind the mercs, up the street, came another shouting mass. Yelling and jumping over the rubble, the freepicks raced toward the plaza. Forty meters away, then thirty-five . . . Nitpicker, rocking from foot to foot, waited in tense silence as Forrest rammed his flexor into the door frame and wrenched at the stubborn metaplas. Spade stepped out between the freepicks and Tsia. In her head Tsia saw the ID dots of the freepicks sweep down the street, the dots of the G-men and miners clash. She could not see herself in the node except as a faint, unverified scan—Horen's ghost lines still set her link in the temple—but in her head, with the cat feet pacing and turning through her thoughts, she felt the bioenergy beat against her body like a tide. Sweat ran down the sides of her face, soaking up the dust in the air. She hung, poised, on the corner of the building as Forrest forced his way in.

On the inside a guild man skidded around the foyer corner and ran toward the doors. The wide disk of a tight-beam breaker was in his hands, and he brought it up with a grim, determined look. *Forrest!* Tsia cried out through her gate. The sense of the cats surged and washed over her thoughts. She felt as if she pushed power into his muscles—into his body—with the very force of her thoughts.

Forrest's shoulders bunched. He made a strangled sound and wrenched one more time at the doors. The metaplas shuddered back. The guild man shouted. And then Forrest's flexor spiked out and caught him in the chest, skewering the man like a frog as the man's own momentum impaled him on the blade. The guilder gave a choking cry. His hands rose up to the thin spike that pierced his ribs, then he began to fall.

Forrest snapped the flexor back and shoved his way inside with his shoulders, his left arm hanging limply by his side. The shadowed planes of his face were sharpened with the tautness of his expression. Tsia darted inside after him. Her senses were heightened by the cats that swarmed in her mind. In her arms the baby wriggled, and she clutched it more tightly, shoving at the cougars that flooded through her gate while Spade shouldered past her and Ramok dragged her to the side.

Three more miners skidded around the corner of the foyer; each one bore a variable sword with the fluctuating laser active. Behind them, two more men raced in.

Nitpicker grinned and leapt forward, but Wren beat her to the first miner. Ramok thrust Tsia back at Spade, but the merc had already jumped one of the guild men. It was Horen who grabbed Tsia's arm and spun her behind him, shoving her to the side, where her back was no longer exposed to the clear crystal door. She staggered from his grip, the cats growling horribly in her head, and then he placed himself in front of her, one hand on her arm to feel her presence, the other with his flexor in front of him and an eager trembling in his limbs. Tsia shrank from his touch, but his grip tightened on her bicep, and his sunburned skin was slick with sweat in spite of the coolness of the inner reception area. He paid her no attention; his mind was in the node, casting webs on the dots of the miners and hiding the mercs' actions in a set of ghosts that spun out, fractured, and re-formed with his thoughts.

In front of Tsia, Wren's flexor cut through the variable blade of the first guilder, and the mining woman's fluctuating laser reformed on the other side of his sweep. Wren did not even hesitate. His flexor, shaped like a club, smashed down on the woman's shoulder, then snapped back, and the guilder dropped to the floor with a scream.

Forrest went straight in and, one-handed, knocked aside the varblade of the miner who had picked him out. With the same hand he snagged the man by his collar and lifted him. The man's laser sword swung wildly. Forrest danced back to keep his body out of the beam and shook the man till he dropped the weapon. Its blade went inactive the instant his hand left the hilt.

Behind him, with her flexor spread into a three-web net, Nitpicker snapped her weapon across a tall woman's varblade. The flex net passed through the variable beam with only a singe of metaplas and caught the wielder's hand. Nitpicker twisted and dodged the flashing laser, then grappled the woman to the ground.

Only Ramok took a burn when he grabbed the weapon of a smaller, lightweight man who twisted incredibly fast and caught him on the side. With a hissed curse, Ramok swung the weapon—

the man hung on to it grimly—in a short, sharp arc. The man slammed into the floor with a groan, half raised his head, then collapsed.

Tsia's feet were dancing to run; cat feet screamed in her head to flee, to fight, to find the safety of the heights, but Horen's hand was immovable. She struggled silently against his grip until finally, with the guilders down on the floor, Horen pulled her up to Ramok and shoved her into the other merc's arms. Without a word, Horen pulled more plugs from his pack and, as he had before, cut off the four still-living miners from the node.

Forrest grabbed two guilders; Spade grabbed the other pair, and all four were dragged, groaning, to a side office where the console inside could be unlinked and the door welded shut. Nitpicker was still grinning, but there was a bruise beginning on her forehead and her eyes were alight with a violent fire.

Tsia felt as if the mercs' emotions were burning her mind—their excitement forced her own heart to pound harder, made the fever sweat run more freely down her back. She clenched the infant, loosened her hold as he cried out, and soothed him with sounds that were more like a low-voiced growling than words.

Ramok grabbed her shoulder. "Up to the walkspan," he ordered.

Forrest ran toward the gravpad, but Horen halted abruptly. "We're registered—" He did not even finish speaking before the gravpad lights dimmed and its door opaqued into shutdown mode.

Imaging into the node, Nitpicker followed Horen's trace. The net of scans that the miners had set up had closed on the foyer and read the fluid traces left on the floor from the guilders. "All lifts are shutting down," she confirmed. "All gravpads are off."

Tsia felt the presence of background energy fading through her gate. The cat feet surged, then washed back into the biolink before the sudden focus with which she shoved them down. She tried to read the bioenergies she felt, but she could sense nothing but the mercs in the foyer and the four miners on the other side of the wall. "Forrest," she said urgently. "They are withdrawing."

Forrest glanced back at her and frowned; Ramok motioned to Horen for confirmation, but the blond merc was still setting his ghost lines, and Nitpicker shook her head first. "Negative," she reported. "There are still thirty guilders in the upper halls."

"The stairs, then. Let's go." Ramok motioned for them to follow him, but Horen held up his hand. "Hold! Those are ghosts, not guilders on the link. The *nyeka* is right. They have withdrawn into the inner halls."

"Outer hall status?" Ramok asked sharply.

"On lockout."

Wren, poised on the balls of his feet, glanced at Ramok. "That's an art guild trick. They use that type of hall access to keep their own work separate from each other."

"They wanted us here," Tsia whispered. "They are driving us."

Ramok swung around, his darkeye piercing Tsia's ice-blue gaze. "Yes," he said softly. His gaze flickered to the infant. "They want us dead." His eyes narrowed. "They have withdrawn completely?" he demanded of Horen.

"Affirmative."

"Then they will loose their deep-salvage snakes. Nitpicker, can you get us into the stairwell?"

"Take me three minutes. Maybe more. They've locked out their own access."

Ramok shoved Tsia toward the manual stairs. "Burn it. Use the mole."

She fumbled for her pocket, and Spade reached for the infant in her arms, but she jerked back. Hu'te was hers, she snarled silently. She yanked the bronze wafer from her pocket and slapped it against the metaplas door of the stairwell. Reaching out, she found that Horen had imaged the node ahead of her; he had already located the pattern of the metaplas and sent it down to her link. The molecular structure almost jumped into her mind. Unaware that her lips were curled back from her teeth and her shoulders had tensed as if she were about to be struck, she closed her eyes to the sense of his imaged voice and focused on the door. One second, then two, and a hot spot appeared. Daya, she snapped at the cats in her mind, why was it so slow?

"They're fighting you." Horen leaned over her shoulder. "There's a nodie on the link. Let me—"

"Get away!" She jerked away from him; the mole faltered, and Ramok wrenched the blond merc back, thrusting him behind Spade.

"Tsia," Forrest said urgently. "Focus."

She caught the mole as the door melted suddenly, its material running down in thick rivulets to the floor. She started to rise, but Wren gripped her shoulder, his stringy arm and huge hand like a monster claw next to her neck. "Nitpicker first." He held her until the other woman crawled through. Forrest was only a second behind. Ramok was third, then Wren.

"Now. Up. Hurry." He pulled her roughly through. "To the walkspan above."

Cat feet urged her up, and her taut legs took the stairs two at a time. Behind her Spade's feet were silent. Horen's boots slapped the stone flight in a hard, pounding rhythm. A part of her brain caught the sounds like the slapping of his hand against her face, and the fevered energy in her limbs drove her to a greater speed.

Up ahead Nitpicker and Forrest slammed through the upper door—not even the art guild could lock out the inside of an emergency stairwell—out of the flight and into the tiny foyer of the second floor. Ramok and Wren were only an instant behind. Tsia, clutching the child and catching her breath with difficulty, felt her energy surge with every pump of her lungs. She pushed the cats back from her gate and ran out onto Ramok's heels, then paused because the faintness hit her hard. She put out her hand and caught at Spade's arm as he jumped up beside her. Her heart was pounding so hard, she had to force herself to see.

A dozen shimmering doors led out from the circular area; three textured corridors curved away. Which way? she cried out in her head. The cats tried to force her to run, but she held her ground, stepping only when Spade drew her forward, out of the stairwell doorway. She thrust back the cats, forced the gate to close down into darkness. She had the control, she snarled at herself stubbornly. She had the will to live.

Nitpicker needed no direction from Ramok. As the woman skidded into the middle of the foyer, she leapt the form chairs in the small area and, imaging into the node, found her link still clear. She darted toward the eastern corridor. Forrest, followed by Ramok and Wren, ran after her. Tsia started to follow the others, but Ramok glanced back.

"Salvage snakes," he explained curtly over his shoulder. He made a sharp gesture for her to wait.

She hesitated, the cat voices surging back, eager in her mind. She shivered, then shook so badly that the child in her arms cried out.

"*Eshe,*" Spade hissed, standing on the balls of his feet and waiting for Horen, crouched in the door of the stairwell, to finish setting his webs.

Tsia's breath came too quickly. She could feel the threat, feel the sense of air moving where it should not. Her ice-blue eyes pierced every corner of the foyer and darted from the stairs to the corridor down which Ramok had almost disappeared. It was behind her, she was certain, but she could see nothing to give her dread a name. Nothing except Horen.

Horen grunted. "Got it." He started to rise.

Spade motioned for Tsia to run beside him and broke into a jog, but Horen made a strange, choking sound behind her. Tsia froze and turned in midstride to see his lips stretch in a grin. He gave a strange cough, and Tsia, the cats in her biogate screaming at her to run, leap high to the chairs—jump up to anything—backed away.

Spade turned and cursed as she did not run. Horen's left hand raised halfway; his back arched; his flexor dropped to the floor. His sunburned face, now ashen, suddenly convulsed, and from his back a length of twisting, coiling metal hovered and flowed back down the steps from between the stairwell doors.

Tsia could only stare. Her legs, once numb, seemed like ice. In a slow-motion leap, Spade came back through the air. His flexor snapped into a razor-thin blade, and he shouted so slowly that the sound seemed to be made only of vowels. The weapon came down behind Horen in a long, sweeping motion that seemed to creep through the air so that she could see the shift of light across the metaplas blade.

Time snapped back suddenly. The writhing salvage snake whipped slightly out of Horen's back. Then Horen staggered forward against Tsia's arms, his hands gripping her biceps as he weakened. She yanked back, hunching to protect the child from his embrace. In the stairwell, jerked down the stairs, Spade hooked his flexor into the still-hovering snake and was slammed brutally against the wall by its headless body.

"Ramok!" Tsia screamed. Horen stared into her eyes. The baby, clutched too tightly in her panic, cried out in a loud, shrill wail. Tsia staggered back, dragging Horen forward. She did not notice the broken-off snake in his back. She did not notice his blood on the floor. All that filled her sight was the leering, blond-haired merc hanging off her arm. All that filled her mind was the smell of him, the feel of his fingers still a threat to her skin, the breath of him clogging her lungs.

His hands were like talons; his eyes were like hooks dragging her down with him to the floor. Tiny flecks of bubbled air pressed out from between the merc's bloody lips. He twisted them into a smile. "You wanted me to share your gate," he whispered. "You wanted me . . ."

She stared at him in horror. His voice in the cabin on the skimmer, his fingers ripping at her chest . . . The baby's wail grew more terrified. The pounding of Ramok's feet was hidden in the pounding of her heart.

"You wanted—me," Horen repeated.

His hands on her arms. His hands on her throat, her neck . . . Tsia's blue eyes went hard and icy. With a desperate snarl, she shook him off, and he hung over the floor, balanced for an instant in time. A naught, she realized, lusting for the gate he could never have. Longing as Tsia had longed, caught in the web of his dreams. If she lost her virus, would she do this to herself—chain her life to her dreams? Tear and hate the gates of others? Tams snarled, and her lips curled back.

She looked into his eyes. There was no expression in the dark-eyes that hid his gaze. She felt her hand curl into a claw. "You aren't even worth my hate," she said softly. Deliberately, she stepped back.

The merc slid to his knees, the bright blood red on his lips, and she did not stoop to help him when he fell. He looked at her, his head sideways on the floor, and the red trail dribbled across his cheek. His eyes never blinked. Tsia stood and watched, her own eyes blazing. Somewhere, as Ramok thrust past her and threw himself down the stairwell after Spade, as the shoulders of the cougars softened in her mind, as the tension of the tams relaxed so that they padded only once more through her gate, the horror let go of her guts, and she saw, without a shudder after all, that the man was dead.

She exhaled the smell of his body and breath from her lungs. In the opening of the hallway Forrest stood, his one arm at his side. Tsia turned and looked at him. Slowly, he nodded.

Within seconds the baby in her arms began to quiet. Waiting, tense in the tortured silence, she rocked on the balls of her feet. She murmured to the infant and stared at him out of eyes too bright in her fever-pale face. Was Hu'te esper enough to feel her fear of Horen, her anger at the guild? The exultation of the cats in her mind? Was that what had made him cry and quiet, wriggle and subside? She took a step toward Forrest, and Ramok and Spade burst back up out of the stairwell. Spade's flexor was charred in one spot, and the blade refused to re-form around the laser-crisped material. He breathed raggedly, and Ramok's face was sweating.

"Light the roof," Ramok ordered Forrest. "Burn it all! That snake was imaged for heat—the fire will confuse the others." He caught his breath. "Tsia, go with Forrest. I'll run anchor with Spade."

Spade, favoring one side like Ramok, pulled a small hisser tube from his harness and, leaning down to jerk Horen's blunter disk from the dead man's jacket, pointed the hisser and smoked the body. Turning purple, then black, Horen's flesh disintegrated, and his clothes faded away until he left only a stain surrounding the smooth metal head of the snake. Wren and Nitpicker, racing back from far down the hall, came to a stop as they saw the smoke in the foyer and the torn snake on the floor. Nitpicker glanced at Spade's hisser impassively.

Ramok did not need to explain. "Nitpicker, you've got the ghost lines; you're on the links. Get the fire codes off line and mask our dots as best you can." He shoved Tsia toward the corridor. "That was a refitted salvage snake, not a rescue worm. It had both lasers and breakers in its mouth."

Behind him, Forrest pointed his matchtube at the fabric ceiling, and a lick of color touched the cloth. The fabric burst into flames, and instantly sparks and cinders fell down on Forrest's head. He wiped at them irritably, ducked to the side, pointed the match at another spot, and torched the roof again.

Tsia watched him, missing Ramok's words as she felt the fever pull the sweat from her skin. Her feet itched: She could dance in this fire, except it was on the roof . . . The sense of the cats in her head swept back in, and she lost her focus on the thought as her eyes were drawn to the flames and mesmerized by the lights that swept across the ceiling.

Ramok grabbed her arm and shook her out of her reverie. "Tsia, listen. The fire will hide us from the sensors in the snakes. Even if they receive instructions through the node for our locations, their physical readings of the other heat sources will confuse them. Your jumpsuit will protect your body, but you don't have a blunter to pull up to protect your hands and head. Can you walk the flames?" He shook her arm. "Feather, dammit, can you stay beneath the fires? You've got to protect your head and hands."

"Yes," she responded slowly. "But the baby . . ."

"Can you shield him? If not, give him to me." He started to reach for the child, but Tsia pulled back.

"No!" She cradled his head protectively to her chest. "I can take him."

"Spade." He turned sharply. "Your e-wrap—"

The other merc dug in his pocket and tossed Ramok the small package.

Ramok snapped the sheet out. "Wrap the boy in this. It's not as good as a blunter, but double-wrapped, it should do for a short run. Stay beneath the flames. Make no sound. Salvage and rescue snakes sense vibration, not just heat." He turned toward the corridor. "Nitpicker, you got the firelinks closed?"

"Affirmative. Heat sensors and fire control are disabled completely. Vents are open; filters and fans are on. I got in under their codes—took their damage-control links out for this floor and the two above us. I could not get street level or anything higher up."

Ramok's face darkened. "Dammit—they'll have traced that snake, and if they have one, they will have at least four in the building." Behind him small, bright fires began to eat their way down the walls. Gases and smoke began to curl down with the orange-red flames. His darkeye glance flicked to Forrest, then Tsia, noting the sweat that ran down each one's face. "Ready?"

"Affirmative," Forrest returned sharply. Tsia nodded silently.

"Then go!"

Above them, the fire raced along the ceiling, and the thick, clean smell of burning fabric began to fill Tsia's nose. With a feral grin she breathed in the hot rushes of air that swept the hall. Heat—flame to kiss her skin ... Had Horen felt this lust even when he became a naught? The fans were still on, and they vented the smoke to the ducts; Tsia savored the traces that were left. The blunter fabric of her jumpsuit shielded her body from the heat, and the sweat protected her head. Her short hair was instantly greased by fluid, and her hands were slick where she tried to hold on to the tiny form of the thickly swathed child. Her feet danced in their boots, longing to leap up into the thick of the flames, and she had to stifle the urge, tell herself to run plainly behind Forrest.

This was the fire of the prophecy—the words pounded into her head with her heartbeat. This, not Cekulu's art, was the fire that burned the babe. She clutched the e-wrap closer, keeping an air passage open and shielding that opening with her chest.

Around her, the mercs covered their heads with the extended collars of their blunters, but Tsia let the sweat flow across her neck. Her body glowed beneath her clothes. She could feel the seared air in her lungs. She grinned and kissed the heat with her glistening lips, unaware of the dark look Forrest cast back. In her head she could feel the cats leaping and swatting at each other through her gate; she could feel the sweat beading and hissing on her forehead. Forrest was energy; he was light; but he was just another dancer who jumped in the flames.

Ten meters, twenty ... The walkspan access was just up ahead, but a hovering line of gray, shining metal cut through the flames at the intersection.

"One up," Nitpicker said urgently.

The mercs skidded to a stop. Their blunters began to smoke as the flames licked down the ceiling toward their heads. Tsia forced herself to stand beneath a tongue of flame that dropped low across her shoulders and flickered against the back of her bowed head. Like fat in a frying pan, her sweat spritzed across her scalp, the balls of moisture sliding and sizzling. It was impossible to hold herself still, to deny the pull of the fire and the yammering of her gate. And then the fever, as if waiting for its chance, shook her.

The snake whipped its smooth, sightless head toward her body. Tsia froze. Her gate was suddenly cold and quiet. The snake wanted the mercs dead, her alive? How could Ramok be sure? Who imaged this snake: the art guild or the miners?

Forrest's eyes flickered. He held himself next to the wall, where the heat waves licked out around his body, and Nitpicker, ahead of him by only a few meters, did the same. The snake, hovering above the floor on its tiny built-in gravpads, hesitated, darted a meter toward Tsia, then paused again. Curling closer, it edged between Forrest and Nitpicker. Its mouth opened to reveal the aperture of a breaker core, ringed with borers and tiny laser mounts used to cut through stone, ships, and shields. It could bore through skin like a screw through water. It approached her in tiny, darting motions, trying to read the heat, knowing that something was there.

Tsia snarled at it in her mind, read its energy, and closed off her gate abruptly. Smoke stained the air to a gray-black seething mass. She breathed shallowly. She could not stay here much longer; the filter fans were not able to handle as much smoke as the fabric ceilings put out.

The salvage snake hovered before her. The baby was immobile. Did it still live? Did it sense the urgency of being still? She stared at the snake, unblinking, not breathing, watching it writhe in the heat, watching its sightless head home in on her body.

The snake's mouth burst open; its head darted forward. From its gullet a short, fingerlong laser beam blazed out. Like a cat, Tsia twisted and leapt, and Forrest snapped his flexor into a spiking hook, ripping into the metaplas back and jerking the snake to his side. Nitpicker lunged forward and rammed her own flexor down. The head of the snake, whipped away by the serpentine motion, lengthened its beam. The laser burned through Tsia's jumpsuit on her side, then bent and flashed across Nitpicker's bicep and chest.

The woman screamed. Forrest, one-handed, jerked his flexor

out and drove it up into the sensor net on the underside of the snake. Tsia curled her body around the baby and jumped through the fire toward Forrest, away from the head of the snake, away from the wildly firing laser.

Forrest seemed to writhe to let her pass. Ramok and Spade, forced back by the beams, cursed. Wren caught Nitpicker as she staggered back, his huge, club-like hands like vises on her slender arms. Forrest, jerking the snake toward himself again, snapped his flexor into the impossible shape of a blade with a dozen hooks and ripped the metaplas claws into the sensor pads.

The silver snake's temple beams flashed out. In an instant they licked the forearm he held at his side. His face went tight, but he did not stop ripping at the sensors. Blackening his blunter, burning through to flesh, the beam finally narrowed, lengthened, flickered, and died. The body of the snake, torn and lifeless, hung motionless in the air, then sank slowly to the floor.

With clenched teeth, Forrest motioned for Ramok to take point. Ramok ran forward. Tsia felt the hot impatience in him, the excitement that caught at her biogate, while the smell of charred flesh caught horribly at her nose. Across from her, Nitpicker's face was twisted and gray with pain, and Wren, coughing, dragged her after Ramok by her elbow. The woman had dropped her flexor, and her fists were now clenched and white-knuckled, but she forced herself into a stumbling run. With her free arm Tsia caught up Nitpicker's weapon and tucked it in with her own.

At a dead run, with the fire already burning out above them, Ramok led them to the walkspan door. Like everything else, it was locked out, and its filter fields were opaque and dull. Ramok's eyes were hard as he turned back. "Tsia—the mole."

Overhead, the ceiling crisped away. A heavy piece of burning fabric dropped onto Wren's shoulder, and Tsia, lunging forward, brushed it off in a shower of sparks. Brittle cinders floated down on them all. Ramok backed off, and she knelt at the door. The mole was cold in her hand. She had to force herself to hold it. There was fear in her heart, but with it, she felt excitement. Her eyes were too bright in her pale, translucent face.

The hallway was black now; the ceiling was bare up to its dark, functional beams and braces. Beneath it, even Tsia's jumpsuit was smoking. Two seconds, four . . . She finally caught the pattern of the door and began to melt it away. As with the crash foam of the skimmer, the door tried to re-form as she cleared it, and with the sudden gap to the outside, the heavy smoke followed the rush of air through the hold and dropped around them so that they all began to choke.

Five seconds, six . . .

"Tsia," Ramok managed urgently.

"It's open," she rasped.

Blinded by the smoke, Ramok found the opening by the tingling shocks of its edge against his hand. He staggered through. Smoke poured out around his feet. Choking, stooping, he whirled and dragged Nitpicker through after him. Wren, at his order, darted through next.

Tsia felt her heart pounding. Her feet wanted to fly through that hole. The smoke that billowed around her burned her throat and lungs as no flame in the firepit had ever done. She could no longer see the door for the tears in her eyes, and the child no longer wriggled in her arms. Daya, she screamed in her mind, willing Spade through as Forrest hung last and scanned the hall. Tsia tried to feel for the baby's star spark in her gate, but the tawny power of the tams surged and crowded her mind with their snarls. Daya, she pleaded, don't let him die . . .

Wren's huge club-fisted hand reached through the opening and yanked Tsia out.

"Snake," Forrest shouted. He dodged through the opening blindly, but he did not see the slowly closing edge, and he caught his limp arm on the rim of the hole. His body locked up for an instant, and Wren had to drag him the rest of the way through after Tsia.

The access door billowed with smoke, and the hole Tsia had made was not closing fast enough. Tsia thrust the mole in her pocket and staggered back, ready to push away and jump. Forrest, impossibly lithe on his massive frame, spun around while still hauled forward by Wren. In the same motion he pulled his match from his harness and pointed it at the door.

"Shield," Wren shouted, thrusting Tsia away from the door. She fell against Ramok, and the merc wrapped his arms around her as she curled around the baby.

Forrest, his head ducked into his blunter, triggered the match. The spout of flame shot out and hit the door; the opaque filter field flared into a pearly white as it tried to absorb the heat, then flashed out a backblast that knocked Forrest back into Wren. Flame blasted between their bodies, engulfing their blunter fabric and crisping the air. Then it was gone.

Wind whipped away the smoke. Heat lingered against their skins; the blunter fabric was hot. There was silence for a second.

Then, as one, they stared at the remains of the walkway. Minutes before, perhaps even as they had entered the building, the span had been atomized by a beam from the coring laser, and its edges still smoked with charred stone. The cutoff span on which the six stood stretched out like an aborted thought above the square.

Ten meters below, all action had come to an abrupt halt. Someone shouted. "Look—look up!"

Ramok pulled his smoking blunter off his head and glanced back. In the shimmering door a small blacked-out spot began to appear. He stared at it for only an instant. "Nitpicker," he said urgently.

The gray-faced woman swayed in Spade's hands. "What—do you need me to do?" she ground the words out between her teeth.

"The snake—it's burning through now. You've got to shut off its link—or ghost the walkways out of its range. Whatever you can do."

She nodded and closed her eyes, and Spade held her steady. Tsia eyed the fighters who stared up at them from below and tried to control her sweat. The smoke from the smoldering blunters stung her eyes, and she loosened the wrap around the infant, feeling for its life force through her gate. It was there, tiny and bright among the hotter animal snarls of the cats.

Below, several fighters halted in midstrike and stared up at the walkway. "Up there!" "Look—the smoking warriors!"

Nitpicker clenched her hands on Wren's arms. "I can't keep it from the spans," she managed hoarsely. "Only the plaza."

"The prophecy!" the shouter yelled again. Miners and freepicks, caught by the smoking figures of the mercs, turned their faces up.

Tsia stared at the blackened circle that widened in the door and began to thin. She could almost see the beams flaring on the other side. Forrest glanced at Ramok.

"Burn it," Ramok ordered. "We need the time."

"Shield," Wren snapped out.

They ducked and hunched their shoulders again. Forrest flicked the match. A second later another backblast forced them to their knees, catching at their jumpsuits and blunters and frying the air around them.

Tsia's gate was wide open and uncontrolled in the fire. The cat feet clawed and urged her to jump from the span, and she wrenched herself from Ramok's arms and staggered to her feet. Behind her, the door had thickened with the fire so that the snake had to burn through its material again. Her gate surged with a fierce joy. Seconds. She now had seconds to flee. But there was nowhere to go. The walkspan hung out over the very guilders who wanted the child in her arms dead.

She shook the boy from the e-wrap to give him air, and a roar rose up from below. Tsia nearly staggered with the sound. "The child!" "The smoking warriors!" "The burning babe!" With both hands she clutched the tiny boy to her chest.

Strangely then, the plaza became still. Ramok and Forrest looked at Tsia. Her eyes were blazing with trapped panic and animal power. The cats surged through her gate. Trembling, she stared down at the gray wisps that rose from her clothes.

On the ground the fighters started to run toward the walkway. One freepick, then two more broke and disappeared between the two guild buildings, heading for the temple. Tsia could taste their excitement as if she had spooned it into her mouth. From the center of the square, carried up by the sharp wind that cleared the smoke from the broken walkway, the smell of dank earth mixed with the odor of ash and melted metaplas so that she choked. The miners and freepicks seemed to be waiting.

"For what?" Wren muttered.

"Down!" Tsia urged Ramok, her feet itching to run.

"That's ten meters," he said sharply.

The black sunspot appeared again in the center of the opaqued door. The cats pressed at her mind. Her skin, hot and sweating even in the wind, seemed to crawl with the sense of their tension. "*I* can jump that," she snarled. She thrust herself away from him and stepped to the edge, but his hand stopped her.

"As you were," Ramok ordered. "Wren first. Then Forrest, then Spade."

The first merc swung down, dangled from the edge of the walkway by his hammer fist, and then dropped lightly to the hard ground below. The miners and freepicks moved back to let him tuck and roll but kept their gazes up, where Tsia shivered with the child. Forrest sat down and put one hand on the edge, while Ramok and Spade grasped him under his arms and helped him swing down, one-handed.

Tsia met Forrest's amber eyes with a burning blue gaze. "What is it?" she demanded. The merc hung for an instant and dropped into the crowd below. Wren helped break his fall as he landed, bent-legged, and rolled. She stared at Ramok. "What is wrong with him?"

"His arm is broken." Ramok motioned to Spade, and the merc dropped easily over the side.

Tsia licked her lips. She clutched the infant tightly, and the cats faded back and forth in her mind. Their snarling mixed with the growing murmur of those who waited below, and she shivered with the sense of their eagerness. To her right, the black spot in the door grew larger.

Ramok took Nitpicker gently by her elbows and dropped her over the side. Crying out in spite of herself, the woman landed as the others had, tucking and rolling across the stones. Ramok motioned for Tsia to give him the child, but she shook her head. She eyed the plaza, unwilling now to jump. Her feet seemed to have claws that dug into the walkspan, and Ramok had to shove her to the edge.

The freepicks seemed to surge forward. The door was beginning to melt through; she could smell the searing energy in the filter field. "No," she started. She twisted against Ramok, but he grabbed her on her rib cage and dangled her over the edge. With one hand clutching the infant, she could only grab at his blunter. Her eyes burned desperately, and a yowl burst from her lips.

"The cougar!" someone shouted from below.

The cats flooded through her gate, and Tsia screamed as Ramok loosened his hold. Her hand ripped from his blunter.

As if they could sense her animal fear, the crowd surged forward as she landed, their hands reaching for her body and the skin of the infant she held. She tucked and rolled up against Spade's legs, and the merc hauled her up roughly and fast.

Faces, hands— Tsia shrank from the grasping, grabbing fingers. Someone trod on her feet, and a hard boot smashed into her shin. She bared her lips and held her breath in the stench of their sweat. She stumbled in the roar of their voices. "The baby of the prophecy!" "Let me touch him." "Give him to us—" It was a miner, and she snarled in his face. "Turn him to us!" "Let us see him—"

Forrest, she cried out through her gate. The infant began to wail in her arms, and the cats leapt against the confines of her skull as she grew more trapped in the crowd. She could not move from Spade's side with the people pressing in. She could not breathe. He tried to shove both guilders and freepicks away, but their weight staggered him. Grimly, Forrest rammed his way through with his shoulders until he made a path into which Spade shoved Tsia. She darted into it almost before it opened, feeling Forrest's intent with the cat sense that filled her mind.

Ducking her head against the tide of freepicks and miners, she clung with one hand to Forrest's back. She buried her face in his blunter until she almost choked with its burning smell. Behind her, Spade and Wren and Nitpicker followed, the woman merc gritting her teeth and stifling her groans in the crush. Tsia glanced up to see Ramok jump down onto the crowd itself. A second later, a sightless silver head snaked through the burned-out door and hung over the edge of the walkway, swaying from side to side as it lost the sense of its prey.

"Nitpicker?" Ramok shouted from behind.

"It's hung," she managed.

A second later, Ramok forced his way through the miners to Wren and Nitpicker's backs, one hand shielding his side where his burn was compounded with torn and bleeding flesh, and his face dark and dangerous as he glared at the men and women who pressed in. He kept his hand on Wren's shoulder to link the line together.

Tsia did not look for Ramok again. She was pressed from all directions. Her weapon was pinned to her side. Only Forrest, towering above the miners, could see where they were headed, and he could no longer stride but had to cramp his feet and kick at the people in front. A priest from the Kumuda temple appeared before him, and Forrest shoved the man aside with less than a glance. Three women dodged beneath his arms, and he caught two of them and flung them away, but they only bounced off the other bodies and pressed back in. Unable to get to the child, the miners tore at Tsia's body.

Tsia cried out as the first hand ripped her collar. The fabric burned across her throat, and her mind lost all thought. Three hands stripped the jumpsuit off her unprotected arm clutching at Forrest's back, and she screamed out. The animal sound that burst from her throat seemed to spur the crowd on. Shouting, they grabbed at her and tripped her feet with their legs.

Spade snatched a man off her back and lifted the struggling miner with a roar, then bodily threw him over the massed faces. His action incensed the crowd to a frenzy, and Wren's fists flashed, their disproportionate size breaking jaws and slapping cheekbones right and left. A miner wrestled his varblade up, and Tsia felt a giant hand squeeze off her breath. Someone tried to tear her off of Forrest's back, and she screamed through her gate until even the cats in her mind cowered with the sound.

Forrest cried out. He stopped suddenly and, flinging out his arms to clear a second's worth of air, threw his head back and screamed out his own inhuman cry. The harsh, piercing sound penetrated the square, and it did not stop. The miner with the varblade dropped the weapon and clapped his hands to his ears. All around him men and women covered their ears and backed away.

Shaking, drawing herself up to Forrest's back and burying her face in his blunter, Tsia hung on numbly while she covered the baby's ears. Still the sound did not stop. The miners' shouting ceased; the priests knelt and huddled on the ground. Tsia's head vibrated—even her biogate was pierced by the shrilling sound. Surely her ears would burst.

And then it stopped, and Forrest lowered his head and shook it as if to rid himself of the sound. Dumbly, the freepicks and fighters stared. A miner, one hand still covering his ears, rose to his unsteady feet. He lifted his fibergun slowly. The mercs shifted, but Tsia twisted the baby away and snarled. The man froze.

"You would kill a child?" she breathed viciously, her eyes blazing with that ice-blue light. "You would kill an infant not even one hour old?" Above her, the salvage snake wavered in the wind at the edge of the walkway, and its silver head shone beneath the heavy, overcast sky.

The man glared at her. His eyes were like holes burning in his face. She stared back, her shoulders and arms bare in the cold wind, her jumpsuit torn in rags where they had ripped it from her body.

"What if this child were yours?" With a curse, she held up the baby and flung off its medwrap, letting it squirm in the cold air for them to see. "Look at him. Look at his tiny hands. Look at his eyes—blind! He cannot see you. He cannot fight you." She trembled with the fever that rose and sapped her limbs, but she forced her arms to hold the infant up. The tiny figure wailed faintly.

"Listen to him!" Her voice rasped. "Listen, damn you all! He cries out for milk and warmth, not blood. He does not live to solve your problems. He lives so that he can breathe the air and seek the warmth of his mother."

The miner who faced her set his jaw; he did not lower the gun.

Tsia felt the rage sweep through her. "This is no leader come to save you from yourselves. This is a child. Look at him!" she shouted. "What is he? A baby! A tiny little boy who has his own destiny, not the one you force upon him." She swept the crowd with her ice-blue gaze, then glared back at the miner. "*You* want to kill him?" she snarled in the tension of the silence. "Kill your own child first."

No one moved.

Finally, in a single motion, Ramok stripped off his blunter and placed it around her shivering shoulders. She did not even glance at him. Instead, she lowered the child to her chest and stalked forward ahead of Forrest, leaving behind the miners and the blind, seeking head of the salvage snake. The crowd parted to let her through; the mercs followed, close and tense. They made the council building entrance in seconds.

Ramok moved to the door. Facing the eyeblock of the door, he linked in. "Contract," he said shortly. "MG433R7. We have business with Feldon of the Pulanese council. Let us in or—" He stretched his lips in a smile that held a grim promise. "—we'll burn your tower around your ears."

Four minutes later they stood in the council chambers.

30

Feldon was a thin man, spare and lean and old. His few white hairs and pockmarked face spoke of two hundred years on Risthmus, and his shirt was decorated with the design that only First Droppers wore. On his left hand he wore a glove made of gem-studded flexan; on his right he wore a band of white gold embossed with the pattern of the pilots. His face was lined and wrinkled, but his light brown eyes were sharp and penetrating. There was no friendliness in his gaze.

Ramok did not step forward. "Contract, MG433R7," he said flatly. "The child is here." He indicated the baby in Tsia's arms. "Verify as you wish."

Tsia stood beside him and clutched the infant to her chest. Her adrenaline was gone; her body felt weak and reeling and she could hardly see beyond the baby in her arms, but the cats clawed at her thoughts, and she could not stop shifting from one foot to the other. The borrowed blunter she wore stank with the charred scent of fabric and flesh, and she did not even care. Her nose was clogged with the scent of the child.

Ramok steadied her subtly. His weapon harness was bare, and the burn on his side was a raw, blackened mess that had stained his jacket as it had stained his shirt. Nitpicker leaned against the back wall, her jaw tight against the pain as she continuously imaged med commands to her brain and tried not to scratch at the grafts that were fusing to her skin.

Spade's darkeyes flicked at every skimmer that crossed before the windows, and his link was tuned to the ID dots of the people in the corridor. Except for a few medtechs and a crew welding temporary metaplas over the coring holes in the street, the plaza below was empty. The miners had retreated to their guild; the freepicks to the tunnels below. Forrest and Wren were silent, each standing at one end of the line of mercs. Forrest's arm was layered in a fastcast, and his side was grafted like Nitpicker's. Wren, his bull fists hanging at his side, stood at Forrest's side.

The councilman turned to the esper who stood behind him. The woman nodded slightly. He turned back then and said, "Contract verified. Sign-off is complete. Leave the child here. You may go."

Tsia glanced at Ramok. His face appeared indifferent, but the tightness around his eyes spoke of anger. He nodded at her, and she stepped forward, then hesitated. "What will you do with him?"

Had it been her imagination, or had the councilman's eyes flickered with anger before they once again went flat?

The aged man shrugged. "Yemene had no relatives. The child is now an orphan. He will be given to the esper guild to raise as they see fit. The council itself has no use for him here. We have other business to see to. The cleanup of the mining conflict, for example."

Still she hesitated, and the councilman raised his eyebrow. "You may go when you give over the child," he repeated.

The dispassion in his voice mocked all Nitpicker's suffering, all of Tsia's struggle with her gate, the breaks and burns that marked the men around her, and the fire that had touched them all. It disclaimed the birth of the child and the death of the mother, and Tsia's hands clenched in a harsh response. The cat gate snarled with her instant fury, and in front of her the esper woman stiffened.

Feldon glanced from the esper to the *nyeka*. His eyes turned cold. "You fulfilled your contract. Set the child down."

"He has a name," she said in a curt voice.

He met her eyes with an icy look. "It is not important."

"His name is Hu'te."

"He belongs now to the guild," he said sharply. "And they will rename him as they wish."

So you take him from the chains of prophecy and give him the chains of the guild? Tsia did not ask the question out loud, but the esper woman's eyes narrowed. Tsia glared at her deliberately, then ducked her head to the infant. With all her strength of mind, she reached into her biogate and forced the thought toward the child. Hu'te, can you hear me? She shouted the thought in silence. Can you understand? If you want your freedom, you have to fight for it. If you want your future, you have to live. Hu'te, can you hear me?

She looked up at the esper and read the shock in the woman's eyes. She smiled, and it was a predatory grin. Hu'te, she thought at the child—she handed him to the esper—your name is Hu'te.

She stared at the boy as the other woman took him from her arms. Your name is Hu'te, she told him strongly. Remember that. You are Hu'te—the star. The star.

Trembling, the esper fled from the room. Feldon's eyes narrowed. Ramok placed his hands on Tsia's shoulders and forestalled the councilman's comment. Without a word, he turned Tsia and propelled her forward until they left the room. Silently, the other mercs followed. They reached the outer office, then stepped into the hall and made their way to the gravpads without comment.

A moment later Spade and Wren were gone; they used the council net to contact Red and the other mercs in the hills. Only Forrest, Ramok, and Nitpicker crossed the plaza with Tsia.

The square was slick beneath Tsia's feet, and she looked up slowly, only to be blinded by the drizzle that now fell from the heavy sky. The clouds kissed her skin with rain. She stared at it, and then, while Forrest gazed at her with his amber eyes, she began to laugh.

"When water shall wash the stink of war from the soil," she quoted the esper prophecy.

Ramok put his hand on her arm.

She shook him off with a bitter, trembling laugh. "The prophecy was right." She pointed at the distant roof of the esper guild, just visible over the other buildings. "The boy has been given to the one guild that will train his talent so that he really could be the greatest diplomat Risthmus has ever seen. So that he can feel thoughts and guide them like I guide the cats." She choked the words out in her irony. "And Pulan—Feldon—does not want him. He will grow up in the shadow of his prophecy. He will be a leader without anyone to lead. Without a county. Without a home."

Her own words struck her as funny, and she began to laugh again. In her head the cat feet padded away, and on her skin the drizzle turned to rain. Forrest touched her face and found it cold.

She reached up and covered his fingers with her hand. *"Ava,"* she whispered. "I need . . ." Her voice trailed off. She needed the cats. There would be no cougars here to help her, no tams that would come at her call. She had to return to the rift. Her hand trembled. Her eyes went to Ramok.

Ramok glanced at Nitpicker. The burned woman's face was pale beneath her tan, and the taut lines around her eyes showed the pain she felt from the burns across her chest and arms.

"Skimmer traffic is still locked out," she said shortly.

"Van'ei," he said softly, using her name. "Please."

"The med commands I'm tapping won't hold me much longer. I need to get to a medical."

"You've taken worse and waited longer."

"This isn't a minor burn."

"So you'll have another scar," he said, his voice suddenly hard. "Tsia will have another life." He dropped his hand to her unburned arm. "I promised her help. And you are the only one who can work around a lockout."

She regarded him silently, then looked at Tsia.

Rsmok released her arm. "Van'ei . . ."

The other merc's black, flat darkeyes bored into Tsia's gray-blue gaze. "We call you puppies," she said softly to Tsia. "New to the guild. New to the world where you have to fight for your rights—where you cannot expect someone else to protect them for you. You do not last. You get yourselves injured. You get us killed." She reached up and touched the jagged white scar that ran across Tsia's face. "The move you made at Cheba Rift—on the heights, to run with the cats—could have destroyed Forrest; it brought the art guild down on us all."

Tsia's cheek flinched as the merc's light fingers rasped unbearably on her skin. In her heightened sensitivity, the bioenergy of the woman trailed like ice along tha scar and dug its accusing chill deep into her flesh.

Nitpicker rested her fingers against the white mark. "Three days you've been riding among us," she said. "Not guild. Not *Merishkan*. But Ramok says you have honor. Red admits you carry your weight well. And Forrest says you are true to your own guild."

Tsia's breath caught in her throat as the merc's touch trailed to her neck. Neither Forrest nor Ramok moved to stop the other merc.

Nitpicker's voice was thoughtful. "You are, I think, like him. Like Forrest. There is something not quite human in your head. Something uncontrolled. Even now, you fight yourself to stay still beneath my touch. I don't trust you." She paused, and her breath was a sweet, smothering cloud drawn into Tsia's mouth. "I should," Nitpicker said, almost to herself. "But I don't."

She stared into Tsia's eyes as if she could read the haunted gaze, and Tsia began to shiver.

Nitpicker's palm rested now against Tsia's chest, and the pain in the merc's strained face burned dully into Tsia's gate, at odds with the chill touch of her hand. The lanky merc pressed hard against Tsia's sternum, as if to feel the strength that was left in the life caught beneath the cage of Tsia's ribs. The pulse she felt, far too rapid in its rhythm, was like that of a wild thing. "You learned on your own to suffer, little Feather." Her voice was a whisper as she read the stoic nightmare-fear and grim determination that warred in Tsia's eyes. "Not even your gate can hide that." Nitpicker's face hardened. "I do not trust you," she said harshly. "But perhaps you belong with us after all." She dropped her hand, and Tsia took a ragged breath.

Ramok gestured. "There is a public pad one kilometer south."

Nitpicker paused, cocked her head and nodded. "I linked it. There are eight skimmers on the pad. I can probably get one of them off the ground, but—" She gave Ramok a grim look. "—I can't guarantee a landing."

"Wind?"

She nodded. "The rain is thickening and moving west. Between the wind and the updrafts, we could crash on the ridge. We could also—" Her gaze flicked toward Tsia and Forrest. "—be torn apart by the cats before we reached the Gea access tunnel to the Rift."

Ramok shrugged. "If she has to, Feather will go in alone."

Nitpicker met Tsia's gaze again. "I hope your *ma'ke ka'eo*— your death victory—is worth this," she said quietly.

Tsia, shivering in the drizzle, did not answer except to regard her with glittering eyes. It was Forrest who growled in return, "It is. She is."

"Better be." The other woman's lips twisted wryly. "Taking a skimmer off contract—even with a lift license—will cost us all our bonuses."

Ramok chuckled. He glanced back at the council building. "What is credit, Van'ei, in a world with plenty of work?"

She linked into the node's skimmer codes. "Meet me at pad seventeen," she retorted. "And bring that lift license. We will take off in ten." She turned and made her way back toward the gravpads in the council building, where she could use the lifts to get into the transport tubes that had not been destroyed.

Forrest and Tsia waited while Ramok imaged the node and set up the lift license for the skimmer. When its credit was tagged to his contract, he nodded, and they made their way back to the sublevels, where they jumped the gravtrain to the skimmer pads. Tsia followed them with feet that danced in her head and dragged on the floors. The cats pulled in her mind, drawing her to them through her gate, but her body was drained and weak, and the shudders, when they shook her, threatened to rock her off her heels.

They had to stop once, and she chafed at the pause. A pair of miners guarded the entrance to the launch area, and they waved the mercs down.

"We're not active," Ramok told them. "This is medical."

Warily, the first man looked them over. "Link in," he returned. "The Ore Wars are on cease-fire again. We're taking no chances on breaking that up."

Restlessly, Tsia watched the miners with a silent feral snarl as, with cold efficiency, Ramok, then Forrest, linked over their ID dots.

"Her?" one of the miners asked, pointing.

"She's on my link," Ramok returned shortly.

"You're logged and clear." The man turned his scanners back to the corridor. "Second door on the left. Main lift just melted from a preset bomb," he explained. "You'll have to use the stairs."

Ramok cursed under his breath. He broke into a jog, and Tsia and Forrest followed, their feet slapping in steady rhythm behind him. They came up to the skimmer pad from the west, then, while the rain dotted their hair, to space seventeen. The access lift on the side of the craft was burned away in a black scar that stretched all the way under the ship's belly, and Tsia had to jump for the already slick hatch.

Nitpicker did not look around. "Hurry up," she snapped over her shoulder. "This ship's already shaking, and the rain is getting worse."

Tsia threw herself at a soft as the two men vaulted in.

"Body check," Nitpicker said sharply. "All in. Foam closing." The foam pieces folded back. "Body check complete." She did not even wait for the sides of the softs to retract completely before she launched the skimmer into a steep rise beneath the clouds.

Tsia grabbed the corner of her seat and dug in her fingers as if they ended in claws. Ramok glared at Nitpicker's back. Linking through the lockout, the pilot banked and accelerated, and the gyros whined to keep up; the cabin tilted fifteen degrees before it leveled.

"Head for Pact Flat," Ramok ordered.

"Affirmative."

Forrest's massive fingers closed over Tsia's hand and felt the pulse in her wrist. His calluses were like rough bark against her skin, and she longed for the smooth, coarse hair of the cougars. She shivered. On her forehead the sweat broke out again and ran down her taut skin. "*Esha*, Tsia," he breathed.

Waves of grass and rising rock fled beneath the skimmer; the cliffs ahead became huge. Tsia felt the presence of the cats grow in her mind. As the distance shrank, their voices began to snarl and their mental feet began to bat at her thoughts. She clenched her hands on the arms of the soft.

"You going to send her through the tunnel?" Nitpicker's voice was short and strained. Ramok noted the ridged muscles on the sides of her mouth. The tension was not all pain.

"Yes."

"We going to wait?"

"Uh huh."

"Get the gear packs, then. With the wind, we might not be able to lift again once I shut her down. Could slide right off instead."

Ramok glanced at the skimmer's holotank. "You can land?"

"It's slick. It's small. Made for a Gea craft, not a transport skimmer like this."

Ramok glanced once more at the holotank, then made his way aft. He hesitated at Tsia's chair and looked at her rigid face. "Do you hear me, Feather?"

She turned her eyes to him, and their blue color was darker than it had been before. "I hear you, Ramok."

"Ten minutes to reach the cliff. That's all."

"I feel like a cat," she said softly, clenching her hands and stretching them out in front of her. Her nails dug into the soft and left long, deep scratches like the marks of a blunt claw. Her wiry thighs tightened and loosened on the seat so that her body was constantly in slow motion, like a cougar that crept through grass.

Ramok and Forrest moved to the back and pulled the survival gear packs from the bays. Nitpicker's voice, when it came, was strained. "Landing in ten. Get soft. This is not going to be smooth." Tsia's eyes were locked on the holotank, and she tensed forward in her seat as the cliffs seemed to rush at the ship.

Nitpicker imaged the skimmer into the wind and aimed the ship at a small open ledge that hung out near the top of the cliff. With the roiling clouds and the clash of hot and cold air, the updrafts swept the cliffs strongly, and the skimmer, built for open air, was barely under control as she brought it alongside. Skimmer vents whooshed and bucked the craft away from the rain-slick rocks. Nitpicker's face was gray.

Ramok and Forrest watched her with remote expressions. Tsia, her hands clenching on the edge of the soft, could think only of the cat feet that pounded in her body with her pulse. Louder, closer, the cats seemed to scream at her with the noise of their snarling and yowling and purrs. She could smell their fur in the rain. She could feel their muscles beneath her skin . . .

The craft edged onto the platform, and Nitpicker cut the engines and let the skimmer stall, leaving only its vents on for balance. She sat still and sweating for a moment. Then she wiped her hand on her trousers and stood up.

Ramok grinned. "You should have been a pilot."

Nitpicker glanced at the holotank. Ramok and Forrest followed her glance. Ramok's smile faded. He raised his eyebrow. The visuals in the tank showed the skimmer two-thirds on, one-third off the ledge. The hatch hung on the edge of the cliff. Nitpicker nodded. "I'll leave the vents on for now," she said obliquely.

Ramok rose and pulled Tsia out of her seat. She staggered, almost collapsed, then shook herself, moving under her own strength to the hatch. Impatiently, tensing from one foot to the other, she waited without speaking while Ramok released the door and jumped down to the slick ground.

The vents of the skimmer had blown the top layer of wet dust into mud on the surface of the flat, and Tsia watched Ramok slip to the very edge of the rock before he caught his balance. Carefully, he moved to make room for Forrest. Ramok reached up to help her down, but she did not wait; she leapt eagerly, her slender legs catching her light weight and her eyes already turning toward the stone tunnel that cut through the ridge.

The two men followed her gaze, and Nitpicker, moving to the hatch, looked as well. At the entrance to the tunnel, where the rain already dripped from its roof, a cougar sat as if carved from the tawny stone. Its paws were just inside the waterline, and the dust mere inches from its face was spuffing up from the rain. In the dull light of midmorning its eyes gleamed. Only its tail flicked while it watched them.

Above the tunnel, where a ridge of broken rock made a rude trail along the rising cliff, a pair of tams crept down. Their fur was tipped with moisture and was ruffled on the knobs between their ears. They crouched in the rain, yowling softly.

Tsia did not notice the rain. Like a sleepwalker, she moved toward the cats until she halted at the tunnel's entrance. Her short hair glistened in the rain. There was a sweetness to the water that fell from the sky, a lightness she had not realized before. She tilted her head back, and as the moisture ran in runnels down her face and neck, her skin seemed to glow. The cougar eyed her silently. She dropped her head and stared back.

Behind her, Forrest halted Ramok with a gesture. "Your Feather can barely stand," he said softly, "let alone climb down from Catmount Ridge."

"Then I will carry her in myself."

Above, the tams watched the three mercs narrowly while their ears twitched forward, registering the subsonic hum of the skimmer's vents. Ramok eyed them with determination. "Wait here," he said to Forrest.

At his words, Tsia stirred. "No. Stay. I cannot protect you from the cats."

"Feather, you haven't the strength to get halfwa—"

He never finished his sentence. With his good arm, Forrest hit Ramok a blinding ridgehand that had behind it every ounce of his whipcord strength. Ramok stumbled and shook his head, and Forrest chopped him across the carotid. Ramok sank down in the mud. Forrest hesitated, then looked at Tsia with a depthless look.

"I cannot focus," she said softly. "I could not keep you safe, either."

"I would take that chance."

"Ava," she whispered. She touched his face. "Not this time."

He smoothed her short, wet hair for a moment in silence, then stepped away. Tsia closed her eyes and felt rain wash her lids. When she opened them again, she turned and walked into the tunnel. Before her, with a low snarl, the cougar turned and slunk away into the darkness, and Tsia did not look back. The shadows of the stone swallowed her up.

"Stay strong," Nitpicker whispered. "Stay alive."

From the other side of the tunnel, Forrest heard a rumble. There was an answering snarl from a tam and the *kai-al nyeka* who challenged it, and then there was silence.

Tsia stumbled out in rain on the other side of the rift. The gray, indifferent light was too glaring for her eyes, and the gray-white sky was unnerving. There was something painfully slow about her movements, something possessive about the gliding feet of the cats. The dampened ground seemed close at first, then far away and fuzzy. Claws no longer scratched her skull; no cat feet tore at her brain—the growling in her ears was not a sound she made herself. Several minutes passed, and when her eyesight cleared, Tsia found herself crouched down on cold knees, facing the cougar that had drawn her into the rift.

The feline eyed her as it would another predator, and slowly Tsia raised her head.

I need the parasite that lives within your claws. Had she spoken those words or imaged them? I need the parasite. I need your touch to be free . . . The cougar hissed. It slunk forward until its hot breath puffed in her face in putrid contrast to the cold buffeting of the wind.

Unsteadily, Tsia stretched out her hand. The white chafing of the chains she had worn still marked her wrists. She ignored the marks. *Please,* she whispered in her mind, the plea echoing into her gate. *I need your touch.*

The cat's eyes gleamed. It raised its paw and batted at her hand, but its claws did not break her skin.

Tsia closed her eyes. Please, she whispered in her head.

Yellow-green eyes glinted. Then the cat's paw slashed across her face, its claws like hooks of lightning as they ripped open her cheek from temple to jaw. Tsia's head rocked back with the blow. Her breath froze in her throat. She locked there and fought against the scream that threatened to rip from her lips with the blinding white fire that had torn open her face. For a long moment there was no sound but the harsh rasp of her breath.

Slowly, Tsia turned and lifted her head while rain washed the blood down in streaks. It dripped from her chin to the ground at her feet and colored the mud with darkness.

The cougar hissed again. *It is done.*

On the ridge, Nitpicker stirred. Her legs ached, and the rain, at first warm and cleansing, was cold. "It has been three hours," she said to Forrest. "Can't you sense her yet?"

The tall merc hesitated. He listened with his senses and realized that there were dark silhouettes in the tunnel. Swiftly, he rose to his feet.

Instantly, Ramok sprang up with him. *"Avya?"* he demanded. "Tsia?"

There was a lean silhouette beside her, and the growl of the cougar was a rumble that filled the stone corridor and echoed in the cold, wet wind. In the shadowed tunnel Tsia swayed. The cougar's muscles rippled, and its eyes were like glowing coals. Tsia's gaze refused to focus. Ahead of her, Ramok was a wavering image in the light at the end of the run. It took all her strength to move again. She moved one foot, then halted, breathed raggedly, and stumbled into the light. The cougar snarled and settled back in the entrance like a guard for the rift beyond.

The rain and sweat glinted in Tsia's short hair. The left side of her face was matted with blood that had turned a muddy color from the dirt of the ridge, and her glittering eyes were clouded.

Nitpicker eyed the woman warily. Forrest nodded to himself. Ramok held out his hand. *"Avya,"* he said softly. "Come."

Epilogue
⚜

It was a month past the killing of her virus, and Tsia vaulted easily into the skimmer, coming abruptly up against Forrest's chest with a smile. He caught her wrists. They were healed of chafe marks, and her arms were tanned around the old skin grafts that had sealed.

Forrest's hand touched the ragged white scars that stretched along the side of her face. The rough callouses of his thumb caught on the edges of the marks, then his long, thick fingers slid around to span her neck from behind. She could feel the strength in those fingers, in the muscles of his hands. She flexed her arms beneath his grip, and his amber eyes glinted. Her own eyes were clear and blue, the deep, sharp blue of the sky before it turned to dusk, and they crinkled with a faint smile as she stepped aside and made her way to the second seat on the right, where Ramok leaned forward and checked his link with the pilot.

Ramok looked back and exchanged glances with Forrest. Behind the heavy, expressionless planes of his face Forrest almost smiled to himself. Tsia: a *kai-al*, like himself. Forever free, forever bound to her gate, not to guilds or men.

Ramok touched her arm as she sat, then scowled into the holotank, and Tsia murmured a greeting to the pilot. Nitpicker glanced back. The burns along her arms and chest had grafted white and smooth, cleanly healed, and Nitpicker, catching Tsia's eye, nodded to the *nyeka*.

At the hatch, Forrest hauled Wren up to the cabin. Wren's quick, birdlike eyes flickered as he noted Tsia's seat by Ramok. He said nothing but settled in beside them and, getting out a slimchim, broke it and offered her half. She took it with a nod, popped it in her mouth, then leaned back and closed her eyes as she chewed. The cats, through her gate, snarled once and shared in silence.

Author's Note

Wolves, wolf-dog hybrids, and exotic and wild cats might seem like romantic pets. The sleekness of the musculature, the mystique and excitement of keeping a wild animal as a companion . . . For many owners, wild and exotic animals symbolize freedom and wilderness. For other owners, wild animals from wolves to bobcats to snakes provide a status symbol—something that makes the owner interesting. Many owners claim they are helping keep an animal species from becoming extinct, that they care adequately for their pet's needs, and that they love their wild creatures.

However, most predator and wild or exotic animals need to range over wide areas. They need to be socialized with their own species. They need to know how to survive, hunt, breed, and raise their young in their own habitat. And each species' needs are different. A solitary wolf, without the companionship of other wolves with whom it forms sophisticated relationships, can become neurotic and unpredictable. A cougar, however, stakes out its own territory and, unless it is mating or is a female raising its young, lives and hunts as a solitary predator. Both wolves and cougars can range fifty to four hundred square miles over the course of a year. Keeping a wolf or cougar as a pet is like raising a child in a closet.

Wild animals are not easily domesticated. Even when raised from birth by humans, these animals are dramatically different from domestic animals. Wild animals are dangerous and unpredictable, even though they might appear calm ot trained, or seem too cute to grow dangerous with age. Wolves and exotic cats make charming, playful pups and kittens, but the adult creatures are still predators. For example, lion kittens are cute, ticklish animals that like to be handled (all kittens are). They mouth things with tiny, kitten teeth. But the adult cats become solitary, highly territorial, and possesive predators. Some will rebel against authority, including that of the handlers they have known since birth. They can show unexpected agression. Virtually all wild and exotic cats, including ocelets, margay, serval, cougar, and bobcat, can turn vicious as they age.

Monkeys and other nonhuman primates also develop frustrating behavior as they age. Monkeys keep themselves clean and give each other much-needed, day-to-day social interaction and reassurance by grooming each other. A monkey kept by itself can become filthy and depressed, and can begin mutilating itself (pulling out its hair and so on.) When a monkey grows up, it climbs on everything, vocalizes loudly, bites, scratches, exhibits sexual behavior toward you and your guests, and, like a wolf, marks everything in its territory with urine. It is almost impossible to housebreak or control a monkey.

Many people think they can train wolves in the same manner that they train dogs. They cannot. Even if well cared for, wolves do not act as dogs do. Wolves howl. They chew through almost anything, including tables, couches, walls, and fences. They excavate 10-foot pits in your back yard. They mark everything with urine and cannot be housetrained. (Domestic canid breeds that still have a bit of wolf in them can also have these traits.) Punishing a wolf for tearing up your recliner or urinating on the living room wall—for instinctive and natural behavior—is like punishing a dog for breathing.

Wolf-dog hybrids have different needs than both wolves and dogs, although they are closer in behavior and needs to wolves than dogs. These hybrids are often misunderstood, missocialized, and mistreated until they become viscious or unpredictable fear-biters. Dissatisfied or frustrated owners cannot simply give their hybrids to new owners; it is almost impossible for a wolf-dog to transfer its attachment to another person. When abandoned or released into the wild by owners, hybrids may also help dilute wolf and coyote strains, creating more hybrids caught between the two disparate worlds of domestic dogs and wild canids. For wild-dog hybrids, the signs of neurosis and aggression that arise from being isolated, mistreated, or misunderstood most often result in the wolf-dogs being euthanized.

Zoos cannot usually accept exotic or wild animals that have been kept as pets. In general, pet animals are not socialized and do not breed well or coexist with other members of their own species. Because such pets do not learn the social skills to reproduce, they are unable to contribute to the preservation of their species. They seem to be miserable in the company of their own kind, yet have become too dangerous to remain with their human owners. Especially with wolves and wolf-dog hybrids, the claim that many owners make about their pets being one-person animals usually means that those animals have been dangerously unsocialized.

Zoo workers may wish they could rescue every mistreated animal from every inappropriate owner, but the zoos simply do not have the resources to take in pets. Zoos and wildlife rehabilitation centers receive hundreds of requests each year to accept animals that can no longer be handled or afforded by owners. State agencies confiscate hundreds more that are abandoned, mistreated, or malnourished.

The dietary requirements of exotic or wild animals are very different from domesticated pets. For example, exotic and wild cats require almost twice as much protein as canids and cannot convert carotene to vitamin A—an essential nutrient in a felid's diet. A single adult cougar requires two to three pounds of prepared meat each day, plus vitamins and bones. A cougar improperly fed on a diet of chicken or turkey parts or red muscle meat can develop rickets and blindness.

The veterinary bills for exotic and wild animals are outrageously expensive—if an owner can find a vet who knows enough about exotic animals to treat the pet. And it is difficult to take out additional insurance in order to keep such an animal as a pet. Standard homeowner's policies do not cover damages or inujuries caused by wild or exotic animals. Some insurance companies will drop clients who keep wild animals as pets.

If you would like to become involved with endangered species or other wildlife, consider supporting a wolf, exotic cat, whale or other wild animal in its own habitat or in a reputable zoo. You can contact your local zoo, conservation organization, or state department of fish and wildlife for information about supporting exotic or wild animals. National and local conservation groups can also give you an opportunity to help sponsor an acre of rainforest, wetlands, temperate forest, or other parcel of land.

There are many legitimate organizations that will use your money to establish preserves in which endangered species can live in their natural habitat. The internationally recognized Nature Conservancy is such an organization. For information about programs sponsored by The Nature Conservancy, please write to:

The Nature Conservancy
1815 N. Lynn Street
Arlington, Virginia 22209

For more information specifically abour wolves, and wolf-dog hybrids or for information about sponsoring a wolf you can write or call Wolf Haven International, another organization which is highly regarded and nationally recognized.

Wolf Haven International
311 Offut Lake Road
Tenino, WA 98589
1 (800) 448-9653

Special thanks to Janice Hixson and Dr. Jill Mellen, Ph.D., and Dr. Mitch Finnegan, D.V.M., Metro Washington Park Zoo; Karen Fishler, The Nature Conservancy; Harley Shaw, General Wildlife Services; Dr. Mary-Beth Nichols, D.V.M.; Brooks Fahy; Cascade Wildlife Rescue; and the many others who provided information, sources, and references for this project.

ABOUT TARA K. HARPER

Friends of Tara K. Harper say that she is opinionated, blunt, far too efficient, unexpectedly patient and kind. About half her friends think she is a thrill-seeker. The rest seem to think she alternates between thinking, dreaming, and working in a passionate frenzy; but they like her cooking and even enjoy the music when she stops playing the same piece three days in a row. Her husband agrees with her friends—on all those points—but he married her, so he has to be more politic about it.

Ms. Harper graduated from the University of Oregon, then went into high-tech, where she has worked for R&D, test-and-measurement companies ever since. Active in community service, she teaches creative writing for alternative schools, trains youth groups in wilderness skills, and serves on the board of directors for a youth treatment center. Ms. Harper is a member of the author's guild.

A martial artist and musician, Ms. Harper also hikes, kayaks, sails, and snowshoes. She admits to being caught in undertows, tidal waves, bogs, quicksand, and river bottom runs. She has slept with bees in her ears and deer at her feet; she has been bear-bashed too many times to count. She paints in oils, sculpts in stone, plays violin and piano, and composes music. She says that, someday, she wants to perform Tchaikovsky's Violin Concerto in D.

Science fiction
at its best
from

Tara K. Harper

Available at your bookstore.

Or call toll free 1-800-733-3000 to order by phone and use your major credit card. Or use this coupon to order by mail.

__LIGHTWING	37161-5	$4.99
__WOLFWALKER	36539-9	$3.95
__SHADOW LEADER	37163-1	$5.95
__STORM RUNNER	37162-	$5.99

Name_____

Address_____

City_____State_____Zip _____

Please send me the DEL REY BOOKS I have checked above.
I am enclosing $_____
     plus
Postage & handling* $_____
Sales tax (where applicable) $_____
Total amount enclosed $_____

*Add $2 for the first book and 50¢ for each additional book.

Send check or money order (no cash or CODs) to:
Del Rey Mail Sales, 400 Hahn Road, Westminster, MD 21157.

Prices and numbers subject to change without notice.
Valid in the U.S. only.
All orders subject to availability.   HARPERT